THRESH

ENGINES OF ASCENDANCY
PART I

GREGORY FIGG

Dear Joan,

Thank you so
much for your
support!

ISBN: 978-1-326-53807-1

PublishNation
www.publishnation.co.uk

Acknowledgements

Many, many people have helped me in the process of completing this book. I would like to thank, in no particular order: Diane, Benjie, my parents and grandparents, Tori, Lucy, Kathryn, Piers, John, Katie, Ox, Clem and all those who have tolerated my endless conversations about writing a story. I would also like to extend special thanks to David and Gwen Morrison at PublishNation for their wonderful work in publishing this book. You all have my deepest gratitude.

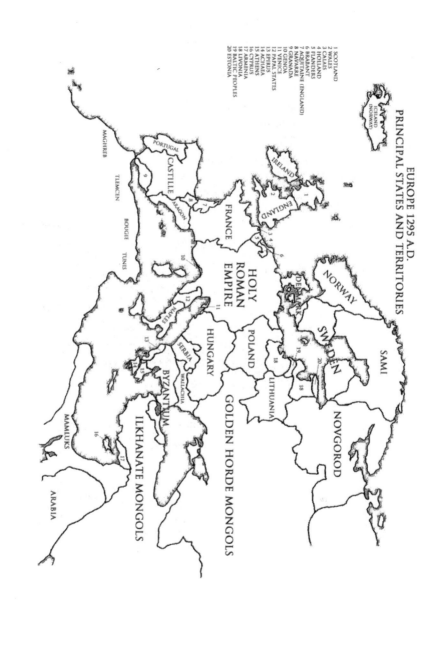

EUROPE 1295 A.D.
PRINCIPAL STATES AND TERRITORIES

1 SCOTLAND
2 WALES
3 CALAIS
4 HOLLAND
5 FLANDERS
6 BRABANT
7 AQUITAINE (ENGLAND)
8 NAVARRE
9 GRANADA
10 GENOA
11 VENICE
12 PAPAL STATES
13 EPIRUS
14 ACHAEA
15 ATHENS
16 CYPRUS
17 ARMENIA
18 LIVONIA
19 BALTIC PEOPLES
20 ESTONIA

ICELAND
(NORWAY)

MAGHREB

PORTUGAL

CASTILLE

ARAGON

TLEMCEN

BOUGIE

TUNIS

IRELAND

ENGLAND

FRANCE

HOLY
ROMAN
EMPIRE

DENMARK

NORWAY

SWEDEN

SAMI

NAPLES

HUNGARY

POLAND

LITHUANIA

NOVGOROD

SERBIA

WALLACHIA

BYZANTIUM

GOLDEN HORDE MONGOLS

ILKHANATE MONGOLS

MAMLUKS

ARABIA

SCOTLAND
Aberdeen
Scone
Stirling
Glasgow
Edinburgh
Ayr
Newcastle
Durham
NORTHUMBERLAND

Coleraine
IRELAND
Athlone
Galway
Dublin
Caernarfon
Rhuddlan
York
ENGLAND
CHESTER
Lincoln
Chester
Nottingham
Clun
WARWICKSHIRE
Norwich
NORFOLK
Coventry
Warwick
HEREFORDSHIRE
Waterford
WALES
Oxford
ESSEX
Ghent
Utrecht
Dolwyddelan
Gloucester
Bristol
London
Bruges
Calais
Aberystwyth
Southampton
Dover
Den Haag
DEVON
Arundel
Antwerp
CORNWALL
FLANDERS
BRABANT

PICARDY
Cologne
HAINAULT
LUXEMBOURG
Mainz
Worms
Rouen
Rheims
Metz
NORMANDY
Paris
HOLY
Chartres
ILE-DE-FRANCE
ROMAN
BRITANNY
Rennes
Troyes
CHAMPAGNE
EMPIRE
ANJOU
Orléans
Nantes
Tours
ORLÉANAIS
Dijon
LORRAINE
FRANCE
Bourges
BURGUNDY
LA MARCHE
Guéret
SAVOY
LIMOUSIN
Clermont-
Geneva
Ferrand
Lyon
Bordeaux
AQUITAINE
Avignon
LANGUEDOC
Arles
PROVENCE
Toulouse
Carcassonne
FOIX
Marseilles
CASTILLE
NAVARRE
Foix
Pamplona
Perpignan
Burgos
ARAGON
Zaragoza
Barcelona

Chapter 1

The wiry man shifted back and forth, uncomfortable despite the inquisitor's reassurances. His shoulders were hunched as if his head were trying to retreat into his body and his eyes rapidly darted around underneath hedge-like eyebrows.

"I can find it for you. The quarry's dark but I can find it," he mumbled through his beard into his chest. "But I don't like this."

The hooded woman did not look at her companion before answering. "You have our word, monsieur. You will not want for anything. To an extent, of course."

The wiry man scratched his head, looked the two inquisitors up and down and cleared his throat softly. "We must be quick." He turned to go, pulling his cloak over his head and shuffling through the door into the moonlight. The two inquisitors moved with impossible silence behind, floating across the straw-covered floor like the cats on the walls outside the hut. The cats froze at the disturbance before scurrying noiselessly into the shadows as the three silhouettes crossed the ten yards of grass before the blackness of the forest swallowed them. No fires flickered at this time, when the full moon was highest in the cloudless summer sky, and the three were the only waking souls in the hamlet.

It did not take long for the three to leave the hamlet along the rough path through the woods. It was not a true path, instead a route of worn-down vegetation cleared by decades of walking. But it was smooth enough to permit travel in exceedingly low light; fortuitous because only here and there did silver shards of moonlight penetrate the tree line. The wiry man moved surprisingly quickly given his ungainly shuffling locomotion though the two companions behind him were nimble on their feet and did not struggle to match his pace. Periodically an owl hooted, or leaves would crunch as some nocturnal mammal scampered away before the soft steps of leather on dried earth came in their direction.

The quarry was only a few minutes' walk from the hamlet. The towering, scarred cliffs carved out of the hillside shone bright grey against the dark blue of the surrounding grass, and enclosed the clearing in the forest on both sides like a ruined Classical theatre. The woman was reminded of the old Roman theatre she had seen once in Marseille. That she would see it now rather than this deserted pit, she mused.

But there was an errand to be run. She had written Guy that evening upon the chance conversation with the wiry man. Guy had always encouraged her to use instinct, and she had done so. It could be a dead end, much as this quarry was from the forest path; or it could represent a conclusion to the decades of searching that the woman's predecessors had carried out even before she had been born.

The wiry man halted in front of them, and the two companions responded in kind with no questions asked. He was as a wary rabbit in the field. There were two men fifty yards ahead, both asleep. It would take a huge effort to thieve from a quarry in the dead of night but the lord thought it prudent to post two sentries to deter any spirited labour gangs. The orders for castle construction were from the King himself, and his earls and barons were encouraged to complete the building with the utmost haste. Any theft of materials from the quarry represented a defiance of the King's will, and therefore the will of God.

The wiry man turned to the companions and whispered in his melodic Welsh accent. "Over them rocks, there. We'll be in."

The woman nodded imperceptibly but the Welshman had already moved off to the left, away from the sleeping guards. The three scrambled up the slope toward the boulders that formed a lip to the steep slope down into the quarry pit. Loose stones rolled with alarming volume down the direction from whence they came, causing the trio to freeze both their movements and their breathing, but because the slope faced away from the guards the sound did not carry. The wiry Welshman hauled himself over the boulders as if he weighed thrice his nine stone frame - the strain of years of quarrying had created a lean yet worn twenty-four year old with the look of a man in his late thirties and the energy of one even older. Yet he did not make so much as a grunt when jumping down to the sandy quarry floor below, bathed in the silver spotlight of the moon like

2

some nightmarish hooded apparition. He did not wait for the two companions and strode off towards the far left wall as he usually did during daylight hours.

Atop the boulder ridge the woman could now see smaller enclaves that had been cleared in what previously appeared to be a backwall of uniform depth. She glanced behind to check on both the slumbering guards and her companion and, satisfied the former remained asleep and the latter had not been left behind, she jumped down after the quarryman. Checking on her companion had only been cursory, merely a symptom of her compulsion to ensure the wellbeing of those close to her; her companion was supremely athletic and would be more likely to have to check on her physical condition the longer the night went on.

They followed the Welshman into a small enclave in the sheer wall, beneath scaffolding that stood like a naked, stoneless castle against the cliff. They were once more in shadow, and had a small hill, one hundred yards and steep between them and the sentries. The woman's companion, a man of average height who had not removed his hood all evening, took a stick of torch wood from his satchel, and from his belt a flint and a small pot of oil. The wiry man continued through the darkness, feeling his way along the familiar walls that he had worked at just hours before. The white exposed limestone seemed to glow even in the shadows, providing a natural guide underneath the scaffolding and around the bulging outcrop of virgin rock awaiting the pick tomorrow or next week. The quarry worker slowed down, and then crouched down as the wall started to arch slowly to the right.

"Here. It is here." He pulled away a cloth cover from the wall, and felt the smooth metal, brushing his right palm up and down without truly realising he was doing so, as if entranced. The woman's companion applied the oil to the torch wood then placed it tail end down on a rock on the floor, and struck the flint spark a few times. The instantaneous orange of the torch seemed to fill the entire world with colour, a world that had been nothing but greys and silvers and blues and blacks since they had left the tavern a few hours previous.

The hooded man brought the flame toward the wall, and the three crowded round the silver metal jutting about the length of a forearm out of the surrounding limestone. It had the appearance of one end of a chest – who knew what form it took, the part of it embedded in the rock? But this was a chest of pure silver, or what appeared to be silver, with flawless craftsmanship and to the woman's naked eye, flawless dimensions. It had no defined corners, and what would have been corners were impossibly soft, rounded edges the craft of which the woman did not think possible. The end jutting from the stone was about a forearm in height, and the same in width. The Welshman had told the inquisitors that he believed he was the only person who had seen it; it was possible, as this was a relatively secluded part of the quarry, underneath the scaffolding to the back of the area. He had worked as much as he could around it before covering it with cloth when the foreman ordered everyone home.

The wiry man had introduced himself to the woman as Brac. She had been sitting at a bench, hood down and long brown hair framing her pale face. Her eyes were kind, and she had a thin mouth that was barely wider than the small nose above it. She was not necessarily a remarkable looking woman, but she was certainly nicer to look at than Ugly Dillan and old Llwyd across the other side of the room. His curiosity was piqued when he had heard her speaking in French with the hooded man in the tavern. Only the highborn in the town spoke French, and none of them had ever so debased themselves to frequent the tavern. The English conquest of Wales had prompted mixed reactions from the Welsh; there were those who welcomed an end to incessant infighting amongst the regions but Brac himself was vehemently anti-English; not a day went by without thoughts of vengeance.

So it seemed to him a natural thing to enquire as to why the French woman was so far from France, and if she'd be interested in buying an unusual find from the quarry - Brac had no intention of allowing the English lords any fine Welsh treasures - he fancied himself an opportunistic man, he figured a woman travelling in a foreign land would surely have connections elsewhere, and be anything but helpless.

This was his opportunity to strike back at the invaders! Denying the brutal Lord de Grey possession of the most magnificent discovery Brac had ever seen in a lifetime of quarrying and stoneworking would be worth a thousand victories in the field. Before approaching, he had made sure to scope their footwear, and sure enough their style of boot was exotic relative to the leather mishmash Brac had tied to his own feet; both wore calf-length leather boots with conspicuously fine stitching, far more precise than any footwear the he had noticed around the town, not that he paid particular mind to the shoes others wore. But with so much of these two characters' physical appearance concealed by hair, hood and cloak he had to make the most from what he could see. Striking accents and very high-quality boots – he had a sure feeling these were not the typical farmers, quarrymen or merchants he usually saw in the area.

At least satisfied the two were neither local nor highborn, the wiry quarryman had puffed his chest with inflated bravado to cover his nerves, and broached the subject with the mysterious duo. His initial optimism drained when it seemed the Frenchwoman was not easily manipulated at the negotiating table. She had taken unexpectedly great interest in the silver stone, and threatened to have the lord anonymously informed of its presence unless Brac took her to it that very evening. He had expected terms to be more favourable but in truth he had too little spine to combat this unnervingly determined woman. And so he had agreed, reluctantly, to lead the woman and the man (who had not said anything to him all evening) to the quarry.

"We must hurry. Get your pick," the Frenchwoman ordered Brac in a quiet tone saturated in authority. He knew better than to disobey this foreigner – but who *is* she? He took a small pick from the belt underneath his cloak and gently nicked off the limestone around the top edge of the silver stone. Brac intended to create a shallow space in the rock the entire way round the silver stone in the hope that it might be wrenched free if the stone was not too deeply embedded. The woman spoke her native tongue to the other man, words utterly alien to Brac, and the other man sprung up towards the slope with the boulders. Brac watched him settle down at the peak of the slope, facing away from them, presumably as a sentry against the sentries.

The wiry man worked quickly and deftly, with nimble hands that caused the pick to dance around the silver stone object without ever touching it, not that it would have made a difference if he had. Earlier in the day before discovering it was there, Brac had hit it with his pickaxe and left neither indent nor even a scratch. As he chipped away at the surrounding rock under the decreasingly friendly eyes of the woman, Brac turned over the situation in his mind. He concluded that this strange, seemingly invulnerable metal object would be better off out of his possession anyway. A quarry worker did not need further uncertainties in his life. But, in case it was valuable, he'd rather the French had it than the English. He'd rather the French had it than the Church; how he saw it, the French could fight the English, but the Church could not.

After a few minutes of chipping, Brac gave the silver object a shove with his right shoulder. Nothing. He grunted. Taking his pick in his right hand once more, he scrambled to the left side of the object and concentrated on the limestone bordering its vertical plane. He made light work of carving a considerably deeper groove and returned to the top, where he did the same. Moving back round to the right, he put his shoulder to it again, and this time there was give; the impact gave Brac a dull ache in his shoulder but this slipped from his mind as he went about the subtle removal of stone from stone, by torchlight, without making a noise.

"Good," uttered the woman, not even looking at Brac but mesmerised on the patterns of the flame reflected on the silver surface. He did not need accolades or congratulations for such work;

he had been praised before, so he ignored the comment and continued chipping away. This time he worked on the right hand side then the underside, and putting the pick down he placed both hands on the left front edge of the stone and yanked back towards him to the right.

Again, a little give, but no more. He skilfully chipped at the loose limestone like a woodpecker on tree bark, and suddenly a clump of limestone the height of the stone itself fell away in one motion on the left hand side. Brac moved back round to the right and gave it another shoulder. The silver stone fell away from the wall, thumping onto the sandy quarry floor. It was flawless – no scratches, no impressions, no details. It was longer than it was wide, with the same rounded edges at the end that had been lodged within the rock. It shone magnificently in the torchlight as if it were a mirror. The two stared at it for a moment.

"It is time," said the woman to the sentry man, in French. Brac couldn't understand. But he wouldn't have noticed if she had spoken in English or Welsh, for he was fixated with the perfection of the stone. *Is it a stone, though?* He had worked around the products of the earth, the cliffs and the mines long enough to know that shapes such as this did not occur naturally, and especially not in silver as this appeared to be. *Is this a gift from God?* Brac felt his heart jump. Was he giving away a gift from God to the French and not the Church? His nerves, allayed by his labour, returned like a bucket of cold water being poured over his head.

Before he knew it, the woman's companion had hauled the stone up into a large sack, and slung it ponderously over his shoulder. By the man's slow movement and the subsequent momentary unbalance in his legs, Brac considered the object to weigh a considerable amount. Yet if it were silver, would it not be beyond the strength of all but the greatest men to carry it so? The woman's companion appeared only of average build, a couple of inches taller than Brac. He pondered what could it be that takes a naturally pure silver appearance yet is patently not entirely silver. And the craftsmanship! Oh, no stonemason in the kingdom could match it. Some entity or being must have forged it, and left it here in the Earth to be discovered. *To be discovered by me.* All anti-English sentiment had

7

evaporated and Brac now just felt nothing but guilt at having crept into the quarry when he was not supposed to, and then having given away a gift made by the angels or God Himself.

But he kept his silence, fearful of the bargaining edge the woman and the man now had over him. They slowly walked back towards the slope, Brac leading, the woman behind him and the struggling man with the stone at the rear. His footsteps were no longer soft crunches but loud scrapes as he hauled the great object across the quarry floor. The woman killed the flame on the torch. Brac noticed for the first time in a while the hooting of the owls, and he suddenly thought of the two sleeping sentries. At the peak of the slope, the two unburdened shadows looked out across the quarry from behind the boulders and saw the two sentries still asleep.

Just as well, thought the woman. Her companion was breathing heavily trying to carry the object up the slope. She hoped he would regain his composure on the way down and away from the quarry. She was already thinking of which route to take back into England and which letters she should send where for armed escort. There were still a few possibilities; the Order's unofficial presence was typically stronger than its official presence. The man Brac would require payment which itself was not straightforward – a quarry worker would not become well off without arousing the suspicions of his neighbours, the sheriff nor the lord.

Should she write Guy again? She implicitly trusted Guy's authority; he had been very precise about the exact nature of the object they were searching for. Was it not a sign from the Lord that the object would find them? After all of this time, a breakthrough! They had not yet left the quarry and the woman's mind was four, five stages ahead.

Her mind was brought back to the current stage when a horn burst through the stillness, causing Brac in front of her to almost jump out of his cloak. The horn had been blown behind them, from the quarry – probably from the sentries, who were probably no longer asleep.

"*Run!*" she hissed, shoving into the sluggish Brac who by now had lost all composure. Her companion lumbered along in pursuit of the first two, who by now had disappeared into the forest. It remained a kaleidoscope of silver and black in the full moonlight, until a few dozen yards ahead a torch was lit, followed by a second and a third. As the eighth torch lit up the two men and the woman had slowed their sprint to a walk, and finally a stop. Some torches were elevated above the others; at least three of the torchbearers were on horseback. The soft, high ringing of steel on steel rustled sporadically.

"Surrender in the name of the King!" commanded a coarse, yet educated English voice. "Lay down your arms and the goods, and his lordship will treat with you as nobility dictates. Of course, there is a limit to the nobility that can be shown to petty thieves. Lay down your arms."

Aware that she, Brac and her companion were still almost completely in shadow, the woman slowly yet noisily crouched down and dropped her knife on the earth. At the same time her companion lowered the bag with the silver stone to the floor with a *thwump*, but did not let go of it. In the same motion the woman had picked up stones and in the process of standing up, launched them at the wall of torches in front. Before her arm had come down she screamed, "*Go!*" and grabbed Brac forcefully by his left shoulder, dragging him right across the path with her and into the trees.

She heard the stones *clang* off armour, and the horses whinnied and reared at the unexpected shower of pebbles. By the time the Englishman with the coarse voice had yelled "After them!" the three were already ten yards into the forest, hurdling branches and roots where they could, and simply running through them and tripping over them where they could not.

Diving into the woods had already eliminated the three horseback torchbearers, but there were presumably at least five who would now be in pursuit, and would not have been burdened by carrying a heavy silver stone or by Brac's ungainly motion. Equally though, the woman thought as she cleared another root from a massive old tree, pitch black and monstrous in the shadow, their pursuers were likely to be wearing at the very least mail armour. The crunching of the stones onto plate and mail had given her no little confidence. She could hear the crashing of the armoured men behind them, the occasional heavy thump as a body fell to the ground, but still the shouts and footfalls came.

"Keep going. *Je traiterai avec eux*," the woman yelled to the two men before stopping dead in her tracks and disappearing from Brac's peripheral vision. He dared to look round to gauge what the Frenchwoman was doing – unable to understand her native tongue, and terrified at the angry armed mob chasing him, the quarryman felt he had little to no grasp on the situation – though he saw nothing but the torch light before the other man grunted "Come!" in a southern English accent. The two men were labouring hard through the forest, the hooded man from the weight on his back and Brac due to his battered body, and compounding the physical difficulties were the problems running through his mind - the Welshman had no idea where they were running, nor how they would escape their pursuers.

Brac's chest hammered with the exertion and fright; never before had he felt a dread like this, never was his own wellbeing so palpably threatened. The threat of violence or illness was always around the corner but the feeling of being hunted was a completely different experience, rendering him unable to consider anything else other than his escape from this situation, not even the destination to where they were heading. It was an all-consuming terror that roared at him with coarse bellows and clashing armour and thunderous footfalls, an unearthly discord threatening doom in the night. If he were caught, he would be hanged for theft from the King's quarry; a miserable end and all for a moment's greed. He had not been a man to covet, beyond the pipedream of striking back at the English.

And yet, Brac had indeed taken the first opportunity to strike back at the English, except the Welshman found himself regretting having done so. Grand ambitions fuelled by years of grieving and poisonous resentment had birthed an urge, that one day would manifest in a symbolic revenge against the invader. But he had not deliberated upon the consequences upon his own safety, let alone his way of life. In the hamlet and the quarry he faced no ostensible personal threats, beyond the occasional drunken scuffle. Brac kept himself quiet and went about his labour with little fuss. The English preferred it that way and, truth be told, so did he. The benefit of Lord de Grey's uncompromising manner of governance was that for years north Flintshire had been largely free of the fighting that had ravaged the country for a hundred years; and now Brac had thrown away that peace.

Hindsight. Everything was obvious with hindsight. Brac had spent a lifetime keeping his head down so as to not require hindsight.

Why did I do this? he asked himself, feeling his straggly hair catch another stray branch before having to dive left around a tall tree of black bark emerging out of the night. In the thick woods, both man and plant were chasing him, trying to bring him down. He knew he must run. The Frenchwoman's companion carrying the stone in the sack was ahead of him somehow, galloping at a remarkable speed through the uneven, cluttered and almost pitch-black terrain. The man must be part-horse or some other beast of burden, Brac imagined, such was his strength and stamina. It was then the wiry quarryman saw that the man with the stone was actually pulling away, and the chasing footfalls and shouts behind him were becoming ever closer. Driven to ever greater panic by the realisation he blundered on even more directly, his desperation removing his willingness to dodge obstacles that, in the briefest of moments he had to judge in the poor visibility, appeared to be sufficiently malleable to run through rather than around or under.

He brushed past the end of one such branch, a great thick arm almost perfectly horizontal across his path, with prying twigs for fingers that snared on the linen covering his right shoulder. It slowed the quarryman down somewhat, causing him to yelp as the twigs hooked through the material of his tunic and into his shoulder. In the instants it took to free himself of the arboreal trap Brac felt he was dragging the branch and its parent tree with him and his voice became ever higher with heightening terror.

He could hear the grunting of his pursuer as the man-at-arms careened through the vegetation his quarry had flattened just moments beforehand, his rattling mail complementing the nightmarish discord. Finally and mercifully the tough tunic material, designed to be nothing but durable, tore and released Brac from the branch's grip. He lumbered away, somehow accelerating despite his twisted body's reluctance to do so. As he did so the great branch sprang back in the opposite direction clothesline and struck the pursuing man-at-arms across the eyes; the great closing speed of man and branch created an impact with the viciousness of a whiplash and the severity of a training sword – the pursuer screamed as he stumbled with nothing to break his fall, clawing as he was at his eyes, one of which now blinded.

The bloodcurdling shriek spurred Brac on even faster than before and beyond what he thought his battered body could produce. The scream definitely belonged to a man, Brac decided in that instant, so it was possible the feisty Frenchwoman was still standing, somewhere, wherever she was in the forest at this point. He did not understand her French when she had last shouted and so did not know where she had gone, but the man with the stone had continued running so Brac thought he should follow suit.

And here they were, still running as the shouts and thumping of feet and clanking of mail diminished with every stride away from the path between the hamlet and the quarry. Brac's lungs burnt with exhaustion and his throat had dried out, caused by both the ferocious pace and the quarry dust he had inhaled almost every day for the past fifteen summers. He knew he would soon be unable to muster much more energy.

Chapter 2

The woman had always been light on her feet. Naturally athletic, she had been a swift runner since she was a girl. There had not been too many days sufficiently cold enough to keep her inside during her childhood, so she would spend months ranging the hills and woods around Carcassonne with her brother and their friends. Her brother was a typical boy, always picking up sticks and fencing with Cedric, the fat boy who lived at the tavern. But the siblings did not play soldiers together - she obeyed their mother's repeated instructions to not fight. The Frenchwoman remembered vividly her mother's fright at the idea of conflict; "be innocent whilst you still can, child," she used to say. But there was nothing to stop her running, climbing, swinging, falling and generally ruining the few clothes that her parents provided her. She remembered her childhood as more an adventure than a struggle because whatever struggles her family encountered, she found a way to climb or run or scramble over it. She had always considered difficulties and setbacks a challenge from God. There were always opportunities to test herself, mentally, physically, spiritually.

And it was so now. Her position in the Order's hierarchy prohibited the necessity of bearing arms, and in theory it was not considered a requirement inside of Christendom anyway. The Church, universal in its spread and influence, was the greatest empire the world had known and soon enough the military orders realised the Church's armies of officials, both clerical and lay, represented a network for the acquisition and transfer of information that dwarfed anything kingdoms were capable of. As the lands west of Outremer were not considered under threat from the Saracens, so the engagement in espionage took ever greater precedence.

The cloudiness of the battlegrounds for knowledge and secrets reflected itself in the makeup of the orders participating. Prior to sneaking into the quarry the Frenchwoman had reflected on her position in the hierarchy; did she even have a position? Who outside of England knew of her presence here, or even in England? Guy knew, and obviously so did Henry. Besides those two, though, she was unsure even if anyone else within the Order knew she was here. Or even if she worked with the Order at all. She wondered if she were truly that alone in the world. There were some in at the London Temple who knew her movements, surely. *If I were to die here, tonight, would anyone know of my whereabouts? Would my body have a name?*

Such fears did not linger long, because action was needed. She was not going to die here, tonight, because she was not going to be fighting anyone. None of the Order members played an active military role within Church lands not threatened by the Saracen, though she had seen enough to know the procurement of information was not only intrinsically risky but also likely to lead to *someone* fighting another. All the same, Guy, like her mother, had forbidden her playing at soldiers – her remit was to procure and provide details with as little fuss as possible. As far as she could help it, this avenue of investigation into the silver stone would be exhausted along such guidelines, with only minor caveats.

The first caveat was the use of the flat of her longsword to batter across the first man's right leg as he burst past her hiding place behind a wide tree. His momentum nearly wrenched the sword from her grip but the blow was sufficient for him to go vaulting over the unseen hurdle, crying out both in pain and fear of the pitch black into which he fell headfirst. The woman saw the man's mail glimmer and then disappear when he crashed with a huge crunch through what sounded like a large bush. She ran to where he had dropped his torch, picked it up and threw it at the next bobbing torch light weaving in her direction about ten yards away. She did not rely on it hitting the man, just to cause enough confusion so as to unbalance him. The torch missed him but the man had tripped ducking it, and collided with another tree with a heaving "*oof.*"

The woman did not stop to admire her work but had already bounded a few steps perpendicular to the angle of the approaching men, to intercept another. Invisible and inaudible amidst the cries of the hunters, she swept her sword flatside-first around her body in a wide arc, arms slightly bent so as to brace for impact with what she hoped to be the man's right shoulder. The blade thudded into his arm and knocked him down roaring in pain. Before she could find his dropped sword in order to throw it away into the dark of the forest, another man, without a torch, came flying into shady view from her left. All she saw was him drop his shoulder before he barged into her with a sickening impact through the middle of her chest as she instinctively turned to face him, sending her flying off her feet. She landed on the hard forest floor, winded and gasping for air and voice. Her sword was gone, she noticed, but she could not have wielded it if it were still in her hand. The man too had fallen following the collision and was shakily getting back to his feet in the shadow before her, grunting as his mail and fatigue tried to pull him down again. Approaching the prone woman, the man kicked her hard in the left thigh, causing her to yelp. Upon hearing a woman's voice, he stopped himself kicking again and instead bent down to lift her off the ground.

The dazed woman was a deadweight offering no assistance to the man picking her up. She heaved as her body flopped onto the man's shoulder, her breathing still not back in its usual rhythm. The shoulder in her midsection did not help. Her head and arms dangled loosely down towards the ground, and she could see nothing aside from the grey outline of the man's mail coat. He tramped forward through the dark without torchlight, but the woman was too weak to take advantage of their seclusion and force an escape. The shouts of the hunters had grown dim, muffled by the woods. All of her senses were deprived save the feeling that her chest had caved in. She then realised that her leg was throbbing from being kicked by her captor.

The softening effect of vegetation on the man's footfalls gave way to the solid thump on bare earth as they reached the path. She heard the same gruff English voice from moments earlier but her head was too foggy to make sense of it. Her English was excellent, but the she had never before taken such a heavy blow and it had disorientated her thinking along with her breathing. With no warning, she was dropped to the ground onto her back, and landed with a soft groan. The woman opened her eyes and saw three solid silhouettes standing over her, but could not tell if they were looking at her. Behind them, the sky was a beautiful inky blue, and for a brief moment she forgot her aching body, until one of the silhouettes kicked at her side with a heavy boot.

"Wake up, love. On your feet. You've been a naughty girl." It was the gruff Englishman who was presumably the leader of this group. The woman rolled over and lifted herself onto her elbows in a plank position, dragging her knees towards her aching chest and then pushed up slowly to her feet. None of the men offered her help. Standing up to her full height, the Frenchwoman could see half of each man's face in the silver moonlight as she silently looked around her. They had harsh faces, all bearded. She turned to face the third man and was greeted with a mailed fist to the side of her head.

She did not feel the impact, but awoke with her head and arms dangling down towards the ground again. They had slung her unconscious body over the back of a horse. It occurred to her that her hands were not bound, neither were her legs. She had no idea if that were through lack of rope, or simply because she was a woman who had been knocked off her feet twice in five minutes. Her head pounded but at least she could breathe, unlike before she'd been punched. She let out a small groan as she came to.

"Glad you're awake, love. I thought we'd never get anything out of you," said the gruff Englishman smugly. "Bit late for a stroll in the woods, don't you think? And a quarry is no place for a lady to go for as stroll at night. Might come into harm's way. Safe now though, love. So what's your name? No name? Ah, not to worry. We'll get some talk out of you tomorrow. Lucky for you, his lordship is in town, and he's a genial enough man. He won't mind silences as much as I do. I'm a talker, you see. Isn't that right, Wilf?"

Another voice, somewhere close, responded. "That's right, sir. You do like to talk." The tone was subservient.

"So it is." The gruff Englishman replied. His lordship will be very interested to hear why you're creeping around his quarry like this. Where are you from, love? And who are those other chaps you were with? No? Not to worry." He had an almost cheery disposition that was entirely out of keeping with the circumstances. He continued chatting away but the woman did not hear much more

16

as her eyelids closed, the gentle swaying of the horse and the concussion she had suffered lulling her to sleep.

The low hum of male voices buzzed around the woman's ears as her dreamless sleep faded away, to be replaced by the grogginess of consciousness. She sat upright, squinting eyes turning every which way, not recognising any of the environs nor remembering what she had been doing before going to sleep. She could make out a wooden floor sprawled around her, and motionless bodies stood either side of her. A man dressed in red was ahead of her, either much taller than those around him, or simply higher up. It was the latter. Her focus came back, though she now remembered why she could not see very well out of her left eye. The man in red was in fact sat on a large wooden chair, with a black hat and a thin, pale beardless face looking down at her whilst talking inaudibly to the men either side of him.

"Wake up, woman. His lordship has been waiting for your testimony." Guttural Welsh tones cut through the hum. She saw it was a man dressed in a brown tunic with wild curly hair and a wilder beard addressing her. He was stood to the red-dressed man's right, a step down from the red-dressed man's chair.

"Thank you, Reeves." The red-dressed man raised his right hand in a dismissive gesture. "You will stand in the presence of a lord, woman. Sir Edward, would you pick her up?" His demand was neither aggressive nor threatening but instructional, as if he were teaching a child. He spoke in the refined manner of the London court. The woman had visited London a few times and her French ears could pick out a few English accents. A hand, presumably belonging to Sir Edward, appeared underneath each of her armpits and the woman was lofted skyward onto her feet. The blood rushed from her head but Sir Edward was still behind her propping her up.

Reeves stepped forwards. "On behalf of King Edward, Lord Reginald de Grey, first Baron Grey de Wilton and Justice of Chester will pass judgement on your crimes," he announced with an air of superiority. The woman thought Reeves looked very pleased with himself. Lord Reginald looked quite bored. From his active role thus far in the proceedings, the woman guessed Reeves to be the manor sheriff.

Reeves continued, "The quarry at Rhuddlan is the personal property of King Edward himself, and theft from the King's own property, if proven, is punishable by death. In your case, woman, you will be drowned until dead." The word 'drowned' made the woman feel sick in her stomach. She thought she saw a smirk forming on the sheriff's face.

Reeves carried on in his pomp. Reginald was checking his fingers as if he had sat through such rehearsed accusations one thousand times before, which he probably had. "Sir Edward de Beauchamp, if you would step forward and speak."

Sir Edward moved from behind the woman and to her left. She could see that it was the gruff Englishman from the night before; he looked handsome, with dark brown hair and a short beard, less harsh than he did in the moonlight. He was above average height and wore a dark grey coat over a fashionable blue tunic. She considered him to be how a knight should look – noble, strong, confident. Of course, how these characteristics would play out in this situation was unclear. The threat of drowning was the first stab of realisation for her. Her and Henry forcing Brac to take them to the quarry, carrying the stone out of it and back into the woods, Sir Edward commanding they give themselves up, taking out three men-at-arms in the woods – that had all been par for course. Even the beating she had taken had not seemed terminal, just like water under the bridge.

But now, faced with authority of this magnitude, and with an accusation such as stealing from the King himself, in the light of day the woman began to consider her own mortality. She was not one to dwell on such thoughts thanks to the daily teachings imparted by the Order. They were reassuring. She was playing her role, and had played it well. There would be a reward for her service to Christ. But that word, 'drowning', it held terrors, and she tried to recompose herself.

Gruff Sir Edward went down on one knee before Lord Reginald. "My lord." He rose. "This woman was caught by my men during the highest moon last night, in the forest by the quarry of Rhuddlan. She was with two companions, both of whom have escaped justice through the woods, no thanks to this woman's remarkable aptitude for trouble. The three had been spotted in the quarry by two sentries posted by myself. An alarm had been raised and it just so happened that I had been at the town gates with some guardsmen, allowing us to make for the forest path. We cut off their escape along the path, but they made off into the woods and we caught this woman. One of her companions appeared to be carrying a large sack, presumably containing an item taken from the quarry. A later report from the sentries confirmed this story. We-" Sir Edward was interrupted.

"Tell me, Sir Edward," Baron de Grey interjected in an honest voice, "how is it that two people, one of whom carrying a rock in a bag, managed to evade capture from ten or so armed guards due to the actions of a woman?"

Looking at his feet, Sir Edward gave a small half-chuckle out of embarrassment rather than amusement. "You see, my lord, it appears this woman sacrificed her freedom for that of her companions, and in the close confines of the night-time forest, managed to disable three of our men through devious cunning. I have men currently hunting down the two companions as we speak. They shan't get far." Sir Edward looked at the woman, his expressionless face almost as bored as Lord Reginald's.

"I should hope your hunting men are more worthy than the three you had disabled," Lord Reginald stated. His curious eyes moved from Sir Edward to the woman. There was an easy nature to Lord Reginald's appearance; the short light grey hair was well trimmed, his resting face not sour like Reeves' but neutral, almost amiable. "So you fought off three men in the dark then, woman, and bought your friends some time. What is it of the King's quarry that you are willing to sacrifice your life so that another may keep it? Sir Edward tells me you have not revealed your identity yet, either. The possessions you carried were certainly not of any tradeswoman, nor your clothes. Yet such business as this is unbecoming of a lady of higher birth. Tell us who you are, woman."

The woman could see that Reginald's disinterested body language was a façade. She had learnt there were two types of noble in

England – the lucky noble and the skilled noble. The lucky noble would also tend to be an incompetent noble. She decided Lord Reginald was a skilled noble. He lacked the self-important haughtiness with which even Reeves suffered, and instead his amiable exterior and calm delivery were vehicles for a keen mind. An incompetent noble would not grasp the unusual circumstances surrounding this incident.

The woman cleared her throat, and the coughing caused her head to pound. "If it pleases my lord, I shall introduce myself." Reeves raised an eyebrow upon hearing the gentle French accent. Lord Reginald remained unmoved. "My name is Eleanor de Molay. If it pleases my lord, I should like opportunity to write to a kinsman for counsel and representation." El lowered her head and curtseyed.

"Excuse me, mademoiselle," Lord Reginald returned in El's and his own native French. It is a rare opportunity to entertain a Frenchwoman here in the north of Wales, particularly with your great name." He returned to English for the benefit of the English and Welsh speakers in the room. "Please, accept my apologies for the treatment you have received. The men responsible for this shall be punished. Sir Edward, please distribute appropriate discipline to those who treated Mademoiselle de Molay in a most unbecoming manner."

Sir Edward, mortified at his conduct towards a woman of such renowned birth, tried to maintain his composure. England was at war with France, yes, but a de Molay, here? "My lord," he said, nodding stiffly at the baron.

"All the same," Reginald continued, "I do wonder, what is it that has brought the blood of Templar Grand Master de Molay to Rhuddlan." Murmurings arose from the onlookers gathered around; Grand Masters of the religious military orders were held in an almost mythical regard. And here was the blood and flesh of one!

"It would seem your name has saved you from the brunt of Sheriff Reeves' professional zeal," Reginald added. He gestured at Reeves, who appeared just as mortified at his treatment of the little Frenchwoman as was Sir Edward. Sir Edward had treated this lady with great disrespect and there was no excusing that, but at least Sir

Edward was of a similar social position. Reeves' threats were inexcusable *and* socially insubordinate.

"I am afraid the King's justice, however, will have to be observed, Mademoiselle de Molay," the baron continued. "You shall be granted your letter to your kinsman. Your counsel shall arrive at Chester immediately for trial, and until such time you shall stay at Rhuddlan castle. Which, incidentally, is where the stones you visited in the quarry last night are headed. No thanks to our Welsh friends, who decided the previous stones would like better back in the earth." Lord Reginald retained his amicable air, as if he were offering El the hospitality between friends and not between accuser and accused.

El nodded her head respectfully. "Thank you, Lord Reginald."

"And should your accomplices be found, they shall also stand trial with you at Chester. Warrants for their arrest shall be issued." Reginald knew this was tantamount to folly – he, nor his men, had no idea what these accomplices were called, let alone what they looked like.

There was no way of extracting such information from the French lady either; if news broke out that Lord Reginald had sanctioned torture against the Grand Master's niece! The King had been on frosty terms with the Order for over a decade since he had raided the Order's treasury at the Temple in the capital. But King Edward Longshanks, a fierce and proud man, knew when and where to tread carefully and he had let it be known to his councillors that the Order was not to be alienated further at this time of conflict with France. Lord Reginald was an old friend of Longshanks and agreed with the sentiment. Further, the new Order Master for England was a formidable man, with whom the Baron de Grey had sought acquaintance and political cooperation as a potential ally against the king of France. Lady de Molay would be looked after as a guest of King Edward whilst awaiting judgement.

El felt a wave of reassurance wash over her. The lord's soothing manner together with his quite reasonable terms of imprisonment had helped stay the adrenaline rush she had been fighting down. She thought she felt her knees knock a little. She did not know if it were relief or a consequence of the previous night's exertions.

"One final thing, my lady." Reginald's tone became icy. El stiffened slightly, as did the others in stuffy hall. The sheriff, still shaken at his accidental insubordination to the lady, turned his eyes to Lord Reginald who was still sat to his left. "You do see the difficulty I face here, Mademoiselle de Molay. King Edward is at war with the French. You are French. King Edward is at war with the Welsh outlaws. You were found sneaking into the quarry being used to rebuild a castle attacked by the Welsh. King Edward is not on good terms with the Templar Order. You are the niece to the Order's Grand Master. As it is, I shall have your letter vetted, for it is not every day, or every night indeed, that we find foreignborn ladies traversing our quarries..."

Lord Reginald paused, and looked out to his left, through the first of the small square windows that lined one side of the small hall. The sun shone fiercely. Reginald was a warrior and an adventurer; he would much rather be out riding the hills than sat here next to John Reeves. The Welsh outlaws were contemptible, but their countryside was a delight. He was rather disappointed the insurgency had been crushed only a few months prior. There would be a lot more sitting around in halls next to John Reeves and a lot less adventure, a lot less *enjoying* himself.

Reginald turned back to El, knowing the effect the pause in his speech was having on the woman. "My friend the King would not look kindly upon any intelligence leaving Rhuddlan under my watch. I'm sure you can understand this requirement, my lady." He stood, and snapped his fingers at some unseen figures over El's shoulder. "My lady," he bowed, and she returned the gesture. Sir Edward appeared at her side once more, taking her arm.

"Lady de Molay, if you would please accept my sincerest apologies." The knight sounded just so. Gone was the knightly air of confidence, replaced by an embarrassed, almost meek tone of deference. Indeed, El thought, if he had not such a knightly look about his face, his height and his clothes, then his body language would appear almost pathetic. "And if you would mind following me this way, my lady. We shall leave for Chester at first light tomorrow morning."

El remained a little flustered at Lord Reginald's parting riposte. She looked the gruff Englishman in the eyes, seeing genuine remorse there. She wondered if there would have been remorse if she had simply been a peasant girl. In her experience, knights tended to be bullies, and bullies tended to be knights. It was an unfortunate state of affairs in both France and England. Her mother had told her stories passed on from her uncle Jacques, of the behaviour he had witnessed from such men. El liked to believe men of the Order such as Uncle Jacques were of a different cloth, both professionally and spiritually.

Chapter 3

"Philippe will not like it. In fact, I do not think even I will be able to stay his temper." Comte Mathieu de la Marche leaned back heavily on his chair, the lamplight illuminating his clean-shaven chin and thin mouth along with the very tops of his hands that were clasped together on his chest. "Norris forgets himself sometimes. These are not the actions of a man of the Church. Are you sure this is what he said?"

The other man, his small, greying, nondescript face covered in grimy stubble, spoke as plainly as he looked. "Le Verre has not been wrong so far. I do not see why we should doubt him now. Le Verre advises action be taken before Norris calls on Rome."

Comte Mathieu despised the little man sat opposite him for so many reasons. One of them was his haughty manner, delivered as it was in the most monotonous manner possible. Who was this lowlife to give orders to the King's councillor? But Comte Mathieu had to tolerate these orders, because the lowlife was only the messenger. Mathieu did not even know his real name. He was referred to as the Le Gris but he did not know if this was his actual name or just a reference to his general colouring, voice, personality or all three. Such a grey aspect was highly prized in this line of work though, and Mathieu did appreciate this. Le Verre, which Mathieu thought was definitely not a real name, required runners who could move *incognito* through the lands, carrying prized morsels of information for clients such as Mathieu. The Comte de la Marche was still leaning back on his chair, hands clasped, when he realised he had not answered Le Gris precisely because he was thinking about how much he despised him.

"Very well." Mathieu leaned forward, bringing his stern face back into the lamplight, his eyes hard as the granite cheekbones that flanked his thin nose. He placed his hands palms down slowly on the table in a subconscious display of intimidation. "Request that Le Verre lean on Norris, to bring him back into line. It is imperative. If Norris does recall those loans, even the Florentines will barely be able to cover the shortfall in the treasury. The Church is of no concern at the moment. The Pope is weak. But our treasury situation… this weakness is a concern. Edward Longshanks and the Emperor Adolphus are in treaty and will soon come. I want news of Norris within the week."

The Comte reflected for a moment on how much he despised Norris as well. He despised many people, actually. He had to. The realm would not prosper if he went easy on those who were not entirely committed to its elevation. Norris was the new Order Master of France and he had proved spiky in his dealings with the Court in the year since his appointment. His obdurateness had solidified further since Philippe's decision to move the Royal Treasury from the Paris Temple to the Louvre, a move Mathieu had cautioned against. And to make matters even worse, Norris was English.

Mathieu clasped his hands together once more. "That is all," he uttered in his rumbling deep voice. Le Gris stood, bowed and turned to leave the room without saying a word. Mathieu sighed. He had suspected for a while that Philippe would eventually turn on the Order, as he had on the Lombardy bankers a few years earlier when repaying their loans became impossible, but Norris' prospective actions would catalyse the entire process. It would be an infinitely more difficult execution than were the Lombard arrests, though equally the payout would be immeasurable. But only financially, he reminded himself, and even then entirely expediently. Almost certainly would the kingdom's enemies some advantage in a conflict between France and the Order, particularly if England or the Empire leant on the Church. And what of the moral repercussions? Mathieu was not convinced the Temple's fiscal cunning was entirely in line with the Lord Jesus' teachings, but even so he knew many Order members for whom the label 'pious' could have been coined. Some of their heroics in the Holy Land were the stuff of legend; surely the Lord would look out for His own in the face of sustained lay pressure and, dare Mathieu think it, persecution.

He leaned back on his chair and rested his clasped hands back on his chest, staring at the sole lamp in the small room. The night was still and the moon was full, but his room received no moonlight, for it was facing away from the Seine, which was magnificently illuminated like some great silver snake lazily slithering to La Manche. There were too many variables at play for his liking were Philippe to somehow strike back at the Order as the Comte knew he would. Le Verre's intercession with Norris was of critical importance.

Mathieu looked out of the window, unable to see anything but bright lights in his eyes from staring at the naked flame. Le Verre had proved entirely reliable in the years Mathieu had dealt with him. They had never met, but this was of no great import to the Comte who considered it to mean there was one fewer person to dislike in the world. He wondered how long it had been since he had willingly held a conversation with someone about something not related to the running of the kingdom. Even the bishop's small talk had all but evaporated. The other courtiers knew to avoid Mathieu in anything other than official state business. He did not hide his contempt for the courtiers' ridiculous dress sense or their snivelling around the King, or their ostentatious spending or their extravagant hunting trips. He looked back at his desk, the dancing lights in his eyes having evaporated, and put his hand to his chin to feel the smooth skin where his stubble had been since a few hours previously. The incident that very morning at the palace, when Guillaume de Troyes had tripped over his own mantle, was a case in point. The garish dark blue fabric fastened about his shoulders with a golden bear clasp on his chest, dragging along the floor at least a pace behind him, was almost as kingly as Philippe's royal blue cloak. De Troyes' effeminate laughter echoing between the palace walls was perhaps even worse. That in turn had set off the sycophantic Geoffroi d'Hainault and his lackeys. Was a mantle really necessary? If a man needed his clothing to let others know of his status, then he was no man of status at all. Mathieu *hmph*ed and leaned back on his chair as was his custom when thinking. At least the next and last part of his evening's work would not grind on him in such a manner. It would be tough, but in an intellectually satisfying manner. Mathieu enjoyed a challenge when it did not involve talking to people he despised.

He then turned further to the back-right corner of the room, where his old retriever lay asleep. Quo had been with him for longer than the King had reigned, and Mathieu could not remember a day when the dog with the white fuzzy face and small build had not accompanied him to his work. The conversations that beast had been privy to! The old boy was sleeping solidly, as he had done in recent months, scarcely stirring despite heavy boots clomping across the floorboards. He was in robust health, just a little slower than he used to be. *Much like myself*, Mathieu thought. The Comte could not bear to think of the old boy not lying in his favourite position in the corner, catching the afternoon sunshine through the window, and then not really moving even after the sun had long disappeared.

"Pascal!" He called. Quo lifted raised his eyes at the sudden increase in volume, without bothering lifting his head off the floor. Pascal, his scribe and secretary, had been writing at a table outside Mathieu's room surrounded as usual by at least eight candles. Pascal had worked for the Comte for countless years and, Mathieu hoped, for countless more following his acquisition of a set of eyeglasses to preserve his eyesight. The Comte had heard that many Lombards and Genovese had taken to reading with such eyeglasses so as to improve their vision; in many instances, so the stories went, men who had almost lost their eyesight were suddenly able to see again as if healed by the Lord Himself. The Comte did not know from where the Italians developed this idea, but he considered it nothing short of marvellous. Pascal always worked hunched over his desk with his nose almost touching the paper on which he wrote and Mathieu wondered why he had never seen another scribe or monk work in such a way. Now the little secretary could sit almost upright in his chair and write noticeably more legibly. The Comte thought Pascal to be at least thirty-five years old, probably more but the extent to which these new eyeglasses had rejuvenated Pascal's eyesight gave the Comte hope he would carry on writing until he was fifty and beyond.

The little man hurried around the corner out of the sun-like glare of his candles into the orange hue of Mathieu's room. He still held his eyeglasses on their thin stick in his left hand. "Yes, my lord?" His voice was respectful, with no hint of fear. Pascal was too good a secretary to need to fear the Comte.

"Please would you send a note to the Master of the Treasury that I would see him now? And have my reports for the King readied to be

27

sent in the morning. I may have an addition or two to make by then, in which case I will catch you beforehand in the morning." Mathieu talked as if Pascal were his equal. The two were by no means alike in status but Mathieu had become familiar with the funny little scribe and his red face, and could not imagine not having him there at his table surrounded by artificial daylight all throughout the year.

"Of course, my lord. And your reports are completed, awaiting your additions and seal, my lord." Pascal bowed and backed out of the room without looking up.

"Thank you, Pascal."

The scribe turned and scurried away. In his movements, Pascal was as close to a mouse as a human could be; never heard, never seen, but always there. He had developed a flair for letters at a young age, when his father was attached to Mathieu's household in Lyon. This was just as well because Pascal was not physically strong, and was worse than useless on the one occasion he had been called to arms in the retinue of Mathieu's father. Mathieu allowed himself a small smile at the memory of Pascal failing to reach a target with his bowshot, let alone hitting it. Mathieu was not one to criticise those patently unsuited to a compulsory practice and requested Pascal be moved to his own retinue when he moved to Paris to serve at the young Philippe's court. For his own part, the scribe had a mental steel and did not allow his martial embarrassment haunt him despite the lifetime of ridicule he had suffered since – the nickname 'Sagittaire' had followed him all the way to the capital, and he had adopted it as an honorary surname.

The Comte took a sip of his red wine. On long days such as this, he would drink many cups of the dark liquid. He savoured the taste but decided against anymore. Even for him, he had drunk a lot. Mathieu had the constitution of an ox and so he never managed to get drunk on the stuff, which gave the other courtiers further reason to avoid him – for what was the purpose of fine Bordeaux claret if not to get one drunk?

But he was beginning to feel a little cloudy, and could not afford to be anything but razor sharp with the Master of the Treasury. Leaning over to the right of his desk he placed the cup as far away as possible from his comfortable sitting position, so that he would not be able to simply reach and take another draught without considerable effort. He leant back again, clasping his hands together over his chest and closed his eyes for a moment. He instantly regretted placing the cup out of easy reach. Yet he was determined to show some resolve against temptation so he chose not to rectify the error. In any case, the Master of the Treasury would take a little while to make his way up from the Louvre, and Mathieu felt he had earned a little rest. He could always take some more wine later.

The Comte awoke, startled by Pascal's nasal pitch announcing the arrival of the Master of the Treasury. The Comte pushed himself forward towards his desk, straightening his tunic down and then rubbing his eyes. He felt a slight wetness on his cheek, and realised with no little mortification he had dribbled during his sleep – for how long had he been dozing? He often worked long into the night, though with the developments of recent months, particularly regarding the kingdom's increasingly complicated diplomatic position, 'often' was becoming 'always'. Still he thrived on it and as he stood, his back and legs welcoming the opportunity to stretch, he reflected that he would probably be closer to the grave if he did not work so hard.

The tall, thin serious man strode in, his dark cloak billowing so dramatically it threatened to extinguish the lamp flame with its draught. He advanced like a malevolent shadow consuming the dim orange light, filling the room with a presence almost more than human. He had permanently cross eyebrows and a snarl carved into his rocky cliff-like face. Lemaître, the Master of the Treasury, was perhaps the only man in the kingdom more sombre than Comte Mathieu.

Mathieu enjoyed his conversations with the Master of the Treasury because of this fact; especially when they immediately followed a conversation with someone as base and contemptuous as Le Gris. Lemaître did not say anything that did not need to be said, which made him ideal for looking after the King's finances. This applied to both positive and negative circumstances, which the headstrong King did not enjoy but accepted.

Mathieu admired how this dour mannered yet sinister looking man was almost entirely invulnerable to the King's tempers and beyond his machinations, much like Mathieu himself. A few of the fellow courtiers had wondered if he were actually a ghost and so beyond physical reproach, hence offering some protection against the King's rages. The Comte considered this unlikely, but did think there was a piece of Lemaître's soul missing, surely. He wondered if Lemaître's face would crack and shatter if he tried to smile. It seemed even the sleeping Quo could sense something different about the man, in that way dogs are sensitive to things beyond the awareness of man. The old boy did not wake for anyone nowadays thanks to his deteriorating hearing and eyesight, except now his ears pricked up in interest at Lemaître's entrance.

"Good evening, my dear Comte Mathieu," stated Lemaître, his voice as monotonous as his black cloak and tunic. "Please advise me of what you have heard from the Order." He did not immediately take the seat opposite Mathieu, a habit that always unnerved the Comte. Mathieu was unsure whether Lemaître deliberately remained standing in situations like this so as to intimidate others. He thought it more likely this were entirely accidentally for the act of intimidation would detract from the efficient delivery of what needed to be said.

"Good evening, my dear Comte Lemaître. Thank you for coming at such an hour. Would you care for some wine? Please, sit." Mathieu knew Lemaître would not partake of the wine, for it wasted time. The snarling man looked to the chair to his left with derision before dragging it slowly across the silent floor and took his seat. "I have word from the Paris Temple. Norris is becoming agitated and is threatening- no, he *will* call in the loans. I am working to at least delay this occurring. He will move before the year is out. You are aware, my dear Comte Lemaître, of what this will mean. I am to meet with the Florentines in the next week but I require your preparation in the event that Norris cannot be tamed. I fear... Philippe will not accept this situation. Even with my assurances. I need your assurances that the King will not react as badly as I fear. You recall what happened with the Lombards." Mathieu leaned back in his chair, clasping his hands together.

There was no hint of acknowledgement in Lemaître's face but from the snarling gap of his mouth his bass voice rumbled in response. "The Paris mint is addressing the silver issue right away, my dear Comte Mathieu. I estimate the proposed debasement of the coinage to save the treasury nearly twenty per cent of silver per *livre* coin, which will add approximately twenty thousand *livres* to our reserves by the close of the year."

Mathieu had hoped Lemaître would not resort to reducing the quantity of silver per coin; like raiding a Templar treasury, it was only an expedient option. He leaned further back in his chair, slowly moving his face out of sight as he had been when dealing with Le Gris, and sighed. It was getting late. The Comte Mathieu was beginning to regret arranging an important discussion at this time. He had assumed the timing of the meeting was neither here nor there for the Master of the Treasury, who looked as if he did not sleep at all.

The Master of the Treasury's plodding voice continued. Mathieu thought Lemaître should have been born something other than French; a Bohemian, definitely a German. Maybe even Norse. English! Yes. Any land with a barbaric tongue. Not the sonorous French, heir to the tongues of Charlemagne and the Empire. He wondered whether Lemaître was so efficient with his language because he was so ponderous at speaking it, or if he had been born like it. If, indeed, he had been born at all – there could be something to the rumours that Lemaître was a phantom of sorts.

"And the English armies in Gascony will not last the autumn," Lemaître droned on. "Their manpower issues are becoming critical. I am willing to pledge you support in order to encourage the Scottish to distract King Edward to the north." Lemaître did not make promises lightly. Mathieu also knew that Lemaître did not make promises with the expectation of repayment; they both put the kingdom above all.

"A most gracious offer, my dear Comte Lemaître." Mathieu inclined his head. "I have been in contact with the Scots, yes. They do not need much encouragement. Should we secure Gascony before the year is out, there should be sufficient *livres* to perhaps tempt some of King Edward's marcher lords in Wales, do you think? I have it on good authority that the English barons are quite dissatisfied with their King's governance and warmongering." Mathieu was testing Lemaître's head for figures as much as he was testing his political nous.

Lemaître's face remained unchanged, giving away no hint as to whether he had considered bribing almost everyone who was not King Edward. "King Philippe is looking to offer the Emperor Adolphus a financial incentive so as to keep the Empire neutral. This is his primary concern." Mathieu knew this already though he did not let his face express this fact, nor show his slight disappointment in the Master of the Treasury's loyalty to the rules. Lemaître was too straight to match Mathieu's political cunning. "This and stopping Norris are my main issues, outside of Gascony. Unfortunately, I cannot offer silver for your purposes in Wales at this time, my dear Comte Mathieu."

"This is not a problem, my friend," replied Mathieu cheerfully, with a big smile on his face. Lemaître did not respond in kind. Mathieu continued, "I fear I get ahead of myself sometimes. But a man in my position, he needs to see the steps ahead. Perhaps once the English have left Gascony and the Paris mint has saved us the silver and Norris has backed down and the Emperor is safe and warm behind the Rhine by the autumn and we have funded a Scottish uprising, then we can discuss my plot to incite Wales once more. They seem to have an inexhaustible supply of princes to rally around."

Without thinking, he leaned across to his right and picked up his cup, taking a deep draught of the wine. He knew that some way or another, the English marcher lords in Wales held the key to this posturing between Philippe and Edward. Mathieu could not remember the names of the marcher lords. They were Edward's loyal retainers. Could he drive a wedge between them and their King? There would be a way - a dynasty built on war as was the Plantagenet would surely fall in the same manner

The Comte de la Marche carefully replaced his cup, only now acknowledging he had given into the lure of the red stuff. "Pascal Sagittaire is delivering my reports to Philippe tomorrow morning; perhaps you will accompany these reports with your own reassurances on the silver coinage issue? I hope you will keep in mind how fruitful an invisible war against the English in Wales could be for us, my dear Comte Lemaître."

Lemaître was sat leaning to his left, with his left thumb underneath his chin and index finger by his temple, framing the permanent snarl. "I am to visit the King tomorrow upon his return from Flanders. I share your concerns over the treasury, Comte Mathieu, I assure you. I would be interested in reading those reports before I meet with him, if you have a copy of them?"

"Indeed I do. I shall have Pascal deliver them to your chamber tonight."

From below the window came urgent hoof-falls and whinnying.

"Riders…" Mathieu sprung out of his chair with a swiftness belying someone of his age and leant out of the window. Quo noticed the movement and lifted his head, ears raised with an intrigued face, waiting for his master to provide an assurance following his sudden movement. "A messenger. I did not expect one quite so soon. My dear Lemaître, I think your discussion with the King should be a little less fraught tomorrow." Mathieu turned on his heels, smiling at the snarling phantom in the chair.

"How do you mean?" Lemaître sounded cynical, unconvinced at Mathieu's predictions. Lemaître did not deal with optimism, nor pessimism for that matter. Pragmatism was all there was.

"Your prediction of a pending English collapse in Gascony is correct, except for the timing. Have more faith in your Frankish brothers-in-arms." Mathieu walked briskly, looking down at the floorboards and deliberately scuffing his heels, approaching the desk moving straight for his cup of wine. He finished it, disappointed there was so little left and subconsciously shook the cup for the dregs. Placing the cup back down, he faced the grim monolith that was Lemaître's face. "Are you sure I cannot interest you in some wine, my dear Comte Lemaître?" Mathieu asked as he picked the cup back up, analysing the simple carved patterns worked into it, spiralling and swirling around in an approximation of a stormy ocean with fish leaping free of the turbulence. He knew it was a rhetorical question and did not need to look expectantly at the Master of the Treasury awaiting the negative response.

"No, thank you," said Lemaître, curt as always.

"A shame, my friend. This is fine Bordeaux red, personally sourced by de Châtillon." Mathieu looked at the doorway, where footsteps accompanied a shadow dancing ever larger across the corridor. Pascal appeared at the door and awaited permission to speak. "You have heard the riders too, Pascal?" Mathieu asked.

"Yes, my lord. They have been sent from the Comte d'Artois. I shall send them up immediately." The little man bowed and scurried off down the corridor, his mouse-like presence having barely registered amongst the big cats in Mathieu's office.

"Do you have an itinerary of the assets likely to be gained in Aquitaine?" asked Mathieu of Lemaître. "I have acquired very recent figures from the merchant houses on the trade situation in the region, if you should like them?"

"Yes, if you would," Lemaître growled, "they should be useful for my discussion tomorrow. If the tidings are as you say, Mathieu, then the treasury figures should benefit to an extent surpassing that of the coinage debasement. Nonetheless, I intend to continue with the debasement. It is prudent to keep the crown wealthier than the population."

Comte Mathieu admired Lemaître for his pragmatism as much as his straight talking, but at times felt the stone-faced man was too rigid in his thinking. This was not unexpected, given the man's temperament and employment. But his stark division of crown and people was unhealthy for the kingdom in the long run – Mathieu suspected that debasement was actually dangerous in the long run, with the previously strong currency being displaced by a weaker one along with the added complication of creditors being paid back in less valuable currency than that in which the loan was issued. Further impoverishment of the commons, financially weakening the crown – the only benefit would fall upon the kingdom's enemies.

"There must be a threshold at which the coinage must be held, my dear Comte Lemaître. The long-term ramifications might be unsustaina-"

Mathieu was interrupted by footfalls out in the corridor, and the breathless arrival of Pascal at the door. "Ah yes, please come in. What tidings do you bring from the Comte d'Artois?"

A bedraggled horseman stepped across the threshold of Mathieu's office and stood to the right of the desk so that the seated Master of the Treasury could remain so whilst seeing him. The rider removed his helmet and nodded in deference to the lords present. Lemaître turned slowly, unsettling the messenger somewhat with his grim visage. The horseman's dark hair was damp with sweat and his blue eyes tried focusing on the standing Mathieu's face, desperately avoiding eye contact with the terrifying apparition sat in the chair. "My lords, I report the complete defeat of the English armies in Aquitaine at the hands of the Comte d'Artois at Château de Bellocq. The English Earl Henry de Lacy has been taken prisoner along with approximately eight thousand soldiers, but Edmund Crouchback, brother to the English king, has escaped. He is being pursued to the coast as we speak."

"'Complete' is a strong word, my man," Mathieu smiled at him. "Can you be sure? The King will want certainties, of course."

"Yes, my lord. Jean de Vendôme is moving south and west from Chateau de Montfort, and the Comte d'Artois has sent soldiers north and east. The remaining English garrison forces in the region have no leadership and will be caught between the two advancing armies." The horseman stood motionless, staring ahead at the open window whilst the Comte de la Marche slowly walked to his right, watching the floorboards as he walked, hands clasped behind his back.

Mathieu turned back to the horseman. "Very good, messenger. I will take your reports." Mathieu gestured for the papers. "Go downstairs, there is beer and wine in the kitchen. Pascal shall show you. I thank you for your good work, my man." Mathieu looked at the doorway where Pascal had been remained during the exchange and the secretary beckoned the horseman go with him. The horseman bowed to the lords and left. In the corner, Quo struggled to his feet, his back legs weakening in his fourteenth year, and padded around in a circle before slumping down in precisely the same position he had occupied all evening. Mathieu walked over and vigorously ruffled the dog's coat around his neck with both hands, at which the dog stretched his legs and arched his back.

"My dear Comte Lemaître, I feel both of our conversations with the King tomorrow shall be that much easier. If our matters are tied up for the evening, I shall walk with you down to the hall." Mathieu stood, leaving Quo wondering where the attention had gone, and walked to the doorway.

"Thank you, my dear Comte Mathieu," grumbled the ghostly Lemaître. Mathieu knew it was not a grumble of dissatisfaction.

Having discovered and broken up a game of dice between the three guards whom had accompanied Lemaître, his own guards Roger and Jean, Berenice the maid and Pascal, Mathieu sent the Master of the Treasury on his way into the night, accompanied by his guardsmen. Watching from the doorway, there seemed nothing more apt than Lemaître melting into the black shadows cast by the trees that punctured the ink-blue night sky. The men-at-arms' plate and swords glinted in the brilliant full moonshine, but Lemaître was, aesthetically, darkness incarnate, and after a few tens of yards he was gone.

Mathieu remained in the doorway for a few moments, looking into the night sky at everything and nothing, mulling over the good tidings from Aquitaine, received sooner than expected, and trying to second-guess what would be Philippe's response.

"Good news, then, my lord?" asked Roger, knowing full well the answer.

Very fatigued, Mathieu cared little for his guardsman's opinions on the Comte d'Artois' victory. If past conversations were anything to go by, and 'conversation' was a generous term, the Comte de la Marche did not think Roger would contribute anything that he and Lemaître had not already thought of. "*Mmm*," was all he replied, at least giving the dark-haired guardsman the courtesy of looking at him whilst retreating back into the dim hallway.

"No more dice games," Mathieu half-heartedly ordered whilst yawning.

Roger and Jean both acknowledged his command but all three knew the guards would not heed it for long; the two had practically exchanged sleep for playing games in the last few weeks and yet somehow remained fit for duty, a resilience to fatigue that bemused the Comte. Not knowing how close it was to dawn but believing it to be answer to be less than he would like, Mathieu cared little for how much the guardsmen played or slept so long as he himself could rest.

He rubbed his eyes and upon opening them saw Pascal had brought Quo downstairs. "Thank you, Pascal. Get some sleep."

"My lord," replied the bespectacled scribe.

The Comte drudged wearily along the stark corridor to his chamber with Quo padding along ahead. A few torchlights burned on the wall mountings, providing small relief from the utter darkness of the windowless path from his office to his bed. It was both his favourite and least favourite time of the day – Mathieu was adept at separating his business from what remained of his private life, yet the transition from the former to the latter was bittersweet. He heaved the door open skillfully so that the wooden creaking was at a minimum. Familiar pitch black welcomed him as the dog slipped into the room silently and sightlessly settled down on his rug by the far corner. Mathieu edged forward, unseeing yet fully aware of his surroundings because he had done this almost every night for over a decade.

As usual, Jaqueline did not rouse as he pulled back the top cover on the bed. Mathieu sighed inaudibly. The Comte thought he and his wife had been in love once; they had married over twenty years ago in Guéret, uniting the leading families of Guéret and Bourganeuf. He had not always been such a serious man; as a youth he had been adventurous, cheeky and passionate. And there had been Jaqueline - as the dashing heir to the County of La Marche, Mathieu had the pick of the daughters of the landed wealth, not to mention any peasant girls he fancied should he have chosen, but he had only ever had eyes for Jaqueline de Bourganeuf.

37

She was the kindest and most gentle soul, with a keen intellect and a wicked sense of humour that Mathieu could not resist. Her mesmeric green eyes were like emeralds captivating all she spoke to, and her infectious smile was breathtaking. They had struck up a friendship during their teenage years having first met when the de Bourganeufs visited their liege lord at Guéret, and as she had matured Mathieu began noticing her blossoming beauty. At her coming of age, the heir to the county of La Manche had asked for her hand in marriage and she had kissed him hard and said yes.

He still loved her desperately, but knew she did not him. Mathieu settled himself down into bed, remembering the days when she would hold him and lock her emerald eyes to his, not needing to say anything to communicate her love for him. He longed for her to roll over and lay an arm across his chest. But her fire for him had died down after only a few years and as the master merchant in the trade of information, Mathieu could not help hear of supposed liaisons between his wife and a courtier here, a knight there. The only solace he could find was in the opportunities afforded by his position to have these whispers stopped very quickly.

He was not angry with her at all; men and women would not be human if feelings did not fluctuate with the passage of time. He just regretted that it was her love for him that had been extinguished. Mathieu lay on his back, staring blindly at the ceiling somewhere above him. He was almost certain the second child she had bore, Luc, was not his though he had never voiced this suspicion and had not let this affect his relationship as father to the boy. The Comte had fostered a reputation as the cold string-puller behind the crown but truly this personality was born of the crushing sadness brought on by the years of rejection he suffered from the one love of his life. The sadness weighed down on his chest as it did every night when he got into bed beside his oblivious wife, and he rolled to his right, away from her, and curled up.

Chapter 4

The cloudless morning sky and motionless tree branches promised another day of oppressive heat, in what had already been a sweltering summer. Sporadic thunderstorms had punctuated the dry weeks, and Henry was glad the rain had held off the past couple of days during their escape from the forest around Rhuddlan. Sleeping in the forest was far more comfortable when it was not raining. The heat itself was of no concern to him. His dark features found it far more bearable than did the fairer-skinned English he had grown up around, and the English and Welsh summers were nothing on what he had experienced in the Holy Land.

The contrast with Brac could not have been starker, however. For a quarryman he was remarkably sensitive to heat and sunlight, his thicket-like hair and the dark brown hedge of a beard that enclosed his face somehow failing to offer protection. Henry thought it just as well that Brac had been born a Welshman, born in what was surely the rainiest corner of all Christendom. Sometimes the tanned Englishman had wondered if the forty days and forty nights of deluge before the Great Flood had anything on springtime in this rugged land. There was a peace about the wild rain on the hills, though, that Henry enjoyed. It represented a simpler existence, more pure and honest, often brutal but not threatening.

The two had spent the hours of darkness on the move since their nigh-on blind run through the forest outside the quarry two nights previous, taking advantage of the full moon lighting their route across the hills towards Chester. Their ensuing journey had unfolded in almost the opposite nature of their original flight from Lord Reginald's men – they had literally stumbled across a sleeping shepherd on the first night, and remarkably the shepherd's dog had chosen to not to raise the alarm, in what Brac considered a blatant dereliction of duty.

Brac felt exhausted. His days in the quarries were long enough without needing to spend consecutive nights running for his life. He envied Henry's effortless ability to fall asleep almost anywhere he put his head down. The knight had dictated they would rest during daylight hours so as to reduce the chances of their being spotted. But even in the shade of the rock outcrop, shielded from the hillside by low hanging beech branches, Brac could not sleep solidly through the heat and his anxiety.

The wiry man had not left much behind in Rhuddlan and had no family there. The English, Lord Reginald himself, had taken care of that. Even so, his newfound independence from the English lord's yoke was unsettling precisely because he now belonged nowhere and to no one. The hamlet was all Brac had known and the quarry wall represented a physical barrier separating him from the rest of the world. He never strayed off the beaten path through the woods to and from the quarry. His mother had taught him that.

The Welshman felt a tinge of regret and swallowed hard, trying to suppress it. He could not remember how long it had been since his family had passed.

Brac blinked slowly and threaded the fingers of his right hand through his beard, tugging on the hair with stress. The wiry man stood up straight and peered down the hill at the track in the distance. He was now a wanted criminal, with no roof over his head and no food on his table, not that he had a table either. Even worse, his only guarantor of safety at this moment was an unarmed Englishman, also a wanted criminal, whom he had only just met. An Englishman!

Brac cursed his rashness in trying to offload the silver stone to the Frenchwoman. She had definitely been the more authoritative of the two inquisitors, and the wiry man did not consider Henry her equal. Yet here he was, with Henry and the stone, whilst the Frenchwoman was presumably in some dungeon under the castle at Lord de Grey's pleasure. He lifted his gaze and stared into the deep blue morning sky, wondering how the fortunes of his life had reversed not only so dramatically but also so cruelly, at a time when he thought he may be able to make something of his life by striking back at the English.

He pondered this seemingly calamitous outcome for a few moments, after which he allowed the outside world into his conflicted mind. There was something about the still warmth that reminded Brac of his childhood. Summer mornings seemed to hold the promise of infinite adventure. In the years before they followed their father to the quarries, Brac and his brother would range the woods, going a whole day without seeing another soul. Only once had they stayed out over night in the forest. It had held no fear for them - no shadows took the form of stalking ghosts and the wind did not whisper malevolently in the darkness. But upon returning home their mother thrashed them harder than he could ever recall, certainly harder than their father had done.

Brac thought he must have been seven or eight years old then. He reflected on how he had not spent a night away from his house since that night and had always equated running away, no matter for how long, with the wrath of punishment from authority. Brac's nostalgia dissipated at this recollection, to be replaced with the overwhelming sense of guilt that had wracked him for the past two days.

Henry clapped Brac on the shoulder, snapping him out of his daydream. The quarryman jumped as he had countless times during their flight. "It's nearly over, my friend." Henry spoke in his typical neutral tone. Brac was not entirely convinced by the knight's reassurance. For the day and a half Brac had shared Henry's company, the knight's calm demeanour had remained steadfast amidst the stress of their situation, yet still the bearded Welshman could not relax.

Henry's illusiveness did not help matters; on the one occasion Brac had enquired as to what exactly he was to do once they reached Chester, the knight had not been forthcoming with details. "You will be looked after, my friend. The Order does not forget its friends," had been his response. Brac had not the slightest clue as to what the Order was, or why he was a friend. Henry did not say anything for a few hours afterwards, which only exacerbated the Welshman's anxiety.

The Englishman was not so much icy in his behaviour towards Brac but indifferent. Brac sensed Henry found the situation unremarkable, as if the developments were expected.

"We'll take the Dee Bridge road in. We'll go in amongst the villagers, separately of course." Henry looked down on the track from the rock outcrop, already busy with the ant-sized villagers pushing and pulling beetle-sized carts. "It is likely the watchmen have been warned of our arrival. But there are too many, and no one knows exactly what we look like. My young Welsh friend, there is no need to worry yourself." The Englishman turned to the wiry man and smiled. He clapped him on the shoulder again. Brac stumbled forward half a pace. Henry was stronger than he appeared, but equally Brac was not expecting another slap.

Brac looked at Henry incredulously, believing his suggestion to be nonsensical – where had this madness been hiding the past two days? Brac thought the Englishman at least appeared composed whilst he himself panicked, but it seemed that foolhardiness was most dangerous when sprung from sense.

Henry laughed; he could have said anything to the wiry man and it would not have shaken him from his terrified state.

"My dear Welsh friend, look at it this way. Which of us is carrying the lord's stone? You are a villager, making his way to town for the market. I am the well-dressed Englishman carrying a sack containing a large stone, similar in dimension to that which was taken from the lord's quarry. We shall meet at the Taverner's Inn, at midday. You shall not acknowledge me, but will come and sit opposite me. I'll take it from there."

The tanned Englishman looked back down the hill to the track. His eyes were carefree, his smile easy. It seemed to Brac that the morning sunlight was shining directly on the Henry and nowhere else on the hillside. Henry turned back to the alcove in the rock and picked up the heavy sack containing the silver stone. He had carried it the thirty miles so far with no audible complaint but the physical strain was very apparent. It had not knocked Henry's persistence though, and he had continued forward, driving Brac with him at a rate almost beyond that of the wiry quarryman. Indeed, the Welshman had never encountered anyone so physically fit. Even Ugly Dillan would have struggled with this pace.

Brac watched him pick the sack up. The Englishman's grey cloak was nearly pristine, his tunic pressed and perfectly fitted to his frame, his belt fine dark leather. The Welshman had so many questions that he dare not ask for fear of the answer – where was Henry taking him? He tried to reason with himself. Henry had carried the stone, with no weapons, the thirty miles from Rhuddlan. If he meant Brac harm, he had a convoluted way of going about it.

42

The Englishman heaved the sack over his left shoulder, steadied himself, and began walking towards the lip of the rock outcrop. The air was still but for the shuffling of Henry's feet under the weight of the stone. This was an Englishman! Brac had approached the Frenchwoman to begin with so as to deny the English this precious silver. And now he was party to an Englishman stealing it! Brac shook his head at just how poorly his plan had played out and urged himself onwards after the stone bearer, fearing being left alone for even a moment in this now hostile terrain.

Henry stopped just shy of the lip as if he had just remembered something of importance. "I don't suppose you have any coins with you, do you. Here, this'll be enough to get you through the gate. If anyone asks, you're coming into the city to see the saddlers for your horses back south. The trade is thriving here these days." Henry fished around in a pocket in his cloak and brought out a small leather purse. For a moment he tried to open it one handed but thought better of it and so gently lowered the sack over his left shoulder to the ground, with the strength and control of a much bigger man.

He handed Brac a number of marks and groats before returning the purse to the pocket, letting the cloak fall back about his shoulders and the pocket subsequently disappeared from sight. Brac fancied that Henry would make a poor choice of target for any outlaws or thieves on the high road, not just for his clear strength and what Brac suspected to be his martial background, but because no one could tell what weaponry the tanned man might be carrying in the countless compartments in his cloak.

Brac took out his own purse, tied to his belt underneath his jacket, and slipped the coins in. They walked together down to where the slope of the hill levelled off on a bend of the rough track, which was known as Handbridge Street. Handbridge Street approached the city of Chester from the south, crossing the River Dee before meeting the city walls at the Bridge Gate. The two marched in silence, as had been the norm since their escape from the forest. It occurred to Brac that he had not said anything for hours.

Henry turned to his wiry companion. "You go ahead. I must find a less conspicuous manner of entrance. The city sergeants will be looking out for two travellers, one carrying a large bag. Godspeed, my friend." Without waiting for a response, the Englishman turned away from Brac and trudged in the opposite direction to the city, travelling around the bend in the road.

Brac was initially puzzled but then thought the stone bearer knew what he was doing. Henry had not been the most forthcoming with details during their short companionship – Brac still had no idea what the Order was, nor how they could help him – but he did seem to know what he was doing. Coming down the slope with a plan and some coin, the man's calm was finally becoming of consolation to the wiry man, who was so far out of his comfort zone it may as well have not existed.

Now, however, that consolation was walking the wrong way, and Brac was on his own. For a moment he was tempted to turn around and run back up the hill, and keep running, away from Chester, the English, Lord de Grey, Henry, the Frenchwoman, his anxiety. The English in particular had always caused disruption and pain whenever they had turned up in his life. Was there anywhere in Wales where the English could not reach him?

No, he thought. He had made his bed and so he resolved to sleep in it. Looking back east at the city only a mile or two away, he pulled his hood over his head and purposefully strode forward. Almost immediately he threw his hood back down, figuring it would draw more attention to him if he had it up in this heat. He looked down at the dusty track worn away by countless footsteps from man and beast. How many of those were the last free footsteps those people would ever make?

He slowed down a little. A few locals shuffled past, paying him no mind. This was good. He looked back over his left shoulder at the spotless sky, and down to the horizon for a sighting of Henry, but Henry had already gone.

Two more men walked past. "Good morning!" The older man cheerily greeted Brac with a huge, genuine smile. His companion, probably the same age as Brac, had an equally upbeat disposition. They were infected with the same cheerfulness as Brac himself had once had on the summer days of his childhood. He faked a closed-mouth smile and nodded his head to them, but his beard was so thick the fake smile was undetectable. Would they have wished him a

44

good morning had they known he was wanted for stealing from the King of England? Probably not. They would probably have apprehended and dragged him to the city sergeants. It would have made them very wealthy. Brac would not have blamed them for it though; they were just English people doing their duty to their King, as Brac had been doing his duty to his people when he tried to sell the silver stone to a Frenchwoman.

He started walking again towards the city. The low murmur of chatter and the occasional laughter from the countryfolk spread haphazardly along Handbridge Street were drowned out by the ever-increasing volume of crickets and insects buzzing in the long grass on the river side of the road. Brac decided to increase his walking pace to something approaching that of everyone else, no mean effort for him given his awkward gait and considerable fatigue, because he did not want to give the appearance of a guilty man reluctantly walking to the gallows. He tried to imitate the purposeful movement of the traders looking to get to the city early so as to occupy the best spots in the market area opposite the abbey. The wiry man almost believed he was actually en route to Chester to see the saddlers.

"Good morrow, friend!" Brac heard an unrecognisable voice behind him. No one answered, so he assumed the greeting was directed at him. He slowed his pace and looked back, his thick beard so huge that it nearly scratched the shoulder of his leather jacket.

"Beautiful day! What business brings you to the city? I haven't seen you before round here." The man spoke in a thick accent, subtly different from Brac's own. He was slightly older than the Welshman, tall and thin with eager blue eyes and a red face bursting out from the confines of dark curly facial hair. Together, Brac and the accented man looked like a pair of walking bushes.

Brac was flushed but regained his composure after a second. "I am seeing the saddlers for my horses. Back down south. I hear trade is thriving here right now." He did not think it sounded a natural response, but the other man replied all the same, his eyes so focused on Brac they were almost popping out of his head.

"So they are!" The man heavily emphasised the soft ending sounds of his words, and the connecting vowels within them, traits that Brac recognised from the English near his part of North Wales.

The man continued, "I'm just off to see them myself. Always needing new leathers for the horses, me. Get through a lot of them for the lord, like. I'm Tom, how are you called?" Tom's eyes were almost manic. His overwrought demeanour was worlds apart from Henry's cool calm.

"I'm Brac, how's it going?" The Welshman offered a hand, which Tom took.

"Not one of those naughty Welsh like, are you Brac? The lord would not like to hear of me making friends with the naughty Welsh, would he!" Tom was laughing at his own comment, but Brac did not know if it was because what he said was actually funny, or if he was just very excitable. Either way, the sombre Welshman felt very uncomfortable. He looked up at the looming castle ahead; they were only a few minutes from the gate, surely.

"Oh no, your lordship has nothing to worry about from me," the Welshman replied. "My family have provided horses to the Lords de Mortimer for many years. We welcome the ending of the bloodshed. Too much bloodshed." Brac felt sorrow rising in him at the recollection of the fighting. What he had told Tom was only half a lie – there had been too much bloodshed.

"Eh, I know that feeling, friend. It was hard." Tom's eyes dimmed a little. "The lordships did well, though. I do think there are good times in front as well, like. Welsh like you wouldn't be able to come up from the south all this way safe like, just for saddles, if it weren't for the lordships and their warring!" The brilliant blue of his eyes returned again. Brac silently conceded that Tom had a point. "So what're you hoping to pick up, like?"

The question hit the Welshman like an arrow. He had no idea what he was hoping to pick up from the saddlers, because he had never worked with horses before. "Ah, you know. The lords like what they like, and want what they want. Same with the horses." The flow of people around them had thickened in the last couple of minutes as they approached the Dee Bridge Gate on the south bank. Hovels had become more frequent as they approached the city, the long grass giving way to small furrows and vegetable plots. The larger gate set within the city walls could be seen over the crowd to the north on the other side of the river, and beyond Greenway Street to the left the castle loomed in the south-west corner of the walls. Brac felt as if every pair of eyes in that castle were watching him.

The low murmur of isolated chatter had become a cauldron of men, women and the occasional child excitedly talking, with the sporadic bark of a dog or lowing of a cow. A man's voice went up behind them. "Make way! I've got a plot to get to. Out of the way!" the man bellowed from the top of his cart, being pulled by a great grey-white speckled horse with white hair. The horse edged forward through the crowd, the cart creaking behind it with two figures perched on top and poles sticking out the back to which were tied countless chickens dangling by their feet and making an incredible racket that Brac somehow had not noticed before he saw it. It seemed that those selling the goods were allowed entry to the city ahead of the buyers such as Tom.

Brac stumbled sideways to his left into Tom to avoid the giant horse's head as it plodded along without any awareness of or care for the maelstrom of excitement and sounds around it. He looked up at the hooded figure next to the bellowing chicken seller. The hooded figure wore a dark brown cloak, obscuring all but his chin. The hooded figure looked down at Brac as the cart rolled past, the wheels and the timbers remaining as one despite the shambolic nature of its upkeep. The shadowy chin moved a little and a smile emerged from the hood, an easy smile that could only belong to Henry. How had he done that? And where did he get these other clothes? Brac's growing admiration for Henry's strategy and resourcefulness was boosted further.

"Get out of the way! You don't want these chickens in your face anymore than I want them on my cart. Get out of the way!" The chicken seller was fuming and cursing. The men-at-arms at the gate called for the crowd to step aside. No one was paying much attention to either.

Tom righted Brac, helping him regain his balance. "Your face there, pal, was like you had never seen a horse before!" His manic eyes matched the colour of the brightening sky. "It's not fair they can walk straight into the city, like. We have to pay as well!"

Brac watched the cart continue to part the sea of countryfolk. "I guess they pay more for the privilege. And anyway, don't tell me you haven't sneaked in on the back of a wagon before?" The Welshman could not remember the last time he broke a smile. He was starting to enjoy this duplicity just a little and felt a semblance of poise return after the little Frenchwoman had shattered it that evening in the tavern.

A few yards ahead, the two men-at-arms hailed the bellowing cart driver to halt. The two soldiers wore simple grey tunics, each with a helmet and small round blue shield with a prominent central boss in their left hand. They held a long spear in their right. Brac thought about the necessity of these men being so conspicuously armed whilst policing a group of generally good-natured countryfolk, with the exception of the bellowing cart driver; it was probably just all for show, particularly in the wake of the recent Welsh rising which admittedly had not directly involved the city itself. The Earldom of Chester was showing the smallfolk that the King's justice was far reaching.

The two soldiers did not appear physically imposing, but they seemed to carry themselves with authority and had obviously been assigned to this position on many occasions. The shorter of the two men-at-arms walked to the driver's side of the cart. Brac could not hear what was being said, for the crowded road was buzzing and the cheek guards of the soldier's helmet obscured his face from the side. The soldier walked round the near side of the cart, on the side towards the river, ducking under the poles to which the chickens were tied, and climbed up to the back of the cart where numerous sacks were piled. Brac figured this was not an ordinary spot-check – the men were probably searching for any item that might appear to have originated in a quarry.

The crowd's reaction confirmed Brac's suspicions as the assembled countryfolk turned their attention to the cart, wondering the meaning of this delay. Another cart driver behind Brac's right shoulder cursed loudly between complaining to someone else about wait. Brac could see a large pile of tied sacks in the back of the cursing cart driver's four-wheel cart. A further heavily-laden cart was trundling along behind that one. A few grumbles could be heard amongst the excited chatter, and the wiry Welshman could sense a changing mood in the crowd awaiting entrance to the city.

"You going to check every chicken as well?" A man behind the cursing cart driver shouted towards the front of the crowd. Intermittent laughs went up but the men-at-arms ignored the sarcasm, and although they were not checking every chicken they had looked the first two bags, and were opening the third. A feeling of dread was rising in the wiry Welshman – surely Henry's bag was in that pile? The soldiers would find the stone soon. Henry was sat with his back to the crowd, so Brac had no clue as to his body language.

An aggressive female voice erupted directly behind Brac. "Oi, what you doing there?"

"Hey, what do you think you're doing, pal?" asked another man.

Brac's curiosity was stoked and he glanced left at Tom, who was already looking at him with his wide eyes, but they were no longer wide with manic enthusiasm. Tom uttered an "*uhm*" with a look of stupidity on his face, all of his bright-eyed confidence drained away.

"He was taking your purse, mate!" said the aggressive woman again as Brac looked back at her. He was met with a scowling face framed by greying light-brown frizzy hair barely contained by a dirty white bonnet. She pointed at Tom's hands which were cradling Brac's purse.

How had he...? The quarryman instinctively patted around his belt for the purse he could see in the man's hands standing before him. He did not feel the purse where he would normally have done and, in spite of being able to see the purse, a dread arising from knowing one has lost something of great consequence rose from his stomach.

As Brac finished briefly patting himself down, Tom gave another hesitant "*uhm*" again before leaping to his right, shouldering between the aggressive woman and the other man who had asked to what Tom was doing. The crowd was heavy with smallfolk milling around but the sudden force of the thin farrier knocked over the aggressive woman and bundled the other man into some of the people behind him.

The woman cried out and a few shouts went up, but Brac was stunned by what was unfolding in front of him – he had not at all expected to be the victim of a pickpocketing, if only because he usually barely had any coins on him. Furthermore, he was a quiet man disinclined to making a scene, particularly in a crowd as large as this. Unfortunately, he reminded himself again, he was no longer in the quarry and in the familiarity of his own hamlet. More people shouted and the crowd as one turned from the men-at-arms to the front to the commotion in the centre, and Brac could see the violent movements of people's heads to either side as Tom bowled through and past them.

The men-at-arms looked up from their inspection and looked to the commotion, their attentions captured by the shouts of *"thief!"* and the increasingly hostile atmosphere amongst the waiting countryfolk. From their perch on the back of the cart, they could see over the heads of the crowd and caught sight of the tall farrier clumsily barging through the crowd. He was still colliding with and knocking down startled merchants and villagers despite the shouts and cries, because the crowd was becoming heavier by the minute and so the people towards the back could not see what was happening up to the front.

"Stop him!" roared the shorter man-at-arms who had spoken with the bellowing cart driver and was presumably the more authoritative of the two, roared at the crowd. Many faces at the front of the group spun round to the back, unaware of what was going on and immediately attentive as anyone would be when offered a dramatic distraction from monotony. The second man-at-arms leaned into the bellowing cart driver, jerking his head in the direction of the bridge and saying something before leaping off the cart and following the first man-at-arms in diving into the crowd to pursue the thief. Behind them the bellowing cart driver whipped the reins and his huge horse pulled on the cart, rumbling forward onto the Dee Bridge. Henry looked round at the crowd that had become like a tumultuous sea of excitement, movement and noise. He regretted being unable to see Brac but accepted the Welshman's fate was in God's hands now.

By now Brac had shaken himself out of his inactivity. With a cry he threw himself forwards in to narrow, uneven corridor through the crowd left by Tom's escape, much like the wake of a boat through the water. The wiry Welshman was ungainly however and succeeded in barging into and through a number of people who had just recovered their balance after being hit by Tom. He felt his bony elbows catch a number of more solid body parts and these were always accompanied by a grunt or curse.

He could see Tom's head just above everyone else's, but even if this were not so the concentration of cries and shouts would tell him the direction he needed to run. Brac tripped over a man who had been floored, landing heavily on his chest and jarring his right shoulder with a winded *oof*, but he sprung up with agility and energy that surprised him. As he launched upwards and forwards he shouldered through the legs of another man who was gawking at the escaping farrier, who promptly collapsed in a mess of brown cloak and dust.

Further back, the men-at-arms were roaring at the crowd to move and despite the awkwardness of carrying a spear and shield found it easier going through the people than did Tom or Brac. Brac looked ahead of the next potential human obstacle, a small woman carrying a basket to her side, and just glimpsed Tom's head disappear downwards and the tops of other hooded and capped heads move together into the vacated space. The Welshman broke through a few more statuesque countryfolk into a small parting in the crowd where he discovered to his initial shock and then gradual delight two men were pinning down Tom on his front. The farrier was not struggling, not that he had much choice; it appeared that he had finally been felled by possibly the biggest men in the entire crowd.

"This yours, mate?" rumbled a heavily bearded tanned man with a barrel chest and long blue jacket that barely contained in his thick arms. He was kneeling on the small of Tom's back and turned to his right and held up Brac's purse to the Welshman. His companion, thinner but still considerably larger than Brac, was holding Tom's arms behind his back securely enough so that the Welshman could see a silent grimace on Tom's face.

"Thank you," murmured the Welshman into his beard, as was his subservient way when talking to anyone physically or socially superior to himself.

The barrel-chested man nodded. "Where are those bridge guards?" he asked everyone but no one in particular. The buzz in the crowd was at a crescendo and not many heard him but more noticed the men-at-arms bundling through the crowd and Brac could see the tips of their spears waving and wobbling erratically above the crowd.

Brac thought again of Henry and the stone. He stood on tiptoes, trying to see the front of the crowd and Henry's cart, but he had no clear view from further down the road. He pulled a dissatisfied face, invisible to the outside world through his bush-like eyebrows and beard. But he had seen two spears above the crowd, which suggested the cart was no longer being inspected. From the little time he had spent with Henry he had learnt that the tanned Englishman was resourceful and certainly not one to panic. Brac relaxed a little.

The men-at-arms broke through to the small clearing and saw Tom being crushed face-first into the dirt by barrel-chested man and his companion. "Our thanks, friends," said the talkative man-at-arms. "Have you proof of his crimes?"

"Aye, we have. The money belt belongs to this man here." The barrel-chested man shared the same accent as Tom, emphasising the long vowel sounds, but with a deeper voice befitting such a broad man. He gestured at Brac, who had taken on the same startled rabbit appearance as had Tom when he was accosted moments before. "We'll leave him to you, if you don't mind."

The talkative soldier nodded. "Aye. The sheriff will be seeing to this one. He's arriving later today with his lordship. Big trial coming up. Should be quite the spectacle. We'll take him now."

Big trial. Brac wondered if the big trial was to involve the Frenchwoman. He looked at Tom, and then at the ground. He idly fiddled with the purse in his right hand. Regardless of whether the Frenchwoman was on trial, the presence of the lord in the city today was not comforting – it seemed Lord de Grey would pursue him anywhere and everywhere. The rush of excitement brought about by his duplicity, the pickpocketing and then the chase was fading, and the Welshman's anxieties flooded back, threatening to drown him. His face went pale and he felt light headed.

"You well, mate?" asked the talkative soldier. "You have everything back?"

"Yes, I do, thank you. And thank you again, friends," Brac replied, trying to inject confidence in his demeanour but not convincing himself he had.

"Very well. Come on, we need to take this one back in. And this crowd's getting restless. The sergeant will not be happy with this build up." The talkative soldier gestured at the men to pick Tom up, which they did before handing him to the men-at-arms. As they dragged him away the temporary clearing amidst the queueing merchants collapsed back into its natural irregular throng.

No longer the joint centre of attention, Brac for once welcomed the enclosure of strangers around him. The thrill of the spectacle had, for the time being, eliminated any discontent in the crowd over the slow process of entering the city, and tongues began wagging lightheartedly as before. Soon enough, the attention that had been foisted upon the quarryman dissipated and he was once more anonymous, the way he liked it.

Chapter 5

El ached all over as she tried to get comfortable in the makeshift carriage. In truth it was more a horse cart than litter and though she had never actually travelled in the latter, she felt a sense of being downgraded, as though she was owed a cushion or some semblance of luxury. Such desirous daydreams were obliterated when she realised such thoughts were unbecoming of a servant of the Lord. What would Uncle Jacques make of her self-pitying? What even the saints? This was not El. She had never had status, or been particularly wealthy or had much in the way of comforts, so why start now?

Lord Reginald was mistaken in thinking she was a lady, but she was not going to correct him. El saw all that happened as pre-ordained and so Lord Reginald's misplaced courtesy from one noble to another was simply a fortuitous circumstance to exploit in the pursuit of her work. Her name was indeed noble, but only in reputation. Her uncle was still renowned and revered throughout Christendom as the Order's Grand Master.

Her father however had held no great lands, commanded no armies, lived in no castles. Along with her name, the material dearth her family faced during her childhood significantly contributed to her joining the Order albeit in an unconventional and largely inconspicuous manner. El considered herself fortunate Lord Reginald had not assumed membership of the Order, presumably on the basis of her gender. This was another pre-ordained circumstance.

She scolded herself again at the self-absorbed introspection regarding the travelling conditions. One has to take the rough with the smooth, Guy had always reminded her, especially when the smooth was so portentous.

The wagon rocked heavily along the track as if its rickety wheels were square. The guards had escorted her down from the castle to the wagon just after daybreak. They had been urgent yet courteous, so far as enquiring to her wellbeing and offering genuinely sympathetic glances; El wondered if any of them had contributed to her bruised face in the forest. Certainly they were under instruction from the gruff knight, Sir Edward, to treat their prisoner with the utmost care and respect. Whilst their motives may have been questionable, she did think about what Guy had said. Rough with the smooth.

The sun was still ascending the Cheshire hills to the east and yet there was a warmth in the air beyond that of any of the scorching hot summer days thus far. The back of the wagon itself, with a hastily and shoddily erected canopy tent roof, was shielded from the sun and yet its entirely enclosed nature created a furnace on the inside that caused beads of sweat to break out on El's forehead. The enclosed canvas tent was beyond stuffy and held that distinctive, overwhelming tent smell that everyone who had spent any time at all in a tent during the summer would recognise. The Frenchwoman longed for fresh air – the heat was only a little less ferocious outside, but the grass sometimes was greener, she mused.

She was still wearing the grey vest, tunic jacket and fitted trousers as she had two nights previously and her cloak was on her lap; thoroughly overdressed for the situation though the Frenchwoman was keen to maintain an air of nobility about her – it would be unbecoming were she to remove even one layer before the common soldiers. Adding to the considerable discomfort, a wheel would at regular intervals practically fall into a divot in the baked earth, the ground having been softened during a thunderstorm, churned up by itinerant merchants and artisans the following morning and then left to solidify like rock in the heat of day.

El had been thrown from her seat on occasion, to be picked up by the guardsman assigned to ensure she did not repeat her feats in the forest. He did not say much, sitting glumly in mail with his helmet covering much of his craggy face. What she could see of his face seemed to be glowing as if he held embers in his cheeks. His dark blue eyes peered out from either side of the noseguard on his dirty helm, above a face that was either unshaven or spattered with caked dust, or both. El could not tell in the shade of the wagon. His stare was unsettling to El, but she figured he was probably wary of her herself following reports of the damage she had dealt in the forest. She reckoned the guard to be more afraid of her than she was of him;

such were the power of soldiers' tales, particularly those originating at night from an unseen source. Rationality held no power against concealed terrors in the dark, and fear was infectious.

Knowing his fears to be largely unjustified confirmed further in El's mind that every particular detail of her mission was being divinely guided. There had always been an option available; find the Welshman, find the stone, find a path through the forest. Even now, loosely bound in the back of a horse cart, she held a trump card in that the men-at-arms in Lord Reginald's retinue viewed her as some noble warrior woman – she had overheard one ostensibly well-versed guard refer to her as Boadicea, though her history was hazy and she could not entirely remember how that story went.

Her lack of sleep was beginning to manifest in a series of deep breaths, sighs and eye rubbing as the adrenaline of the early morning wake up and hurried transfer from her holding room in Rhuddlan's castle to the cart wore off. The chances of falling asleep were slim though with the hard wooden bench's unyielding surface exacerbated by the rocking motion of the cart, worse than any ship on which she had sailed. El was reminded why she always preferred to travel on horseback.

Even sat upfront driving a wagon still left one at the mercy of unnatural and unforeseeable jolts and jerks; the occasional jarring bump when atop an otherwise graceful mount could be excused for the beauty and fluidity of the beast's motion. The Frenchwoman felt at home, free like when she was a child, when riding in the open. The restrictive and cumbersome method of travelling by wagon seemed like imprisonment, even when she was not being transported as an actual prisoner.

A heavy, concentrated *thud* woke up El and the guardsman from their respective early morning doldrums. *Thud*. *Thud*. Two more in quick succession on the guardsman's side of the wagon. El's eyes met with the guard's and she immediately knew that such noises were both unexpected and unwelcome. Somewhere outside a man cried and horses began whinnying, and the wagon jerked to a halt, nearly throwing its two passengers into the bare front wooden panel of their carriage. Further shouting went up, all of it undecipherable, as did a scream which spurred El's guard to feverishly right himself from his half seated, half kneeling position following the cart's sudden stop. Readjusting his grimy helmet and grabbing his round blue shield he made his way to the back of the cart.

"Stay here," he ordered as he passed her, looking at El only briefly but long enough for her to know he would prefer to stay put with her.

On her part, El could not imagine any scenario that would make her want to go outside. The guard skilfully drew his sword from its sheath and brought it up in a diagonal motion from behind his elevated shield across his body, all the more impressive given the cramped space of their carriage, and used the shield in his left hand to carve through the canvas sheet that acted as a 'door' to the back of the cart. Amidst the jumbled and confused shouting from all around the wagon train he leapt out and back to the right behind his shield, presumably to use the wagon as cover whilst he assessed the situation.

The glare outside meant that El could not immediately see anything beyond the end of the cart, though her day vision returned in the space of two more thuds in the side of the cart opposite where she was sitting. She saw an arrow head drilled through the side panel of the wagon, and then with a *whoosh* another arrow shot through the canvas at head height just an arm's length away to her right. El dived to the floor of the cart, clenching her robe tightly and looked out through the gaping canvas material at the back. *What is going on?* she almost cried out loud.

What had been a calm and ponderous morning's journey to Chester, just thirty or so miles from Rhuddlan, had descended into chaos. El feared looking outside in case the chaos would further deteriorate into a nightmare. Men shouted all around and cries went up periodically, interspersed by the *whoosh* and *thud* of bow shots and the stomping and neighing of terrified and confused horses. The quiet peace of a summer morning in the green Welsh countryside had been obliterated by what El could only guess was a brigand attack on Lord Reginald's men. Where was the baron? Was he travelling with the train? Her eyes had become familiarised with the contrasting brightness of the world outside the carriage, and she saw a soldier taking aim with a bow from behind another cart, this one open topped, and beside him another man slouched against a cart wheel, almost lifeless with two arrow shafts stuck fast in his right shoulder and side.

With a heavy *thud* another huge arrow stuck in the cart behind and the archer behind it ducked. He was not wearing a helmet but was otherwise dressed as was El's guard, with the exception that he had a quiver over his right shoulder. The wounded man on the floor was also lacking a helmet. It was likely, El thought, that none of these men, except her own guardsman, would have worn a helmet in this heat, and certainly would not have felt it necessary this close to the castles at Rhuddlan and Chester so soon after the destruction of the Welsh rising. The men-at-arms she had seen that morning had not seemed in the slightest perturbed by the prospective journey; they were hurrying, yes, but only because their superiors were apparently so insistent upon a timely departure.

A horrifying scream snapped El out of her observations and deductions. She could still not really make out what was happening, which in her mind insulated her from the danger simply because she could not see it. But no sooner had that scream gone up then the sound of steel clattering steel rang through the air, a harsher and unnaturally sharper sound than any of the shouting and crying of men and screaming of horses. El reckoned the clash was just to the front and right of the wagon, which as she was lying was behind her left shoulder. She could hear the voices more distinctly now – some shouting was in English, which she could comprehend, and other in a tongue she did not understand. She guessed it to be Welsh. A few grunts and shouts accompanied the clattering of sword on sword, and then a sickening *squelch* was accompanied by a man shrieking. The shrieking was cut short merely a second later, and then a gruff English voice began roaring orders.

"To the ridge, on the left!" bellowed Sir Edward de Beauchamp, who El had not actually seen that morning – she had been escorted directly from the gates to the wagon with little fanfare, but as a result with at least a shred of dignity; she had not been paraded in front of the populace and workers of the castle.

"Archers, forward! Swords, on me." The gruff knight had a confidence about him that suggested he knew what he was doing, much to El's relief. The archer she had seen firing from behind the next wagon sprang round his temporary hideout and bound forward, out of sight. El saw the slumped man now had his head lolling to his left shoulder. She could not take her eyes off him, in spite of the cacophony outside of the wagon and the occasional arrow that thudded into the front – *there must be a man using the driver's bench for cover*, El thought. She was always perceptive, even in times of stress, and she had experienced a few stressful encounters during her time with the Order but none more than this. A few years previously the Moors at Granada had taken countless shots at her, but their archery skills were dreadful and her heart rate had barely registered the potential danger.

But now, El was gripping her cloak beneath her chest so tightly her palms were sweating. She felt the need to use and dissipate this nervous energy. The sound of clashing steel sounded a little further away, and so she chanced an escape from what was probably one of the least safe positions in the entire train, judging by how low were the wooden side panels in her carriage, the only arrow-proof material around her, compared with those on the cart behind. She crawled forward to the opening of the carriage and in one flowing motion that belied her aching body and throbbing joints she brought her knees up to her chest and launched herself forwards, out of the cart and towards the wagon behind and the slumped man.

The Frenchwoman had jumped out of countless trees as a child and so it came naturally to her land her feet one-two, left then right, allowing her forward momentum to continue into a roll over her shoulder, taking the force of her weight. She came to a stop by the slumped man. The two arrows had lodged so far into his shoulder and side that glancing down to his left side, El expected to see arrow tips poking out. She softly lifted the man's chin with her right hand, but his eyes were closed and the blood that had been brought up to his mouth by the internal injuries was already drying black. The arrows had penetrated his mail shirt as if it were cloth. El reckoned them to have been fired from a longbow – surely there could no Welsh brigands left with the will to fight Lord Reginald? She gently let go of his head and it fell forward so his chin rested on the top of his chest. The man was dead, and so would be El if she did not afford herself more protection that the wheel of a wagon.

Looking up, she could see a scuffle coming into view from behind the last wagon at the end of the train, no more than twenty paces away, with a number of men in a mishmash of outfits battering each other with swords and clubs, shouting and screaming. The men-at-arms, clad in grey with their blue shields, steel occasionally flashing against the backdrop of green and brown, were heavily outnumbered by the brigands in their dark browns and reds. El saw one man-at-arms strike forward with his spear, skewering a brigand through the stomach, but in that moment he had left himself open to an attack from his right. He could not bring the shield in his left hand up and over the spear, which had gone all the way through the brigand, in time to block an attack from the huge brigand approaching. The second brigand swung with both hands his terrifying mace once round his head, a monstrous great spiked club that looked heavy enough to cleave a horse in half, and brought it down ferociously onto the head of the man-at-arms who, like the dead man next to El, was without a helmet.

The top half of the soldier's head exploded spectacularly in a shower of red gore, and the mace ball lodged itself in the remaining bottom part of the man's head, pulling the weapon down with it as the man's body immediately collapsed. El watched in morbid curiosity, beyond revolted by the spectacle but intrigued as the brigand took two heaves to remove the embedded mace from the stump that was once the man-at-arms' head. All of the helmets in Christendom would not have saved the poor soldier, his body now crumpled atop the skewered first brigand.

A distressed white horse trotted into view in between El's wagon and the fighting around the end wagon, throwing its head back and forth with flaring nostrils and wide eyes. It had no rider, but was saddled and reined. It appeared a fine example of a swift palfrey, an ideal horse for escorting or raiding a wagon train. Its rider was either one of the brigands or of Lord Reginald's banner, but evidently he or she had chanced their hand on foot in the close quarters combat that had evidently developed.

The thought of escape sprung into El's mind and took over her thoughts as if nothing else was happening right at that moment, no slaughter, no arrows, nor exploding heads. She saw a long spear on the ground to her right, and grabbed it in the motion of moving forward along the length of the wooden cart towards the horse. The horse trotted further so it was now entirely behind the imaginary line that formed the 'defensive' position of the single-file carts in the train. It wheeled round on the spot and revealed a huge spatter of blood along its left flank. El could not immediately see any wound on the animal and nor was its movement impaired beyond the effects of its terror upon its locomotion, so the blood was presumably that of one of the combatants on the other side of the wagon line.

The little Frenchwoman peeked over underneath the wagon and could see a number of dancing feet, a few bodies lying motionless in the dust and then a dark haired man in a brown and black patchwork of cloth dropping to the track followed quickly by a sword brutally thrust down into his chest. He was nailed to the ground by the sword of one of the heavier-armed soldiers, and almost immediately the sword retracted and the clad boots scurried off forwards and right.

El stood up a little straighter again and approached the horse slowly, putting her finger to her mouth as one would to elicit silence in another. "*Sssssshhh* my darling, it's ok," and she attempted to sooth the horse by stroking its head with her left hand and patting its neck with her right. She led it back a little closer to the wagon, and then, ducking as she went, pulled it by the reins towards the canvassed carriage in which she had travelled. The canvas offered no protection against arrows, but would at least block anyone's view of her mounting the saddle. The horse continued shaking its head and stamping its hooves, but moved forwards with El easily enough until they reached the cover of the canvassed cart, which was stopped underneath a tall poplar tree.

She looked up and down the line behind the wagon train and it seemed everyone was fighting out in front. The din from the fighting had not diminished; it seemed as if two armies had clashed on this small stretch of track between the wooded hill on the south and the less vegetated slope down to the river to the north. El used the side of the cart as a spring from which to mount the tall horse, landing gracefully considering she was still holding her cloak and had the spear in the other hand. Even before taking the reins she had kicked the horse's flanks and it bolted, as full of nervous energy as its rider, and in the shadow of the trees to the left and the wagons to the right, El raced along in the direction of Chester. The terrain to the left was not suitable for a horse at high speed, and she did not want to return in the direction of Rhuddlan where she knew many of Lord Reginald's men were garrisoned. Towards Chester it was, but intending to turn south before reaching the city and onto one of the churches housing a friend of the Order.

For the first few score paces El felt as if the entire battle had stopped and was watching her, despite the continuing clanging of steel and shouting of soldiers. After about thirty paces, up to the third cart from the front, which was a great vehicle loaded with barrels of some wine or other, a few riddled with arrows and one with a dead soldier lying across the top, El noticed the fighting was threatening to break through the line of the train and block her escape off at the front end. A man-at-arms to the right noticed the woman riding at breakneck speed through the shade on a great white horse and yelled, *"The prisoner!"* Slowing the horse a little so she could duck under a few wayward branches, El heard the alarm and looked to the right where she thought she spotted Sir Edward, bloody longsword in hand, arching his neck round in disbelief at the sight.

The gruff knight mouthed something that she could not hear, and she turned back to the direction in which the horse was racing. A soldier was clambering up the side of the next wagon and raised his spear arm to thrust at the horse as he cut off El's angle of escape, but in his haste the soldier tripped at the last moment and fell from the cart into the horse's wake. El gripped the reins with her left hand tighter than she thought possible, still holding onto her cloak as if that were as important as the silver stone, and held the long spear out in her right. She cleared the first wagon and there appeared to be no obstacles ahead as far as one could see. The hill to the south gently rolled down to a sloping end ahead and to the right, with the track winding around it to the left, boxed in by a few trees to the north. It was to this gap that El directed the horse, thundering along to escape the carnage of the ambush behind.

The promise of escape was no further than sixty paces away when figures appeared on the crest of the gentle slope above the track, four of them.

"Oh, shit," El cursed to herself and the horse. She kicked hard to accelerate, if it were possible, for the horse in its terror was already flying at an incredible pace. Fifty paces. One of the figures was holding what looked like a long spear perhaps, or maybe a longbow? The longbow was quite often far taller than its user. Forty paces. El could see it was a longbow, and could see the longbowman had already loaded an arrow and was drawing the string. Thirty paces. If the arrow hit her, she'd be dead for sure, and if it hit the horse at this speed, she would be killed in the fall. She prayed this archer were as terrible a shot as the Moors of Granada.

In a snap decision El turned the horse slightly right towards the slope, throwing the longbowman's aim off. Twenty paces. The three other men, all armed with swords, began to scatter at the approaching beast, its rider carrying the spear as if it were a lance. The bowman remained stationary, startled by the horse turning towards him, but bravely and, for El, disconcertingly steadfast.

He let fly the arrow without having had opportunity to truly readjust his aim, and the arrow fizzed towards El and the horse. Ten paces. The arrow screamed past El's left shoulder, flying through her trailing cloak and carried on to an unknown destination. The horse tore on up the slope straight towards the now terrified longbowman, who released his bow and dived to his left just in time as the horse thundered through his recently vacated position. The man had left his escape so late that the bow was still fleetingly standing upright on its own before the impact of the horse's chest on the tall bow shattered the curved yew into three huge shards. El and the horse crested the slope and hammered down the other side, sending grass and dirt flying as the shouts of the longbowman's companions died down with the ever-increasing distance between them.

A few minutes passed before El slowed the horse from a gallop to a canter. Both woman and beast were breathing heavily, and the horse's mouth was foaming with exertion. The track had smoother ground along this stretch, allowing for a horse to sprint without risk of breaking a leg in the divots that had plagued El's carriage journey earlier in the morning. She had not even realised the risk that the horse's speed posed along such surfaces – but given the brush with death she had just experienced courtesy of the longbowman's arrow there was no room for worrying over what could have been.

El said a short prayer of thanks and, transferring the reins awkwardly to her right, spear, hand, reached to her neck with her left hand, pulling out the cross necklace she had and kissed it. The noises of the skirmish were no longer audible and the deep blue sky was filled with only birdsong and the heavy hooves and snorting of the white horse. The greens of the woods to the right and the wild weeds to the left were more intense than El could remember seeing, and the daffodils and sunflowers amongst the long grasses down the slope to the left of the track grew high and proud thanks to the frequency of alternating sunshine and thunderstorms. The little Frenchwoman thought it remarkable that such an idyll could exist so close to the awful slaughter from which she had barely escaped; and here now she was sullying this paradise's purity with her bruises, blood, sweat and spear.

Two blurred figures came into view on the horizon, and El wondered if somehow a messenger had been dispatched from the train to bring help back from the city. As the white horse continued to canter down the apparently endlessly straight track, the two figures became four, two large and two small, and none of the four gave the impression of rapid movement. Still, the sun was in El's eyes and so she was basing this assumption on outline alone – even with her sharp eyesight she could not make out any details, but guessed they were two people guiding two horses.

Another few minutes passed and she had caught up with them, urging her exhausted horse on with urgency. The little group consisted of a man and a woman, the one dressed in a yellow shirt with brown trousers and a woollen jacket with long leather boots, and the other in a long brown-red tunic over a linen smock with similar leather boots to her companion. They were pulling along a horse each, the man with a speckled grey and the woman a black one, rounceys both. The man and woman turned simultaneously at El's approach, and each hailed her with morning greetings.

"Good day to you, my friends," replied El amiably. The man and woman appeared a little taken aback; either at El's unusual, un-English and un-Welsh accent or at her windswept and perspiring appearance atop the blood-spattered, steaming palfrey. "Please, if you will mount your horses and ride as quickly as you can to your destination." El's tone turned authoritarian as it had with Brac before and in the quarry. "I have just ridden from a train of wagons belonging to the Lord Reginald. It has been attacked by Welsh outlaws, and many men are dead." The woman turned to the man, open-mouthed, to find he was already looking at her fearfully.

"How many are there?" The woman looked shocked.

"It is hard to say, my lady. But I have nearly been hit with an arrow whilst trying to escape, so please, I urge you to mount your horses and escape quickly," she insisted, unconsciously pulling at the now-ripped cloak. "Any people you see, you must warn them too. If you are going to Chester, you must raise the alarm and send for help. Sir Edward de Beauchamp is fighting and in great danger." El's plea was impassioned and strictly speaking factually correct, if not a little manipulated.

"Y-yes, of course... We'll go now. Pauline, quickly!" The man's nerves appeared to fall to pieces within moments of El delivering the news. He scrambled onto his horse and turned to El. "Thank you for this, friend. Godspeed."

"Thank you and Godspeed," echoed the diminutive Pauline, who had clambered atop the black rouncey like a squirrel racing up a tree. The pair kicked their heels in and their horses flew off east down the road, dust flying in their trails, quickly obscuring them from view.

El watched them go, for a moment feeling as if she had just passed the torch on to the couple, feeling as if she now had no responsibilities. Looking back west up the road, she could see a small cloud of dust over a rocky slope on the south side of the road. A wave of nausea hit her, and she leaned to her right wretching but bringing nothing up. She felt dizzy from dehydration as she recalled the sight of the soldier's head being obliterated just moments before.

Having stopped running, the ordeals of the past two days caught up with the Frenchwoman. She had taken a physical and psychological battering, and although she had seen men die before

65

she had never witnessed such barbaric violence. And how close to her own death had she been? Every day in her work, prayers and reading the concept of the next life was ubiquitous but having been truly and tangibly confronted by her own mortality was more disturbing than she imagined it would be.

El had passed that test, however. There was no shying away from the longbowman, her would-be executioner, and in actual fact she had challenged the situation face on. And won! She was still alive and now with at least some country between her and the warring skirmishers. El then reflected that facing the challenge head on had arguably saved the lives of Pauline and her companion, presumably her husband. The little Frenchwoman always faced obstacles head on and now she had seen the rewards for passing her most dangerous physical task yet.

Hacking and coughing she lifted her head up, remembering where she was. The rising cloud of dust brought her back to the present and decided not to wait for the colours of the approaching horsemen to reveal themselves. Spurring the horse, El galloped in the direction of Chester. The rush of riding was a welcome cure to her queasiness and she drunk in the fresh air, which in turn almost caused her to fall from the horse as the subsequent head rush brought the blood back.

The day wore on though, and its ever rising heat allowed neither rider nor horse get comfortable and the foam and spittle flew from the horse's mouth, spraying El's legs, and its flanks felt like they were on fire beneath. The pair she had met earlier were still in sight but steadily pulling away thanks to their own mounts' relative freshness. *Come on, come on.* Understandably, the frightened, blood-spattered mount was becoming increasingly fatigued and El regretted the woodland on the slope to her right was unsuitable for both of them. Staying on the road was dangerous for the presence of Lord Reginald's men, but equally it seemed the hills and woods were harbouring Welsh rebels, a scenario many she had spoken with considered very unlikely.

Henry had been particularly confident that Lord Reginald had stamped out all resistance following the crushing Welsh defeat at Maes Moydog earlier in the year and El had been inclined to agree. She still preferred her chances off the road; in the forest she may not encounter anyone, but as a lone woman riding on a great white, blood soaked horse, she could hardly be any more conspicuous. If El were to encounter brigands she believed they would treat her better given that she was French. Over the past year El had generally found it easier to get along with Welsh than English, although this was limited to the Anglophone Welsh such as Brac; she found the Welsh tongue quite impenetrable.

The sun was now at its zenith in the deep blue sky. El could no longer see dust rising over the slope to the south-west so she slowed the horse down. Though El was not familiar with this stretch of road on the way to Chester, Guy had been a stickler for studying and always emphasised the importance of geography to her role. Hours and hours she had spent hunched over the most modern scrolls drawn by the finest cartographers the Order could find, or so Guy had said. He was an enthusiastic man, though sometimes prone to exaggeration and El accepted this with good humour.

Nonetheless, the Frenchwoman could see in her mind's eye all of the routes inked around the north of Wales, and more importantly the settlements along the way. Her prodigious memory also allowed her to recall exactly which of these settlements had which Church order; Benedictine, Franciscan, Poor Clares, Dominicans; and which of those Church orders could offer what support to the Order. The closest town with an Order house was Garway, but that was perhaps one hundred miles away to the south-east, so El would have to work with what resources she could find in the villages here.

El could not tell how long it had been since meeting the two riders. There had been no one else on the road, so presumably the peasants had spread the word about the brigands to anyone they had encountered. Slowing the horse to a canter, El afforded herself another look behind. The thinning woods on the left and the bushy slope down to the right were all brilliant green and framed the dirt road, itself so bright in the sunlight it almost appeared grey. There were no visual or audible indicators of pursuit from either Welsh or English. The midday sun mercilessly beat down on horse and rider, and evidently on the wildlife of the woods as well for the morning's birdsong had all but disappeared. The buzzing and clicking of insects and grasshoppers were the only accompaniment to the heavy footfalls and snorting of the great white palfrey.

El had always been a free spirit and felt the great temptation to remove her long tunic in the oppressive sunlight, but her sensibilities rejected the notion. She missed the freedom of childhood in the hot French south, where her and her brother and their friends had no concept of modesty, when finding a pool meant immediately throwing off her smock and jumping in, her friends likewise discarding their clothes; it was an age of innocence that she knew would never be experienced again. El knew her vulnerability to nostalgia was her greatest weakness. She had mental fortitude, a resilience to impure thoughts that had only become steelier since coming under Guy's tutelage, and was not easily swayed by the temptations of the flesh as was required by the Church and the Order. She had her fair share of suitors wherever she went and initially suspected Brac to have been just such upon his initial approach in the tavern, though it quickly became very clear that he was very definitely not of that ilk.

But daydreaming about those summers... Why could she not control that? Of course, a day like today with its irresistible heat and the emptiness of these tracks through the threshold of the forest could only stir memories of years past – *all* of her memories of those carefree days were framed by copious sunshine in and around the woodlands. But predominantly it was always the same type of scenario that played over and over in her mind; running free, being chased and climbing. From whom and whence were she and her brother and friends running? It would be impossible to remember the roles they played in each and every game, though not being able to recall was starting to eat away at her given how often she found herself inadvertently reminiscing about those days.

Indeed, as she patted down the white palfrey as it regained its composure and cooled in the shade of an imperious ash tree, the little Frenchwoman imagined this current scenario, escaping the brigands and Baron de Grey's men, was one she had already experienced. El resolved to speak with Guy about these recurring memories and in the meantime to pray for strength.

And so here El was, thinking about the freedom of those summers whilst riding a horse in the midday sun and covered shoulder to foot. She mused how odd it was that as a fugitive from the King's justice she still observed acceptable and traditional customs of moral behaviour and dress, even more so on a road she knew to be deserted. But still, the next village could just be over the lip of the next slope, or behind the copse of trees ahead. Unlike in the old days of running and chasing with her brother and friends, it paid to be prepared and she could not afford to let her guard slip.

Chapter 6

The wiry man lumbered awkwardly into the crowded inn. The smell of ale and sweat was heavy in the air and low ceiling was hazy with unventilated smoke from the kitchen. Unsurprisingly, business was heaving on such a fine day and the atmosphere suggested that the intrusive and laborious checks at the gates had not permanently soured spirits inside the walls; it was not long past the ringing from the abbey and church bells signalling the terce prayers and already a number of the inn's patrons appeared more than a little merry.

Brac hated rowdy and cramped conditions such as this. The largest alehouse at Rhuddlan was of similar size but barely a quarter as busy, though he would be at the quarry at this time of day and was thus unsure whether Rhuddlan had a thriving midmorning drinking scene. The quarryman contemplated the choice of location for the rendezvous with Henry and concluded that, despite his own dislike of the surroundings, the Englishman had chosen well. From an initial glance practically everyone was too busy with their own conversation and beer to pay attention to Brac's self-consciousness. And anyhow, the more drunk people got, the less they would be able to listen in on Brac and Henry's conversation.

The downside of this arrangement, however, also represented the major obstacle to having a conversation with the Englishman in the first place. With all of the heads facing this way and that, long, short, brown, black, blond hair, how was he supposed to find Henry?

He shuffled forward, his small eyes darting back and forward from their lookout post amidst his hairy face, scanning every which way in the rowdy tavern. Even if most of the tavern's clientele were engrossed in the happenings at their own bench or table, Brac was conscious of how much an outsider he was; everyone here seemed to be with someone else, and Brac was a loner. A fugitive loner, at that. A strong hand gripped his right wrist and he looked down, eyes wide with terror. Henry's kind face looked back at him with a gentle smile. Nothing seemed to bother Henry.

"Welcome, friend. We have ale for you. It's been a long journey. Sit," the tanned Englishman insisted.

Brac hesitated. He thought that after a slow start, Henry had really warmed to him. Brac did not think Henry had been particularly antagonistic, but did have the feeling the Englishman had been suspicious of him. In hindsight, Brac considered this a fair stance. The wiry man wondered if managing his own entrance to the city had been some sort of test set by the Englishman, a rite of passage from which he could make more qualified judgements about the quarryman. By his own admission Brac had been almost useless during the flight from Rhuddlan and so felt relieved that he had managed to actually achieve something under the scrutiny of his protector.

Brac nodded curtly and nervously at the Englishman's words. It was now the absurdity of his situation dawned on him – that he was trying to impress an Englishman, one of those who had taken everything from him. He was all alone in the world because of what the English had done.

In general, he thought, sneaking into a city in order to visit a tavern before the sun had reached its highest in the sky was absurd.

Henry slid to his right along the small bench so that he was sitting up against the wall, three or four benches in from the front of the inn. The tanned Englishman was now sat opposite a man wearing the simple black cloak of the Benedictine order. He looked about forty, his dark hair streaked with iron grey and its hairline accentuated by the monk's haircut. His light eyes and pale skin gave him an almost ghost-like appearance in contrast with his black attire, emphasised all the more by the faint steel-coloured stubble around his chin and cheeks. He had a stern look about him that suggested a degree of seriousness befitting a man of the cloth. The temperature in the tavern almost matched that outside and yet still the monk was in his full garb, scapula and cowl over a tunic, topped off with a prominent wooden crucifix.

"Thanks," mumbled Brac, shuffling in and trying not to knock the woman sat behind him.

"Brac, please meet Prior Simon of the abbey. Prior Simon is prior at the abbey, which allows him leave to come recline with us in

71

such a colourful location." Henry grinned at the monk, whose expression did not change. "Most people would find it unusual to see a man of the prior's calling in here, but it is fortunate for our friendship that many of the Chester flock enjoy partaking of the ale."

"Blessings to you, Brac," spoke Prior Simon, slightly inclining his head as he did so. His voice sounded far less sombre than his face looked. It was as if they did not match up.

"Blessings, brother," Brac meekly replied.

"Prior Simon has some good news for us," Henry chimed, "of course, I shan't elaborate too extensively nor loudly here... but we have passage to London tomorrow, with the sisters of St Mary's. All we need to do, is hole up with the brothers tonight, and we'll be on our way." Henry clapped his hands together and took a long draught of ale from the big wooden cup, as if he had no further tasks to undertake in his life.

Prior Simon spoke. "I have heard of your tribulations, Brac, and I assure you there will be nothing to worry about from hereon in. Just so long as no mention is made to my brothers about the bag here." Brac could not see where the bag was, but he assumed it was under the table. Prior Simon spoke slowly and deliberately, befitting the contemplative nature of the Benedictine monks. His accent was from the south of England, like Henry's. Brac noticed he did not seem to blink, and indeed the monk had not taken his eyes off the Welshman since the latter's arrival at the table. The Welshman felt that Prior Simon should instil a feeling of reassurance; as prior, Prior Simon would be going out into the community more often than any other brother, and was the most publicly accessible of the fraternity. Brac, however, just found him unnerving. He probably had some other redeeming qualities, though, Brac thought. *Everyone is something for a reason.*

The wiry man spoke up. "They know we're here?" He looked at Prior Simon but was asking both men.

"No chance, especially after that stunt you pulled back there," replied Henry. Brac thought him remarkably jovial for someone who had spent two days and nights running for his life whilst carrying a large stone in a bag. Henry took another draught of his ale. Prior Simon finally took his eyes from Brac and looked disapprovingly at the knight. Brac had no idea who it was that Henry or the Frenchwoman were bound to, but seemingly they were relaxed enough for the knight to afford to drink on the job. The thought of drinking ale in the quarry was quite alien to the Welshman, not to mention inadvisable – the brewers of Rhuddlan were renowned for the strength of their drinks. Henry continued, "how exactly did you pull that off?"

"Well," the Welshman stuttered, conscious of his strong Welsh accent amongst the English tongues around him, "I had my purse stolen, and a woman behind me sees the thief take it, and then everyone joined in."

Henry grinned, drawing another disapproving glance from Prior Simon.

"I must apologise for such behaviour; we try to set a good example here in the city," explained Prior Simon. The monk brought his elbows up on to the table and put one hand on top of the other just under his chin. "But it seems it is more difficult to extend our lessons further beyond the walls," he trailed off, looking saddened.

"Sounds like assistance from the Lord, Brother," interjected Henry. "There is something about the stone, don't you think?"

"It is not for us to know the Lord's plans, Sir Henry. You know that better than anyone." The prior spoke firmly but without scolding the tanned man.

Brac's attention perked at the title with which Prior Simon addressed Henry. *Sir? This man is a knight?* Brac had not before encountered a knight of such a nature! A knight never allowed one to forget they were a knight. The absurdity increased.

Henry's jocular nature evaporated, and he became more serious and almost childlike in his inquisitiveness. "But how are we to reconcile that which we are told is to happen regarding the salvation of our souls with a rejection of divining the nature of the Lord's plans?"

"Sir Henry, we can discuss this this afternoon; I feel it shall become easier for you to understand once we have returned to the abbey. Tell me, when *was* the last time you attended a service? You as well, Brac. In fact, I daresay you'd probably be required to attend a sermon anyway, if you're hiding out from Lord Reginald and the King."

Prior Simon finished his cup. Brac assumed it was ale. The Welshman was not sure what the clergy were allowed to do regards ale – there were so many orders and rules, he could not remember. Presumably Henry was in some way affiliated with the Church, because he repeatedly mentioned 'the Order' and a Church as smuggling service. On the other hand, the knight was apparently very fond of ale, so Brac remained as much in the dark about Henry's affiliations as he was about all that had unfolded over the past few days.

Not for the first time over the past two days, Henry interrupted Brac's daydreaming. "Anyway, it pays to be vigilant, morally and physically, so let's head over to the Abbey before we get arrested. You going to finish that? Or even start it?" Henry looked accusingly at Brac, and then Brac's cup of ale.

The wiry man looked down stupidly, stared for a moment then took the cup in his right hand and emptied it in one go, as his father used to do. Most of it was caught by his beard however, and Henry noticed that some even managed to find its way to the Welshman's great eyebrows.

"… That happens quite a lot," Brac grinned.

The three emerged into the blinding sunshine and their senses were assaulted by colours, smells and sounds far in excess of those experienced in the tavern. Eastgate Street was heaving with bodies, human and animal, large and small. The refuse puddles down the sides of the partially cobbled road had dried in the blazing sunshine and it was difficult to see where the waste ended and the earth began. They trod gingerly over the eroded ditch in front of the inn and on to the south side of the street, avoiding a number of cart drivers, goatherds and running children. Prior Simon walked to the left, beckoning his two guests to follow. They weaved along, leaning towards the north side of the street where the bakers and the dairy sellers had their shops; here the smell of fresh bread overpowered the stench on the road itself and the people on it.

Brac looked ahead and saw St Peter's Church towering high above the haphazard thatched roofs, marking the centre of the walled city and home to much of the secular business of the city. It was on the northwest of The Cross, the junction of Northgate, Eastgate, Bridge and Watergate Streets. Countless people and sights and shades and noises crammed the three men from all sides, but their progress was unimpeded for it seemed everyone would step aside and allow the prior through with a cheerful greeting.

"Keep up, Brac. We are just around the corner." Prior Simon marched on, moving like a grey and black phantom through the multi-coloured throng. He turned right onto Northgate Street, towards the market hall. The market hall rose up in the centre of the widened southern end of Northgate Street. Dwarfed by the abbey on its east side, it nonetheless stood proud like an immovable wooden rock in a sea of merchants, hawkers, peddlers and buyers. The market hall and the stalls around it were a mosaic of colour supporting the din of tradesmen and victuallers crying out and customers shouting, all to the steady rhythm of laughter from all directions.

It seemed the ale and the sunshine had created an ambience that relaxed even Prior Simon's stern features. The three weaved through the vegetable sellers and the woodworkers, meandering around idle wanderers interspersed with wellwishers turning to greet the prior as he passed. To the right a plump woman in a light blue smock and white bonnet was hawking the sweetest looking apples Brac had ever seen; his stomach grumbled spectacularly yet noticeable only to himself. He had not yet eaten today. He considered how ale for breakfast had not generally produced enjoyable or particularly productive days.

Over Prior Simon's head did Brac spot a commotion in the crowd, identical to a scene from earlier in the morning; spears waving and wobbling about above the mass of heads, and the violent jerking movements of those heads as the bodies to which they were connected were shoved out of the way by helmeted men-at-arms.

Instantly Brac felt an icy touch of fear, and was on the verge of spinning and running but for Henry placing his left hand on the Welshman's right forearm, giving him a knowing look.

"Out of the way, in the name of the King!" ordered a soldier. Prior Simon looked back at Henry with an uncertain glance. Soldiers simply moving from A to B did not invoke the name of the King to provide a clear path. The jostling came closer, until the men-at-arms were almost on top of the group, for Prior Simon had moved to intercept the soldiers.

"What is the meaning of this roughhousing?" demanded the monk, who stood squarely in front of the three soldiers. A number of tradesmen and commonfolk turned to watch the confrontation, and a hush fell over this small part of the market. A boy climbed on top of a barrel up against the market hall wall, and a woman pointed to the group from atop her horse cart. The soldiers' shouts died in their throats and the last soldier almost crashed into the suddenly halted second. Prior Simon evidently held no mean standing in the city; Brac had never seen anyone of common stock stop soldiers in that way before.

"Apologies, brother," said the first man-at-arms, his helmet askew from the effort of wading through the thick sea of bodies. Rivulets of perspiration could be seen flowing down the man's neck – roughhousing he may have been, but in these conditions this was likely the last location the man-at-arms would want to be. "Welsh outlaws have attacked a train of Lord de Grey travelling from Rhuddlan. Huge number of them, so it is said." Many of the witnesses to the exchange began muttering and whispering to each other with looks of disbelief.

"Are there many dead, my friend?" asked Prior Simon, his stern features reforming following a lull.

"Don't know yet, Prior. But we've orders to close the city and go out and hunt them." The man-at-arms replied matter-of-factly, but his two comrades could not keep still through nervous energy. Brac thought they looked scared. Next to them, Henry too had fear in his eyes, and the knight caught Brac looking at him. Uncomfortable that he had been spotted noticing an expression of weakness in a knight, Brac turned away quickly back to Prior Simon.

The monk nodded and stepped aside. "Very well, William, and may the Lord protect you and your brothers," he said as he touched the man-at-arms' shoulder.

"My thanks, Prior," William responded, before bounding off through the crowd again towards The Cross and presumably Bridge Street beyond, followed by the other two men.

"Did he say 'Welsh', Prior?" asked a young woman carrying cloth. She looked as terrified as Prior Simon looked concerned. News was evidently spreading through the crowds with pace, for the laughter and shouting died down almost within an instant. Confirmation for those hearing the information by word of mouth was found in the sight of men-at-arms running this way and that, the occasional glimpse of a spearhead waving along the street or the glint of sunlight on steel.

"I thought they was gone!" exclaimed another woman.

A ruddy-faced man carrying a belt full of hammers piped up. "How will we get home?" He looked around as if expecting an answer.

Prior Simon sensed panic brewing. "Please remember, my friends, that this city stood tall during the rebellion! And now the rebellion is crushed, and a few of the rebels are out attacking easy targets. Rhuddlan is thirty miles away. The Welsh have never come this far into England before."

The ruddy-faced man fretted further. "But brother, how do I get home?"

Brac was beginning to see why Prior Simon was the abbey's prior even if the Welshman personally found the prior somehow unnerving. The monk answered the ruddy-faced man and in doing so addressed the surrounding crowd. "I shall visit Lord de Grey this very afternoon. I am sure his men will comfortably disperse the troublemakers. And as our Lord Jesus Christ taught, there is nothing to be gained in worrying, for it shall add not a single hour to your life. You shall go home, John Blacksmith."

Prior Simon's reassurances calmed John Blacksmith and a few around him, but bad news travelled quicker than did the monk's message and the cheerful ambience in the market area had completely dissipated. Henry tugged almost imperceptibly at Prior

Simon's arm, nodding back at Brac. The silent communication was understood perfectly; the prior and the knight were concerned at the fearful response of the English crowd to the news of the Welsh brigands; a fearful response could quite easily turn into an angry response, and they both knew angry was interchangeable with violent. Brac stayed close to Henry, mouse-like in his wariness.

"Please, make way for the Prior!" commanded the knight. Brac had not heard Henry raise his voice before. It demanded attention and obedience with which it was met, and previously fretting woodworkers and vegetable sellers instinctively cleared a path for the black-clad monk and his companions. Brac followed in Henry's footsteps, reflecting on how unusual it was for once to be in a party for whom everyone else stepped aside – the commonfolk unconsciously moved aside for those in authority.

The three navigated the sea of worrying traders and merchants, reaching the edge of the market area with a sense of relief from escaping the immediate threat of violence breaking out at the slightest provocation, and also feeling able to breathe having fought clear of the choking atmosphere of fear. They approached the imposing abbey gates, over twenty feet high and thicker than the city walls. Indeed, the abbey complex was virtually impregnable. Brac had been to Chester on a few occasions and had always wondered at the majesty of the abbey and its grounds, which covered about one-sixth of the city's walled area. Never did ten feet-thick gates look so comforting to the wiry Welshman as they did now.

"Brother Stephen, would you open the gate for us, please?" yelled the prior, barely audible above the cacophony of the crowd behind them. Prior Simon hammered at the heavy oak door, a giant slab more befitting the gate of a castle than a religious community. The prior had often commented on this feature of the abbey's security – the Benedictines were contemplative, and less communally active than other orders such as the Franciscans, but the prior believed it completely unnecessary to hide away from the world as if in a stronghold under siege. He wondered, was not a Christian house supposed to welcome the world? The prior knew he could not do anything about the walls and gate buildings, for they were too magnificent to tear down. But an alteration could be effected with the gate door. If he had his way, he would simply have it ripped off.

A few moments passed and a previously inconspicuous wooden panel slid to the left at Prior Simon's head height. Two blue eyes and a long nose peered out from the viewing port. If Brac thought that Prior Simon spoke in a methodical manner, then Brother Stephen may as well have been asleep when talking.

"Of course, brother. A moment, if you will." Brother Stephen was slow and ponderous in his speech, though not in a deliberate way. Years of silence and private study seemed to have left the long-nosed man unfamiliar with his own vocal chords.

Henry had always been fascinated with the rota system in the abbey, specifically the reasoning behind putting the community's oldest member on the gate duty. Whenever he had visited the brothers at Chester he had asked the prior whether it would be wiser to place a greener brother at the gate, to assist in teaching patience and attentiveness through long periods of silence, physical inactivity and introspection. Brother Stephen had an entire lifetime's worth of practice under his belt. Furthermore, the knight wondered how it was that moving the heaviest individual object in the entire complex, the majestic gate door, was the responsibility of the abbey's least physically capable man. Every time Prior Simon had assured him that he would find answers to these questions. Henry was still waiting.

The wooden panel closed and three heavy clunks echoed about the monumental archway, slowly and evenly spaced in a fashion remarkably similar to how Brother Stephen spoke. Prior Simon looked back at Henry and Brac, anticipating a comment or question on the gatekeeper's lack of urgency. Henry answered the prior's expectation with a knowing smirk.

Chapter 7

Prior Simon led them across from the gate to the main building itself. Larger than all other structures in the city except for the castle, St Werbaugh's Abbey was a magnificent stone monument to God and His Son, watching over the city diagonally opposite the castle; power in one corner of the walled perimeter and reverence in the other. Reverence was, of course, power under another name; the rulers of that majestic construct were as canny and influential as their counterparts in the other towering bastion across the city.

The monastery and the resolute monks within had stood fast through two hundred years of social upheaval and war, of which the Welsh uprising earlier in the year was just the latest feature. Inside the walls of the abbey's enclosure Brac was able to forget his weariness and fears. He was now under protection from the Lord. The English could not reach him here.

"Brother John, the Lord has sent us a delightful day. Please, would you happen to know where Father Thomas is?" Prior Simon hailed an unsuspecting young monk walking away to their right, towards the south end of the abbey building. Brother John spun around and courteously bowed for the Prior. He looked no older than Brac, his hair fine and not so much as a single facial hair in sight.

"Blessings to you, Prior Simon, and your guests. The abbot is presently in his quarters, with his writing."

Simon smiled at the young monk. "Thank you, brother. Come, we must see Father Thomas. Sir Henry, it has been a while since you were here – the abbot remains as strong as ever." The iron-grey man unintentionally and dramatically swept his cloak around as he walked away to the left, towards a small building on the north side of the abbey.

Henry and Brac eyed each other, mirth in the former's eyes at the sober prior's uncharacteristically theatrical exit, before the knight heaved the bag higher on his shoulder and marched after Simon.

Brac looked around, noticing a couple of monks carrying sacks near the south wall, presumably where Brother John was headed.

As John had said, Abbot Thomas Birchills was indeed in his quarters with his papers. Thomas disliked the huge bureaucratic responsibilities of running the abbey, but did not grumble for he knew this was his calling and endurance was the only way he knew. Benedictine discipline was drilled into his very bones. It was not so much the drudgery of the bills and lists and supplies and communication to which he had to attend that dragged him down; more that it detracted from prayer, contemplation and study.

Thomas thought back four years to the death of the previous abbot, Simon Whitchurch. Thomas was the only realistic choice to replace him and he knew things would not have turned out any other way. He often reflected on and drew solace from how his sacrifice in running the abbey and conducting diplomacy enabled his flock the opportunity to undertake the prayer, contemplation and study he so craved.

Three knocks rapped the door, breaking him out of his daydream. "Enter," requested Thomas.

Prior Simon slid in, bowing as he did so but trying to keep moving to allow Henry and Brac space in the room also. "Good day, Father Thomas."

Thomas looked up from his papers and felt warmer for the company of his friend. "My dear Simon, good day. Blessings to you and your guests. Is that, Sir Henry? I almost did not recognise you. How long has it been since you last visited?" The abbot had a warmth about his face that the prior did not.

Henry beamed. "Good day, father! Indeed it has been quite some years. I trust the Holy Land has not aged me too prematurely."

"Not in the slightest, my boy. You have a wonderful glow. And I do not believe we have met, young man?" He gestured with his right palm open to Brac.

"Greetings, father, I am Brac of Rhuddlan." The wiry man uncomfortably stooped low, as smoothly as his rickety back allowed.

"Welcome, Brac of Rhuddlan. A surprise and a delight to see one of our Welsh flock here in Chester. Are you searching for some accommodation?" The abbot leaned a little in the direction of the Welshman, all ears.

Prior Simon spoke up. "Sir Henry is also, father. They have come into some trouble with Lord Reginald." Abbot Thomas leant back to his original sitting position. Simon continued, "With the help of Brac, Sir Henry has obtained a stone from the King's quarry at Rhuddlan at the request of the Temple... They are to ride for London tomorrow with our sisters by the castle."

The abbot's face contorted in confusion. "Brother Simon, I am not quite sure why you have become tangled in this unusual matter. Far be it for me to judge the Temple's actions and orders. Sir Henry, I should like to observe this stone, if I may. What business does the Temple have with stealing from the King's quarry?" Abbot Thomas viewed the knight and Brac with a little contempt, raising his head and looking down his nose at them.

"I'm afraid you have us wrong, father," Henry said, with an easy air about him and a disarming smile. "'Stealing' is a strong term. Master Guy has requested an object of this description be brought under the Order's care." He shifted the sack off his shoulder and lowered it to the stone floor with a heavy *thump*. His shoulder ached from having supported the silver stone's weight for the best part of two days, but he did not complain. It was not Henry's way to complain. Master Guy had liked that about the knight; he and El simply got on with things with no grumbling. Master Guy knew El's piety gave her extra steel, but guessed that Henry's character was so relaxed that he could be asked to carry the stone all the way to the Holy Land and he would not show concern. Henry patted down his dishevelled tunic, still wearing the one Brac had spotted him wearing on the bellowing man's cart outside the city, and rose up to his full height again.

Abbot Thomas remained unimpressed. "And why does Master Guy presume to sanction theft?" His voice dripped with derision.

The knight chuckled softly and scratched his dark hair. "This 'theft' was sanctioned by the Grand Master."

Thomas looked to Simon for support. Prior Simon raised his eyebrows and pursed his lips in an expression recognising just how high this matter went in the Church hierarchy.

Henry continued. "I'm sure you can appreciate that I am merely a servant undertaking my duties... I have reservations myself, Father Thomas, but it is not my place to question plans and orders." The knight gave a knowing glance to Prior Simon, whose annoyed, narrowed eyes betrayed a recollection of their earlier conversation in the Taverner's Inn.

Abbot Thomas sighed. "You put me in a difficult position here, and you know the laws on sanctuary rights for felons." His tone had softened, nearly sympathetic. He was not entirely inflexible.

"But would this not be in service to the Lord?" Henry replied, gesturing at the sack on the floor. "I appreciate your difficulties, but we must be practical. No blame or scorn shall fall on your head. You are assisting the Temple, one order to another, and tomorrow I shall say the same to your sisters, too." He shifted his weight from one foot to the other, looking down at his feet. "I don't know for what purpose the Grand Master has requested possession of this, or another thing just like it, but all I know is that for the Grand Master to sanction what some may term as 'theft', then there must be something of great consequence afoot." The knight's eyes were honest and his delivery impassioned. Brac, who had not uttered a word since being introduced to the Abbot, looked expectantly at Thomas.

The abbot clasped his hands behind back and bobbed on his heels. "Our Lord Saviour taught us to render unto Caesar what is Caesar's... this object is rightfully the King's. How does the Grand Master even know that this is what he is searching for?" The prior and the quarryman turned back to Henry. Brac had never felt more out of place in his life.

"The Grand Master trusts Master Guy, and Master Guy trusts Eleanor..." The knight trailed off and his eyes dimmed a little at the thought of his absent friend. "And Eleanor trusts her own judgement." Henry snapped back to his former unflappable self. "And you know the reputation of the Grand Master, my dear Abbot! Name me one bishop of England or France or Italy who is more reputable than Jacques. Bishoprics are more or less duchies. You know that."

Abbot Thomas breathed heavily through his nose as he pondered the situation. "I do hope you are not naming any names there, Sir Henry. We all share the same Church, remember," he cautioned the knight. "And what are we to say to Lord Reginald when he comes knocking in the city, asking anyone and everyone of the whereabouts of a mysterious piece of quarry rock?"

"You won't have seen it, my dear brother," replied Henry, the twinkle back in his eye. And if Lord Reginald doesn't believe you, he can request a warrant to search the abbey. There will be no trace of any mysterious stone after tomorrow."

"I suppose the only thing for it, is to see the object itself," interjected Prior Simon in his slow and deliberate tone. The prior met eyes with Abbot Thomas, who nodded. Henry took his cue and lifted the silver object out of the old woven bag, letting it drop to the floor in an untidy heap. Henry held it in two hands at stomach height, the silver surface reflecting the lamp flame and candlelight beautifully across its untarnished surface. Thomas and Simon gawped wide-eyed at the flawless stone. Brac too was mesmerised, even though he had spent more time with it than anyone.

"May I place this somewhere, Father Thomas?" asked Henry, his body language suggesting it was not so easy holding the stone in his hands.

"Yes, yes, of course. Here." Abbot Thomas haphazardly swept aside some papers from his heavy oak desk, a hulking great table that could have originated from the same mighty tree as the gate door of the abbey. Henry hauled the stone a few steps and swung it down onto the desk, landing with a deep *thunk* that rang through the thick oak foundations. Thomas looked it over, brushing his right hand over the top and the curved edge closest to him. "Wonderful craftsmanship... what metal is this? I have not seen its like before. Simon, are you familiar with this?"

Prior Simon approached the desk and with equal care caressed the top and side of the stone, and was equally confounded by its conspicuous properties. "If this is the work of man, he has God with him," the prior solemnly declared. "I think I should like to investigate this a little closely, if we are not losing possession of it until the morrow?"

The abbot smiled. "I should say it behoves us to investigate further, brother. Just so long as henceforth you don't renounce your vows in favour of a life of alchemy. Technically, I have some responsibility for your soul, so I'd rather you stay with us."

Prior Simon nodded to the abbot. "I'm sure the venerable Doctor Bacon would have appreciated your concern, brother." The prior was referring to the great Franciscan friar and philosopher Roger Bacon who had died only three years before. Thomas and Simon had met him on one occasion and had been as awed by his gravitas in the flesh as they had by his reputation beforehand. Prior Simon had since applied himself to investigating the natural world at any opportunity he could, determined to solve the myriad mysteries of the Lord's creation.

Simon turned to Henry and Brac. "My friends, may I trouble you for a penny?"

"It cost us everything just to get into the city, brother!" Henry laughed, and even Brac broke a smile. The knight pulled out a silver penny and handed it to the prior. The prior studied it carefully, turning it round and flipping it in his right hand, left hand still behind his back. "You can trust me, Prior Simon. We may be thieves, but we have real money." Henry looked at Brac with big grin and the wiry Welshman chuckled into his thick beard.

The prior smiled for the first time since the meeting at the inn. "You are a trustworthy man, Sir Henry, we have no qualms about that." He clenched his fist around the coin and turned back to the desk. Holding his right hand out over the stone about half a foot above, Prior Simon released the coin and it hit the stone with a dull ring. "Well, this is not silver. Or, at least, not pure silver. Which may explain why you were able to carry it so easily over such a distance." Simon picked the coin up and lightly dragged it across the stone, no sound emanating from either object. His eyes lost focus as he gazed into the perfect silver, mindlessly dragging the coin back and forth across the surface.

"That is rather conclusive, prior," offered Thomas.

"Were this pure silver, the coin would have rendered a sweet ringing sound upon its surface," explained Simon rather distractedly, still absently contemplating the hypnotic surface. He was not patronising, however. Straight-laced he may have been and with rarely any excitement in his delivery, but the prior was certainly not an impatient man when it came to teaching. He appreciated his audience would often unlikely possess the knowledge about which he taught – otherwise they would not be his audience - and resolved to educate in an unpatronising manner. After all, Simon could hardly claim ownership of that knowledge; he was merely a vector for the transmission of God's knowledge.

Henry looked to Abbot Thomas. The abbot eyed him back, silently suggesting he allow the prior some thinking time. The knight struggled to determine whether he had known that characteristic about silver or if hearing the prior discuss it suggested to his own mind that he already knew it.

"Brac, did you know that?" Henry asked the quarryman.

Not expecting direct involvement in this, or any, discussion in the abbot's quarters, Brac was taken aback somewhat. "I, yes, I did," he affirmed nervously. The Welshman deemed himself too lowly to have ventured his own answer to the abbot's question, however.

Prior Simon broke away from the silver and raised his head to Abbot Thomas. "I'm afraid my curiosity is getting the better of me, Father Thomas. Some heat would not go amiss. With a miniscule risk of burnishing what is clearly a magnificent artefact, the application of some heat can give us a few hints as to what this may consist of. Given this stone's apparent imperviousness to any damage or even scratch, I'm confident there will be no permanent effect. I hear our young quarryman here hit it square on with a pick and it remains flawless." The prior scraped the coin back and forth vigorously and carelessly on the top surface, grinning at Henry and Brac. "Brac, please pass me the lamp over there."

The wiry man turned and lifted the plain ceramic bowl from a shelf, and carefully carried it to the prior. The ceramic was warm to the touch, and the flame vibrant; it had evidently been freshly lit. Prior Simon put the coin down on the stone floor and stood back up, groaning as he did. The prior seemed to temporarily drown in his multitude of black robes and hood before emerging upright from the quagmire.

"We shall see, with this coin, the heat of the flame will not affect its appearance. A little space, please. Now, this is only the most basic cupellation, but it is the best that we can provide here, in the abbot's quarters." Henry and Brac backed off a step or two, and Abbot Thomas leaned forward over his desk as tall as his small frame would allow. Prior Simon carefully poured some of the flaming oil onto the coin, which fizzled momentarily before burning itself out in a wisp of smoke. Simon gave the lamp back to Brac before thoroughly wrapping his right hand up in his robes and cloak and bent down, picking the coin up. He blew on it as one would anything hot, as if such an action would noticeably cool fire-treated metal. Abbot Thomas walked round his desk to join the other three in peering at the coin.

"No markings on the coin, no evidence of flame, no burnishing. This is a good piece of silver. Sir Henry, your Temple knows their money." The four men laughed, but only Brac was unaware of the in-joke about the expansive Templar banking system; the first to encompass the entirety of Christendom. "Brac, the lamp again, if you will. Sir Henry, please place the stone on the floor. Neither Father Thomas nor I are as young as we used to be."

Henry obliged and then stepped back with Brac and Thomas, as Simon once more held the ceramic lamp out, slowly and deliberately poured out a slight dripping of oil. The superheated oil splashed on to the top of the stone, fizzled and with a small *whoosh* completely disappeared. Startled, Simon leant in closer. There was no trace of the flame nor oil. He looked at the spot where the coin had lain, which had stained the stone floor with a dark residue of the oil. But the stone was bare, with no indicator of any heat treatment whatsoever.

"I... I must confess, I'm not entirely sure what to make of that," said Prior Simon, clearly taken aback. "The object is not silver, and so should temporarily mark... which it has not done. Once more, as investigation dictates."

The prior looked at the other three in turn, intense curiosity in all four sets of eyes. He poured a greater quantity onto the stone, with the same result – a fizzling then immediately a *whoosh*, before the flame and oil completely disappeared.

"Did you see the colour?" Brac asked excitedly, eyes so wide through his bushy face they were almost completely visible. "The blue. I've not seen something like that."

"Aye, I did," answered Simon, "and neither have I."

"So we are unsure as to what that blue might indicate?" enquired Abbot Thomas. The edginess in his voice was returning, having earlier been quelled a little following Henry assuaging his apprehension over the stone's theft.

Simon shook his head and jutted his jaw forward as he thought. "I have heard the horsemen of the east have learned to manipulate fire in such a way so as to control its distribution and colouration, but..." he trailed off again, trawling his memory for a solution to the puzzle before him.

"As in, Greek fire?" asked Henry. The English knight had not seen it used, but had been told the walls of Constantinople still stood thanks partially to its devastating employment against the Turks.

Again Prior Simon shook his head. "That's far more chaotic." He looked to Henry as he explained. "This seems entirely controlled, so controlled as to completely disappear with no trace of the fire ever having existed. The men of the east have used fire in this way, delivering fire to a target which then explodes and vanishes from what I have read, though this surpasses even their control."

Henry was relieved he had not encountered these controlled fire-explosions during a battle. He could not imagine the terror such a display could instil in already frayed nerves.

Prior Simon rocked on the balls of his feet. "As representative of the Grand Master, Sir Henry, I request your permission to pour the rest of this lamp over this stone?"

Henry muttered an affirmative under his breath, unable to remove his gaze from the stone. Prior Simon poured the remaining fiery oil over the stone, which splashed and *whoosh*ed once more, throwing up a slight blue flash before disappearing, along with the stone flooring immediately surrounding the stone. It dropped a foot or so into a newly formed pit and *whoomp*ed to the ground.

The four men stood with jaws open, completely incapable of comprehending what had just transpired.

"What is this...?" Abbot Thomas, crossing himself, could not find the words to complete his question. "That's a solid stone floor, and it's just disappeared?"

Henry and Simon both also crossed themselves and asked the same question. Brac stepped forward, mumbling a request for protection from God, knees clicking loudly as he bent down to observe the stone in its new pit. The earth beneath the stone foundations of the abbot's room was there, with half a worm poking through in the far corner as Brac viewed it.

The stone itself remained flawless, still no hint of any heat treatment, and absolutely no hint of where the flooring stones had gone. The Welshman tentatively reached out to the stone and poked the top of it with his left index finger. It was cool to the touch. He pulled his finger back and studied his fingertip, finding no unusual markings amidst the encrusted dirt.

"This is beyond the understanding of man!" Abbot Thomas proclaimed, backing away slowly. "This must be some sort of sorcery. Sir Henry, you are not to make mention of this to anyone, and as soon as day breaks on the morrow, you are to remove this object from this abbey and this city." The abbot was becoming increasingly red-faced and began to tremble. "The Lord's house will not be further defiled! Brother Simon, please find appropriate storage for this cursed thing. Sir Henry, it is only my respect for your Order that is preventing me from having this object removed from the abbey immediately! There shall be no mention made, not today, not tomorrow to the sisters, not any time." Thomas sat down heavily on his chair behind the desk, gripping the arms of the chair tightly.

Prior Simon slowly acknowledged the abbot with a nod, but found he could not look away from the hole in the ground where the floor should have been. "Sir Henry... please can you place the stone in its sack and follow me. Brac, you shall come too."

The knight hesitated. "It is... not necessarily accursed, Abbot," Henry suggested, "could it be some sort of relic?" His question was more hopeful than expectant.

Prior Simon murmured an agreement of sort, rubbing his hand over the grey stubble that seamlessly blended into his grey face.

89

"He's right. The Devil has no power within these walls. A holy environment is the best place for this object, one where its mysteries can be investigated under safe and controlled conditions."

"Need I remind you, Prior Simon, that a number of floor stones have simply disappeared?" Abbot Thomas stood up again, bewilderment exacerbating into stress, palms flat on the table. "Are you suggesting we continue investigating how much more of the abbey can disappear?"

The abbot had raised his voice, but once he realised he had done so he shrank down to his seat again as if physically atoning for such an outburst. Or at least, what would be considered an outburst for a monk. "My apologies, brother, Henry, Brac. That was unbecoming of me and may the Lord forgive my lack of faith." He crossed himself again. "I agree that this object should remain in Church possession at least until such time when we can ascertain its true nature."

Henry approached the stone, sunken in its pit, and felt the smooth, cool surface. "The Grand Master is a clever man," he said to no one in particular.

"Indeed, he must be," replied Prior Simon. "What brings you to such a conclusion at this point in time?"

The knight straightened up. "The Temple is to keep this object away from man, for the safety of man. Could you imagine the nefarious purposes to which this object could be put by ill-minded individuals?" He turned to Brac. "My Welsh friend, your scheme to con the English lords could save many people much hardship."

Brac had never before been praised for anything, let alone touted as a hero, albeit an accidental one. He smiled a genuine smile at the knight, who replied in kind.

Prior Simon interjected. "Before Sir Henry's penchant for hyperbole fills you too full of pride, young Brac, I must remind you that we are to guard against such sins, and also that we do not yet know what this object is capable of, or indeed designed for." Brac visibly appeared to deflate at the prior's pragmatism. "Sir Henry, you are taking this to the London Temple?"

"The very one," said the knight, narrowing his eyes trying to deduce Prior Simon's next sentence.

90

Simon looked back at Abbot Thomas. "Oxford to London would take two, three days?"

Abbot Thomas smiled and nodded, "The man you have in mind is young; two days will be sufficient."

"Very well. If you would not mind, father, perhaps a letter of recommendation to John Duns at Oxford would serve the Temple well? I'm sure he would find much upon which to speculate with this item." Prior Simon gestured dramatically at the silver stone on the floor.

"Master Guy would probably undertake the very same," reflected Abbot Thomas. "Prior Simon, please show our guests to the visitors' quarters, and ensure the stone remains hidden. Even our brothers might be tempted a peak if they hear of what has transpired here."

The abbot did not look up again from his desk as the three shuffled about the room following his instructions. As he reached for his quill he heard the heaving and clunking of the stone being lifted out of the small pit, presumably by Sir Henry, and the effort and laboured breathing accompanying it. Taking a fresh piece of scroll, he began writing.

Brother John, a most just man and follower of our Lord Jesus Christ from your dear Brother Thomas Birchills,

Blessings to you and your brothers and sisters. I sincerely request you undertake a journey to the London Temple, for there awaits a gift truly beyond the realm of man. You must ask for the silver stone, and it shall be delivered unto you. I have delivered instructions to the Temple ahead of you so that your attendance will not be without foreknowledge. Cupellation is recommended, but with extensive consideration for your physical wellness and that of those around you, you can consult with Sir Henry of the Temple on this matter.

Believe me your most loyal servant and humble petitioner while I live.

Rolling the scroll, Abbot Thomas sealed it with hot wax and made his way out of the now empty quarters, the other three having left during his writing. He made for the stable by the gate where the messenger should be waiting. Exiting the door to his quarters he strode across the dirt path, initially blinded by the midday sun. The heat enveloped him and immediately he felt sweat forming on his brow and his back. The messenger boy was standing in the shade, kicking the dirt and apparently thoroughly bored. His small, round face was almost as caked in dust as his leather-wrapped shoes, and his blond hair was matted and darkened by the dirt.

"Boy, come here," commanded Thomas. The boy looked up, bright blue eyes shining expectantly. He had prayed for an interruption to his boredom and God had answered his prayers. Thomas looked down at him amiably. "Please take this to William the Farrier, down on Saddler's Row. Tell him the abbot requests he ride for the university of Oxford immediately. Good lad."

Turning about and scuffing a brown sandal on the temporary ruts in the ground created by the carts trundled through the mud after the last rains, Abbot Thomas headed in the direction of the main door, his mind heavy with contemplation. A few brothers ambled here and there and the abbot greeted them as they passed, more instinctively than consciously as he pondered the remarkable events, nay miracles, they had just witnessed. Gazing without really viewing, he saw ahead by the door Prior Simon with Henry and Brac, the former leading the latter across the enclosure seemingly in the direction of Thomas' quarters. Henry was carrying the stone in its sack. Presumably the prior had pressed the strong knight into some manual labour whilst he showed them to their quarters. Simon was taking an unusual route, Thomas judged, but the abbot quickly disregarded it as he refocused on the more pressing mystery of the silver object.

At the periphery of the abbey estate, Brother Stephen began opening the gate door painfully slowly and no sooner had a foot-wide gap appeared did the thin boy slip out into the chaos of the market square. He paused, looking left and right and assessing the traffic of people, before taking off. Barely two strides into his run he was jerked back by his right arm, the grip biting into his upper arm causing him to yelp like a dog.

"Woah, little man, running through crowds is dangerous." A girl, no older than sixteen, looked down at him. She was taller than he by over a head, but herself was of average height. Her long and frizzy dark hair was tied back and she wore a dark blue shirt as grubby as the messenger boy's." You might get lost. What's this you have here?" Her right hand darted forward faster than the boy could react and wrested the rolled up letter free from the boy's grip, all the while not letting go of his other arm with her left hand. "I'll deliver this for you. Much safer that way. Run along, boy." Her voice was friendly but her face was most certainly not, and the messenger boy, suddenly free of her grip, ran off into the crowd with tears forming in his blue eyes.

Chapter 8

The council meeting had been more lively than usual, Mathieu de la Marche thought. This owed in no small part to the resounding victory of Comte Robert d'Artois in the south west against the English. Mathieu's report on d'Artois' success to the Grand Chamberman Robert de Bourgogne had been recounted to the King with all of the level-headed coolness that characterised de Bourgogne. Comte Mathieu was a great admirer of de Bourgogne, the Duke of Burgundy, but mainly from afar. They had last met on unofficial business a few years before, prior to the outbreak of fighting in Gascony, but they shared so much time together at court Mathieu believed it superfluous to meet outside of it. He felt de Bourgogne to be the archetypal Grand Chamberman, the second most powerful man in the kingdom, and one of the few capable men, including himself and Lemaître, surrounding the King – strong, precise, focused, and utterly, utterly ruthless.

The assembled noblemen and retainers had maintained an air of excitement throughout the more mundane discussions of state for which the likes of Guillaume de Troyes and Geoffroi d'Hainault had no time. To the Comte, it seemed as if the chaotic market in front of the Notre Dame cathedral had come to the Louvre; the colours, the energy, the verve, all underneath the hastily constructed awnings bordering the garden at the end of the palatial grounds. Across the grass, Mathieu even saw the abbot of Cluny and the archbishop of Sens, the King's confessor Guillaume de Paris, in heated conversation like two boys caught up in the excitement of the joust or the fair. The Comte found himself wondering what King Philippe Augustus would make of this rabble of children, holding court in the palace he built a century beforehand.

Mathieu had remained silent for the entirety of the meeting thus far. Robert de Bourgogne was again standing on the grass, the central point between the three banks of awnings; the Maison du Roi, the King's household, on one side, the Parisian elite on the other, and the King and Queen in between. The Duke was addressing the

94

assembly on wine supplies for the city; Mathieu could see the Duke knew this was mere child's play for a statesman and warrior such as he, but still, keeping the Bordeaux supplies open *was* of import. It had gone past the midday and the Comte had not yet had a cup of red. It was tiresome enough having to tolerate even looking at de Troyes and d'Hainault without this season's finest de Châtillon to hand.

He scanned the seats around him. De Troyes was there, d'Hainault, Guido da Vigevano, the Queen's physician – he was wearing a pair of the eyeglasses Pascal had. Pascal probably obtained his pair from him – Guido did have contacts in Genoa, after all. There was something weasel-like about Guido, but he seemed harmless enough, and neither the Comte nor consequently Philippe had any qualms about his presence in the Maison. There, too, was the Constable of France, the fearsome Raoul de Clermont; long, black hair down either side of his scarred head, week-old beard complimenting his heavy eyebrows under a furrowed brow, sitting more uncomfortably through the proceedings than anyone else in view. He was a true *comes stabuli*, 'count of the stables', an ancient Roman office – he lived in the saddle and Mathieu had not seen him beaten in the joust. No doubt he was aching to hear of Philippe's plans for Flanders and perhaps even beyond.

Behind him brooded Lemaître. The shade in which the Maison du Roi sheltered from the sun seemed not to come from the awnings above but from the menacing Master of the Treasury himself. In a rainbow of vibrant colours and designs, Mathieu had spotted Lemaître immediately when approaching his seat – he was again wearing entirely black; oftentimes from behind and the side Mathieu had mistaken Lemaître for a Benedictine monk in their black habit. Mathieu watched Lemaître for a while and yet the latter did not take his eyes off the Duke of Burgundy, either because he did not sense Mathieu's stare, or that the duties of state were above such distractions. Mathieu figured it was the latter.

The Duke had finished his discussion, followed by the King and a few of the leading citizens of the city. The heat did not seem to wear down the debaters nor the length of the debates; as usual everyone had been eager for their chance to talk with the King. Mathieu

95

approved of Philippe's patience throughout – he had engaged in every topic brought up and demonstrated a balanced concern for the city and the kingdom, as far as he could. Philippe had created his fair share of enemies amongst the Church leaders particularly, but the Comte had his finger on those pulses so that any concerns would not surprise the King. If only those critics could see him here, Mathieu thought. *He is neither human nor beast. He is a statue,* the cantankerous bishop of Pamiers had said about him. But inflexible Philippe was not. What did the old bishop know about running a kingdom, anyway?

The Comte sat back and clasped his hands over his chest in his customary manner, watching as the impetuous de Troyes strode forward onto the grass like a cockerel strutting amongst the hens to add his voice to proceedings. Mathieu studied the young nobleman with his magnificent blue mantel, deliberately coloured to emulate that of the King and the royal *fleur-de-lis* emblem. Surely today was too hot to be wearing such a superfluous item of clothing? To his credit, the boy is durable, the Comte thought.

De Troyes predictably questioned the plans for Flanders, in the light of the English collapse in the south-west, a discussion that drew periodic murmurs of approval from the enthusiastic audience. Even the archbishop of Sens could be seen nodding vigorously – Mathieu had always suspected the archbishop to be of questionable moral fibre and had unsuccessfully counselled against his instatement as Philippe's confessor; Mathieu believed those at the helm of the kingdom on occasion may be required to undertake morally dubious activities – he was not innocent of this – but archbishops should not be amongst that number. The Comte lamented the politicisation of church offices and with it the evolution of clerical responsibilities and concerns. Archbishop Guillaume was no shepherd to the flock. Mathieu knew from sources the Archbishop was not even close to being morally suitable as a shepherd.

A few points made by de Troyes on relations with the Aragonese impressed the Comte, who generally held a monopoly on matters of foreign affairs amongst the courtiers. The majority of the Maison and the leading citizens were apparently mesmerised by the young nobleman's demagoguery, Mathieu noticed. The simpleton Geoffroi d'Hainault was having the time of his life as his hero lectured. The Comte began drifting in and out of listening to de Troyes' speech, and began considering seriously for the first time the threat that such a popular figure could pose to the stability of the crown. Not many in France knew their Alcibiades from their Pericles, but Mathieu did and he wanted to deduce which of the two de Troyes most closely mirrored.

"It's simple, sire. You have no enemies at your back, move against Flanders and drive the English allies in to the sea. Edward will taste French steel soon enough." Guillaume de Troyes was young and brash, which the King liked. Idolised by the younger and less influential at court and their hangers on, thoroughly detested by the more established; the only point on which everyone could agree was that he was very effective at gaining attention. That the sunlight made his golden bear clasp shine like the very sun itself only reinforced his position as centrepiece at court.

"Remember this man's youth," Queen Jeanne whispered in to the King's ear.

Philippe turned to his right where Jeanne was sitting. "He's the same age as me, my dear. Does this mean I have to remember my youth as well?"

Jeanne smiled affectionately. "You don't, because you're not an idiot." She kissed him softly on the cheek, knowing that such a display was completely anathema whilst the court was in session, but she did not care, and neither did the King.

Philippe took Jeanne's hand and squeezed it as he stood up from the gilded and carved high-backed chair set on the grass in front of the palace residence. Walking forward with impeccable posture so that he cleared well over six feet, his blond hair fell perfectly over his shoulders and the pearls on his padded jacket blazed like countless stars in the deep blue night sky. Mathieu watched him closely, aware of just how well drilled Philippe was in looking the part.

Physically, perhaps, the Bishop of Pamiers had it right when accusing him of being a statue, but the Greeks themselves had never carved something so magnificent. Philippe le Bel, they call him. It was not a misplaced nickname, for sure. Upon arriving in the morning, Pascal had suggested to him that the King must be the likeness of Achilles, but then quickly retracted the statement on account of Achilles' early demise. Mathieu had found that amusing; the learned Pascal should have known better than to assume saying such a thing would automatically lead to the same outcome occurring.

The murmuring fell silent as the King stopped abruptly before de Troyes. The nobleman looked on in anticipation of agreement from Philippe. De Troyes had become very good at guessing the King's moods, which meant that many of his suggestions matched the King's own plans. Some interpreted this as de Troyes having the King's ear, but Mathieu knew de Troyes was merely reactive, with little originality of his own.

"I appreciate your enthusiasm, Comte Guillaume, but I feel now is not the time for expansion. Have we not just expelled the Duke of Aquitaine from Gascony? That is expansion enough for now. Comte Dampierre will be talked round. I feel consolidation is in order." De Troyes nodded solemnly, and overhead a cloud passed over briefly, dimming the sunlight reflecting off his golden bear clasp. Mathieu smiled to himself.

Philippe continued. "I have been in discussion with the archbishop here," waving a hand at the archbishop of Sens, who gracefully nodded in acknowledgement, "and he has offered some advice regards the sanctity of my soul, in the light of all this fighting. The Lord has sent me advice, and I shall follow it, and as your King I am extending this advice to you all. All hostilities with the King of England are henceforth ceased." A silent yet conspicuous shock went up from the bank of leading citizens; only de Troyes and d'Hainault followed suit amongst the Maison. Mathieu sucked on his cheeks as he mused on the King's words, this visual indicator of thought masked by the light stubble on his granite cheekbones. It was a prerequisite of his vocation to be difficult to read and yet this moment had caught him by surprise – but sharp as ever, he snapped himself out of it, not realising his fresh beard hid the evidence anyway.

Philippe had not previously given any indication of dropping hostilities against King Edward; the armies under Comte Robert d'Artois had been instructed to clear Gascony of the English lords, and the fearsome Raoul de Clermont had nearly four hundred knights and over three thousand footmen camped outside Paris to move imminently against Comte Dampierre, the count of neighbouring Flanders to the north. Flanders, on friendly terms with England and the Holy Roman Empire, was integral to the wool trade between England and the rest of Christendom – a strategic economic chokepoint for whosoever could control it.

There was deceit afoot; Mathieu could feel it. The King was not inflexible but he was certainly not unpredictable, which had made the Comte's job easier, until this very moment. He had a clever cover story as well; in very poor taste, he thought, but clever nonetheless, for it was entirely plausible. Mathieu hoped the Lord would permit the King this one use of His name as a cover. The Comte unclasped his hands, brought his left arm across his stomach and rested his right elbow in his left hand, running his right index finger over his mouth. It was definitely deceit, and Mathieu did not like being deceived.

The King had paused for dramatic effect after delivering his decision. He knew not one of the citizens would be capable of masking their surprise. Philippe turned and faced the Maison. He saw the flamboyant Guillaume de Troyes and Geoffroi d'Hainault puzzling over his words as if he had spoken in Coptic to them. The King made eye contact with de Clermont, his face as blank as the boulder his massive body was probably carved from, and Comte Mathieu who moved a little but otherwise did not appear caught out.

"My dear Mathieu, if you may prepare letters for King Edward and his commanders, and I shall meet you this afternoon to discuss specifics. The terms of this peace are dependent on King Edward renouncing his title as Duke of Aquitaine," – at which another silent shock went out – "and to renounce in my presence, here, before the summer is out. The very fear of our martial prowess will be sufficient to keep Edward in line. And when he sees Edward kneeling, Comte Dampierre will do so too – if he can still kneel, that is."

The rows of leading men laughed, except for de Bourgogne, de Clermont and Mathieu, all three of whom had too much respect for the ancient Comte Dampierre - who must have been at least eighty years old - and Lemaître, who simply did not know how to laugh.

The sun shone again and the King basked in its warmth whilst the murmurs died down." For now, I am fatigued from the ride. It is time we dined!" he exclaimed, clapping his hands and smiling broadly. As one the assembled council members rose and bowed and the Queen curtseyed, and they began filing back to the palace along the smooth paving slabs set in the cut grass. Mathieu remembered hearing of Philippe's peculiar desire to have the palace garden grass cut to a low length for the first time. Of course no one said anything of it, but the Comte could tell some people found it unusual behaviour for a king and whispers of suspected unusual behaviour from a king could quickly become dangerous. Mathieu knew the King almost as well as he did himself and thought it simply reflected Philippe's nature – a king who keeps his appearances so well maintained will keep his country well maintained.

"My dear Comte de la Marche," said Philippe, "You shall dine later. Please, walk with me." The King beckoned Mathieu with an open hand and a genuine smile. The Comte approached the King as Philippe looked out over the Seine, and Mathieu removed his hat. The wind picked up a little, blowing the King's hair off his shoulders around his neck, whilst the rest of his body stood firm like a rock in the ocean. "I trust you saw through that." Philippe stated.

Mathieu stood next to him and also looked out on the river, clasping his hands behind his back. A few boats rowed along, tiny and nondescript. Anyone could have pulled up their boat at the base of the wall should they have been so inclined, but the wall was forbidding and the men-at-arms standing here and there imposing. At this point on the wall the King had asked a few soldiers to stand elsewhere, however.

"That I did, although I must say I didn't think you had it in you," replied the Comte.

Philippe laughed a little through his nose. "I might be able to do your job soon. One can never have too many strings to one's bow." The King watched a couple of rowboats lazily drift by. "Old Dampierre is stubborn and I fear outright conflict will soon arise. His disrespect for my kingship is wearing my patience thin. I wonder if you could lean on some people for me, in this respect? De Clermont's forces will remain ready to march at the earliest, but not at least until d'Artois returns from Gascony. And I met with Lemaître this morning before the council, as you are aware. He did not bring positive tidings, but it is difficult for someone of his disposition to be positive about anything. Therefore, I have deemed it necessary to investigate alternative methods of financing, which would also serve to strengthen the kingdom's standing amongst our rivals." The King turned to Mathieu with a stern face. Mathieu feared what the King would say next, thinking of Norris and the Temple loans.

The King continued, "I'd like you to start investigating the leading townsmen of Calais, drum up some opposition to the Flemish merchants. We shall need mischief there before too long."

Mathieu considered for a moment, casting his gaze out over the river and the slow rowboats that still had yet to pass their section of the wall. "The Flemings are well established, and have much support from the English," said the Comte, trying not to sound dismissive. Philippe was the lord of Calais, but the town's merchants had become far more powerful than any absent feudal lord. The cosmopolitan population further contributed to this – the inhabitants primarily spoke Dutch or Flemish, not French.

Philippe laughed but without humour. "Well, what do I pay you for, Mathieu? A stranglehold on the English wool route to Flanders gives us a huge platform upon which to further the kingdom. Edward won't come and kneel, so we will show him what happens when the Duke of Aquitaine does not show fealty to his liege lord." Philippe's eyes became fierce.

Mathieu looked up at the tall king and could sense the conqueror's ambition radiating. The Comte was not looking forward to revealing Norris' plans to the King in this mood. "Very well, I shall commence my investigations. I assume that de Clermont is in position in preparation for the end game?"

"They shall not move until I order; for now they will be used simply to keep Dampierre in check. I trust you do not need any further information, Comte de la Marche?"

Mathieu knew the King was not happy with his initial scepticism. The idea behind the strategy was sound – gaining control of the English wool trade route through Calais to the Flemish clothiers made sounds financial sense, and politically it physically cut off the Flemings from their sympathisers at Edward's court.

But the manner of going about it was clumsy. Mathieu delayed the King with a short *hmm*. He clasped his hands behind his back and pondered - it would be far more subtle to take back Calais through mercantile pressure; it would be far less conspicuous and provocative, far less disruptive to existing trading patterns and not to mention a lot less bloody. Additionally, other merchant cities in the region, Ghent and Bruges being the most significant, would become more susceptible to influence if Calais fell further into the French sphere.

"Sire, if I may ask," Mathieu hesitated, looking at the ground, before looking back up at the King, stood so regally he could have been having an impression taken for a sculpture, left arm on his hip, right hand on across his waist, "are you looking to *England*...?" Mathieu trailed off, knowing the answer already.

"Duke William the Conqueror left the north of France and united the kingdoms; for too long the English lands of the house of Anjou have been separated from their ancestral French home... All we need to do is go fishing for the king of England." Philippe bought his right arm up and clenched his fist. Lowering his voice to almost a growl, he continued. "Edward shall yield or shall be removed; either way England and France shall return to the rule of one king, not a descendent of the Angevin kings like Edward Longshanks, but a Capétien king, *me*." Fire blazed in the King's crystal blue eyes and the wind blew the ends of his long hair around his shoulders. For a moment even the Comte became carried away, imagining Alexander the Great himself stood before him.

Gathering himself following the unexpected flood of ambition, Mathieu looked the King in the eyes. "I shall make arrangements regarding Calais. Also Bruges. It will not take long for Edward to react to our movement against the Flemish, though the Scottish and Welsh are waiting in the wings to play their turn."

"Good!" The smile returned to Philippe's face. "I shall let you get on then, my dear Comte. I am tremendously hungry, so I think I shall join the Queen and Enguerrand at lunch." Philippe turned and began walking away, impeccably upright as usual.

"One more thing, Sire, if I may," Mathieu blurted out, with little formality and more than a hint of a command. Mathieu was prone to speak as an equal with the King, and in light of his age, the counsel he had provided and his position as spymaster, sometimes down to Philippe. He had been with the King for many years, since he first ascended to the throne as a mere sixteen year old. Equally, Philippe did not usually question Mathieu's occasionally lofty manner, though recently Philippe had developed a more headstrong attitude that Mathieu attributed to the influence of Jeanne as she matured. Philippe, regressing from world conqueror to the boy-king of years before, stopped and looked round expectantly at his old advisor.

Mathieu approached him. "The Temple are causing us a few difficulties. Norris is... threatening to call in the loans." The Comte saw the slightest of responses in the King's expression. "I have means of dissuading him from this course of action, but I fear they would only be a temporary measure."

Grimacing, Philippe looked down at the ground, at the neatly cut grass. "I thought the Temple was supposed to be a religious institution, and here we are with our gold and silver balls in their hands. That Norris is far more trouble than he's worth. See that you delay the loan recollection. For now, that is my only concern in respect of this matter. We shall meet in a week, by which time I want suggestions from you and Lemaître on how we shall proceed with Norris. Good day, my dear Comte." At that, Philippe abruptly turned about face and marched imperiously up the path towards the palace. There were to be no further questions.

Mathieu habitually inclined his head even though Philippe's long strides had already taken him a few paces away along the path. *Not bad*, he mused. The news from last night had worked wonders for the King's mood and blunted the impact of the revelation about Norris at the Temple. But still... the King's ambitions were risky. He saw the King approach Jeanne, who had been waiting with Guido and the Grand Chamberlain, Enguerrand de Marigny, a small, dark-haired man who grew ever bulkier by the week. Mathieu thought he looked like someone had fashioned a puppet head and stuck it on a bale of hay wrapped up in a carpet, much like a fat scarecrow. He could not stand de Marigny, and for once he was not alone in disliking someone – the Grand Chamberlain was almost universally hated for his ingratiating manner and the insufferable pomposity that came with his position within the Maison du Roi. As for sources of inspiration for Philippe's grand plans, Mathieu suspected the fat scarecrow had some input, and probably the Queen as well. Guido removed his hat and bowed to the King before scurrying away, leaving the three to walk toward the palace.

Jeanne was a calming influence on Philippe, as suggested by his more frequent outbursts of anger in her absence. As a princess and then Countess of Champagne, and Queen of Navarre, she spent some time in the former. It seemed the whole court would welcome her back to the capital simply for the hold she had over Philippe, but as it were she was also well loved by the court and populace alike. Her political acumen was second to none and she was a *de facto* adviser to Philippe, although masculine pride did not allow the King to acknowledge this too conspicuously at court.

Mathieu thought about the combination of Jeanne and de Marigny, the two closest to Philippe, whispering in either ear and the effects this may have. More work, and tough work at that. Not impossible, but tough – the Comte de la Marche had whisperers in and around the Maison du Roi, including a handmaiden in Jeanne's retinue, Camille, who was so thorough in reporting that Mathieu wondered how she actually completed any of her own tasks. He would have to ask Camille to keep an eye on any collaboration between the Grand Chamberlain and the Queen.

He would also, that afternoon, have to start planning for Calais! But for now the Comte wanted nothing more than to return to his house on the other side of the Seine, find Quo and sit in the sunshine. The old boy was struggling in the heat, lacking for energy at all times. Mathieu also considered again bringing his desk downstairs to cater for Quo's weakening hind legs; Pascal was practically carrying the old dog down the steps at the end of the day nowadays. He might even see Jaqueline more often if he were on the ground floor. She never climbed those stairs, for all that was up those stairs of significance was Mathieu himself.

He sighed. The rowboats were still sauntering past with painfully slow progress, no strings to pull and no pulses to check, their sailors probably delivering some artisanal products to and from the Notre Dame market. Having concentrated their attention throughout the day on a market plot no wider than ten paces, those merchants could return at sundown to their beds and wives and not concern themselves with the machinations of the leather maker three shops down or the financial irregularities of the cooper across the square.

On Mathieu's shoulders fell the responsibility for clearing a path for a clean military campaign, to be conducted on the backs of lies and the ill-advised suggestions of partial courtiers. Philippe had grown from a boy to a man and the kingdom was to reap the fruit of this maturity, be they plentiful or rotten. The Comte foresaw that he would soon be asked, nay expected, to assume the duties of physician to the state in addition to those he already held.

Chapter 9

El could see the church rising above the jumbled assortment of thatched roofs scattered haphazardly around, in the manner of just about every village she had seen since landing at Southampton a few years previous. The arrangement, or lack thereof, was always the same – single room houses were placed all around as if they were dice dropped at random from a giant bag in the sky. Every time the church stood tall in their midst, quite literally a stone shepherd watching over the milling and disorganized flock of hovels. Occasionally she had seen a stone house for the more well-to-do peasant, but only in the west of England; there was barely a stone to quarry in areas such as Hampshire so all of their villages had wood-framed houses. Any useful quantity of limestone had usually already been requisitioned for castle construction; King Edward's zeal for permanent fortifications was not just a means of staying the Welsh only but stretched the length and breadth of his realm. He had castles built and enhanced from Winchester in the south to Northumberland in the north.

The ubiquity of the Norman and Celtic village's aesthetics reduced the chances that she would recognise this particular settlement based on appearance and landmarks. As it were, Guy's cartography lessons would have to suffice but even those could not help her here. The dust road continued eastwards and skirted to the north of the village, along past the haphazard strips of vegetable plots and occasional cow braving the temperature by wandering the common land away from the shade of the encroaching forest. El turned her exhausted mount right down a smaller path, worn away as it lay on the most direct route towards the church from the larger road.

The tall stone church stood proud just off the track down into the village, shielding most of the houses behind it like a sentry tower at the gates of a city looking out for the souls of its wards within and for the trustworthiness of visitors without. Gazing upon that spiritual sentinel built of stone and slate made El realise she was still carrying the spear from the battle at the wagon train, and she threw it aside, dismayed that she had grown so familiar with bearing a weapon as to not even be aware of its presence. The finely crafted spear tip and shaft sank into the brittle and largely untrodden yellow grass beside the path without trace.

A few obscure figures further down the road crossed back and forth, shimmering in the haze. El was utterly drained; she could not imagine how the blood-spattered palfrey was suffering in this heat and prayed for the animal's resolve in such trying conditions. Enough life had been lost today; the horse would not be added to that list. The Frenchwoman already carried enough guilt for the casualties taken during the attack on her prison train. The horse lolled its head up and down as it slowly walked into the town and El was struggling to maintain her riding posture in the saddle, fatigue and dehydration causing her to lean almost precariously forward. Both horse and rider were lifeless as puppets on slack strings.

El mumbled a prayer for a cup of water. She would have welcomed being caught by Lord Reginald's men if they brought with them flasks of water. About fifty yards ahead a child watched for a few moments on the side of the road before darting back into the nearest house. A few more people along the road began noticing the lone horse and rider slinking into the village. Any visible activity would puncture the slumbering midday atmosphere in this village, El imagined; especially a slumped woman riding a blood-spattered white horse. By now, however, she was far too fatigued for self-consciousness. She was becoming too fatigued for consciousness itself.

Only a few houses lay between her and the church and from the first of them re-emerged the curious child with a man in tow, now around twenty paces away. El lifted her head, unconcernedly watching the man and child materialise from the darkness under the thatch roof that comprehensively covered a house below. The thatch appeared so heavy and low that it was surely drowning the building underneath it. In her delirious state the little Frenchwoman thought she saw the thatch growing up over the house from the long and dry yellow grass surrounding the house, but she could not confirm this as a fact once the small lights started turning at the edges of her vision.

The slim man, wearing a grubby-looking reddish-brown tunic, projected a surprisingly deep voice at her.

"*Cyfarchion, ffrind. Ble ydych chi wedi teithio o? O, eich ceffyl!*"

El could not tell if the man spoke in English, French or Welsh. Involuntarily closing her eyes through lightheadedness did not increase the acuity of her hearing either. One hand dropped the reins and she fell forward, planting her nose into the back of the palfrey's neck. Sensing the sudden absence of commands the blood-spattered horse halted and gave a pathetic whinny, the last breath in its lungs from a traumatic and arduous morning.

The man's face quickly turned to concern, noticing the dirty orange smears on the horse's flank where blood had mixed with sweat. He turned to the child and barked something at him in the same incomprehensible tongue before turning back and approaching El, arms aloft as if to lift her from her saddle. The child ran back inside the house, shouting something else that El could not understand. Even if she could the little Frenchwoman lacked the energy to respond, and she had no Welsh in her vocabulary in any case.

She simply slipped further forward so that she was almost cuddling the horse's neck. The man was not tall and did not look particularly strong but with little fuss and even less exertion he pulled El from the horse on her left side, slipping her down the side of the horse into his arms, cradling her head into his left shoulder and lifting her legs under the knees with his right arm. El was momentarily roused from her fatigue by the acrid smell of sweat as her face was held into his shoulder, and she heard the child's voice again as he ran past once more in the direction of the horse. A woman's voice answered the man's urgent bellowing; she sounded far closer than justified the volume of the man's chattering. El slowly slipped back into the comfortable dream-state, a cocoon where she was neither tired nor thirsty nor required to use her limbs for locomotion or balance. By contrast all around her was clamouring and busyness and yet she was not aware of this kindness on her account.

Opening her eyes El saw that the man, woman and child lived in the single-roomed house typical of those who worked the land.

Regardless of the man's strong odour, she enjoyed the sensation of being carried without any need for effort on her part, and the feeling of being laid down on the rushes on the floor was almost blissful. The chattering in Welsh continued above as invisible hands held her head up and the woman appeared before her face with a cup of water, pouring it through her parched lips and down her cracked throat. El felt a weight lift from her body and for the third time in as many days, passed out.

The Frenchwoman opened her eyes and saw the blackness that hung from the underside of the looming thatch through the low light of the dusty and poorly ventilated house. El was lying on her back and felt the itchiness of the straw on the parts of her neck not covered by her grey hood. The Welshwoman was scurrying around in the corner but what she was doing El could not guess; having not caught the woman's notice, she was not keen to engage in conversation whilst she did not need to.

Her enforced silence ended abruptly as she coughed, however, feeling wheezy and sore as she did from another enforced bout of unconsciousness. This brought the attention of the woman who dropped whatever it was she was holding and rushed over to kneel by the prone Frenchwoman's side. The Welshwoman had a kind face with big round cheeks and a compassionate, motherly gaze that was looking through El's eyes, peering into her mind for the answer to questions as yet unasked.

Without averting her eyes, the woman reached out to the table and took the cup of water and brought it down in front of her chest. El tried to move her head forward to the cup again, jutting her chin out which brought forth liquid relief, tasting sweeter than any wine she could remember. Drinking, the Frenchwoman wondered why she had regressed to a childlike state just because she did not share a language with her rescuers.

"*Annwyl wraig, ble wyt ti'n dod? Beth sydd wedi digwydd?*" asked the woman with worry in her voice and a troubled expression.

"English... English?" El croaked.

"English? Yes, English, English, yes! Of course, where are you from, lady?" The Welshwoman's concern for this stranger's health was briefly blown away by her inquisitiveness – this stranger's accent was clearly not English, neither was it like the Norman English of the English lords.

El smiled at the Welshwoman's curiosity, partially out of relief at encountering someone who did not want to arrest her or shoot her with a longbow, but mostly because the round-faced woman was so delighted by simply talking to someone from an unknown land. A sense of wonder and wandering permeated El's soul, which helped greatly in her line of work. Encountering others with a similar sense was a joy. It was of course highly unlikely that the vast majority of people El encountered on her travels would ever have left their village, but talking with those who dreamt that there was something tangible and fascinating beyond the fields allowed El to feed off their enthusiasm and both to indulge in the escapist fantasies of travel.

El tried sitting up and as she did the man behind her shuffled out of the way, pulling a seat up for her to rest against before he scrabbled round besides the round-faced woman and sat on his haunches, the same curious gaze combing El's face for clues. "Thank you for your kind hospitality, friends; my name is Eleanor, and I am from France. I-" El was cut off as the round-faced woman began speaking to the man in Welsh, bemusing the Frenchwoman before she realised the woman was translating for the man.

"Please, continue, Miss Eleanor. My husband, Dywel, does not speak English I'm afraid. Oh, and my name is Morwen." Morwen's round cheeks bunched up as she broke into a huge smile, to which El could not help but respond in kind. Dywel raised a smile too, before a child shouting outside startled the man. He swiftly stood and raced outside. Everyone around here seemed to run, El thought, even in such oppressive heat.

"Have some water!" insisted Morwen.

"Thank you, friend," El responded with a warmth she had not felt in days. Not having smiled in days either, the combination of muscles required to do so ached and reminded her of the beating she had taken at the hands of Sir Edward de Beauchamp and his men two nights previously. She moved her hand to her cheek and temple, wincing a little.

Morwen's eyes scoured the dark marking around El's left eye and cheek and brushed the Frenchwoman's sweat-drenched hair away from the bruising. "What's happened to you? This is terrible!" Morwen did not look El in the eyes but fussily scanned her head for further injuries.

El turned her head away to the side, allowing Morwen to continue her inspection. The Frenchwoman replied in a quiet, labored voice. "It is nothing. An accident, I fell from my horse, and could not bring my arm up," she lied. White lies were permissible, Guy had told her. She had been initially uncomfortable with this deceit though the young Templar had quickly learned that discretion was a more than adequate substitute, removing the necessity of white lies entirely.

El knew she should have attempted discretion in this instance as Morwen saw right through the fib. "I have a child, lady; I know when someone is not speaking truth." She smiled again. "You cannot ride here with a bloodied horse and appearing as you do, and say you have fallen from your horse."

"I encountered some trouble with your lord," El admitted. She felt the woman should know that Lord Reginald was searching for her, for the woman's own safety. The round-faced woman looked flushed.

"He's not my lord," she replied sharply, the kindness in her eyes concealed behind steeliness. "Are you being chased?" Morwen shuffled back a little and spoke not angrily but with noticeable worry. The hospitable air of the crowded little house chilled a little.

El understood her concern. Harbouring a fugitive was viewed as dimly as the original crime itself, so El did not intend to loiter in this kind woman's home for too long.

"I am, yes," El said whilst struggling to sit up further, her head pounding from dehydration but her body welcoming the rest. "I will not stay long; thank you for your kindness. I am to go to the church here, for I have taken my vows and am a woman of God." El went to stand up. "Please tell me, what is the name of this village?"

Morwen's faced betrayed further confusion. "This is Llaneurgain, and the church is of St Eurgain. You are a sister of the Church? But why… we must get you to there. Come," she ordered the Frenchwoman, getting to her feet far quicker than El could, and she leant down to offer a hand. "I won't ask you what happened, sister, but I don't think it is too good for us to be hiding you – I'm sorry, sister, I am a good woman and my husband a good man, but the English lord does not like us Welsh… I have heard terrible things about what he does to us Welsh." Morwen was becoming visibly agitated which prompted El to redouble her efforts to stand and go outside.

"Of course, of course, I am sorry for this trouble; you and your husband are good Christians and you shall not suffer for this." El held Morwen's hand as the round-faced woman was turning to walk out of the dark house, pulling her back. "Thank you, friend." El smiled through the bruising, the dark marking on one side of her face divided perfectly from the ruddy colouring on the other by her small nose and thin mouth. Morwen could not tell if the El looked so vulnerable despite her words, or whether her words were reassuring despite her vulnerability.

At that moment the heavy summer silence outside was punctured by the hammering of hooves coming from the rock-like earth road into the village. Morwen dropped El's hand and spun to the door, lifting the bottom of her shawl to allow her to run out from under the drooping thatch, with El in her footsteps until the little Frenchwoman reached the doorway to the house and grasped the folly of exposing her identity to a number of unknown horsemen. She stayed in the shadow inside the doorway, concealed behind the dark grey thatch, momentarily blinded by the fierce afternoon sunshine as she had been when her wagon was opened up earlier that day.

Morwen had stopped a few paces ahead, standing noiselessly looking out in the direction of the church. Three horsemen were slowing their steeds to a stop, clad in steel that blazed in the sunlight, further adding to their alien nature in such a sleepy setting.

Morwen let out a gasp at seeing Dywel and their son stood next to a riderless white horse tied to a post in the shadow of the church, facing the horsemen who were now dismounting. El immediately recognised the horse as her blood-spattered mount, the mount that she had taken from Lord Reginald's men, the mount that those horsemen had seen her ride off from the fighting. How could she have forgotten the horse! Lord Reginald had found her and now her promise of safety to Morwen and her family was now up in the air, and as soon as that promise was up in the air was it then shattered as the dismounted horsemen approached Dywel and his son.

Morwen picked her shawl back up and rushed over to her husband and son as quickly as her legs could carry her – she was clearly unaccustomed to such movement and her shoulders rocked back and forth in an exaggerated manner as she ran across the dusty road.

El had to do something. She had watched as the men-at-arms jumped down from the horses and walk up to Dywel and his son, their spears in hand. The soldiers were like grotesque brutes, not men. The blazing reflection on their mail was extinguished as they entered the shadow of the tall church, and even from this distance El could see the battered state of their armour. Black stains marred the steel grey, and one man-at-arms had a heavy bandage around his left arm. A second limped, leaning on his spear more than his right leg. They surely had fought the Welsh brigands earlier in the day, a savage encounter from which no man could have emerged unscathed.

I have heard terrible things about what he does to us Welsh, Morwen had said of Lord Reginald. The treatment El had received at the hands of Sir Edward and his men flashed through her mind and spurred her forwards. She did not know the ins and outs of the relations between the English war hero Lord Reginald and individual Welsh villages but assumed a resurgence in violence attributable to the brigands would inevitably increase the chance of reprisals against the Welsh villagers. The political vicissitudes of kings, princes, lords and chiefs were beyond the Order, but the physical and spiritual security of all four categories of people plus everyone beneath were of concern to El. In this moment, that meant the security of Dywel and his son.

But she was one girl with no weapons and they were three men-at-arms who would be baying for vengeance, fired by having survived the slaughter on the Chester road and the opportunity to

113

hold someone, anyone, accountable for what had happened. They would be both angry and scared, understandable reactions to the horrors they had witnessed. El had seen all too often the results of such anger and fright in times of war – such base demonstrations of man's fragility and weakness - and knew it was at odds with the Church's teachings on turning the other cheek and disregarding mortal peril in favour of the next life. That these teachings were correct El had no doubt – she considered the following of these rules to be amongst the most challenging for man to accomplish.

What could she do to protect Dywel and his son from three armed men? Confrontation was inevitable and with it misunderstanding. In this environment misunderstanding was always a precursor to bloodshed. She was scared. Dywel had moved his son behind his back and next to the horse, and the son ran round the animal so he was between it and the church. The horse stood, ears flicking but otherwise stationary and oblivious to the escalating danger it had unwittingly sparked.

The three soldiers had surrounded Dywel but knowing that the man did not speak English, El could imagine the conversation was not getting very far. A soldier jabbed a finger at Dywel's chest and then pointed at the horse. Violence was likely – these soldiers had just been attacked by Welsh and seen death just this afternoon. Violence was likely regardless or not of whether the Frenchwoman intervened. Morwen had got as far as the shadow of the church when she started shouting at the soldiers; the soldier with the bandaged arm turned round and immediately struck her across the face with the back of his gloved hand. The round-faced woman dropped to the hard-baked earth like a stone and her son behind the horse screamed. She did not put out her hands to break her fall and her head slammed to the dirt.

El gripped the decaying wood beam of the doorframe as her heart rate jumped with the rising tension. She could not leave these Samaritans to such a fate, could she? Dywel shouted something and shoved at the bandaged soldier; the uninjured soldier to Dywel's right retaliated by punching Dywel square in the jaw, knocking him down. The church's front door opened and a bald man poked his head out at the disturbance; upon seeing the two people on the floor he stepped out and began shouting at the soldiers, who responded in kind in between kicking Dywel in the head and stomach. The battered Welshman tried to shield his head from the kicks that rained in from all sides, though with each booted strike his arms weakened and the impacts became proportionately more dangerous.

The soldiers were only focused on their immediate environment, at which point El slipped under the thatch in front of the doorway and slid left around the front of the house, keeping against the wall under the thatch. More shouts went up. The Frenchwoman turned round the back of the house away from the church, guilt dragging down on her far more than her battered body had done over the past few days, her stomach knotted in worry and her mind turning over and over the thought of how she consciously allowed a man and woman to be beaten on her behalf. Without instruction from her mind El's legs began pumping and she ran around a number of obstacles, a barrow here, some buckets there, to the back of the next house along. It was another small building with a disproportionately large and strong thatch roof to keep the usual north Welsh weather at bay. Behind the various obstacles and the low hanging roofs El managed to stay out of sight of the soldiers, who themselves were now dragging Dywel up and untying the blood-spattered white horse.

El peeked out from behind a freshly harvested hay pile at the unfolding incident. Her conscience was torn between serving the Lord by offering protection to these people, protection from the suffering she had brought upon them, and her own self-preservation. This choice was easy to settle in theory and frightful in practice. The soldiers tied Dywel up with the very rope he had used to tie the white horse before they slung him over the exhausted palfrey. The churchman was still yelling, bringing the attention of two women who emerged from the other side of the church building and promptly screamed at the carnage playing out in the shadow of that hallowed building.

The frightened child behind the horse screamed and ran to his mother. The poor woman lifted her bleeding head from the ground and now caught sight of what had happened during her momentary concussion. Morwen began incoherently screaming and groggily trying to get to her feet whilst her son cried and dragged at her shawl, his high-pitch bawling pitifully audible above the deeper cries of the adults around him.

El was susceptible to bouts of guilt, guilt over almost anything. Temptation, unwanted thoughts, things said in the heat of the moment. She would fret over the guilt for minutes or hours, sometimes even days if she were sufficiently distracted, unsure whether or not the guilt was warranted; she found it difficult to discuss this with others, even Guy; were the temptations, unwanted thoughts and regrettable comments of her own volition, or her mind just playing tricks on her? The little Frenchwoman could sense the weight of guilt slowly building upon her mind, threatening to consume her.

Another man with pitch black hair emerged from the church doors, from a distance El could see he was at least a head taller than the bald man and broad with it. He did not take long to gauge the situation, roaring and barging through the yelling bald man he ran shoulder first into the bandaged soldier, crushing him into the solid stone wall of the church. The bandaged soldier fell to the ground with no resistance from any limbs, knocked out or dead El did not know. Watching from the safety of a distant mound of hay, she scolded herself for her cowardice and hoped it would not be too late to rectify the situation both for the Welsh villagers and in the eyes of the Lord. This was not the woman who threw herself through branches and bushes at dark shadows to buy Henry and Brac more time. That woman had a sword, of course. But guilt was stronger than a sword.

Her adrenaline kicked in once more and furthermore she experienced a sense of increased perception and awareness, a feeling Henry had spoken of from his time fighting in the Holy Land. This enhanced consciousness of experience was not something that had before happened to her and yet El was not surprised or unsettled by it; it had a reassuring and comforting feel to it, despite the stress of the situation. He had said that during melee combat with Saracens when death lurked behind every sword swing, he felt that passing moments blurred into something more than temporary; a calm came over him and he neither panicked nor rushed any movement as if he could see things developing before they happened. He credited this

116

as a gift from the Lord. It exhausted him afterwards, but at least he had experienced an afterwards.

El scanned the assorted implements around her; a thresher, a plank of wood, a hammer; a mix of tools from a mix of professions, likely shared communally. The people in this second house were likely friends with Morwen and Dywel's family, and it would only be appropriate for their own implement to be of support. Grabbing the hammer El leapt from her hiding place and darted across the road with the speed and intent of an eagle plunging from the sky into a flight of unsuspecting starlings.

The huge man's assault taking them by surprise, the other two soldiers dropped the ropes they were carrying and scrambled to pick up their spears before the huge man reached them. One was too slow as the huge man slammed his considerable bulk into the soldier's side as the soldier tried to spin and face his attacker. He too was knocked to the ground with an enormous punch that crunched him square in the face, probably breaking his nose instantly. The man-at-arms flew backwards and cracked his head on the ground, plate rattling on plate and then the hard earth, somehow audible above the yelling of the bald man, the roaring of the huge man and the screaming of Morwen and her son.

The uninjured man-at-arms was quicker than his comrade and no sooner had the huge man floored the second soldier did the uninjured man-at-arms run his spear into the huge man's back and clean through his belly, skewering him through his torn grey tunic and soiling the ground in front of him with black blood. El could run with the speed of a whippet but was still ten paces away when the huge man's head drooped forwards and he fell to his knees in silence, toppling as if all of the bones had been removed from his body. He nearly took the soldier with him until the soldier let go of his grip, so cleanly had the spear been thrust and so perfectly had the shaft driven through.

El's subconscious locomotion took over once more and she launched herself at the remaining soldier, hammer high in her right hand, landing a terrible blow to the soldier's left shoulder, denting the plate and shattering bone underneath. The soldier howled in pain, clutching at his now useless left arm and spinning around to find the unseen assailant whose hammer had dropped from her hand with the impact.

"*Arrêtez!* Stop this now!" El's eyes burned through the sweat-soaked hair that dangled in front of her bright red face, panting heavily from the exertion as she raged at the injured soldier. He immediately stopped howling in shock at the monstrous command from the slight, ragged and strangely-accented woman in front of him, and slumped to his knees. The bald man at the church door began shouting in Welsh and ran to his huge friend lying face down with a spear standing four feet out of his back, the bald man breaking down in tears as he utterly failed to roll the man over onto his back; in his grief he could not make sense of the huge man's bulk nor the spear that had nailed him to the ground.

El watched the soldier with the broken arm for a moment whilst he knelt in the shadow of the church bewildered and dazed by what had just happened, then rushed over to Morwen. The round-faced woman was sobbing as her son was still trying to help her stand up, her short hair veiling her face from the Frenchwoman. El approached and bent down to help her up, prompting Morwen to lift her head to see who was supporting. The right side of her face was swollen and her eye barely open from where she had taken a gloved fist from the man-at-arms, and dried blood caked her nose and chin. She screamed in fury at the sight of the Frenchwoman, pulling her arm away from El's grip and falling back into her small son.

"You! This is you! You did this! You brought this here!" she shrieked through gasping breaths and flooding tears. "*Dywel, ble mae Dywel?*"

Her son replied with soft words between his own tears, pointing to the white horse that had trotted further down the side of the church and away from the commotion. Dywel's motionless body was lying on the earth nearby, presumably having fallen off the horse's back when it became startled by the commotion.

El backed away from Morwen as the woman wailed and struggled to her feet. The blow she had taken looked sickening from the distance El had seen it and the little Frenchwoman felt her own bruising with her free hand. The acute awareness that had assisted her in facing up to the English soldier dissipated as El watched

Morwen shrieking at her, and it was replaced by a numbness that descended and clouded her eyes and mind. What the fevered Welshwoman was saying was beyond El's comprehension; she just heard sounds.

Hoof falls and shouts that increased in volume and began to eclipse the wailing and crying of those already present. El surveyed the chaos; Dywel lying face down and partially bound ten or so paces away, a soldier lying on his side by the church wall, the bald man sobbing over the body of his friend, the shocked soldier with the broken arm crouching, fear heavy on his tired face.

The other soldier lay on his back, stirring slowly and holding a hand to his face that shot up in a protective manner when he noticed the two new figures looming above with raised swords. The two simultaneously brought their blades down before the wounded soldier could beg for mercy, one biting through the chest armour and the other hacking into the ring mail covering the man's stomach. The dying soldier drew in a sharp breath but did not exhale.

It seemed to El that these two somehow embodied the most surreal part of this horrific situation. She could not have said where they had come from, because she had not been paying attention to the approaching villagers. They pulled their swords out of the English soldier's body, the straight blades making a *squelch* as the one that had cut into the stomach brought entrails with it. They were a woman and man, both wearing dark crimson cloaks fitted tightly with belts in which were tucked what looked like large knives. Their heads were uncovered and they both had fair hair tied back; from a distance El fancied them to be twins – it seemed only the man's full beard differentiated the two.

But for El, the most striking aspect of the duo's appearance was not their near-identical appearance and clothing but the utter impassiveness with which they brutally murdered an injured man before casually walking away - towards El, she noted – were they going to finish her off as well? What was more, neither the bald man nor the wailing women further away down the side of the church seemed to even notice them. El wondered if she were having a vision, of two crimson-robed angels of death, commanded by St Eurgain himself, finishing off the sinful combatants in the shadow of

119

his church and condemning them to hellfire. She could not move but was desperate to do so, inexplicably rooted to the spot where she had dropped the hammer. The cloaked woman veered off to her left to where the unconscious soldier was lying whilst the man continued towards El, eyeing her with no hint of recognition or any emotion as if he were indeed beyond human, brushing past her to the whimpering soldier with the broken arm crouching down; El watched the soldier look up and mouth 'no' as the cloaked man brought his great sword down across the soldier's left shoulder and through the shoulder plate; his useless left arm was almost completely severed as the black blood ran down between the ringmail across his chest. The cloaked man put his right boot on the soldier's chest and pulled out his sword, kicking the his body down as if he were a sack of potatoes.

The crimson-cloaked man turned to El. "Now tell me, mademoiselle, why is a Frenchwoman fighting English soldiers in Wales?" He approached, sheathing his sword to his left side before crossing his hands at his stomach, his right hand clasping his left wrist. His Welsh accent was melodic and serene and certainly more in keeping with his calm appearance than the callous brutality he had just displayed. More villagers were arriving, bringing with them further weeping for the loss of the huge man and the injuries to Dywel and Morwen. Morwen had by now limped over to her unconscious husband, her face half swollen and the other half streamed with tears. El looked around, her mind racing. No one paid the crimson angels any mind! How could this be?

The blonde woman glided to the cloaked man's side. She was strikingly beautiful, adding to the shocking features of these people's appearance and behaviour. Her blue eyes were like the sky, her wide and pale cheeks as much flawless as the man's cheeks were bearded. "You are chasing someone, and being chased, are you not?" the crimson-cloaked woman asked, her voice sounding almost bored. "We share more than just one ambition, friend… but for different ends."

"I do not understand," El stumbled, at a complete loss as to what had unfolded over the past few minutes.

"We shall not hinder you, Templar," interjected the man.

"How do-" El managed to say before she was cut off by the woman.

"We will not compromise your identity. We must move quickly – Lord de Grey mustn't know these soldiers died here," the woman stated, turning away before finishing speaking to El. Instantly she switched to Welsh and began gesturing at the three dead Englishmen, prompting a flurry of activity from the milling villagers.

The crimson-cloaked man leaned close to El's face as she looked on, the Frenchwoman smelling his sweat before she saw him from the corner of her eye, making her jump. Her already fraught nerves were close to snapping.

"I'd take your horse and slip out quietly, friend," whispered the man, his breath hot on El's hair. "They do not understand the mechanisms of a predetermined action, which is why they will blame you for this man's death." He extended an arm in the direction of the huge man who was being carried by three villagers. "Quickly now."

"What objective are you seeking? Murder is no way to settle it," El sneered defiantly, unwilling to completely lose control of a situation that had got drastically out of hand.

The man dwelled on her words a moment. "And you are not party to murder?" he asked.

It was a devastatingly simple and effective riposte. If the man was not an angel of death then he was the embodiment of El's guilt. Her eyes darted away from the blond man's to the tree tops away to the north. "I ask you, what objective are you seeking?" she repeated.

"Knowledge has its price, Templar," the crimson-cloaked man said threateningly as he put his hand to his sword handle.

El saw this movement and tensed a little.

The blond man continued. "You haven't paid a price for this knowledge. Your experiences these past few days have been nothing on what is necessary for that." He removed his hand from the sword handle and returned to grasping his left wrist in front of his stomach, assured of his intimidation's success.

El was unnerved by the man's rhetoric, as callous and direct as were his actions and disturbing in its details. "You do not carry out the Lord's work, sir."

The blond man retained his composure. El found it increasingly intolerable, partially disturbing and partially arrogant.

"We keep the sheep safe from the wolves, Templar. What do you do?"

Large numbers of villagers were congregating at the scene and El suspected more than a few eyes on her conversation with this man wearing a crimson cloak. The longer she stayed here the greater chance of harm.

Somehow the blond man intuited El's unease over the growing crowd. "Your window of opportunity shrinks, mademoiselle. Your horse awaits you."

Without ceremony the blond man strode past after his companion, who was directing the villagers to their horses about fifty paces away, carrying the bodies of the English men-at-arms. The sleepy summer afternoon had become like a beehive in the shadow of the church of St Eurgain. El looked down at the baked earth, stained with patches of blood. Morwen was cradling Dywel's head in her lap willing him to wake up. El felt terrible about what had happened to the family who took her in, the remorse burning away inside. Yet she could not approach them; Morwen would not want her support.

The crimson-cloaked man was right; she would need to leave immediately. The priest of the church was there now, tending to Dywel, and the huge man was being carried away behind the church. And there was her white horse, the rope tied round it not connected to anything at the other end, clearly agitated at the traumatic afternoon that had followed the traumatic morning. The Frenchwoman ran to it and vaulted up into the saddle in one movement; her rest this afternoon restoring her considerable athletic prowess. She wanted to use the horse's nervous energy as a means of escaping, so she kicked in and sent the horse into a gallop back to the road that lead to Chester, passing the crimson-cloaked pair who were leading the three English soldiers' horses, carrying the bodies of their unfortunate riders, up to the road as well. The two crimson riders watched the Frenchwoman ride past without acknowledgement.

The feeling of agitation induced by the crimson-cloaked riders compounded the burning guilt over what happened to Morwen,

Dywel and the huge man, and facing back to the road ahead El kicked in again and set the horse off quicker than before. Something was not right. She was not meant to visit this place; having done so cost the lives of four men, possibly five if Dywel did not wake up. She needed to get out of here, get off this road and get back to Guy and Henry.

Chapter 10

Having completed his first prayers of the day, Brother Stephen walked slowly but purposefully from the main building out to the gate, pulling his hood over his head to keep out the early morning chill. It seemed another cloudless day was in prospect, but the sun had not yet risen above the Abbey's walls and so the courtyard itself remained very cool. A few other monks were scurrying off to attend their chores and errands; one seeing to the chickens, another to fetch water, a third to sweep. Like all of the brothers, Stephen had many duties, and he undertook them all with the diligence and patience of a man truly living in faith. His monastic discipline was excellent to the extent that he gave no thought to the concept of 'discipline', because it was so inherent to his being. Some brothers had made unfair comments on the speed with which Stephen went about his business, usually drawing a rebuke from Abbot Thomas or another of the more senior brothers. On the whole, however, Brother Stephen's low-paced style was considered as much a part of his person as was his disproportionately long nose, or his slightly curved back. How could a man as old as he be expected to move any quicker?

He had reached the gate by the third loud *knock* slammed on the other side of the hefty wooden monolith. Raising his black-sleeved arm to the viewport, Brother Stephen slid the wooden panel back and pressed his face forward to peer through. Dawn visits to the Abbey such as this were not common but certainly not completely unexpected. What was unexpected, though, were a group of men-at-arms greeting Brother Stephen's blue eyes.

"Open up, brother, in the name of the King," a deep voice from within a helmet bluntly demanded. In his countless years at the abbey Stephen had known many soldiers and knights coming for guidance and repentance, but not often in large groups and certainly never in armour and with weapons.

Brother Stephen cleared his throat before responding. "On whose authority would you demand entrance here so attired?" he asked, the volume of his laborious speech increased as if he were a herald. A

124

small light of defiance sparked within the elderly monk. There would be no secular bullies acting as if they owned the place on his watch.

The lack of compliance and speed of the monk's response infuriated the talking helmet, the nose protection and cheek plates of which left only a small area of the soldier's face uncovered and even that was in shadow. For all Stephen knew, the soldier to whom he was speaking might not have had any facial features at all. Perhaps his head was just that helmet. "On the authority of the Bishop of Lichfield and the Lord de Grey," said the helmet, malice lacing his words.

Brother Stephen looked down for a moment, weighing the gravity of the situation. His body may have been slow and his manner quiet, but his mind was perceptive and analytical. A lifetime of reading had honed his brain as his body had slowly faded. The ancient Bishop of Lichfield, Roger de Meyland, had not left his see at Coventry for years – it was well known that the bishop was a dying man. So why was he sending soldiers under Lord Reginald? Armed men in the Abbey complex would be unacceptable!

"Open the gate, brother!" demanded the helmet, slamming his fist against the gate three times. His anger seemed all the more intense for the otherwise silent morning air; even the birds were yet to rise. They soon would if the talking helmet's belligerence continued.

Stephen reached to his right and with an effort that almost exceeded his elderly frame's capacity he rang a small bell four times, *ding-ding, ding-ding*. Brother Stephen was not one to use it very often solely because he felt its use unnecessary in all but the most consequential of circumstances. Unlike many of the younger brothers, the old monk had seen enough to distinguish between an occurrence and an incident. He turned back and began unbolting the great locks that did justice to the size of the gate door. Within moments a distant bell responded in kind, *ding-ding, ding-ding*, and after that a further distant ring of the same kind.

By the second reply the elderly monk had undone the locks and was heaving the door backwards. Its creaking frame cracked hideously as if it were about to splinter into a thousand pieces, louder than the ringing of the bells, penetrating the still morning air like some terrible alarm call to the city. Brother Stephen thought it appropriate such a warning would cry out now given the ostensibly serious nature of this visit under the supposed auspices of the principal spiritual and political authorities of the area.

It was the talking helmet who trooped through first, full of self-importance holding his long spear in his right hand. The men-at-arms wore the blue tunic of Baron de Grey's retinue and in the pale early morning light it looked almost as grey as the mail armour over the top of it. Brother Stephen stood back and watched the peacocks enter the courtyard, six, seven, eight of them, followed by Reginald de Grey himself, resplendent in navy blue tunic and white fitted sleeves atop his famous black destrier, Arthur.

Another horseman followed the lord, his identity unknown to Brother Stephen. Like the men-at-arms, he too was armoured, though wore no helm so his dark hair and features were there for all to see. Stephen imagined it would not be long before his identity would become known. His armour was finer than that of the footmen, heavier and fitted. This dark-haired man with a beard impeccably trimmed was clearly a knight, and even without the armour and the pomp and the horses one could tell Lord Reginald and the knight were of a different caste to the talking helmet and his fellow footmen.

Reginald looked down kindly to Brother Stephen, unlike the menacing glare he had received from the talking helmet. The knight followed suit, a practiced look of the upper classes when dealing with the lower-ranked religious orders. The bishops of the realm were essentially noblemen themselves, many being richer than their laymen counterparts. Though Baron de Grey had a reputation for honesty, Brother Stephen knew in the case of the knight that such cordial greetings were likely a mask covering the impatience beneath. The elderly monk sighed at the value placed on aesthetics by men in power, and those working for them.

Lord Reginald stopped his horse and dismounted with the grace of a man thirty years younger. His dashing leadership during the suppression of Llywelyn ap Gruffudd's rebellion had become almost legendary throughout the realm and it was apparent the man was not one to rest on past glories – he carried with him an energy and drive

126

that manifested itself in a steeled expression and trim physique. Brother Stephen had met the lord on a few previous occasions, and almost disturbingly the man never seemed to age, with the exception of his greying hair.

"Brother Stephen, it has been a long time," Lord Reginald said, no smile on his face but nor iciness in his voice. "Please, excuse the manner of my men, they aren't as familiar with this time of day as are you. May we speak with Abbot Thomas?"

Brother Stephen bowed his head. "Welcome, my lord. There is nothing to excuse. Please, this way. But I must close the gate."

Fearing the elderly monk would take as long closing the gate as he did to open it, Baron Reginald interrupted him. "We shall close the gate for you, brother. Come, I should like to speak with the abbot."

The bearded knight, still atop his horse, barked an order at one of the footmen who promptly attended the open gate. A few monks stood idly by, gawking at the spectacle unfolding until a voice from an unseen source caught their attention over their shoulders, and they dispersed back to their tasks.

Handing Arthur's reins to another footman, Lord Reginald began following Brother Stephen's steady footsteps across the courtyard to the main abbey building. But before reaching the entrance, Abbot Thomas burst through the door followed by Prior Simon and a third monk. The abbot's expression was as dark as his black cloak, a look of thunder spoiling his usually genial face and at that moment he appeared so much larger than his five and a half feet frame.

"My lord, I must ask - what is the meaning of this?" Abbot Thomas asked cordially, but struggled to keep his rage in check. "When is it necessary to bring armed men into the house of our Lord?"

The baron responded coolly. "Good morning, Abbot Thomas. These men are here for the stone. I have the bishop's permission to bring them into the complex with me."

Sensitive enough to not inflame the situation, Lord Reginald did not comment on how easily for a monk the abbot's temper was stoked.

Abbot Thomas appeared on the verge of exploding, but Prior Simon, standing just behind the abbot's right shoulder, had the same characteristic stoic look about him as usual. The third monk, Brother Francis, was bemused by Lord Reginald's explanation, but knew it was not his place to question at this moment. He was young, barely a hint of beard growth about him, but had quickly picked up the hierarchical rules upon joining the Abbey. A highly literate man, Brother Francis was attached to Abbot Thomas' retinue and knew better than most when to keep quiet, even for a Benedictine monk.

Thomas knew the Bishop Lichfield had not granted Lord de Grey permission to bring soldiers into the complex, because the stone had only arrived the previous day. The bishop's palace at Coventry was well over one hundred miles from Chester; it would take nearly a week for riders to complete a return trip between the two cities. The abbot had heard stories about the lord that ran contrary to the heroic figure renowned the length and breadth of the land for his exploits against the Welsh; stories that the lord had certainly not confessed to the abbot.

"You are bringing soldiers with spears to collect a stone from us, my lord?" Abbot Thomas was a terrible actor and his indignation was barely concealed with his pithy rhetorical question.

Reginald sighed. "Unfortunately, quite the debacle has arisen over this stone, father. And this letter," he said as he pulled out the note Abbot Thomas had written the previous day for John Duns at Oxford, "has stoked my interest further. 'Sir Henry of the Temple' is a man I'd like to meet, if you know him. May we come in, father?"

He held the letter aloft in his left hand. Lord Reginald maintained a composed demeanour, quite dissimilar to the gloating smirk of Sir Edward de Beauchamp who still remained atop his horse. Abbot Thomas regretted Sir Edward's arrogance, narrowing his eyes a little before realising what he was doing.

Thomas regained his composure. Intercepting the letter for John Duns was a cheap shot, entirely unexpected. Was no institution sacred these days? "Very well, but you'll see how it is prudent for the stone to remain in the possession of the Church, my lord."

The abbot clasped his hands behind his back, standing a little taller than naturally, knowing Lord Reginald would come right back at him. Being a monk, he was not an aggressive man, but being an abbot, he knew how and when to be combative.

"I think the King would have a say in this matter, father, especially when he discovers the manner in which the stone was removed from his quarry," Lord Reginald replied matter-of-factly. "And *especially* now that the stone is being held right under the nose of the Earl of Chester, who happens to be his son."

The baron's name-dropping did not perturb the abbot. "I think the King would be interested in seeing what this stone can do, my lord." Behind him, Prior Simon looked to Sir Edward for a reaction. The knight was idly patting his mount but it was apparent his mind was working hard to decipher Abbot Thomas' reply.

"I'm not sure I follow." The baron narrowed his eyes, trying to ascertain the abbot's intentions.

"It is as I say, my lord. Prior Simon here is my witness." Thomas turned to his right and gestured to the prior, before once again facing the lord and his men. "And if it is as you say, that the King himself has ownership of the stone, then I should like to treaty with the King himself over the gifting of the stone to the Church."

Sir Edward scoffed. "Is it not enough that the holy houses take in tithes and taxes, without resorting to precious stones as well? I thought you were brothers of poverty, not treasure hunters," he said, the derision in his voice amplified by his being atop a horse whilst the monks were on foot.

"And if you had seen what we have seen, good sir, you would know that this is not treasure as you would know. Truly, the work of the Lord is in this stone." Thomas crossed himself.

The knight walked his horse a couple of paces forward, ahead of the other soldiers and just behind Reginald's left shoulder. "We all know the stories around the relics, father, and we all know the value attached to these stories." Sir Edward spoke with force but not condescendingly. Lord Reginald continued watching the abbot, waiting for any clue that he was hiding something.

"I am truly sorry to hear of your dissatisfaction in the history of our Church, sir, but I beg you visit more often, and we can convince you of the folly of your doubts." Abbot Thomas answered genuinely and resolutely.

129

"A theft is still a theft, father!" Edward raised his voice further. "Even the Church cannot escape justice! It-"

"Thank you, Sir Edward," Reginald interrupted, as if rebuking a child. The knight quietened immediately, glaring at the back of the lord's head.

At the abbot's side Prior Simon watched Sir Edward's response with barely concealed mirth on his face. The prior did not smile often but found the Lord Reginald's unintentionally blithe dismissal of the knight as a welcome tonic to the subliminally bitter exchange between baron and abbot.

"Enough of this bickering. Neither of us enjoy idle chatter, do we, father?" The baron's question was loaded and the abbot knew it.

"The devil sends many afflictions to us, my lord, and we avoid them as best we can," Abbot Thomas responded dryly.

Reginald looked down to the dusty courtyard ground and kicked at some dirt with his booted foot in a move that betrayed growing impatience. "Would you be so kind as to lead us to this stone, father?"

The steely baron stopped scuffing at the ground and looked up, staring the abbot in the eyes. He did not intend for his request to be negotiable.

"You can see the stone, my lord, but on the proviso that it remain in Church custody until such time as when the King can judge on the matter." Thomas remained statue-like with hands behind his back. Brother Francis adopted the same pose, attempting to emulate the abbot.

Reginald looked to the sky, and the roofline of the abbey that blocked out so much of the rising sun. He breathed deeply of the cool morning air, taking a lungful before answering. "*I* am the King's Justice here, father, and I also have the blessing of your bishop. I'm not sure how well regarded would be an accusation of theft against your name." The lord raised his right hand and gestured with his fingers for his men to approach, at which Sir Edward dismounted with a clattering sound completely alien to an abbey courtyard at sunrise.

"I have no intention of going against your authority or that of the bishop, my lord, but before passing judgement, please at least await a response to my letter to the Pope regarding this matter." The three monks' faces remained unchanged; monastic discipline was holding.

The baron raised his head slightly, his eyes wandering over the façade of the abbey of St Werbaugh, momentarily captivated by the blotchy colouring of the sandstone still visible even in the early morning shadow, before looking back down at Abbot Thomas. Masking his rising anger with a pensive, gentle expression, lips pursed and eyes locked onto those of Thomas, the baron took a deep breath again. His exasperation betrayed despite his best efforts, the Reginald looked down at the ground and kicked the dust once more. The messenger for the Pope would be long gone by now, even if the baron could spare men to catch him. And how would they know what the messenger looked like?

"Very well, father. The King will have to be notified, of course." He paused, mulling over the abbot's purported letter to Rome. The abbot was displaying unexpected obduracy - suspicious obduracy – and Reginald was certain the issue was beyond just a simple stone from a quarry. He certainly did not believe the abbot's cryptic talk of what the stone could 'do', and was more than a little surprised Thomas had resorted to such outlandish language – had it really been such a long time since the lord had spoken with Thomas? Surely his mind could not have deteriorated so quickly. Had he really written to the Pope? That could be a ploy for time or position. Many questions.

This was not the straightforward arrest he anticipated. But it was a welcome change from the tedium of tending to administrative duties with the likes of John Reeves, and would help take the men's mind off the bloody fighting the previous day when the Welsh brigands attacked the caravan. Retribution would be swift on that front.

He turned to face Sir Edward, who thankfully had escaped unscathed from the ambush, though he knew it was a close run thing. The de Molay girl would need to be found as well; Lord Reginald grimaced at the events of the previous day and the embarrassment it had caused to English rule in the northern Marches, not to mention issues of stability.

131

Abbot Thomas interrupted the lord's silence. "So it shall be. Would you like to join us, my lord? We have a much business to attend here in the Abbey, as you can appreciate, so I feel we should get proceedings underway. The Lord frowns upon sloth." He nodded at Prior Simon, who turned and headed back towards the great oak door of the abbey, a monstrous construct that almost rivalled the gate door in sheer presence. The abbey door was more aesthetically developed, however, adorned as it was with tinned nails in decorative patterns that were primarily practical but, as was customary with large expanses of woodwork that required extensive nailwork, took on an ornamental role owing to the lack of space allowed for carvings and motifs.

Thomas spun and took a step before pausing as a thought hit him. "Come to think of it, my lord, we'll stay in the open air. Why waste such a glorious day provided by the Lord?"

"Alright, let's go, boys," bellowed Sir Edward, unnecessarily loud given the proximity of the soldiers and the near-complete silence of the courtyard bar the occasional rustling of leather and clanking metal plate. There were not many trees within the city walls and only a couple within the Abbey's estate, but a few blackbirds had woken and began singing at each other, whilst somewhere in the city a pigeon was hooting.

Abbot Thomas, standing with hands clasped behind his back, motionless in his black robes as if he were part of the shadows created by the Abbey behind him, turned his gaze to Sir Edward. "Your men are permitted in the abbey grounds, but not as soldiers," his tone stern and uncompromising. Sir Edward was not familiar with receiving orders from anyone bar Lord Reginald and indeed had not done so since joining the lord's retinue from that of his uncle, the Earl of Warwick, William de Beauchamp, the previous year. Warwick had broken a two-month Welsh siege of Conwy Castle where the King himself had been trapped. Sir Edward himself had stormed the Welsh commander's tent and put him to the sword, earning personal congratulations from the King.

The Earl sent his nephew to Reginald's retinue to free his promising military career from future accusations of nepotism. The young man's arrogance and sense of self-importance was catalysed by the freedom granted him by his uncle and the responsibilities given by Baron de Grey. The knight sneered at Thomas, acutely aware that the latter's ecclesiastical authority permitted a butcher's son to give orders to the nephew of an earl. Reginald noticed Sir Edward's displeasure and it gave him no little satisfaction, for the knight's egotism ran roughshod over all and sundry and so a lesson in humility was overdue. Reginald also knew that Abbot Thomas enjoyed it. Even in the heat of verbal combat, he could allow the abbot that pleasure.

"One more thing, my lord," stated Abbot Thomas, now fully with the upper hand over Reginald, "I think it will be good to have the Prioress Alice here as a witness also. We are all branches of the same tree, after all."

Reginald maintained his neutral exterior but the shift from having the initiative to merely being reactive irked him, particularly in front of Sir Edward, a talented soldier but also difficult to control. The baron knew that Sir Edward was still sufficiently immature that an indication of weakness on the part of his superiors would be interpreted as complete character failure. "Of course, father," he replied, smiling consciously ensuring his eyes matched the purported happiness indicated by his grin.

"Thank you, my lord. Brother Francis, would you be so kind as to send the younger Brother John to the convent and request Prioress Alice join us, please? Pass on the message that both the Lord de Grey and I would dearly welcome her presence. She will understand." Brother Francis nodded, clasping his hands together before him in the long sleeves of his pitch-black robes and noiselessly slipped away. His catlike silence in movement suggested that he was indeed the shadow his Benedictine habit so resembled.

Abbot Thomas watched his young assistant glide away. The nunnery was in the shade of the castle in the south-west corner of the city, at the junction of the eponymously named Castle Street and Nunnery Lane. Brother Francis knew where Brother John was at this moment – all the monks were at prayer – but it would take John much longer to traverse across the city, down Northgate and Bridge Streets before cutting right onto Cuppin Street leading to Nunnery Lane. Thomas knew he was trying Reginald's patience, but patience

133

was commendable and the baron could take this as a lesson in humility.

"There is the other matter, father," Reginald said, so solemnly it was almost a whisper, "regarding the thieves, and the letter has revealed the identity of one of them. I find it curious how Sir Henry of the Temple *and* the niece of the Grand Master were in collusion in this instance-"

The abbot jumped in before the steely baron could continue. "Sir Henry was here, yes, but he has since ridden ahead to London. As for thieves *plural*, I know not of an accomplice, unless you are referring to the niece of the Grand Master, the pleasure of whose company I am yet to experience."

Reginald was testing the abbot, challenging him in his own courtyard. In their psychological contest neither baron nor abbot wanted to be the first to break eye contact; the two heads of their respective households were verbally jousting before their right-hand men, Sir Edward one and Prior Simon the other. But it was not for pride; Abbot Thomas had long lost all concern for that and Lord Reginald was above the pretentions of the men about court such as Sir Edward.

No, this was about authority, pre-eminence in the city, the right to lead, power. Each respected the other and their basis for authority, but both considered this contest to fall within their domain. And both knew that despite the lord having the element of surprise, the abbot was currently in the ascendance. Prior Simon too forced himself to keep looking at Reginald despite the surprise and discomfort at the abbot's lie over Henry working alone – how much fabrication would Thomas spin to prevent a full display of the King's justice for those who took the stone?

Reginald considered what Abbot Thomas had said, not trusting he was telling the truth. Being a terrible actor, the abbot was also naturally a terrible liar; in fairness, he had never desired nor needed to hone that talent. The lord grinded his teeth, as was his habit when faced with a conundrum. For over forty years his wife, Matilda, had warned him against grinding his teeth – he would lose enough teeth without reducing them to dust, she would tell him. Usually Reginald listened to his wife's advice, and she was privy to most of his work for the King, but in the case of his teeth the lord refused to heed her warnings, pointing out that having almost a full set of teeth at sixty was not only a remarkable achievement but also evidence his teeth were tougher than anyone else's he knew.

Reginald continued grinding his teeth together, the movement of his jaw just visible through the iron stubble. What option was there but to take the word of the much-loved and widely-esteemed abbot? What Reginald considered to be the actual truth – that Sir Henry had an accomplice and they were both hiding in the abbey – would only come to light through unofficial means. A guard would have to be posted at the gate at the very least.

Reginald frowned at the abbot. Speaking far louder than before, he lectured Thomas. "Stealing from the King is a grave offence, father, you are aware. Should events have transpired otherwise to how you say, neither the bishop nor the Pope would be too happy." He turned away choosing not to accompany his thinly-veiled threat with aggressive posturing, and ordered five of the footmen to drop their arms.

Amidst the *clank*ing and *clang*ing of spears and swords crashing to the hard ground, Abbot Thomas looked to Prior Simon, the two holding a knowing look for a brief moment, two expressionless faces speaking volumes to one another, before Thomas spun round to Reginald once more.

"Would you and your men like something to drink, my lord?" he asked.

Prioress Alice arrived with the younger Brother John. She was busy and bustling as she walked with Sister Agnes, her second in command. Both wore black head to toe, both indistinguishable at the distance between the gathering in the open area behind the abbot's quarters and the gate. It had been a while since the prioress had visited the abbey, and her and Thomas were old friends. She was full of life and enthusiasm and when she put her mind to it, she never failed to raise spirits in her audience. The current circumstances were highly unusual and not necessarily benevolent but Thomas always found reassurance in Alice's presence.

Brother Francis, who was waiting by Brother Stephen's post at the gate, was first to welcome the nuns and did so with open arms. "Good morning to you both, Prioress Alice, Sister Agnes. May the Lord bless you this day."

Francis enjoyed his occasional conversations with Alice and Agnes. They were both sharp in their own ways and offered insights into scriptural matters and points of nature that differed from the largely homogenous perspectives found in the abbey.

Prioress Alice beamed at him from underneath the white veil upon her brown hair. "Brother Francis! May the Lord bless you too. Young Brother John here has us all a stir with his request for our presence before Lord Reginald, but in true Benedictine fashion has chosen to retain his silence over the nature of the matter. Would you care to enlighten us?" Her demeanour was cheery as always.

The young Brother John looked sheepishly to Francis, unsure whether to take Alice's comments as a compliment or criticism.

Francis had seen as many winters as John but carried a far more refined mind, and the latter looked up to him in almost all matters requiring an opinion. Unfortunately for John, he could not read Francis' amused reaction.

"Brother John has yet to be informed as to what the matter is, which I suppose is one way of ensuring our Benedictine discipline remains strong," Francis joked, again drawing a smile from Alice and even one from the poker-faced Agnes beside her. Joviality over, Francis' expression straightened. "A relic has been found with mystifying capabilities. I myself have not witnessed them yet, but the abbot and prior have both seen them and are adamant it is of heavenly provenance." Francis' voice lowered as if he were confiding in the three present. "I've not seen either as flustered as they have been about this object," he said, leaning in slightly.

"Where was it found?" Alice asked.

"Rhuddlan, mother. In a quarry."

"Thus it ever was, brother, that the most auspicious items are found in the least auspicious locations. It's the reward for honest labour."

"I'll let you decide for yourself," Francis added. "This way, please, sisters."

The young Francis led the nuns to the congregation in the clearing of the yard, where Abbot Thomas greeted them. Behind him stood Simon and Reginald, whilst the soldiers were standing a little away, relaxing in the sunshine and taking advantage of an unexpected moment of leisure.

"Excellent timing as always, Mother Alice," quipped the abbot with a wry smile.

"At Creation our Heavenly Father kept to a timetable and so should we," replied the prioress cheerily, the anticipation not having dampened her disposition just yet.

Abbot Thomas nodded. "Quite so. I am keen to hear of your and Sister Agnes' thoughts on the following demonstration, which *should*," emphasising the word, "produce results as we witnessed yesterday."

"So it is a holy relic, you say?" asked Alice, inquisitiveness written large on her face.

"Yes, we think so," Thomas answered hesitantly. He looked at Simon and then Lord Reginald before returning to the prioress and Agnes. "We have classed it as such, preliminarily, because quite simply we could not find a satisfactory explanation for it yesterday-"

Simon gently interrupted his abbot. "I fear the abbot is not giving sufficient justice to the display we witnessed. This, Mother Alice, is something truly powerful, certainly beyond man's capability."

"Has the Lord spoken to you in your prayers on this matter, father?" Alice enquired keenly.

"He... has not, yet," admitted Thomas. "And the same goes for Simon here, I believe." The abbot looked sheepish at not having received divine communication in the matter, and felt a little embarrassed that so many people were witness to what he considered to be his own spiritual shortcoming.

"The Lord would not be our Lord if He gave us all the answers straightaway," offered the prioress. Peering over Thomas' shoulder as well as she could given her small stature, she noticed a man approaching who was awkwardly carrying a large cloth sack over his right shoulder. "I assume this is the object in question?"

With little announcement or fuss, Lord Reginald's right-hand man, Sir Edward de Beauchamp, trod carefully and deliberately along towards the circular gathering, with the others stepping aside to allow the man and his unwieldy cargo space. He had bristled at the Reginald's request to fetch the stone from Abbot Thomas' office but the baron did not see it fit to ask a monk to engage in manual labour, and did not want a common soldier tramping through an Abbot's quarters.

Sir Edward placed the brown sack containing the stone on the rock-like earth, all vegetation long since worn away from hundreds of daily sandal footsteps over hundreds of years. His flawless armour creaked as he struggled to lower it slowly, prompting Abbot Thomas to recall Sir Henry's seemingly effortless strength in handling the same object the previous day. Once it had landed with a soft *thud* Sir Edward retreated back, ludicrously overdressed relative to the severe plainness of the garments worn by the monks and nuns. Even Reginald seemed underdressed standing next to him.

The morning sun was now coming over the city wall at the back of the abbey's estate and the perfectly burnished steel plate on Sir Edward's armour burned bright in stark contrast to the Benedictine brothers and sisters' solid black habits. It was this shining human torch that first attracted the attentions of a number of brothers to the gathering of monks, nuns, soldiers, a knight and a lord - a most unusual occurrence within the walls of the abbey. Curiosity in matters apart from one's own tasks was discouraged in the monastic community, but upon noticing the brothers approaching their circle Prior Simon did not warn them away. Knowing how she was a force of nature both within and without the convent, Thomas expected Alice to comment on the momentary breakdown in monastic discipline but the prioress was as silent as the monks standing a few paces behind their little group.

Prior Simon approached the sack and loosened the string around the neck before pulling its sides down, for the sack was rough, worn wool that more or less held its form when unsupported. Even without direct access to sunlight, the silver object had a perfect varnish about it that could not be dimmed by the shadows covering it. Thomas watched the eyes of Reginald, Sir Edward, Alice and Agnes widen at the sight. War leader, spoiled bully, nun – it did not matter who looked at it, the reaction was the same, though Thomas would have rather the sight of shiny treasure had less impact on Alice and Agnes.

"A candle, please, Brother Francis," requested the abbot. Brother Francis lifted one of the candles from the ground next to him and passed it to the abbot. The air was still so the flame was in no danger of dying; so the monk took no care to shelter it, and neither did Thomas upon receiving the bowl. "I shall now recreate the experiment conducted by Prior Simon just yesterday, whereby it was discovered that this object is of a most baffling origin." Prior Simon smiled and thought the abbot was being a little dramatic. Abbot Thomas cast his voice around the circle of onlookers. "Please, some room."

Lord Reginald gave the abbot a sceptical look before taking two steps backwards. Sir Edward waited for Reginald's lead before *clunk*ing backwards in turn. As usual, Alice's emotions were written large on her face and her brown eyes widened even further in alarm so she wasted no time in falling in line. Agnes was wordlessly compliant. Even before joining the convent she had tended to be wordlessly compliant, not through being meek but simply through an incredibly tranquil disposition.

As Simon had done yesterday, so Thomas did today. He slowly poured a drop of the candle wax onto the stone, which fizzled instantly and then instantly ceased. The abbot faced up his audience; Reginald and Sir Edward to his right, Alice and Agnes to his left. He could see the two Brother Johns behind Reginald, peering over the baron's shoulder. It was an administrative and organisational inconvenience that the only two brothers by the name of John tended to found side by side. And then there was Brother Pierre and Brother Ederick, and the tall Brother Peter, looming high above the others as he always did. He was like a thin, leafless tree planted behind the prioress, who was nearly two heads shorter. A few more brothers were approaching from around the corner of his lodging. Thomas reflected that the abbey would be quite unproductive this morning.

Thomas was met with blank stares. Reginald was stood with his arms behind his back, before bringing his right hand up to scratch his stubble. "Forgive me my rashness, father, but I'm not sure his Holiness will consider this worthy of his attention." There was sarcasm in neither his voice nor intention.

The abbot knew this, even if others did not. Alice shot an indignant look to the lord, who paid her no mind. "Indeed, my lord. But this is no mere trick... if you would please take another step back."

The crowd shuffled back a little further. "The tongs please, Francis," he asked his young assistant. Francis obliged picking up the yard tongs he had found in the storage room. Having handed the candle to Prior Simon, Thomas gripped the candle bowl in the tongs and, standing a good couple of paces away, stretched out his arms and poured half of the melted wax over the stone. The surface of the stone sizzled and *whooshed*, sending up the same blue flash of light as had been seen yesterday before the stone once again dropped into what had previously been solid ground. There appeared a crater roughly three feet deep and three feet wide, the dark brown soil contrasting with the light dusty surface, severed ends of roots poking through, pebbles here and there.

The silver stone lay at the bottom of the crater, flawless and glinting even without direct illumination. There was no hint that it had been subjected to hot candle wax or falling from heights into earthy pits. Nor was there any steam or smoke or any evidence of the process that had created such a phenomenon.

A few onlookers gasped. Without saying a word, Abbot Thomas placed the tongs and candle bowl down and then once more surveyed the audience. No one spoke, but just stared vacantly at what had just happened. Prioress Alice and Sister Agnes both crossed themselves, and even Agnes had an expression of surprise on her face. The finely bearded Sir Edward was open-mouthed in shock. Lord Reginald, one of the greatest actors of the nobility and renowned for his ability to disguise any emotion, the nature of which were debated in jest by his men at the drinking table, let his guard slip and had frozen mid-stubble scratch, his hand glued to his face in an unnatural pose. The Johns and Brother Pierre dropped to their knees in penitence and humility before such an awesome demonstration of the Lord's power. In the distance two more monks stopped walking and looked over at the ever-increasing gathering of onlookers.

"Here is the reason that I have written to the Pope, brothers, sisters and friends. Here is the reason why I wanted Brother John Duns to investigate it himself, that most subtle doctor, whom some say possesses the finest mind in all Christendom. Who better to assist us in this matter? I have no knowledge of any material capable of such effects, nor does Prior Simon. Mother Alice, have you encountered anything of this nature? Sister Agnes?" The abbot was beginning to shake a little at the adrenaline rush from witnessing the mystifying event, a power surely granted by God, and then immediately trying to address a crowd in a calm and logical manner. Prior Simon approached from his left and put a hand on his shoulder, steadying him.

Alice patted down her habit, not because it was out of place but as a subconscious attempt to regain composure. She fixed her eyes on the abbot. "All of my instincts are telling me this is some very, very clever trick, father," she paused, expecting Thomas to grimace at an unintended accusation, but the abbot did not rise to it. "But that is not you. I have never seen anything of this type. Though I must say that I have heard of the Mongols of the east throwing bursts of fire at Christians. Perhaps there is some element of eastern fire... *bursting* at play here?"

The prioress' insight into military history surprised all of her audience bar Agnes, who was privy to Alice's voracious appetite for reading. Sir Edward appeared almost as stunned at Alice's conclusion as he had been at the preceding events. The Bishop of Lichfield, or, because of his advanced age, his lackeys, had cracked down on what was considered unnecessary reading in the convent at Chester and had gone so far as to politely warn Alice against misusing her time on this Earth. Abbot Thomas maintained a neutral position in the matter, refusing to either counsel Alice against her enquiring into matters beyond the remit of a prioress or defend her right to intellectual curiosity before the authorities of the see.

141

Alice knew Thomas' hands were tied in such matters and both were saddened that the upper echelons of the Church were more political than the kingdoms over which they kept watch; it was said that Bishop Anthony Bek of Durham had been invested with such secular, military and diplomatic responsibility by King Edward that he was himself a king in the north.

Lord Reginald finally removed his hand from his chin. "I believe you are on to something here, mother. I too have heard tales of the eastern horsemen and their flaming barrels, though why one should be found here is puzzling. The Earl's court would have informed me of a visit by a Mongol ambassador."

"Neither have I had any word of such a visit, my lord," added Sir Edward, eyes still on the crater.

The Baron de Grey stepped forwards to the edge of the small hole in the ground and peered in. "All the same, a weapon of war does not belong in an abbey, father. It is hardly fair for you to request my men disarm themselves, when it is you who has the most potent weaponry." Sir Edward grinned.

Thomas glanced expectantly at Prior Simon. The prior had long been the abbot's fixer in all manner of circumstances - regarding supplies, organisation, politics - and here Simon did not disappoint.

"Pardon me, my lord, but this is no weapon," Simon's tone as melancholy as ever, "and what manner of fire are you familiar with is capable of causing solid earth to vanish?" The prior was another learned reader, like Alice, but he was far subtler about it and so had avoided the displeasure of Bishop Roger's immediate circle.

"Come now, Prior Simon. We all know the destructive nature of fire, unfortunately." Lord Reginald was not looking for a fight, but felt the situation was returning to his control.

Prior Simon's attention was caught by an occasional glint in the distance. He looked past Lord Reginald to one of the men-at-arms by the gate. The man-at-arms' spearhead glinted like a beacon in the increasingly bright sunlight, as did the steel rings of his mail overcoat. The man must be getting uncomfortably hot, the prior thought. *Steel... hot...yes!*

"You are quite correct; fire is incredibly destructive. Would your men mind if I borrowed some of their armour, my lord? I am a great believer in the empirical method so faithfully adhered to by our own *Doctor Mirabilis*, the learned Bacon."

Sir Edward spoke up. "My lord, this has gone on long enough. The men drop their weapons and now the Church would seize them to add to their own here?" The bearded knight spoke to Reginald but his dark brown eyes glared at the prior.

"I quite agree, Sir Edward, but my curiosity has been piqued by Prior Simon. He is a learned man himself, you know." Reginald turned back from the knight to the prior. "Of course. I imagine such an establishment as this will not suffer to repay any costs incurred to my men's armour this morning." Lord Reginald was a reasonable man and a pragmatic man. He knew the prior to be onto something here, but he also knew exactly the state of the abbey's finances, Abbot Thomas thought; it was well known that during his abbacy and that of Abbot Simon Whitchurch before him there had been a number of grants made to the abbey, and successful defences of the rights of the abbey against disgruntled heirs of benefactors. "Sir Edward, would you bring three of the men over, please."

With no fanfare the knight marched off towards the gate where a few of the soldiers were lolling in the rising heat. Even so early in the morning, the direct sunlight felt oppressive to those wearing armour. Yet Sir Edward's knightly appearance remained immaculate, barely a bead of sweat beneath his jet-black cropped hair. Even when shouting at the men-at-arms his face did not attain a beetroot shade.

The knight strode back with three men-at-arms, swords and mail vests in hand. They were all red-faced, with the inexplicable exception of the physically unflappable Sir Edward, suggesting the command to remove their mail jackets was welcome. The soldiers' eyes widened at the bizarre sight before them. The iron-grey prior ordered the three swords and three vests laid around the silver object in the pit.

The men-at-arms, all youths with fresh faces, were cautious in approaching the pit, holding back from the edge of the crater. They could sense the unease in the crowded audience and did not want to come any closer to what they guessed to be the source of the onlookers' interests – having been lounging near the gate, they had

143

not witnessed any of the investigation thus far. The lead soldier eyed Prior Simon uneasily, silently fishing for instruction and reassurance. The soldier was recognisable to Simon even when helmed; he was William, a good lad with a sharp mind about him. Simon had lamented William's choice of career given his natural flare for letters. There was still time to talk him round for he had not long turned twenty years of age, but this was not it. What William saw was the unsympathetic face of the prior, his sober expression emphasised by the general greyness of his features. The only response elicited was a slight turn of the head and eyes down to the pit.

William looked back at the other two soldiers, both of whom conspicuously devoid of initiative or action. As usual, it would be William who took the lead. The slender young man removed his suffocating helmet so as to aid his visibility as he crouched down and clambered into the pit. Lord Reginald had already noted the young soldier's fearlessness and Sir Edward had seen firsthand his courage in the attack by the Welsh the previous day.

Treading carefully to maintain his balance in the limited space available around the object, he reached up for his own sword and mail on the lip of the crater. In turn, the two other soldiers handed down their own arms. Having distributed his own arms and those of his companions William climbed out from the pit and scurried clear to a safe distance behind the circle of nobles, knights and holy people. The swords and mail jackets were arranged haphazardly around three edges of the stone, the three sides facing Reginald and Sir Edward, Alice and Agnes, and Thomas and Simon.

"We know a naked flame to be hot, but not to the same degree as the flame of the smith's forge. A case in point: Brother Francis, please pass me the candle. Thank you. Here, I am able to extinguish the flame with my fingers," Prior Simon demonstrated as he pinched the flame, "with no damage to my skin. We are able to heat bowls without melting them. We can cook food without melting it. All of this is impossible in the forge – the forge where iron is melted and steel is moulded."

His monotonous voice was strangely captivating in the circumstances, and even Sir Edward had unconsciously discarded his contempt at being lectured by the lower orders.

Prior Simon continued, "And so, is it not reasonable to conclude that if the *wax* of a naked flame – not even the flame itself, but just the wax – when applied to this object, can cause the iron and steel surrounding it to not just melt but – like the earth before it – *disappear*, then we have something beyond the capabilities of the science and weapons of man and instead something of far greater origin? Surely it cannot be that the eastern horsemen's firebursts create conditions hotter than those of the smithy."

By now more monks had gathered round, and the assembled audience were enthralled with the prior's impromptu lecture, monks, nuns, soldiers, knights all. His ponderous voice carried far over the still morning air, its almost sorrowful tone adding gravitas to the heady words he spoke.

"Francis, please." Simon gestured to Brother Francis for the second candle. "Again, if we could have some room please." The prior paused as the closest onlookers shuffled backwards a little. Over their heads over by the gate, the prior saw one brother discussing with another before the other took off with great haste towards the gate. The former started towards the demonstration. Ever observant, Prior Simon could not think who was scheduled to leave the estate at this time – that would need to be a matter to pursue later, however.

Turning back to the crater before him, Simon took the candle in the long tongs and steadily poured the entirety of the bowl's wax into the crater and onto the stone. The wax instantly vapourised with the same blue flash as before, accompanied by the sound of a gust of wind for all but a second. Once the blue flash had disappeared, it became apparent that wherever it had gone, the swords and armour and surrounding earth had gone as well and the stone was now nearly six feet deep in its pit. The front row of the circle of observers rushed forward to get a better view, all sense of decorum forgotten as Agnes jostled with Thomas and Reginald shoved Sir Edward. Again they collectively gasped as they were met with the sight of the silver object, on its own, still unmarked.

145

Lord Reginald closed his mouth following the sharp intake of breath and, putting his hands behind his back, stepped backwards and turned to his right, toward Abbot Thomas.

"Father, I'd like you to write a further letter to His Holiness, detailing that the stone is to be transported to London for inspection by the King, Archbishop Robert, John Duns and the leading men of the realm. His Holiness is to be informed of the proceedings here today, with Prioress Alice, Prior Simon, Sir Edward and myself as signatory witnesses, and the house of St Werbaugh as attendees. And gather your things, most importantly your pens and papers, because we are leaving immediately and you will write all of the archbishops and bishops in the land." It was as if the earlier debating had all been for nought; when a decision was to be made, the air of authority Reginald could muster was irresistible.

Abbot Thomas lifted his gaze away from the seemingly innocent pit in the ground. "Yes, my lord, right away." His voice sounded as if it were getting lost on the way out of his mouth for the words were not aimed at anyone, nor did they really matter relative to what he had just witnessed. Was this the greatest miracle of the age? The baron was right in insisting – no, stating – the stone go to London. It would arrive in London eventually anyhow, and the baron was a straight-talking man; if Thomas himself were joining the caravan, there were surely no tricks being played.

"Mother Alice, if you would join us too," Reginald requested, with the implication of a command.

The prioress looked at Agnes and back at Reginald. "Of course, my lord. If you would excuse us, my lord, father, brothers." With that the two nuns spun and hurried off towards the gate, manoeuvring through the assorted crowd of monks loitering behind the main actors at the front.

Lord Reginald walked closer to Abbot Thomas, tall and regal next to the small, black-cloaked abbot. The lord's face softened. "This is bigger than you and I, father." Paradoxically given the burst of orders just delivered, this was the first time Thomas had seen the lord appear at a complete loss.

"That it is," the abbot replied, trying to allay the lord's concerns without really believing he could.

Chapter 11

The five days since escaping the abbey had been largely uneventful, and their good fortune had continued with a cooling in temperature. Both men and horse found the cool westerly breezes coming down from the mountains a welcome tonic after the endless heat wave. The late afternoon sky was as clear as it had been since the last thunderstorm a week previous, keeping the humidity down, allowing the two to cover greater distances and bypass more villages because the horses did not need to be bathed so regularly. Brac had seen so many horses succumb to heat exhaustion through overwork already this summer in Rhuddlan alone. These palfreys supplied by the abbey were sturdy and Brac had grown attached to his one, a steady, silent and reliable companion. He welcomed consistency in these troubled times.

As the days past, the vivid lush green of the north Welsh and English hills had given way to a sad brown-yellow in the English midlands. The crops they had passed were healthy, but Henry had prayed for rain that the harvest would not fail. The villagers with whom they had spoken were not yet overly concerned, but each day without so much as a cloud rendered the wheat stalks ever more brittle; it was a blessing to no longer toil under the most oppressive heat in living memory but at least that heat brought with it rainfall.

"Do you think they're following us?" Brac broke the silence that had held since cresting the sweeping hill dominating the horizon behind them.

His melancholy accent seemed richer and more vivid since he had shaved, Henry thought. The amount of hair he had had around his mouth could only have muffled his voice. And it probably weighed down his head as well; for the wiry Welshman did not look at the floor or talk into his own chest half as much as he used to. Brac had even intentionally made Henry laugh on occasion.

"I believe they are." Henry could not have sounded less concerned.

The English knight did not take his gaze away from the wide expanse in front of them, the road snaking gently downhill from amidst overgrown meadows in sore need of tending from grazing animals to the patchwork strips of cultivation around the edges of the next village. If the distribution of houses appeared to have little planning regarding layout, then the strips had none at all. The dark browns, light browns, yellows, the odd green here and there, were mishmashes like a shattered stain glass window; sense could be made of the overall shape, but not of its constituent parts.

Brac was taken aback by his companion's nonchalance.

"Aren't you worried?" The wiry man looked round again over his left shoulder at the two horsemen cresting the hill, a little closer now than they had been for the majority of the day, shielding his eyes from the sun with his right hand. Relative to their journey into Chester, their ride across England had so far been almost comfortable.

Even the escape from the abbey's grounds had been straightforward; upon a chain of bell ringing signalling the approach of unwelcome attention, Brother Francis had arrived early and escorted the two stowaways to the subterranean gate at the rear of the estate. The tunnel passed underneath the city walls against which the abbey backed onto, and the two waited here until two horses were provided on Baglone Street outside the walls. With an entire abbey complex and the city walls between them and their pursuers, the English knight and the Welsh quarryman were afforded ample opportunity to take flight to London.

Nevertheless, Brac could feel the familiar and unwelcome sensation of nervousness beginning to riddle his core, from his stomach and up through his throat. He turned back to Henry. The Englishman was slouched in his saddle, his horse lolloping along in perfect synchronicity with its very relaxed rider. There was nothing that could faze this man.

Henry, whose horse was a few paces ahead of Brac's, could sense the Welshman was watching him and was expecting an active response.

"If they were looking for trouble, they'd have caught up with us days ago." The knight stopped his horse and directed it to turn

149

across the road, blocking Brac's horse which itself was forced to a halt, and allowing him a view of the figures behind them. "Let's see what they want." He glanced at Brac, eyes narrowed to shield from the sun overhead, tight-lipped as if he were not expecting any further discussion on the matter.

Brac could not believe what he was hearing, but found his desire to argue restricted by his timidity and respect for the knight.

"We need to go," he urged Henry. Brac's agitation was transferring to his horse, a brown palfrey with a magnificent mane of fine black hair, and it began stamping periodically.

Looking to prevent his own horse from picking up the other mount's tension, Henry patted down the animal's right flank and the right side of its neck and ruffled its mane.

"We'll talk to these people. You faced up to the thief in the crowd last week, didn't you? This is just the same, but with two people instead of one. And we don't even know if they want to thieve anything from us. So, twice the people, but half the risk, so it's the equivalent of one person, which you've already dealt with. See?" Henry looked up at the clean-shaven man, knowing Brac would be incapable of countering his convoluted logic.

The knight steered his black horse further round so that it was facing the direction they had travelled from and paced slowly to Brac's left side. The Welshman looked the Englishman in the eyes as the latter approached closer.

Henry placed his left hand on Brac's left shoulder, sighing before he spoke.

"In the Holy Land, I could not run. I wanted to, believe me, but could not. I was younger than you are now, the first time I saw the Saracen horsemen, stretching from one end of the horizon to the other; I thought the whole of the orient had amassed for a battle that would be the end of the world. I couldn't turn my horse around though because there were tens, hundreds just like me lined up behind me. They were all thinking the same as me but all unable to run away, because they had tens, hundreds just like them lined up behind them."

Henry's hand dropped to his side. He absent-mindedly brushed down the left arm of his shirt as he spoke, not because it was grubby, which it was, but as was his habit when talking at length.

"Necessity planted a seed of courage in us all that day; without necessity, courage cannot take root because necessity provides the fuel needed for courage to grow. Today, I am the tens and hundreds of knights behind you, stopping you from running away. This is where your courage will grow, here, on some road between some villages in some part of some country that isn't yours. Like my courage grew on some road between some villages in some part of a country that wasn't mine." Henry looked Brac in the eyes. "Let's go find out what they want."

The knight spurred his mount forwards in the same lazy manner as he had previously been travelling the opposite direction. The slow *clip-clop* rang through Brac's head as the wiry man pondered Henry's words. He had never heard such words before; then again, he had never spoken to a knight before, and certainly never had a knight speak to him in this way. He had always been spoken down to, not engaged in conversation by the lords and knights, if they had ever deigned to do so. This man was remarkable, and not a little strange in his disobedience to social norms, he mused.

He watched Henry roll slightly in his saddle with the motion of his horse's slow walk. Brac was so very envious of the man. The Englishman had more or less kept to the promise the Frenchwoman had made a week ago that Brac would not want for anything, and here, a week later, Henry was still with him, leading him to the London Temple. Clearly circumstances were not ideal and Brac blamed no one but himself for this. By protecting and encouraging him, a complete stranger, Henry was playing the ideal of the knight to perfection, the knights of the tales and stories, not the knights of the English conquest of Wales.

Brac had never had a real, solid, physically conceivable figure to inspire him – all Welsh knew the heroes in the stories: Owain Gwynedd, Llywelyn ap Gruffudd, all the way back to Camber. But Brac had always struggled to relate to these stories like those around him did because he had no means of connecting their heroic ideals to everyday life. He did not encounter people or situations that could plausibly or genuinely embody those ideals. Losing his family as he did, he was unable to connect these heroic ideas with everyday life, for he had no mother to nurture him like the great Owain nurtured the Welsh kingdom, nor a father to protect him like Llywelyn defended their kingdom.

The powerful influences on his life had neither nurtured him nor protected him. He thought back to his cruel guardianship under his family's neighbour Morgan Saermaen, the stonemason. There was also the brutal knight Sir Hugh and his often-sadistic dislike of the natives under his purported watch. At this moment, Brac realised that Henry was both an ideal *and* real. And so he now, against his better judgement, knew why he felt an uncharacteristic attachment to the knight's companionship. Who would have thought, an English knight!

With the sun to their backs the two approaching riders were silhouetted but Henry could see they rode straight-backed in the saddle, their horses ambling slowly which produced an eerie sense of purpose and composure about their movement. Henry was not apprehensive; what he had said to Brac was not merely placatory – if they were looking for trouble, they would indeed have announced such intentions days ago.

The two groups had now closed to about fifty paces of one another. Henry noticed they were wearing cloaks both, long and crimson with hoods down. The Englishman fancied they must be extremely uncomfortable in this heat, but knowing the significance of the crimson cloaks he was not surprised that they retained what regular folk would consider inappropriate attire for this time of year.

"I know who these people are," Henry said to Brac over his right shoulder. He did not turn round to face the Welshman though, instead keeping his eyes on the two figures now thirty paces ahead. Henry raised his right hand to his forehead to shield his eyes from the sun, which allowed him to make out details of the two crimson-cloaked figures' appearance. They were a man and woman, both with long blond hair tied back. The man was heavily bearded, but at this distance that seemed the only difference between the two.

Brac's sonorous voice responded to Brac's reassurance. "Is that a good thing, or bad thing?"

The English knight did not respond.

The crimson-cloaked riders stopped their horses, but Henry continued his gentle progress with Brac following suit. The knight closed so that he could make out their eyes, no longer hidden in silhouette, and halted his mount ten paces from the two cloaked riders.

"What business have you in this part of God's good Earth, Templar?" asked the woman. She spoke with neither scorn nor threat.

She was strikingly beautiful, the most beautiful woman Henry could remember having seen since... when was the last time he had seen such a beautiful woman? He thought of El. She was not conventionally beautiful, but Henry did enjoy simply watching El's face as she spoke, her small thin mouth beneath her tiny nose, the way her eyelids fluttered. He never thought of it as attraction. That would be absurd. Where was El?

Henry dismounted in silence, brushing himself down as he landed with the softness of a cat. He patted his palfrey and plucked an apple out of a hidden pocket in his cloak, possibly the same hidden pocket from which he retrieved coin for a week previously, and fed it to the horse. The tanned English knight faced the two strangers, clasping his hands together in front of his stomach.

"What business have you in this part of King Edward's land, Dragon?" Henry walked closer to the mounted woman, whose grey speckled rouncey snorted in the dry air and stamped the ground, quite a lot more excitable than its master. "And what makes you think you are addressing a knight of the Temple? I am flattered to be viewed as either a knight or a Templar. Sadly, I'm not. My friend and I, we've noticed you trailing us for the best part of three days now. You must be very shy for not coming to say hello sooner."

Henry had long suspected their stalkers were Dragons, the class of warriors leading the Welsh brigands in their revolt against the English. The knight was at a loss to explain quite how the Dragons knew who he was, however, and also Brac. Their organisation was assumed to be efficient but even the Temple did not credit the brigands with anything resembling an information network.

The crimson-cloaked woman dismounted with equal grace and even less sound than did Henry just moments before. She handed the reins of her grey to the man, who remained atop his steed, golden hair burning bright like some heavenly aura.

Henry scrutinised her and her movements, and there was nothing to suggest she was concealing anything larger than a dagger under the billowing cloak, if she were carrying any weapons at all. He imagined it likely she was. After all, Henry himself had a knife stowed up each of his shirtsleeves. And, so the stories went, Dragons were dangerous creatures.

She walked slowly towards the Englishman, stopping so that her nose was barely a foot from his own. She was tall with an almost hypnotising beauty, though it would take more than simple aesthetics to break a man of Henry's resolve. The Holy Land had seen to that.

She spoke again, her northern Welsh accent unmistakeable. "We do not encounter many of your kind, Templar, but when we do, we know who they are." She scanned his face for a response, which was not forthcoming. "Strange how two of you turn up, and then suddenly the Lord Justice of Chester is taking half of his army to London in an armed caravan, calling on the King and the lords of the land to gather."

Two of you? She had said 'two of you', Henry thought; had she seen El?

The crimson-cloaked woman continued. "We know what they're taking to London. You know it too." She looked back over her right shoulder to the crimson-cloaked man who retained his vacant expression, almost as if he were staring right through Henry. "We have followed you to give our thanks, for the work you've undertaken on our behalf. We would have shared our gratitude sooner, but we simply wanted confirmation of our suspicions. Taking the quarry worker to London, very predictable," she chided.

The man on the horse suddenly came to life, sharing the strangely serene manner of speech as his female companion. "Marvellous work, indeed. You have acted as would a good Christian," he stated matter-of-factly.

Henry snorted. "What would you know of good Christian behaviour?" The question was genuine but also delivered with

154

bluster to cover the knight's concern over their purported knowledge of the stone – too little time had passed and far too little exposure allowed for any interested parties to become aware of the stone's existence, let alone where it was right now and where it was headed.

"Guiding and protecting the lambs constitutes good Christian behaviour, Templar, you know this," the blond man replied.

"I think we differ in our definition of 'guiding' and 'protecting'," Henry countered. English villages throughout the Welsh Marches were rife with rumours of savage attacks directed by the brigands. The knight preferred not to rely on tales fuelled by mistrust and paranoia but equally had witnessed the truly base capabilities of men driven by blood-frenzy in times of war. An exaggerated truth was still at its essence a truth.

Henry was watching the crimson-cloaked man but noticed out of the corner of his eye the woman's right arm slowly begin to slide down the side of her cloak. In less than the blink of an eye, Henry had grabbed the handles of the knives that were tied to the topside of either wrist inside his sleeves and drawn them, and in the same motion held the blade in his right hand up to the woman's throat and the left against her right wrist.

"Don't move, Dragon. I might slip," the knight hissed, his eyes furious and teeth gritted.

The crimson-cloaked woman did as commanded, remaining still as a statue. A huge blade dropped from her right arm sleeve and thumped to the ground, momentarily interrupting the ubiquitous chorus of grasshoppers and crickets in the long, drying grass of the surrounding meadows. The woman's face remained steady, though Henry could she see was blinking more regularly than before the dagger was at her neck.

"We have no quarrel with you, Templar," she uttered, quieter than before though with the same neutral delivery.

"I doubt that. Riding as far as you have in these showy uniforms is somewhat inflammatory, isn't it?" Henry was in no mood for games.

The woman's eyes looked fleetingly to her crimson cloak before darting back to Henry again. "We choose not the path of cowardice and deceit through merging with the crowd as some do, Templar. We know who we are and do not pretend to be otherwise."

"Cowardice?" Henry spat back. "Hiding behind the flames you ignite sounds like cowardice to me."

"*Dewch gyda ni, ffrind,*" the man said, staring straight at Brac.

"What's he saying?" Henry asked Brac, aggressively and urgently.

Brac stumbled a reply. "He... he says for me to go with them." The quarryman lifted his eyes back to the mounted man. Speaking in his native tongue, Brac spoke quickly. "How do you know I'm Welsh? Who are you? And why are you chasing us?"

Even without understanding a single word of what the wiry man had said, Henry knew exactly the questions asked. The knight kept his eyes on the crimson-cloaked woman, who herself retained eye contact.

The crimson-cloaked man replied in a mellow manner, as if the answer was obvious. "You don't belong in London, friend. You have a greater destination, if you'd come with us."

The woman spoke up, feeling the blade against her neck as her throat moved with speech. "And tell your knight that he will live, if you come with us." She stared at Henry and it seemed as if her eyes were mirrors reflecting the perfect blue of the sky.

"What are they saying, Brac?" Henry asked again, increasingly unsettled. His grip on the knife became ever tighter and saturated in sweat. He knew he needed to retain his composure, something that the man and woman seemed to possess in abundance even with Henry's knife against the woman's throat.

Brac wrestled with the reins; his horse was still stamping and rearing its head in stark contrast to the other three animals, feeding off his own nervousness. "They say that if I go with them, you will live..." he said, trailing off a little as he considered the gravity of the threat.

The knight pushed his knife closer to the woman's throat, slightly piercing the skin in two places so that tiny drops of dark red blood trickled down the iron blade and soaked into wooden handle. In response the woman's blinking became more ever more rapid, but this was the only indication of discomfort in her admirable display of cool.

Henry's eyes darkened like an impending storm. "Threatening a knight of the Temple is not wise, Dragon," he warned, "turn around and return to whence you came and the Lord might look kindly upon your transgressions. You might only suffer repercussions in this life and not the next."

The woman broke her eye contact with Henry, her eyes scooting to Brac whose horse was still dancing behind Henry's left shoulder and then back to the knight. She began speaking in Welsh again. "The discovery you made, it means more than you can imagine right now, and you won't understand how much it means for us unless you come with us. God is with all four of us here, but He does not want you to go to England with the Knight. Madog ap Llywelyn is not the Prince of Wales; the battle at Maes Moydog was not decisive."

The woman's throat pulsated increasingly quickly as her breathing became ever more shallow, the slow trickle of red from the nicks on her neck continually replenished by the instability of Henry's own shaking, knife-holding right hand.

The wiry man thought his heart was trying to explode from his chest. What did the woman mean about the discovery? And what did Madog ap Llywelyn have to do with this? Henry had promised him safety in London, and there was no chance he could return to Rhuddlan having disappeared immediately following a theft at the quarry; he would be as good as dead.

But they had threatened to kill Henry! Their composure was unsettling and Brac did not doubt they would carry through such a threat, especially given the woman had been carrying a huge knife... though Henry had been carrying two, and Brac was not sure that Henry was the type to outright kill someone, though he clearly had fought in battles in the Holy Land years before. A week previous Brac had had no idea of Henry's existence, nor for that matter these Welsh riders.

Henry growled at the woman again. "I said, turn around and leave us. Tell your man to turn his horse around and leave. Then you will go with him."

157

The Englishman recognised the name of Madog ap Llywelyn, the last Prince of Wales. He had heard of Madog's defeat to the Earl of Warwick at Maes Moydog earlier in the year and rumour suggested the prince had been captured by the Earl of Arundel's men in recent weeks. These Dragons were almost certainly appealing to Brac's sense of partisanship.

Silence fell heavily over the group, the buzzing of crickets and insects melting seamlessly into the background, catalysed by the tension of the standoff. The man addressed Brac once more, in Welsh. "This is not your fight, friend. Your fight is back in your own land. Come with us, and the knight will not have to die. You have our word."

It had been a few days since Brac had last wished he had never said anything to the Frenchwoman and the Englishman in the tavern that night, and presently once more that regret washed over him like rainfall. He was pretty sure he had made a terrible mistake that evening but resolved that he would not make such errors again in future. Especially an error that would lead to Henry being killed, as unlikely as that circumstance currently appeared what with the knight holding two knives to the woman.

But these Dragons – that was what Henry had called them - repeated and discomfortingly calm threats in spite of the woman's position suggested they were confident of overcoming such difficulties and delivering on their promise. Anxieties raced through Brac's mind, threatening to overwhelm him; he did not know what these people would do to him if they were to kill Henry. What would anyone do to him if Henry were killed? He could not travel through England alone.

"I'll come with you," Brac said in his typical low and almost embarrassed tone. It was a snap decision. The wiry man had previously heard of these Dragons only through hearsay; it was difficult to come by information of the revolt from other areas because many in Rhuddlan were actually sympathetic to the English, chief among them the sheriff John Reeves, toady to the Lord de Grey.

The bearded blond man smiled, which was the first indicator of any emotion from either of the crimson-cloaked pair since the confrontation began. He spoke in English to Brac, for Henry's benefit. "Very good. The Templar will go free with his life."

Henry was startled a little by the sudden and rather audacious decree, glancing up and left at the man who remained upon his horse. At this momentary slip in concentration the woman kicked her right leg up with very little back lift and crashed her knee into Henry's groin, throwing her head backwards away from the blade. The knight grunted and doubled over in pain, falling to his knees and dropping the knife from his left hand, the grip remaining strong on the one in his right. The woman regained her balance and swiftly crouched to pick up her own discarded blade in her right hand. She stood up before Henry; the knight straightened his body in time to see the woman's boot come flying as she kicked him viciously in the left side of his head.

In the one or two seconds it had taken the woman to nullify the knight's threat, her colleague had skilfully driven his horse up alongside Brac's mount and drawn his own dagger at Brac. Brac was watching the scene unfold with gaping mouth, and when he turned his head at the approach of the blond man he froze rigidly in his saddle at the sight of the blade. The blond man maintained his mellow expression, slightly inclining his head to the left and blinking slowly in a non-verbal demand that Brac not do anything rash.

Henry slumped to the road and smashed his face into the hard earth. Immediately a heavy cloud of pain came down over his eyes. The impact of the woman's boot had been sickening and he rolled over clutching his head with both hands momentarily, before sitting up and seeing the woman climbing onto her horse. His survival instincts successfully battled the intense desire to just lie down and close his eyes and he roared at the woman.

"Where is your honour, Dragon?" The knight groggily climbed to his feet, clearly unbalanced and now without his knives. "This is no way to fight!"

He shambled towards the blond rider as composed as he could. Given the sick feeling he had in his stomach from taking the knee to his groin, and the fog of pain around his head, his body screamed for him to curl up on the floor but the Englishman's mental fortitude and dedication to duty was not to be outdone.

Brac rode his horse between Henry and the crimson-cloaked woman, blocking the knight's path and forcing him to a stop. The wiry Welshman looked down at the bloodied Englishman with sorrow on his face.

"Please, stop, Sir Henry Please," he beseeched the knight, hoping the use of his full title would cut through the concussion and appeal to Henry's senses.

Henry placed a hand on the flank of Brac's horse to steady and compose himself. Brac had not called him 'Sir' before; not many people did, and in doing so it had reminded Henry of who he was; a knight of the Temple charged with carrying the burdens of a gentleman and a monk. This fight was over. Vengeance and retribution were unbecoming behaviour in anyone, let alone a man in his position, and he could not possibly win this fight. They were two skilled combatants on horseback, and he was an unarmed man with concussion.

Henry squinted as he looked up at Brac, the afternoon sun just behind Brac's head from his perspective. "God be with you, friend. Perhaps our paths will cross once more, hopefully in less stressful circumstances." He offered his right hand to Brac, who grasped it with his own before Henry slapped the top of the horse's hind leg to set it off on a trot.

The man and woman in crimson cloaks trotted after the wiry Welshman without turning back to the English knight, who was left standing alone on the deserted road. Henry put his hand to his head, partially cradling his aching temple and also to shield his eyes from the sun. *At least they didn't take the horse*, he mused, determining to concentrate on the victories and not the defeats.

Retaining possession of the black palfrey was more than crucial to the knight. He needed to return to the Temple to warn of the aggregating list of groups who were compromising the stone's secrecy, of which the Dragons were the latest but perhaps most worrying.

Chapter 12

The Comte de la Marche slapped his hand to his face and dragged his palm down his cheek in a sign of conspicuous exasperation before puffing his cheeks and blowing out of his mouth. Matthew Norris was still bolt upright in his chair on the other side of the broad desk. He was uncompromising; a solid wall at the negotiating table against which all of Mathieu's arguments had bounced off. Mathieu did not know if Norris's impeccable posture in his chair was a conscious decision to physically resemble a solid wall so as to match his debating style.

Norris was as livid as he was uncompromising. "The winter. The winter. It's always the winter. Your master is no more than a boy in man's clothing. Does he even know how to count? We're not talking *livres* that you can count on an abacus! *Two hundred thousand livres*. Councillor, this has gone on too long. The money is coming in and your king will learn the true meaning of rendering unto Caesar what is Caesar's."

Norris was a magnificent exponent of the vitriolic; Mathieu respected him for that. He did not like Norris but could appreciate the man's acerbic turn in times of displeasure. Mathieu wondered for a moment how it was that such a prickly man became an Order Master, but then considered the bitter and very personal political infighting across the upper reaches of the wider Church. The Temple was just a microcosm of the whole.

Mathieu leaned back in the high backed chair, resting his elbows on the arms and clasping his hands together over his chest. "Gascony has been opened up to us, father." Mathieu saw Norris roll his light blue eyes. The Master's face was sour like his personality, with jowls hanging down below sharp eyes that in turn were circled by heavy lines, the product of years of frowning. "Within the month, the restoration of wine trade in the south-west will be back to pre-war levels, and revenues doubled given the seizure of the English tariffs. The next-"

161

Norris cut him off. "We have a requirement to consider fiscal *and* moral issues. By contrast, the King only has expedient, military means of raising fresh coin." The Englishman Norris placed his palms flat down on the large desk, his flawless French accent resonating throughout the small room. His voice was not particularly deep but had a piercing quality that could travel though any medium, a wonderful trait for someone required to continually fight against everything Philippe did, Mathieu thought. Norris continued. "My stewardship of this Order will not be tarred with money procured with the spilling of blood." He pursed his lips, slightly inclining his head in a subconscious challenge to the Comte, like a stag facing down a rival.

"Where did your silver come from in the first place, father?" Mathieu was not to allow Norris an easy victory. He deliberately kept his voice down, far quieter than the Englishman's resounding speech.

Norris snapped back instantly. "I have been tasked with cleaning this house and it begins with this house's biggest debtor," he said through almost gritted teeth. "The Temple is not the treasure trove for the King of France, nor any king."

Mathieu paused for a moment and sat upright, slightly leaning over the table. "If I may talk frankly and from an unofficial perspective, father, I dearly beg of you to hold off the recollection – you know what the King did to the Lombards, don't you?" The Comte maintained his soft approach and his request had thus far not elicited a reaction from Norris.

This was only because Norris was already angry. Norris was permanently angry, Mathieu thought. How could a monk be permanently angry? And more pertinently, how could a permanently angry man be a monk? The Temple was a more opaque organisation than the wider Church and the Comte resolved to investigate it more deeply. He lamented that Le Verre's contact was unable to stop Norris as Mathieu had requested – he would have words with Le Gris about this. How he detested Le Gris.

The Order Master volleyed back, incredulous. "Do you think we are some merchants ripe for recruitment into the King's personal treasury, Comte Mathieu? He is a sinful man who refuses the mother

Church its due, that which would pay back our innocent benefactors who have risked their lives for Christendom. And yet your king keeps their money as his own, in order to wage war against Christians! Philippe is tarring his name with his creditors as we speak, Comte Mathieu, and you know it. Rein him in, before he brings ruin to this kingdom. We have no more to discuss."

No sooner had he finished speaking did Norris stand and walk to the door to his right. He was a remarkably average looking man, average height, dark wavy hair sporadically greying, drowning in a dark brown cloth overcoat that was far too large for him, a brown belt tied around the middle indicating the actual position of his body in the huge garment.

Mathieu too, stood. He picked his wine cup and drained it without thinking, as if it were integral to the locomotion of standing up from a chair. Norris looked disapprovingly as he opened the door, and it juddered and creaked as the wooden panel swung inwards. Mathieu placed the cup back on the desk and walked purposefully across the stone flooring, stopping in front of Norris, looking him in the eye. "Thank you for your time, father. I hope our next meeting may be under more auspicious circumstances."

Norris smiled. "May God bless you, Comte Mathieu. I know you are merely serving. We are ultimately all serving, and may you draw strength from this."

Mathieu nodded his head and turned through the door. Walking along the long corridor that ran through Caesar's Tower, the smaller tower of the Paris Temple, he pondered the predicament. Breaking the news to Philippe in the afternoon would be difficult, but Lemaître's presence would absorb some of the damage from the King's anger.

Just as well it were he taking responsibility. A lesser man would see his career at court cut short for a failure of this magnitude. Mathieu clenched his fists as he walked, his wide shoulders rolling with his strides through the remarkably well-lit corridor. He did not know how one corridor with one window at one end could remain as illuminated as if it had no roof. There were barely any candles! The Paris Temple complex was truly a wondrous construction; and it was to be expected, because the Order could call on the finest stonemasons and builders in the kingdom. It was seldom Mathieu visited, but when he did, he always took the time in spite of the business at hand to appreciate the architecture of Caesar's Tower and its bigger brother, the Great Tower. It allowed him to consider that there was an existence outside of court machinations and state politics, an actual, physically conceivable and accessible world, the world provided by God, the world above and beyond the petty scheming of fallen man.

The ornately carved double doors, heavy as were those at the entrance to the Great Tower, required no little effort to open. But Mathieu was a strong man and he almost smashed through them in to the sunlight; he drew peculiar satisfaction from bursting through double doors. The mid-morning sun was beating down with the intensity of a blacksmith's forge, surprising him every time he exited a building.

Outside, to the right of the doorway, Roger and Jean were sat in the shade of the tower, helmets off and one shield upside down on the grass between them. The spymaster's dramatic appearance through the doors gave them both the fright of their life, which also lost them the wherewithal to hide the dice they were throwing before Mathieu caught them.

He stopped walking forward looked down at the two men-at-arms, both with gormless looks of surprise on their faces. After a brief moment they both scurried to their feet, throwing helmets on and fiddling around with the shields trying to strap them to their respective left arms. Mathieu watched the flurry of panic and activity for a few seconds before deciding to put the soldiers out of their misery.

"Well, gentlemen. What would Father Norris say if he caught you sullying this house's name with your gambling and games?" Mathieu did not expect them to answer, and they did not. Every time he caught them gambling and playing games they offered him nothing but dull eyes in return.

"Sorry, my lord," Roger stumbled, acutely embarrassed and consciously trying not to right his helmet having hurriedly put it on askew. He was a tough man, Roger; probably in his mid-thirties,

164

always dependable and industrious, rarely drunk, only failing to maintain discipline with his penchant for gambling.

"My lord," repeated the younger Jean. His curly blond hair billowed out from underneath his open face helm and together with in his perturbed state he had the appearance of a man just dragged through a hedge.

Mathieu regarded the two guards and pulled his lower lip under his upper in a thoughtful expression. "*Mmm.*" Unimpressed, though cutting short the admonishment, the Comte turned abruptly and strode to where his horse Pinto stood placid in the shade of a young apple tree.

The bay chestnut mare, a fine rouncey he had owned from a foal, was lazily inspecting the low-hanging branch for any fruit the burgeoning tree had to offer. One or two partially-mushed apples strewn on the long grass suggested she had quite enjoyed her time whilst her master tried to save the kingdom's finances.

Mathieu brushed his hand through the mare's mane and fiddled with the tied reins. He mounted swiftly and beckoned the guards join him return back across the city. They would be needed to clear a path through the congested central streets, even the wide avenues around Notre Dame, filled as they were with the most ungodly of traders and hawkers. The Comte often wondered when someone would remind them of the Lord Jesus casting out the moneylenders from the temple in Jerusalem.

Dismissing Roger and Jean, Mathieu dismounted and unenthusiastically walked over the hot dirt towards the doorway of his house. The heat during the ride had been almost insufferable. He lifted the cross latch and shouldered open the old grey door, beyond which was a murky shadow that overwhelmed the hallway, punctuated only by slight reflections of the newly admitted daylight on edges and surfaces that faced the door. Knowing his eyes would quickly adjust to the change in light conditions Mathieu marched forwards into the dark. Up ahead the maid Berenice crossed from one room to another. She noticed the fatigued-looking Comte and stopped in her tracks.

"My lord," she greeted him, curtseying with a smile that was clearly forced. Mathieu did not consider himself too hard on his staff, reasoning that if he were working his fingers to the bone in service of the kingdom then so should the household he headed. Berenice's almost ragged appearance suggested otherwise, however; even with the rings around her eyes and the puffy cheeks below them, she still looked less than thirty years old, but were she to remove her bonnet her greying hair was testimony to practically a lifetime of service to the Comte's family.

Of course, even if Mathieu had not been one of the least approachable men in the kingdom neither Berenice nor any of the other servants would have complained, such was their station. They were good Christians and persevered diligently - was there any other way? For years the Comte had been very content with his staff, because they went about their work with minimal fuss - they had no choice - and whilst not all as stealthy as the mouselike Pascal, Mathieu sometimes went days barely noticing their presence.

"Good morning, Berenice. Have you seen Jaqueline?" he curtly asked. Mathieu had always found it bitterly ironic that he was a man with strong distaste for talking to the vast majority of people but possessed skills that required him to do so, *and yet* he could barely exchange a word with the one person with whom he desired to converse. He had the means to obtain, attain or accomplish anything of he so fancied but could barely talk to his own wife.

"The Lady Jaqueline is in your chamber, my lord," replied Berenice, whilst looking down at the floor as form dictated.

"Thank you," Mathieu sighed, almost ruefully. He was partially hoping his wife would not be in so he would be spared the torment of seeing her whilst enduring the heartache of being her husband in name only. Straightening his posture to his full height, which was almost as tall as the ceiling, he strode past Berenice, the timid maid not slinking away until she heard him open the door further down the corridor.

The Comte entered the room and discovered his wife sat in a chair facing away from the door, hunched over with something on her lap. He guessed it was her vielle, her favourite instrument, a most beautiful specimen she had had commissioned at a woodworkers' in the city. He did not know why she had taken up such a lowly instrument, usually the preserve of minstrels and the occasional beggar, but Mathieu had not heard a more gifted player.

"I'm leaving the city, soon," Mathieu stated, expecting Jaqueline to look up from her vielle.

"*Mmm.*" She continued scrutinising the strings on the instrument, meticulously fiddling with the wooden screws in the pegbox at the top end of it, leaning close in so that a few strands of her long, dark brown hair cascaded down to brush her nimble hands. "And where are you going?" she asked, though Mathieu suspected she was asking merely from courteous habit rather than genuine interest.

The spymaster walked to the bench underneath the window and took in the warmth. The great window in their bedchamber looked out to the south, across the gardens, and the faded quilts and cushions piled up on the bench were testimony to the years of sunlight streaming through into the room. It was a wonderful position from which to watch the outside world, if he had the leisure time in which to do so. Mathieu saw very quickly that he was blocking Jaqueline's light and so danced to the right, into the shade, before turning to see his wife illuminated, almost as if the heavens were shining on her alone in the world.

"I have to meet with the Flemings... again," he finally replied, rubbing the base of his palm against his right eye and then left for the relief it provided him from the morning's stress. "Will you be coming with me?"

She looked up and her emerald eyes caught the light so that they appeared an unnaturally bright shade of green, like the colour of the first leaves of spring on a sunny day. "Dampierre could probably do with something nice to look at when he's being told off in his own house," she said playfully. "It's the least the old man deserves."

"Well, the Queen shall be in attendance, so what would you be offering?" Mathieu jested. The Comte's gaze lingered on Jaqueline's face long enough to see the corners of her mouth twitch

167

as she tried to suppress a smirk before he looked back out of the window.

Jaqueline plucked a string on the instrument, and then another. Satisfied with her handiwork, she picked up the bow and put her finger to the black horse hair, enjoying the fine sensation on the pad of her fingertip, then lifted the instrument to her chin and began playing. It was a song with which Mathieu was familiar, a piece usually accompanied by singing, entitled 'The Miller's Daughter'. The tune was light and pacey in keeping with the humorous lyrics, which depicted a young man's pursuit of a fair maiden who continually rejects him and yet he is not to be dissuaded, conjuring ever more imaginative ways to woo her. It was popular in the taverns of Paris, and even Mathieu enjoyed hearing it, despite the fitness of the lyrics to his current predicament. When he first presented Jaqueline with an instrument all those years ago, they would sit in the evening, her playing and him singing. He smiled at the thought.

Mathieu was still leaning his right arm up against the window frame, watching the butterflies erratically weave in and amongst the flowers when Jaqueline finished playing. She noiselessly placed the vielle down on the stool to the left of her chair and lightly placed the bow on top, so gently as if daring it to unbalance and fall to the floor. She stood, slender and willowy in a magnificent long-sleeved royal blue tunic with a fitted white chemise underneath. Not just any tunic, but the finest product of Jerome le Couturier down on the Rue Neuve. The shimmering golden seams somehow added form to the shapeless garment; Mathieu could see the sharp angle of her wide, thin shoulders and the curve of her hips. The Comte had learned of splendid Greek statuary throughout the old Roman Empire, all extolling the perfect human form, and imagined that none matched the perfection embodied by Jaqueline.

"I'm not coming to Flanders, Mathieu," she leaned on the left-hand side of the window frame, the long sleeve of her tunic slightly falling down her arm exposing the chemise sleeve underneath. The chemise became almost transparent in the sunlight, silhouetting her arm. Mathieu had noticed this and thought about the fact that he had not seen her bare arm, or bare anything, in months.

168

The Comte looked over at her, sullenly. He had expected her to say this, but the rejection was no less crushing. She had always let him down in that manner - delaying an answer long enough for her husband's hopes to rise before inevitably dashing them. "Attendance isn't mandatory, anyway. I'll have Berenice assemble my things…"

Jaqueline spun away from the window and back to the side table, picking up the vielle and once more scrutinised the sleek animal gut strings. "Luc is coming up to see me, with Mathilda and the baby. He wrote me a few days ago." Her voice sounded disinterested, as if such information about Mathieu's own son and grandchild were of no interest to him.

"I didn't see any letter!" the Comte responded, the volume of his booming voice rising high. He immediately readjusted it to better suit the proximity of the two, but the hurt remained. "How is a man in my position not aware his own grandchild is coming up from Guéret?"

Jaqueline walked round to her side of their bed and moved around assorted pots and casks on a long bench up against the wall. Mathieu never knew what she kept in those pots and casks nor did he have any interest in finding out, but the revelation of secret letters between his wife and their youngest son was sparking his curiosity.

"Your powers aren't waning yet. Luc just sent the letter to Saint-Germain-des-Prés. He guessed we're not often in, so he went for the next most obvious option." Her tone was almost condescending and it grated on the Comte.

"So he wrote you, but not us? The first time he's bringing his child to the capital and he doesn't tell his own father?" said Mathieu incredulously. Beyond the immediate question of why Luc was only informing his mother and not his father, Mathieu suspected something was not quite right about the letter being delivered to the abbey at Saint-Germain-des-Prés, just down the road from the de la Marche household.

Jaqueline stopped rearranging the pots and casks, the new organisation of which seemed to make no difference to Mathieu, and considered the annoyance carved into her husband's usually stern features. "He appreciates what you do and doesn't want to step on your toes. Not every son has a father who's at the beck and call of

169

the King. And to prove his point, you'll be in Flanders anyway." She turned back to her ostensibly purposeless rearranging.

Mathieu knew he was not going to win this one. He rolled his eyes up to the timber beamed-ceiling and took in a deep breath, breathing out heavily through his nose. "And how many letters has he sent to the abbey?"

"Just the one or two. Like I said, he doesn't want to burden his father."

Mathieu's ire was rising. "One or two? And when were you going to tell me about these letters? A man should know how things are with his grandchild."

"You have plenty of people in plenty of places, Mathieu. You would hear on the grapevine eventually." Jaqueline remained by the pots, keeping her back to her husband, her composure remaining ice cold.

No one in the kingdom could better the Comte in debate except Jaqueline. He felt he had at some long distant moment past been cursed to love and obsess over this woman regardless of her actions. Mathieu just fell to pieces whenever she was near.

He went to reply, to ask for how long his wife had excluded him from the conversations with their son, but no words came out. He knew he personally could have written Luc. Where was the time for familial correspondence, though? Being the eyes and ears of an entire kingdom was a time consuming responsibility.

The spymaster sighed dejectedly, defeated in the domestic sphere once again. He was not truly the head of his household. "Where's the dog?" he finally said, trying to not sound too despondent.

"He's in the kitchen," Jaqueline said, without stopping what she was doing, "he hasn't moved since you left this morning."

Mathieu reluctantly hauled himself away from the window. "Things would have been better if I hadn't moved since this morning," he grumbled under his breath, aware that Jaqueline would not have been paying attention to him anyway. As the sun's direct warmth gave way to the cooler, shaded innards of the house, Mathieu thought how apt the light and temperature change was – the outside world was bright and glorious, but nowadays every building he entered just seemed cold and unwelcoming, bringing only discontent and unfulfilment. Whilst in the sunlight, Jaqueline had been the girl he married; joking, content, musical; but when she retreated into the shadow, she told him she was not joining him because their second son had been secretly communicating with her regarding a visit. Excluding Mathieu. His father! And the less said about the room in which he talked with Norris earlier in the day, the better.

It did not take long for the Comte to cast aside his malaise upon finding the old retriever sprawled square in the middle of the stone kitchen flooring, the majority of his white coat bathed in the light flooding in through the large south-facing window. It was unlikely Jaqueline had exaggerated when she said Quo had not moved all morning. Mathieu walked around the large, heavy table in the centre of the room – a monstrous artifice built to withstand all manner of chopping and beating in the name of dinner preparation – and crouched down next to the old boy, his knees clicking as he did so. Even so Quo still did not stir. Mathieu watched the dog's abdomen rise and fall with long, slow breaths, and occasionally his front left paw would twitch, then the back two also, as he dreamt. Mathieu thought of how much time he must have spent whilst at his desk in the office, watching his friend dreaming; it had a mesmeric quality to it.

The Comte reached out with his right hand and gently stroked the back of the dog's neck and after a few moments he slowly and not without a struggle opened his eyes, blinking in the light as would a man waking up with the dawn, before lifting his head up and round to his master. Immediately his unusually bushy tail, which seemed to feather out in all directions at the end as if it were a huge brush rather than the usual vertical manner typical of retrievers, began sweeping the floor and he bared his teeth in his characteristic smile. Mathieu leant forward, cradling the old boy's head against his chest and pressing his own forehead down on top.

"Hello boy! How are you today? I have missed you, boy, yes." Quo responded with a strained whining sound that substituted for talking. "You're talkative today, aren't you, Quo. Come on, let's go outside. I'm tired of this house."

Man and dog rose to their feet in a laboured fashion, both lacking the youth of their prime, but once up and about there was a spring in

171

the step of both. Mathieu and Quo seemed to perk each other up, as if each were dependent on the other for energy and vigour. Watching the old boy trot along ahead, out of the open door into the gardens, Mathieu knew they had a mutual dependence for *joie de vivre* at the very least. He stood on the yellowing grass and saw the white retriever almost bounce along the rows of roses, violets and marigolds that Jaqueline had painstakingly planted, sniffing out anything of interest as dogs are wont to do.

The plants were holding up remarkably well given the lack of rainfall, again probably Jaqueline's doing. The quiet of the immediate surroundings was glorious; to the south, the hum of the residential areas along Rue de la Harpe and the commercial district on Grand Rue Saint-Jacques was carried far on the wind. To the west, the old Merovingian palace rose high, commanding a view of the entire city from its central point on the Île de la Cité. Beyond that was the Louvre Palace of Philippe Augustus, preferred by the King. But the relative tranquillity of this little garden in Les Augustins, with Quo and the roses and violets and marigolds, could have been on the other side of the world from Norris and the court as far as Mathieu was concerned.

"My lord," a small voice murmured behind him. The Comte nearly jumped out of his skin.

"For the love of... Pascal, don't do that to me!" Mathieu patted down his black overcoat to restore the appearance of composure, taking a couple of deep breaths.

"I'm sorry, my lord," Pascal stated, more authoritatively this time. There was a lack of sincerity in his apology, but Mathieu did not really care. Pascal was attached to the Maison de la Marche for the matters of business, and Mathieu knew that Pascal would *only* request his attention for matters of business. If he needed to be shocked out of a daydream then so be it.

"What happy tidings do you bring me today?" asked Mathieu sardonically. "In exchange, I have news for you regarding the Norris problem."

"Unfortunately, my lord, the King has news for *you* regarding the Norris problem. He's calling forward your scheduled meeting, to now." Pascal looked at Mathieu, then away at Quo, who was rolling on his back on the grass, sneezing with the exertion and excitement. *He is a peculiar dog*, Pascal thought.

Mathieu sucked his upper lip, exposing his bottom front teeth. "Hmm," he pondered, "news indeed." He did not fancy traversing the heaving city quite so soon having just returned from the other side of the river. "Who will be present?"

"The King, the Queen, yourself, Lemaître, de Clermont, de Bourgogne and the King's brother. He's not in a good mood." Pascal was blunt as ever.

"I don't blame him," rumbled Mathieu with the air of a man about to attend his own execution. "I mean, I'm furious with this whole mess, and I'm not the man with no money." Mathieu smiled a little at his own joke, but quickly forgot such human emotion as humour in favour of his usual solemnity – only Jaqueline and Quo were familiar with this side of the Comte's personality. "Go tell Roger and Jean they are needed again. And confiscate their dice if they're playing. I'll find Pinto."

"Yes, my lord," Pascal said whilst bowing, turning to leave before he had returned fully upright.

"Oh, and Pascal," added Mathieu, causing the scribe to spin back to face him, still not upright, "who do we know in the abbey down at Saint-Germain-des-Prés?"

The mouse-like man paused and stared over the ashlar-faced limestone garden walls. He searched his library-like mind for the name of the young, bright-eyed sister at the convent. "Clémentine," he announced finally.

"Ah, yes. Be sure to ensure she keeps an eye on correspondences in and out of the abbey, please, particularly those to and from Guéret."

Again Pascal bowed in his funny little way and shot off to look for the two men-at-arms whilst Mathieu called for Quo to come in. Much like the blond Jean earlier scrambling to dress correctly having been caught playing dice, the dog looked as if he had been dragged through a bush, which he practically had done so himself. Unlike the blond Jean, Quo could not have looked happier, tongue out, eyes wide and tail wagging manically. Mathieu bent down to give his old friend a fuss and held Quo's head between his hands, ruffling the dog's ears and neck whilst kissing the top of his head.

"If only I could bring you to the palace with me, boy. You'd like it there. The King wouldn't, but you would." He stood and began walking back to the kitchen door. Mathieu thought about it and concluded that there were two things stopping him taking Quo to the palace, and neither of them involved the King; one was that the journey was too far for the old boy, and the other being Lemaître's presence at court. Mathieu would not wish Lemaître's presence on any man or beast.

Chapter 13

The King's council chamber was the largest room in the palace, larger than the kitchens and even the larder; with a long beech table running down the middle flanked by high-backed oak chairs, cumbersome brutes built to withstand any bouts of emotion or anger from their users. Along the walls were the torch and candleholders fixed with iron rivets into the sheer oak wall panes, interspersed with hanging banners and pennants in royal blue adorned with the *fleur-de-lis*. There were no windows yet the illumination was superb without the accompanying risk of fire – no one in Christendom underestimated the risk of fire.

Mathieu was the last to arrive, he noticed to his regret. The King and Queen were at the centre of the table on the right hand side as the Comte entered. On the opposite side were Jean Lemaître de Chartres, as ever a void of darkness in an otherwise colourful environment; fearsome Raoul de Clermont with his scars and brooding eyes; there also was Duke Robert de Bourgogne with an amiable expression juxtaposed with the hostile atmosphere around him; and beyond him Charles de Valois, the King's brother – not as striking as Philippe, with a wide face and long, flat nose ending in a rather bulbous manner, and limp brown hair hanging down the sides of his face underneath a black hat.

As usual Charles looked daggers at Mathieu. The Comte de Valois had never taken to the Comte de la Marche. Mathieu suspected that Charles believed the Comte de la Marche had disproportionate access to and influence over the King. Philippe knew Charles' strengths and weaknesses and it was simply unfortunate for the latter that the strengths only manifested on the battlefield. But family was family, and the county of Valois was sufficiently close to Paris that Philippe had no choice but to extend invitations to his younger brother.

"My king, my queen," Mathieu said deferentially, bowing as he did so. Straightening up, he turned his gaze to the four men across the table from the King and Queen and greeted them in turn. "My lords," he announced solemnly, inclining his head as he did so. Queen Jeanne smiled at him and the lords across the table nodded their head in return. Philippe did not acknowledge Mathieu's entrance, giving the impression that he was reading a letter in front of him.

As he walked to his seat next to Charles, Mathieu studied King Philippe's face, all furrowed brow and clenched jaw. He knew Philippe was not truly reading the letter but instead simply stared at it indignantly so that everyone present knew he was unhappy with its content, probably as a show to intimidate the Comte de la Marche.

It was only natural to have an aversion to the anger of others but there was no escape from the hostile atmosphere in this royal bear pit. Fortunately for him, Mathieu was particularly thick-skinned and so the King's conspicuous and deliberate show of displeasure was water off the Comte's back. He pulled out the high-backed chair, ornately carved at the top and centre with the royal crown of France and Navarre, the *fleur-de-lis* repeated five times around the centre supporting the roof of the crown, itself topped by a further fleur and eased himself down. The spymaster shuffled the chair forward and with it the scraping of the legs across the stone floor was uncomfortably loud in the heavily tense silence.

Philippe placed the letter down, straightening it fussily so the bottom edge lined up perpendicular to the table. He placed his elbows either side of the paper and slowly crossed his arms, lifting his eyes up to meet Mathieu's.

"Tell me, Mathieu, why it is that the Temple have called in the loans?" The King spoke coolly, his words loaded with the suggestion that he would pay no heed to any response given.

Mathieu placed a hand on either arm of the high-backed chair before replying. "Sire, I have spoken with Norris to-"

"I don't care if you've spoken to Rome!" Philippe barked as he stood up, not slamming his palms on the table but certainly ensuring everyone heard it. "You had one task, Mathieu. Norris does not know his place." Philippe looked up and down the table for signs of support. Lemaître and de Clermont, men not well versed in the art of empathy, remained stony-faced. Duke Robert shook his head almost imperceptibly, catching Philippe's eye, which prompted the King to sit back down.

Mathieu spoke up, unperturbed by the King's outburst. "It is unfortunate, yes, but not disastrous. It does not necessitate a rash response on our part, Sire," he spoke, intending to come across as reassuring, trying to defuse the situation.

"Are you patronising me, Comte?" the King shot back, blue eyes piercing and mouth sneering. Jeanne placed a hand on the King's right arm to temper his fury. Mathieu thought of the Bishop of Pamiers' description of Philippe as an emotionless statue. The Bishop had clearly not seen many statues.

"The Comte makes a valid point, my King," said the Queen, gently. The effect was immediate and at once Philippe's grimace softened, and he sat a little further back in his chair. Jeanne continued, "and in all of this, there is opportunity. Norris is playing our games now, and it would be fair to show him how our games are played."

She took her hand away from her husband's arm, clasping her hands together on her lap and looked at Mathieu. The Comte responded with a shrewd smile. She was not much older than twenty years and yet here she was, quelling the King's anger and putting ideas to the table that had evidently left at least two of Philippe's closest circle bemused; the Duke narrowed his eyes in contemplation, and Charles shared his brother's blank expression. Her rounded face, pretty but not striking, was the very picture of innocence and virtue but behind it was an intellect more in keeping with Mathieu's calculating mindset than her husband's more direct approach.

"Her Majesty is on to something here, Sire," he spoke, lifting his head so as to address the table rather than just the King directly, and then looked left down the table before continuing, "my dear Comte Lemaître, I assume you have seen the particulars of the Temple's demands?"

The great stone monolith cloaked in black tunic and overcoat sitting at the far end of the small congregation responded as bleakly as he always did. "I have." No further elaboration was necessary, because Lemaître had answered the question at hand.

Robert de Bourgogne hefted himself round in his chair to face the master of the treasury. "Are the Temple loans propping up this kingdom, my dear Comte? Please, a little detail if you would." The Duke knew Lemaître well and was familiar with the need to pry for further information.

"The recollection of the loans will be problematic if the King wishes to continue funding the enemies of King Edward, whilst maintaining armies in the field," he boomed. If the manner of speech of the King and his circle were like deer flitting about the forest, delicate and subtle, then Lemaître's speaking style was slow, heavy and unwieldy as a pregnant cow. "The Comte d'Artois reports that the Gascon wine trade is weeks away from full rehabilitation. He also reports that the English Earl de Lacy did not have a great treasury with him when he was taken prisoner, nor have the English castles provided much silver."

Mathieu, who was now sat with his right elbow planted on the table, scratching his stubble, spoke up. "The money is there, somewhere, but the population are hiding it. With the greatest respect, Philippe, there is little love for northern French kings in Aquitaine."

Lemaître spoke up once more, startling people as if had just materialised from thin air. His intercession also took the table's attention away from the uncomfortable truth regarding Philippe's popularity in the southwest of the country, of which they all, including the King, were aware. "Both Robert d'Artois and Jean de Vendôme have used a great deal of their personal treasuries, and the crown is currently unable to offer loans."

"Which places our consolidation in Aquitaine in jeopardy, were Edward to strike back in force," said the Duke de Bourgogne, adding a conclusion where Lemaître would not have.

The King, now calmer than earlier and altogether more recognisable as the restrained and contemplative figure he was seen as by those outside the Maison du Roi, glanced at Mathieu. "*Will* the English come back?"

Mathieu removed his right hand from his face and placed it over his left on the table. "Unlikely. King Edward has as little money as do we, and fewer ships. I am working on the Scottish and Welsh to

178

keep him occupied. The latter have been particularly cooperative." The spymaster thought it appropriate to not delve too far into his machinations in that theatre.

Raoul de Clermont's bass voice rumbled across the table, the acoustic interpretation of a landslide of stone and rock. "All the same, Comte Mathieu, I should recommend moving the Marseilles fleet to Normandy, keep Edward pinned down on three sides."

"And prevent any English movement to Flanders," said the Duke, jumping in again and nodding his approval of de Clermont's plan.

Philippe agreed. "Yes, very well. Mathieu, have the fleet move immediately. The Mediterranean is quiet – neither the Aragonese nor the Italians have stomach for a fight."

"Very well, Sire," Mathieu replied, enjoying the business of serious politics far more now the King had recovered from his tantrum. He eyed Jeanne. *She's good at this. Very good*, he thought. She was oblivious to the Comte's scrutiny. "The Aragonese and Italians have not the capacity to fight even if they had stomachs in the first place."

Lemaître shattered the positivity of the previous decision with a blunt interjection. "There are sufficient reserves to pay the Emperor, but after that, we shall require new creditors."

The Queen replied to the Master of the Treasury, the two representing a strange dichotomy in appearance, vocals and perspective, and yet each integral to the Maison's work. Her voice was so young but possessing a learnedness that commanded attention and respect. Mathieu had often mused on the importance of gravitas in one's voice; pure aesthetics were essential, of course; but without gravitas, the aesthetics counted for nought. Those around the table possessed the right combination of appearance forcefulness of speech. Without these two traits, one could have the intellect of Thomas Aquinas yet no one would notice a word one said.

"There are still a few weeks until the harvest," said Jeanne suggestively and cryptically. *She is very clever*, thought Mathieu.

She looked to Philippe, who appeared to have understand to what his wife was alluding. "Raoul," he asked, "how ready are your men?"

"They could march now, Sire. The Comte de Valois has kept them from boredom," said the heavily scarred man, his long, greased, black hair surely covering further cuts and wounds underneath. The soldiers in camp often referred to him as 'Butch', an abbreviation of 'the Butcher's block', on account of how many hacks he could take without breaking.

"Robert, you are to muster men in the Île-de-France and surrounding countryside. You have three days, and they are to be armed as can afford," commanded Philippe. The King was not often inclined to make spur-of-the-moment decisions, and Mathieu suspected Philippe's proactivity was at least partially catalysed by some of the adrenaline from his earlier rage.

The Duke was taken aback. "You can't mean to attack the Flemings now?"

"We shall make hay whilst the sun shines, my dear Duke," answered the King.

"His Holiness will not like this, and it will make the Emperor nervous... I would counsel against such a move." The Duke was respectful but uncompromising, taking a paternal tone as he usually did.

"The Emperor would not dare make a move," Philippe asserted, not if we let it be known that d'Artois and de Vendôme are marching back east." He spoke with an air of nonchalance as if he had already conquered Flanders. "And Pope Boniface, he knows that it is God's Will that kings rule, not counts or dukes. The Comte Dampierre too shall understand this soon enough, just as the Duke of Aquitaine has discovered. Raoul, you shall take my brother with you and capture Bruges and Ghent. That shall be enough the secure our finances until a solution can be found for the Norris problem."

A moment's hush descended on the table as the councillors digested the instructions laid out. Mathieu was uneasy with this strategy and the feeling translated itself into physical discomfort, causing him to shuffle around in his chair. Tactically it was a well-connected plan, but strategically it could be disastrous, he reflected. The Flemings were fierce and under no circumstances friends of the French. And regardless of how stretched they found themselves, the

English would never allow the Flemish cloth markets to fall into French hands.

Further, in battle the French levies would be largely untrustworthy in the event of a setback. The fighting would be decided by de Clermont's usage of his knights, far greater in number than their Flemish counterparts and perhaps the largest concentration of heavy cavalry in Christendom. Mathieu finally sat back in his chair, hands clasped, running through the difficulties to be faced. He knew Philippe would have struck at the Flemish eventually, but did not expect it quite so soon.

"Perhaps I could accompany the Comtes, given the preliminary work I have undertaken in the region," offered Mathieu.

The King nodded. "Raoul, you will move out on the fourth day, picking up levies en route to Arras. By the time you reach the city, I expect the Flemings to have begun levying. Bring me the keys to Bruges and Ghent." Philippe paused, tapping his finger against his cleanshaven chin. "And I want Guy Dampierre and his daughter alive. And tell me, de Clermont, where is that son-in-law of yours, Guy Dampierre's son?"

De Clermont inclined his head, his menacing eyes disappearing beneath the heavy brow. Upon lifting that massive head back up, he spoke in reply. "My brother has taken Guillaume Dampierre into custody; my son-in-law shall not be of assistance to his father."

"Good," concluded Philippe, "which now leaves the Temple."

Duke Robert intervened before Philippe could continue. "We ought to leave the Temple alone for now, Philippe. We are not in a position to fight Rome on this."

The King did not a say anything, but turned to Mathieu, expectantly.

The Comte de la Marche's eyes darted from the King to Duke Robert and back again. It had come to this. He knew it would. A straight debate between two differing types of duty lay ahead – the duty of upholding morality in the eyes of God or the duty towards a king. If he did not mention it now then the Queen would only suggest it instead – the Comte reasoned that if he were to broach the topic he might be able to rein in the debate and bury it. *Better the enemy you know.*

Taking a deep breath, he offered his opinion. "Robert is right. Norris is untouchable, for the moment. *But*, the only opportunity we might have, I believe our lady Queen alluded to earlier." The Queen retained her enigmatic, passive expression. Mathieu continued, "Perhaps we should consider an indirect method of attack. I am not sure of the exact scriptural justification for the Church's exemption from taxation, but I do recall that our Lord Jesus Christ taught us to render unto God what is God's, and render unto Caesar what is Caesar's. In short, tax the Church."

Mathieu immediately felt the need for penance after such a suggestion and shifted uncomfortably. Feeling hot around the collar, Mathieu speculated if he could already feel the flames of hell lapping at him.

The King once more leaned back in his chair, resting his head on the high back so that the carved royal crown on it appeared instead to be sat perfectly on his blond hair. "It has not been done before... Is this not a sacrilege to consider? How will the Church react?" he asked the table, but only expecting answers from Robert and Mathieu. The King used the term 'sacrilege', but his lack of surprise at such an inflammatory suggestion as taxing the Church in turn surprised Mathieu a little; Philippe generally preferred doing things by the book. This council meeting suggested otherwise, however. The Queen must previously have hinted at this suggestion.

Attempting to atone for what he considered his sinful suggestion, Mathieu responded quickest to Philippe. "Badly. This will drag Pope Boniface in, not to mention some of your critics within the kingdom."

"I can talk over the clergy around the city, but the southern bishops will be obstinate," offered Duke Robert, as every the voice of reason to the young king.

"You could quite easily do so, my dear Duke, but perhaps we ought to ponder whether we *should* talk over the clergy around the city," Mathieu offered.

King Philippe rocked forwards and ran both hands through his long, golden hair as he mulled Mathieu's suggestion. "The Pope will fight this, will he not?"

"Undoubtedly," replied de Bourgogne in an uncompromising manner, "but if we were to fully commit to the legal and scriptural

182

minutiae then Rome will have to back down. The Archbishop of Sens is no ally of Boniface and I am sure we can rally more to our side."

Charles de Valois finally spoke up. "Think hard on this, Philippe. You have already gone back on your word of peace, remember."

The King inhaled deeply in a barely concealed display of annoyance. It was particularly galling to Philippe to have his younger brother bring up such a valid yet so personally damning point.

"The King has no need to explain or defend his deeds and words," Jeanne quickly countered.

"I'd say he does, my lady," Charles replied, "otherwise what would be the point of these meetings?"

Mathieu watched and listened to the exchange with curiosity. There was palpable tension between brother- and sister-in-law, perhaps an expression of the greater yet still subtle friction between brother and king.

"The King's words with the Archbishop are his own concern," Duke Robert asserted, speaking down to the Comte de Valois.

"I'd say they were the concern of the men of the Ile-de-France, wouldn't you?" Charles scoffed in return.

"Don't be so naïve," Robert responded. Mathieu thought the two sounded like bickering children but they did make important points, the likes of which the council existed to debate.

"I don't think it's naïve to expect a king to be held accountable for his actions," countered Charles. "The Germans sack their kings if they aren't pleasing enough for the nobles."

Duke Robert laughed. "This is a nonsense, Charles. What do the Germans have to do with this? Have you seen how weak their system is? It is incredible that union stands. It runs on its name alone, and even that's a sham. It's neither holy, nor Roman, nor an empire."

Charles raised an eyebrow, backing down from direct confrontation with one of the realm's greatest statesmen. "Being able to do something doesn't mean it should be done."

Mathieu conceded the Duke of Valois had a point. Mathieu was also surprised that Charles had not only made such an astute observation but that this observation correlated with his own thinking. *Strange and heady times*, he mused.

"The Lord has chosen Philippe as your king and you would have him wallow instead of strengthening the kingdom?" asked Jeanne with an acerbic tongue.

Her question was like a scythe across Charles' argument. There was no way of effectively countering it without sounding either treasonous or blasphemous. Mathieu could see the Queen had a knack for hitting the nail on the head. She would have to be watched.

The Comte de la Marche decided it was time for the sniping to cease. "The Duke is as concerned for the strength of the kingdom as the next man, my Queen. I feel he is merely reiterating the stance I earlier proffered."

"And where do you stand, Comte de la Marche?" Jeanne questioned him, her youthful eyes unblinking and expectant.

Mathieu sighed. He had not expected to be put on trial by one so young, nor a woman and yet here she was, more perceptive than most of the royal inner circle. He noticed the King regarding him with a neutral expression beside Jeanne, leaning against the back and right side of his chair. Philippe seemed perfectly content to allow Jeanne to carry out her own investigation in this matter.

"I merely offered the suggestion for the King's consideration, my lady. I am not afraid to speak my mind," which he almost always did with Philippe, "and admit I have shortcomings over the spiritual validity of such a move, even if it is for the furtherance of this most holy kingdom's strength."

"I didn't have you down for an ally of my brother here, Comte Mathieu," said the King with a slight smile.

"More an ally of Boniface," remarked Jeanne whilst looking accusingly at Mathieu.

The Comte was rather taken aback by the Queen's swipe. "I serve God, and His servants, my lady. Your husband is God's servant and my master," he offered blandly, though not untruthfully. He did not feel the need to defend himself too vigorously precisely because he did not feel there was anything to defend.

"Mathieu is right," Philippe declared grandly, all eyes turning to him. "As a servant of God I have been offered this opportunity to cut down the political and monetary vices that plague our Church. As ever, my dear Comte Mathieu is the voice of balance, and now

184

accompanied by my brother, it would seem. Which is a pleasant addition to your ranks, as opposed to the sycophants in the general council."

Mathieu felt he could see a slight glint of light in what appeared to be a tunnel of gloom, and that was Philippe's continued recognition of the value of a diverse council. His kingship would likely recover from this rash taxation venture, but the day the King stocked his council with the likes of Guillaume de Troyes or Geoffroi d'Hainault then he was truly beyond saving.

All eyes in the room were on the King as he pondered for a moment before slowly standing to his towering full height. At that, the other six at the table stood also, not taking their gaze from the King's fair face. "We have had a productive session, my dear lords. Duke Robert and Comte Jean, you are to work on the tax issue, once the Robert has raised the levies. Mathieu, you are to join Comte de Clermont and my brother in Flanders. Now, *ma chère* Queen," he spoke as he turned to Jeanne on his right, "a spot of lunch?"

Mathieu climbed into the saddle atop Pinto, scratching the mare behind her ears once he had made himself as comfortable as one can in a long tunic on a hot saddle. Pinto and Quo both enjoyed being scratched behind their ears. The only friends he had in the world enjoyed being scratched behind the ears. *Perhaps this is the criterion required for friendship with me,* he contemplated.

Glancing around to check on the progress of his men-at-arms, the Comte saw Jean and Roger were already mounted with reins in their left hands and spears held vertically in their right. Encased in armour, rounded iron helms flashing in the August sunlight, mail *clink*ing sporadically with the slightest of movement, they seemed to Mathieu to be an entirely unforgiving pair and he was grateful for this. His years in the capital had largely been uneventful so far as personal security was concerned though it was of course always prudent to avoid complacency: were an enemy of the kingdom to catch a hint of

Mathieu's significance to the machinery of government and act on it, the two guards could save not only Mathieu but Philippe's crown itself.

Quite simply, there was no other who could accomplish the work he did.

The Comte sat back round in his saddle, satisfied his men-at-arms were set to leave the grounds of the Louvre and move out onto Rue Sainte-Honore. Absentmindedly thinking of how glorious would be a cup of red wine at this very moment, he took the reins in his left hand and his right delved into his pocket, retrieving the small, rolled letter. He had broken the wax seal and read it almost immediately after receiving it from Pascal that morning. He unfurled it and reread its contents, refocusing his mind back to the matters of business. The message in the letter was at once ambiguous yet sufficiently specific to warrant direct and immediate investigation:

English Temple has discovered powerful relic. Now in hands of Edward Longshanks. The power of God is with it and him.

The last sentence unsettled the Comte. He rolled the letter and replaced it in his pocket. "Let's go," he ordered sullenly, and Pinto and the guards' horses rolled forwards, gently and rhythmically rocking their riders in their saddles.

The power of God is with it and him. The letter was sourced from his most trusted English contact, one whom had proved entirely reliable for many years. Whatever the precise meaning, Mathieu had a strange feeling the contrast between the present contexts surrounding the two kings. Edward had obtained this relic whilst Philippe had set about taxing the Church on the Comte's own recommendation. How else could the Lord's favour be interpreted? And what did this mean for Mathieu's own soul?

Such apprehension bordering on distress was an unusual and unwelcome experience for the Comte. But the Maison du Roi had needed to act, and plans had been set into action, and all he wanted to do now was find a cup of wine.

What a shit day. A cup would not be enough, he decided.

Chapter 14

Brac was sore with severely chafed inner thighs and aching legs from three days in the saddle. He was unaccustomed to prolonged periods of riding, and it was remarkable that he was able to ride at all given his upbringing – it was entirely unnecessary for a poor quarryboy to learn how to ride and even more unlikely that one would ever learn how to. Somehow the saddle came naturally to him for reasons he did not care to investigate – he would take any benefits that came his way right now, no questions asked.

Nonetheless three days' solid riding was not natural for him. His long ride with Henry had at least been punctuated with frequent breaks - even the veteran knight needed to stretch his thighs and relieve the pressure on his groin. Furthermore, the morning after leaving Henry, the roasting hot sunshine had given way to a day of sporadic showers, transforming the dusty earth to a soft and fine dark loam that stuck to shoes, clothing and skin with the slightest contact, and since then a muggy atmosphere had prevailed. Accordingly, sweat had been joined by damp and so when Brac had removed his breeches to relieve himself he noticed angry rashes on the insides of his legs. They burnt regardless of how much or little he scratched at them.

He thought about his home, a tiny thatched-roof holding, dark and dank but furnished with a generous grounding of straw that he could afford to replace weekly in the summer thanks to the proximity of the fields to the quarrymen's hamlet. Such luxury, would he know its like again?

His companions were not entirely forthcoming with details of what awaited them at their destination, if indeed a destination awaited them. They seemed comfortable with riding for a whole day, only pausing to allow the horses to rest but never specifically for themselves or Brac. The wiry man figured they had leather for skin under their crimson cloaks. Brac was also adamant the man could not have had balls.

Perhaps these two blond riders lived with horses, like horses, simply roaming. It was a wonderful idea, to be free of obligations to foreign lords and hard toil from dawn until dusk. Perhaps their murky plans, as yet impenetrable to Brac's comprehension, revolved around an itinerant existence. The more he thought about it, the more it made sense, and the more he accepted the apparently endless ride through woodland and across hills, avoiding settlements as they went. It occurred to him they had not passed so much as a hamlet, let alone a walled town or castle. Then again, he reasoned, he had not travelled this far east or south before, so it could well be this part of England was simply empty.

What was it Henry had said to them? Brac could not remember the exact words, but undoubtedly it had been aggressive, a trait he had not seen in the Englishman during their time together. Henry had gone on the offensive even before he was assaulted - after their shared experiences, the wiry man thought it was surely only a significant irritant that would rile the jocular knight.

Poor Henry. The English knight had done everything he could to protect Brac, even when threatened and outnumbered by the crimson-cloaked pair, only for Brac to then abandoned him and leave him shambling on the road after their goodbye, with goodness knows what injuries to his face and elsewhere. The woman had savagely slammed a knee into Henry's groin – maybe these crimson people did not like balls? They were, after all, a hindrance to a life in the saddle - before kicking him around the head.

Brac had thought about Henry a great deal during the ride, about how he had betrayed him. Though had not Henry told him to stand up for himself? The knight may not have expected such a result from his teaching, but Brac's actions were certainly in keeping with them. Even so, the grace with which the English knight had seen him off! Brac almost wished that Henry had cursed him, tried to attack him as he left, but that was not the knight's way. Henry truly was a gentleman; the least English Englishman he had encountered.

In the present, the empty silence was becoming ever more infuriating. Even the hawfinches and wood warblers were not to be heard; these riders truly were masters of avoiding any form of life. Even such a quiet man as Brac needed distraction on occasion. He had asked for clarification of their destination and why he was so integral to their journey, only to be met with platitudes at best and silence at worst. He was pretty sure the most he had heard them speak had been during their exchange three days previously on the road with Henry.

The man rode before him noiselessly but for the soft *clomp* of his light brown mount's broad hooves in the damp earth, muffled by the long, coarse hair around each hoof. Brac had not seen the man's face all morning, or was it now afternoon? The sun was nowhere to be seen because a uniform white-grey canopy wholly covered the heavens and if his time with the two long-haired riders was anything to go by, they would not be stopping to hunt or forage. For all Brac knew, the man ahead could have been asleep for hours and their solemn, miserable caravan was simply being led wherever the man's horse fancied wandering.

So this is it. I'm being led by a horse. Brac mulled over this ludicrous possibility and really hoped he was not losing his mind. He had always been a follower, occasionally chancing his arm only when the risks were low; the exception being the stone that was the source of this misadventure and introspection. *I am being led by a horse because I could not return to my village because I tried to sell a stone to a Frenchwoman.* Adventures did not happen to him or anyone like him. Adventures were for people like Henry who could comprehend the events that were playing out and perhaps, more pertinently, influence those events. *I'm just being led by a horse being ridden by a man who is asleep.*

The slow pace along the rudimentary path through the woods continued. The forest was only lightly wooded and so it was possible to traverse in many directions. Ahead to the right, the low hanging branch belonging to a juvenile acorn tree threatened the blond man's head, and yet he made no attempt to avoid it. The branch almost brushed the blond man's hair. Brac himself leant forwards in an exaggerated motion and then looked over his right shoulder, feeling the stiffness in his neck, and watched the blond woman and her enigmatic face. She too bowed forwards in the saddle to comfortably clear the branch. In a way, Brac found the blond woman terrifying for what she had done to Henry and mostly her inhuman lack of emotions. He was following a horse carrying a sleeping man and was followed by a horse carrying a statue woman.

The wiry quarryman noticed a simple parallel between the glorious sunshine of his travels with Henry and the grey existence of his time with the crimson-cloaked riders. It was no more than an existence, because he was not doing or achieving anything. His companions were achieving the same accomplishments, the accomplishment of simply being, just by being a statue or asleep. Brac needed to do something – working all day with his hands was all he had known since before he could remember; it may not have required conversation or discussion and he would have likely shirked such requirements anyhow, but the variation between clumsy bludgeoning and fine manipulation of the rock of the earth not only caused time to fly but also provided a realisation of his efforts and existence. In short, riding a horse for days with no discernible endpoint was not for him. Brac needed to do something.

And so he did, stopping his horse. The sleeping man's horse halted a few steps later having somehow detected its immediate companion was no longer moving, and the statue's horse followed suit a moment later. The soft hoof-falls were eliminated and the woodland returned to its eerie natural silence. The crimson riders had promised a 'greater destination' than London for him, and to spare Henry's life, thus through these two promises Brac had accepted the journey without disobedience. Now he had stopped his horse at an unscheduled and unpermitted time; this was his first little rebellion.

"You are not happy?" the woman asked without sounding particularly interested in the reply.

Brac shifted in his saddle and turned to the woman, bringing his horse around perpendicular to hers. Stopping his horse was a spur-of-the-moment action, and he had not really considered what he would do to follow it up.

"What is this, this journey? You've not told me anything for days," he complained through his thick beard.

"You agreed to come with us. This was your choice," deadpanned the woman.

191

"You said I should come with you, not to London, and you attacked my friend. It's… it's not my place to argue with… people with swords."

"Your choice," the woman repeated, to Brac's infuriation.

"You have *swords*! When your countrymen find you and threaten your friend and tell you to return to Wales, not England, you go with them!" the quarryman exclaimed, exasperated. He'd quarried rocks with more conversation than these two.

Still the woman remained illusory. "You will see."

Even with the silence of the preceding three days, the quarryman was astounded at the lack of progress in this exchange. "I will *see*? I'm exhausted. Give me a chance to rest today, at least," he entreated with little conviction. He had no stomach for a mental fight with these people, let alone an actual struggle.

The woman did not react, rather continuing to stare with unaffected gaze, but from over his shoulder Brac heard the man's composed voice, sonorous and fluid meandering through the still woodland air, as natural as the gently rustling leaves. "You need to be stronger, there are tougher times to come."

Tougher times, Brac pondered. *Oh good.*

"We are sorry for your friend, but it was necessary," said the blond man with little in the way of genuine remorse. "Casualties are inevitable in times of war, the Englishman is fortunate the Lord showed him mercy."

The blond man looked around, quite disinterested in the conversation. His lack of concern for what had transpired and for the current circumstances unsettled the quarryman, who himself was so inclined to playing over circumstances and decisions both long gone or recent in his mind.

Brac wished he could discard problems from his memory so readily. He had spent too much of the past few weeks thinking over and over the decision to approach the Frenchwoman and the Englishman that evening in the tavern.

But these long-haired riders were of a different, unfamiliar cloth, despite their Welsh accents and clear dislike for the English. Brac needed to know how intensely they disliked the English on account of their apparent propensity for violence. Brac had no strong feelings towards the English himself, of course, but found Henry's treatment particularly difficult to bear, especially given that such treatment was entirely unnecessary – Brac would have gone with them in any case, thanks in no small part to Henry's own words about standing up for oneself.

The blond man continued. "You need to be stronger. You are a quarryman, no? This should be child's play for you. Are you not born of the Clwydian hills? There will be taxing times ahead, most of which being of greater significance than you could imagine." The blond man continued to elicit little in the way of emotion and remained detached from the presumably heavy subject matter to which he was referring. It was as if he was to have no part in it, which Brac doubted very much.

Brac remained unsatisfied with the explanations he had been offered. Pursing his lips as he pulled a troubled expression, he took in a deep breath through his nose that gently swayed the thick bristles of his uncontrolled moustache. Despite having been shaved only a few days previously at the Abbey his facial hair was already returning to its usual bush-like state. He had always found it burdensome in the summer for its insulating properties and so back in the hamlet he frequently sought Rhonwen's assistance in keeping it manageable, for after a few days his beard maintenance became a two-man job. She was a wonderful woman, and what he felt for her on the occasions they spoke was as close to love as he thought he would ever get. Did Rhonwen remember him? Probably not, he had concluded. She was happily married to Glewlwyd the gateman; why would she think about the quiet quarryman when she was married to the Rhuddlan castle gatekeeper?

In any case, Brac stood no chance with Rhonwen now, not after having committed the grave crime of stealing from the King's own quarry. His name would be known across the Flint area as a thief and a coward. The crimson cloaks knew his identity... they were here to take him to Lord de Grey! The realisation struck him and raised the hairs on his arms. The wiry Welshman's eyes darted between the serene faces of his eerie companions. He must have been so blind not to see this before!

193

He had been duped. *Henry was right to not trust them!* How could he have been so gullible? Going with the crimson cloaks was beyond the recklessness of the theft of the stone; at least he ran away after stealing the stone, but now he had meekly handed himself over for certain execution on the back of empty promises of adventure. The empty promises had been exposed after a few days of evasive answers and intense observation, even during the night. On more than one occasion the quarryman had awoken from his grass and weed bedding beneath the trees and stars to find one or the other of the long-haired riders watching over him with the patience and infallibility of the statues he suspected them to be actually be. They were terrible, lifelike statues animated for the sole purpose of bringing him to justice for his crime, able to search and work day and night without fatigue.

Brac saw the woman's jaw clench. He guessed she was anticipating he would take flight. Was this divine justice? It was possible these two otherworldly figures, human but somehow not entirely so, were agents of justice sent by the Lord to seize him and see he receive the punishment he deserved in this life, a punishment that would further lead to the punishment he suspected was waiting in the next.

The idea of fleeing was tempting yet too obvious. The woman had apparently speculated Brac would flee before he himself had decided. His paranoia began spiralling.

Brac then glanced at the man, whose serene expression remained, the picture of calm and with no conspicuous physical indicator of heightened preparation for activity. The wiry man was certain the crimson-cloaked riders had detected his unease though, and a small panic was rising from inside. Brac could hear the blood pumping in his ears and his cheeks were heating up, he was sure of it – though he did not realise his thick whiskers kept his reddening face hidden from view.

Without conscious command the quarryman kicked his horse in its flanks, startling the beast and sending it into a frenzied gallop towards the blond man's horse. Stones and clumps of dark earth flew up from the animal's hooves as its nostrils flared and it snorted loud, and the sudden acceleration threatened to dismount its equally

194

frightened rider. Before Brac could realise what he had done he was almost upon the blond man's horse, Brac's own mount delivering a glancing blow to the other horse's right hip causing it to whinny and jump forward. This movement meant the blond man's sword swing missed Brac's horse by an arm length or so, a lightning draw and cut delivered with unfathomable speed. Brac's horse leapt clear into a small clearing in the trees and thundered forward as if it recognised the open canopy above it as much an opportunity for freedom as did its rider.

The galloping motion of his horse now steadying into a manageable rhythm, Brac managed to stand a little and look down past his left arm at what he expected to be his pursuers. The blond man was indeed there, about twenty yards back on his light brown mount, shouting encouragements to the beast. Behind him could be seen the blond woman similarly agitated with crimson cloak billowing like a sail. It had not taken long for the unflappable pair to burst into life.

The wiry quarryman sat back down and looked ahead at a rapidly approaching thicket of trees over a slight rise in the earth. It resembled a small natural motte, lined to the left with impenetrable nettles but fortuitously clear to the right just before earth rose. Brac steered his ride right and the horse slowed dramatically, much to its rider's chagrin. The angle of turn was too tight for the speed they had built up however and the necessity of slowing was made clear to the quarryman when the nettles of the heavy brush to the right scratched across his bare arm and ripped at his breeches, prying at the tender skin beneath.

The quarryman sucked in his breath sharply at the pain. He gripped tighter at the reins whilst leaning in to the turn, gritting his teeth and forgetting to breath as he concentrated on not falling off. Around the corner the going was good with relatively flat ground uninterrupted by the trees that predominated to the left. The dangers of unseen divots and rabbit holes were not unknown to Brac, however, but his fear of his pursuers overwhelmed any sense of caution he may have had and he kicked again at the horse's flanks, yelling unintelligible commands to induce as much pace as he could from the swift beast's churning legs.

The heartbeat hammering in his ears and the earth-shattering impact of his horse's hooves deafened Brac and so he could not tell whether the crimson riders were still on his tail after the sharp right-hand turn at the earth wall. Fifty paces ahead he saw an opening into the heavily wooded area to the left where the earth ridge sloped down and the trees gave way, an enticing invitation to ostensible safety amidst the trees and vegetation. Heading the horse left and reluctantly slowing down once more, Brac dived into the thicket, immediately noting to his relief that the forest floor here was relatively clear of the plants that shrouded the lay of the previous stretch. He imagined a flat out sprint would be possible on this perfectly flat earthy ground though no sooner had this registered did he notice the grey form far to the left, flying through the trees like a ghost, no concern for the perils and obstacles of the forest.

His heart jumped even faster at the sight of the blond woman on her flying grey speckled palfrey, blonde hair and crimson cloak flowing as she raced forward on a trajectory that would surely converge with his own. He lashed at his horse for additional speed all the while attempting to duck and weave through the dark green leaves of the acorn trees that were increasingly obscuring his and his horse's visibility. This did not deter either party, though, and they recklessly tore through the low hanging branches and foliage unheeded until after perhaps thirty or forty paces Brac could see the blonde woman and her horse fall in just behind. She was up in her saddle but crouching forward, holding a tight rein in her left hand close to the palfrey's neck whilst she pulled her right arm back behind her. Brac turned back to the route ahead which was becoming ever narrower as the nettles thickened on either side of the path they followed, presumably forged by as a semi-regular route by unknown denizens of the area both human and animal, hemming them in close about their sides.

The going became ever more treacherous underfoot as the soft, dark brown soil gave way to churned black peat where the denser vegetation cover had not allowed the rain of two days' prior to fully dry out. The pitch earth was dashed about the legs and flanks of Brac's horse as it careered into the enclosing nettles and blackberry bushes. Unbeknownst to the quarryman, the blond woman held a knife in her right hand that she threw with venom at his horse, striking about its right hip and glancing away into the undergrowth.

The animal immediately leapt in fright and pain, launching its rider from its back before it landed and thundered off along the makeshift path through the trees, wounded but not critically.

Brac heard the horse scream and then inexplicably saw nothing but green leaves blurring past his eyes before experiencing a heavy, shocking *crunch* to his right shoulder and the sensation of stillness after the exhilaration of the chase.

The pain was stunning and then numbing, and Brac could not comprehend how he was lying in the dirt. He groaned and spluttered the slightly wet yet fine and crumbly earth from his mouth and laboriously rolled off his right side onto his back. Dazed, the sound of approaching hooves sparked awareness of the circumstances back into the quarryman and he frantically attempted to sit up to avoid being run over by the pursuing horse. Despairingly he found his body, aching from perpetual running, hiding and riding and battered from falling off a horse at speed, could not match his spirit's endeavour. Discomfort shooting through his neck and shoulders, the wiry man heaved himself up from the woodland floor and in the same movement brought his knees to his chest so as to spring forward and continue his escape on foot.

Before he could spring forward, however, the quarryman felt the ground shuddering behind him which was joined almost instantly by the crashing noise of a horse rapidly slowing from a gallop, the combination of thudding hoof falls and snorting and whinnying momentarily becoming the loudest sound Brac had ever heard.

A breathless female voice broke out above it all. "That was," she took a deep breath before continuing, "a fine horse. And now it is gone."

Still on his haunches, Brac craned his neck around tenderly to avoid aggravating the severe strain he could feel but the agonisingly slow movement caused him to lose his balance and he half-fell back onto the path and lightly brushing the lowermost nettles and weeds. He threw out his left hand to break his fall but the arm gave way and so crashed unceremoniously to the forest floor, though mercifully with less impact than he had done moments earlier.

The woman had reined in her horse a few paces from where the wiry quarryman lay sprawled and she athletically vaulted down from the saddle, waiting a moment upon landing for her cloak to settle and then strode towards Brac, drawing her sword and directing it at the quarryman's throat.

Alarm swelled in Brac's stomach and rose through his chest leaving him with a disturbing, sickly sensation in his throat as the realisation set in that he probably would not live for much longer. Almost immediately, and much to his horror, it dawned on Brac that *this* was the punishment he deserved for running away from God's justice at Rhuddlan, not just once following the original theft but now twice from those taking him back to Rhuddlan. He would now not face Baron de Grey because his justice was to be served here.

The woman stalked over to him and looked down with pity. "This is not an avoidable fate," she said coldly, her eyes narrowing as sharp as the knife with which she had slowed his horse. "This means more than your hunger or lack of sleep. You have spent your life running away but now is the time to stand and fight."

Her message seemed a little contrived given it was relayed down the blade of her sword, its deadly point directed accusingly at him. *Stand and fight?* Brac could barely stand in his current situation, let alone fight.

The woman continued. "We see correlation in your fate and that of our people, quarryman; for too long it has been driven down and worked hard with little opportunity for representation or relief."

Brac was taken aback by the appraisal of his life. "But, how do you know…"

"You have seen the stone; you found it. You know what it does. It is a gift," interjected the man, newly arrived, his long blond hair only a little dishevelled from the chase but his face glowing from the exertion. Even statues had to expend effort on occasion, it seemed. "It is a gift," he repeated, "discovered by us in our land. Just as we have no purpose but this, you had no purpose but to find the stone." He took a deep breath, further chipping away the statue-like persona they had carved for themselves.

Between laboured and uncomfortable breaths the wiry man coughed into his sullied beard before speaking. The fall from his horse had winded him but then Brac thought for a moment for the poor beast itself, in greater danger and long gone in the woodland with what could be a grievous wound to its hindquarters. Guilt washed over him again – an inescapable sense of responsibility for the ills of the world that bore down on his bony shoulders. He had run away from responsibility and justice. How had he become such a coward? His small voice crawled through the tangled beard. "Just please, get it done with, if you will punish me," he said in the tone of a man resigned to an inescapable fate. He could not fight them and he could not escape them. "If you got the Lord's mercy in you, be quick. I have nothing left." Brac felt tears forming in his eyes but he swallowed hard and resolved to see out his days with the dignity that life had not shown him during his short and often brutal time on Earth.

The woman considered him for a moment with her wide and expressionless face, stray blonde hairs falling over her forehead and adhering to it in places through the sweat that even a statue woman could produce. She then flashed the blade to the side. The sword's sudden movement panicked Brac, fearing the final cut.

The quarryman was still of this world though. She had simply angled the sword in order to sheath it before crouching onto her haunches beside the prone quarryman, knees clicking loudly as she did so, but the sound did not elicit any sign of discomfort. Her proximity allowed Brac to feel the warmth that radiated off her body, an inevitability given the unseasonal heaviness of the cloak she wore. "I promise you this, you are not in peril in our company," the woman said in a characteristically hushed tone. "We are not returning to Rhuddlan nor to the Lord de Grey. We are heading in the wrong direction for Rhuddlan. We have travelled west for the past three days, did you not notice?"

Brac did not feel of sufficiently stable mind to answer rhetorical questions.

"Do you know exactly what it is you discovered in that quarry?" the woman asked him plainly.

"The Lord's work," he replied, quietly, eyes still brimming with fear as he looked up at her.

"It is the Lord's *gift*," she corrected him.

199

"I tell you, I really don't know any more than what I saw. I don't even know what happened when I saw it. I can't answer any more questions," the wiry man pleaded. "Please, just tell me what you want with me. You said my purpose was to find it, but if it's already been found, what use am I now?" Brac did not believe in fortune tellers and the like; everything that could happen, had happened - that is why history was full of great deeds, because they had already happened. From his perspective, great deeds no longer occurred, otherwise there would be stories about modern adventures.

"You do not know the value of that which you have discovered, friend. The stone... it is the stone of Cynon and Owain. You have seen it, you have seen what it has done." The woman's eyes were wide and full of life, a brilliant sky blue blazing forth from her pale face and seeming to light up the shaded woodland around them. Brac had not before witnessed such vigour from his generally languid companions; of course, they had incapacitated Henry but in such a manner as appeared routine and with little to no expenditure of effort. Now, though, he could finally see the passion that drove these mysterious individuals, a passion itself driven by unshakeable adherence to a manifest destiny they would only feed to him in morsels here and there.

Cynon and Owain. Brac knew those names well. He knew the great knight Cynon, who was out for glory and adventure, had found the fountain in the domain of the Lady of the Fountain, defended by her husband the Black Knight. The Lady had been told that if she could not defend the fountain, she could not defend the kingdom. *The stone!* Brac had a moment of clarity. The Black Knight was only summoned by throwing water on the stone slab at the fountain. That was the story, was it not? Was it water? Throwing the water on the stone slab brought forth a terrible thunderstorm, giant hailstones crashing to the earth and howling rains and mighty lightning that nearly killed the knight and his horse.

He tried to remember the story as it had been passed to him from Morgan Saermaen. Morgan was a cruel man but did insist on reciting the tales to Brac and his own children. Had Morgan's repeated recitals meant more than simply keeping the Welsh flame alive within his household? It was a dark time, during the English conquest. Was there something greater at play? Surely not. The wiry Welshman was too unremarkable to be anything other than a pawn in history; indeed he had never even considered his existence was worthy even of a pawn – at least a pawn contributes in some manner.

Brac unconsciously gazed blankly into the blond woman's bright eyes and tried to make sense of the ideas that were forming in his head, various ends of various threads that began to snake around each other into something resembling a cohesive whole. He had never taken the old tales on anything more than face value. Life had taught him of the struggles of the present, a world away from the glory of the old knights such as Owain, Geraint or Peredur. Brac had enjoyed listening to them for their romantic and idealised appeal, though he did sometimes wonder if this was mainly the case because they offered respite from the brutal guardianship of Morgan. However, the church had been his guide and had taught humility, penance and industry in the face of the world's ills, and he knew first hand that the circumstances of war and battle were not at all as they were in the stories. Brac had always known the stories were just that – stories.

And yet the unusual and flawless silver stone he discovered in the quarry displayed remarkable though indescribable properties. Who knew what it could spew forth in less controlled circumstances than in an abbey – perhaps thunderstorms, hail, lightning and amid the fanfare and woeful dirge the defender of the kingdom? Brac thought he remembered the tale depending on water rather than fire as a catalyst. There was something there, nagging at him, something seemingly out of place. The story of Cynon and Owain's stone had not even occurred to him upon watching the strange and frightening display in the abbot's quarters, where Prior Simon somehow conjured some divine performance from the object. In fact before the woman had discussed it Brac had not given a single thought to the old tale.

"Are you saying the old stories are true?" Brac asked dubiously.

"Not all of them. But their prophetic qualities cannot be ignored, quarryman," she explained. "We cannot ignore the gifts we are blessed with."

The woman continued. "Your discovery, it is the beginning of the end of the cycle towards which we have been working. The Lord has sent us a gift, discovered long ago by Cynon and recovered by Owain at the fountain. Can you not see it, friend? You are the Black Knight, defender of the kingdom, given life by the stone you have found. Those who desire the kingdom of the Welsh have not yet fought the Black Knight, the guardian of the fountain."

Standing unsteadily on his bowed legs and feeling the jarring impact of the fall through his right shoulder, Brac groaned both from physical exertion and with the difficulty of persuading these people that he was not who they thought he was.

"I really don't know how I can help you," he mumbled, "I've not fought anyone before. I can't use a sword. I'll never forget what the English have done to my family, but I don't think I can help you." Brac looked at his tattered leather shoes and shuffled his feet, noticing a new hole on the outside of his right shoes. He could not remember the last time he had taken them off.

At last, the crux of the matter. The English. It was because of the English conquest that Brac had lost his family. With a sadness heavier than any he had before endured, he realised he could not even remember what his parents looked like, yet here he was, rejecting a second chance to strike back at them. Brac wondered what exactly his purpose was in life.

The quarryman raised his head again and jumped a little upon seeing the blond man approaching him, raising his arms to Brac's shoulders and clasping them strongly. Brac felt the man's fingers firmly grasping at his bony shoulders; the crimson-cloaked rider was much stronger than he appeared and certainly more so than Brac, who himself was not weak by any means but possessed strength of a different kind – it was more rooted in endurance built up from years of quarrying with pick and hammer from dawn until sunset. The quarryman felt he could not escape the clamp-like grip if he tried.

The blond man's wide and seemingly unblinking blue eyes met the hazel irises of Brac's. The latter's eyebrows formed a concerned arch over his nose and burgeoning curling moustache and beard hair, a scrubby untidy mess a mere foot away from the miraculously tidy and controlled whiskers and tied hair of the blond man facing him.

"What you say is correct, friend," said the blond man, "but matters not. Did not our Lord Jesus tell us, that the last shall be first, and the first last? Shall not the meek inherit the Earth? What has been promised shall come to pass, and you are that will come to pass. You have spirit – spirit of which even your Templar friend does not possess. He stood his ground, weapon in hand and with opponents in sight, but you showed your back to your enemy; it is a brave man who bares his back with neither sword nor shield for protection…"

Brac interrupted the blond man. "I ran away. It's not brave."

The blond man paused before resuming. "We are restricted, friend. We cannot confront the invader head on, lest we are overwhelmed by the devil's legions. We choose our battles. You choose your battles. Your Templar friend did not choose his battle and yet he resolved to fight. It is admirable, but foolhardy." The man raised his eyebrows and continued to stare at Brac as if he were awaiting a response to the statement he had just made, or at least an indicator of understanding on Brac's part.

Brac looked down to his shoes again, the straps of leather becoming ever more decrepit with every view. He did not know how one should respond to praise, or what he thought could be considered praise. The concept of receiving congratulations or recommendations was beyond alien. Were these people suggesting he somehow possessed a courage beyond that of Henry? Or greater than that of the Frenchwoman? All he did was run away! He ran away from the quarry, and ran away from Chester, and tried to run away here in whichever forest this was. That was not brave! What are these people talking about? *I found a stone.* That was it. That does not make me the hero they are looking for. How could two people overthrow the English, regardless of how strong the man is and how skilled a fighter the woman?

He looked back up again at the expectant face before him, unnervingly still and poised as if the blond man were not even breathing. Ever since encountering them, Brac had found the man and woman disquieting in their demeanour and perhaps at no point more so than now. Brac glanced over the man's left shoulder to the blond woman and her broad face and sky blue eyes, and back again to the man.

The wiry man was in no position to negotiate, however. Brac saw no escape from his current situation. He needed them in order to remain alive, and recognised the irony in any additional attempt to flee being considered further evidence for his own bravery.

"Why me? Anyone could have found that stone. I didn't even make it work. That was the prior," Brac offered in increasing exasperation, questioning and explaining at the same time. "Anyone could have found it." He scratched his beard and looked to the floor, stretching his neck on the right side. He could not remember a time when the right side of his neck was not sore, from the way he slept or from the strain of repeated lifting over his shoulder he did not know. The fall from his horse had certainly not helped.

His physical discomfort was complemented by an intense self-consciousness brought about by the crimson riders' scrutiny and the disturbing revelations about exactly how much they knew about Brac's life and character. Further, there were many ways in which a shy man could be helped to feel more at ease, and being proclaimed a vehicle of destiny was not amongst them.

The blonde woman listened to Brac's objections with an impassive face and without the impetuosity of someone who knew the answer to a question before that question had been completed.

"I do not blame you your ignorance, friend, for many and varied are the stories and histories that stretch across the Lord's earth. You are a fragment in the whole tapestry of Welsh destiny. Look how the Angevin kings have invaded and conquered despite the Princes of Wales assembled against them; even Llywelyn the Great could not withstand them. Luned asked the Lady of the Fountain how she might defend her kingdom if she could not even defend her fountain. The kingdom is God's kingdom; the kingdom of our Lord Jesus Christ the Saviour; Wales is our fountain."

The fervour was returning to her eyes and she took on a manner more devout and impassioned than any priest Brac had seen. "We must defend the fountain from the legions of demons that would and have sullied our waters. Only once we have defended the fountain can we defend the kingdom."

The wiry man stood rooted, attempting to comprehend the gravity of what he had heard. "I... I...," he spluttered.

"...don't understand?" offered the blond man, finishing Brac's proclamation for him. "It is quite simple. The stone has returned and already the English are seeing ruin visit their borders; the Scots ceaselessly harry their lands and King Philippe has vanquished the Englishmen from Aquitaine. Imagine the speed with which the warmongering Edward Longshanks, the Hammer of the Scots, will crumble when the stone is brought to bear on him."

The man's confidence and eloquence was potent and something in Brac switched. The persuasiveness of the crimson riders were complemented by their almost hypnotic delivery; controlled volume, even distribution of emphasis across words and sentences and yet an incessant suggestion of truth that underpinned their whole structure of speech – to Brac, they sounded very much like Welsh-speaking versions of Lord de Grey but with greater authority and none of the noble airs. He had never heard such a wonderful use of the Welsh tongue back home. Becoming self-conscious now even about the manner in which he spoke, Brac realised his stumbling and ragged speech was akin to a rock being thrown into the perfectly still pool of crimson riders' measured delivery.

"You have been tested, quarryman, and we see you have strength. You are preoccupied with your failings. Come, we have nearly reached our destination. We shall reunite you with the stone," explained the man, gesturing for Brac to join the woman on her horse.

Every which way, Brac had found his objections countered and overrun. He had endlessly protested his patent unsuitability for whatever role they planned for him and still they maintained their desire to take him with them.

"We continue our journey. Enough time has been lost, and that was a good horse," stated the blond man blandly.

Brac felt normal service had been resumed as the platitudes were replaced by blame. It was true, that horse was a fine animal.

"You have a duty to your people, quarryman," the blonde woman reminded him.

Responsibility of this magnitude was certainly not normal service for the wiry man. Was he predestined for this? Brac wondered. He suspected he had simply been in a lot of wrong places for the past few weeks. But now he was far too far gone to turn back.

Chapter 15

The sobbing quietened down just enough for the woman's voice to be heard. The voice's softness and tranquility was out of place in the dark and dank environment around them, illuminated by a few torches mounted on the wall with flames that danced lazily in the heavy atmosphere.

"Do you know how many children died?" she asked, for the fourth time.

The man's head was lolling, his lank, brown hair hanging before his downturned face, all congealed with the blood from countless cuts and the sweat from abject fear. He whimpered through the scraggly beard that had been left to grow unchecked for days, weeks maybe. He could not remember. Nor could he remember how long he had been on the run before capture, though his judgement was impaired considerably by the treatment he had received, both physical and non-physical. To be on the outside, in the fresh air, with the sky above and the grass below and with movement in his legs. How long had he been here? And what was the question this woman was asking? Something about the children. He did not know.

She asked again. "Do you know how many children died?" Five times she had asked, five times she waited for a response that went beyond reflex audible responses to pain. "I'll have to start delivering on my promise, you know. One finger for every babe. I don't think you have enough fingers for that."

Her tone was casual, as if such a conversation were a regular occurrence. There was no hint of enjoyment in her voice, though. The earl had recognised such a level temperament in the woman and thus entrusted her with all matters pertaining to justice outside of court. He had referred to these circumstances as 'special sessions of court', reserved only for significant cases concerning the security of the border regions. Before leaving, the earl had left which cases would be considered as significant to her discretion, trusting in her sagacity which he believed to be very similar to his own.

Neither she nor the earl were bloodthirsty like so many of those petty provincial sheriffs and gaolers, but nor were they idealists who lay their faith in concepts alone. Pure ideals and concepts were fine for the teachers and thinkers, but the art of ruling and keeping order, particularly in times such as these, required the embodiment of these ideals and concepts in deeds. The earl had insisted, however, on the basis of the long-haired man's value as a prisoner that he retain full control of his faculties; the blonde woman would not dream of disobeying her lord.

But she had not previously found one who had been at the village on the day of the attack.

The long-haired man whimpered again but managed to lift his head to face his questioner. Through the tangled strands he could see her neutral face, pale and dominated by shapely dark eyebrows above sharp eyes that were either hazel or green, he could not tell. If September were to be represented by a colour, it would be this woman's hazel-green eyes. They were compelling, until the ringing of iron on iron snapped him out of his stupor and, looking down to his right in the direction of the noise, he saw the woman picking up the clamp device that she had brought with her on the first morning of his ordeal. Since placing it down on the table she had not even so much as glanced at it, but its mere presence had been a crucial component in her strategy. Initially he could only guess for what purpose the woman had brought the clamp.

She saw his eyes widen as she raised the clamp up so he could see it clearly. It was an old vice she had borrowed from the blacksmith and its condition befitted its origins in the smithy; battered, scarred, chipped yet ostensibly durable and therefore functional. It was small enough to be carried in one hand and to be operated with the other by means of a thin, cylindrical handle on an axis for tightening and loosening, which was perfectly suited to the woman's intentions. The man was strapped to an upright wooden frame, lashed in across his arms, chest and legs. The ties around his wrists were wide and tight, covering the joint between hand and wrist, severely restricting movement in the former and completely in the latter.

"I was there, when the fire started," she said, "and I can still hear the screaming and the crying, and all them timber frames crackling and bursting." She seemed not to blink as if she were in a trance, seeing the things of which she spoke right before her eyes, rather than the long-haired man. "My girl, she was only five, she didn't have a chance. You know what they did? What they did to a little girl?" The woman began twirling the clamp's handle, all the while looking at the man with unseeing, unblinking eyes. "They pretty much *cut her in half*. Was it you? You were there, they said."

The man sobbed once more, for he had been there, and he too could see the flames and hear the screams. He too could see the horsemen riding down anyone and everyone. But he had not been one of those horsemen, and he had not killed any children. "No," he croaked, barely distinguishable from a grunt.

"I might take a finger for each year my girl lived. Her name was Matilda. Makes it worse, doesn't it, knowing the name." She broke her gaze and brought the clamp down to her right side, down to the man's left hand, and placed the jaws of the clamp around the bottommost joint of his little finger, eliciting a high-pitched whimper. "After this, you won't be able to light fires again."

The woman started to slowly rotate the handle, which tightened the jaws and caused the volume of the man's panicking to increase. "And when I'm done on this hand, I'll take your fingers from your right hand, so that you can't use a sword ever again." She looked back up at the man who by now was attempting to shake himself free of the leather bonds and was heavily sweating, drenching his ragged cloth shirt and trousers.

"Please, please, no more, I don't know the children! I didn't kill them!" he begged rapidly and loudly, "I didn't do it! Please! Oh, God, please!" before shouting phrases in a tongue the woman did not understand.

The woman stopped tightening the vice and left it dangling from the man's little finger as she moved away to the stool behind the table, from where she picked up a rag of cloth. "If you're going to make so much noise, I need to give you this," she stated bluntly as if scolding a child.

The man's elation at her ceasing to tighten the clamp quickly dissipated when he realised she was actually going to gag him and then continue with procedure. She wrapped the cloth around his mouth and tied it at the back of his head, which she was able to do because the frame to which he was strapped only came up to his shoulders. Consequently, he was denied any support against which to rest his head.

"You know how many children died? Twenty-eight." She returned to the clamp and turned the handle, causing the man to emit a muffled noise of terror, and she continued turning until the resistance on the handle required two hands to overcome. She pressed the clamp against the frame and maintaining that horizontal force she wrenched the handle round whilst ignoring the rattling and shuddering to her left as the man's panic gave way to muted screams of agony. The woman's face was a picture of concentration on the task at hand, which was to overcome the physical resistance offered by a bone encased in a thin layer of skin and tissue. Blood started oozing from the vice and the resistance increased to the point where, almost completely closed, her strength was no longer up to the task and so she stopped.

"Now you know, I'm actually here to ask you questions on topics I don't know much about. Not just questions on things I do know about, such as the number of children you killed." She let go of the clamp and stood back up to her full height, half a head shorter than the shackled man. The clamp dangled and then fell to the floor, tearing the pitiful remnant of the man's little finger with it, and he continued wailing behind the cloth gag. He could not coherently vocalise his terror nor pain but his eyes told the woman everything she needed to know about his current state of mind. His eyebrows were raised towards the middle and two, then three tears were beginning to make their way down his cheeks to his thick beard along with the droplets of sweat from his lined forehead.

"And even more luckily for you, there is someone even more important than my lord who would like to speak to you, and he's got someone in my position with even more toys to play with, so I best leave him some fingers, shouldn't I?"

Her use of grammar and the occasional dropped letter suggested humble beginnings but evidently she had climbed high into the esteem of the lord whom she served, the lord who had captured this long-haired man tied to the makeshift wood support. Her accent also implied she was a long way from home, unusual for a lowborn.

For these reasons and others the man was discovering by the minute, the small woman was enigmatic. She had introduced herself, if such a meeting could be considered an introduction, that very morning. The long-haired man initially believed the young woman to be a maid of the castle, perhaps visiting the prisoner to provide a semblance of medicine, even simply to bathe his wounds or some such. He had not been *directly* mistreated during his incarceration; it was more what his gaolers had *not* done to and for him over the day and weeks that had worn him down. Meals were sporadic, if they could be considered meals; illumination infrequent; and bedding virtually non-existent after the few handfuls of hay had effectively rotted away in the damp environment of his stone cell. But when two unknown men, dressed in the clothing worn under the armour of soldiers, carried in a large wooden frame with leather and cloth materials and tools, the long-haired man had sensed the indirectly atrocious treatment was to be replaced with active punishment.

The woman continued speaking, standing only a foot or so away from him, looking up to his watering eyes between the shaggy strands of limp, dark hair. "Although, all this being said, it would look a *little* suspicious if you had just *one* finger missing. I'd have to explain that one, wouldn't I? Much better for me to say you were injured in combat, or something."

She bent down to retrieve the clamp, still with the majority of his little finger between the jaws, and loosened the device. The finger fell to the floor with a light *smack* and the woman paid it no mind, instead studying the operating handle to ensure its functionality remained after the first removal.

Upon their introduction it had quickly become apparent to the long-haired man that the young woman was not a maid bringing some medicine or even food, but someone a world away from being a healer. It had also quickly become apparent that this lowborn woman did not care for the man's higher status. She did not even suggest she was aware of it. The man resigned himself to worse treatment on account of how cold and meticulous she was; as if he were simply another object requiring treating, moulding and

210

remoulding. He could have been flour and yeast and then dough and she the baker, and she would have been as disconnected from the flour and yeast's provenance as she was with him. He was the bread; just a thing with which the little woman worked but from which she was utterly detached. His present fear and the throbbing pain resulting from the crushing and then removal of his finger fogged his mind and prevented him grasping the remarkable calmness she displayed even with the revelation about her young daughter.

She loosened the clamp further and bent down to her right again, to the man's left hand, and slipped the jaws over his ring finger. His frightened blubbing became louder and higher as he felt the jaws swallow another of his digits and press up against the bloody mess representing what remained of his little finger.

"So I'm only going to take a little bit off this one," she explained indifferently. "Make it look like a sword cut, at an angle, you know?" She started spinning the handle at the same pace as before, slowly intensifying the tension that in turn caused a seemingly exponential increase in the volume of the man's gagged wailing. He ineffectually struggled against the bonds holding him upright and prone as the vice's grip was now firm enough for the woman to take her left hand away and assist her right in turning the handle. As before, the resistance of the muscle, tissue and bone grew as the jaws closed, ever slowing the speed at which the woman could turn the handle. The long-haired man threw his head back, desperately searching for a way out, the whites of his eyes bright against the filthy visage in which they were set, sweat pouring like a waterfall and the blood vessels throbbing in his temple and neck. The woman ground the handle with all the strength she could apply given the awkward angle of both her position and that of the clamp, and finally with a sickening *squelch* barely audible above his stifled screams the man's ring finger was crushed down to the top joint.

Once again, the woman left the iron clamp to dangle solely by the remaining intact tissue within its victim before it became too heavy for the sinews and dropped to the stone below with a clumsy *clunk*. She regarded her handiwork and noted the pitiful state of the man's fingers, hideously maimed in a manner no one would mistake for a clean sword cut. *I can only work with the instruments provided*, she mused.

"Now, if you're going to shut the fuck up, you'll give me answers to the questions my lord has requested." She then balled her right fist and punched him hard in the nose, jarring his head back and instantly quietening his howling. The shock of the punch and its impact stunned the man and allowed the woman to hear herself as she continued to talk at the same level volume as she had done since arriving in the cell that morning. "Good. Now, you'll stay quiet once I take off the gag, yes?" She had a natural strength that belied her slight appearance, and wiry arms toughened like taut rope on the rigging of a ship through years as a milkmaid.

The man drowsily brought his head forward down to the physical embodiment of a nightmare stood before him. She did not look like someone who tied people up and tore off their fingers with an iron clamp. Upon her unassumingly walking into the dark stone cell, her face lit up by her own torch and those of the soldiers around her, she took the appearance of an angel in the darkness. Her blonde hair was curled and her eyes kind and after weeks of solitude and misery the man thought her the most beautiful creature on God's Earth.

"You're going to tell me," she started, walking around behind the wooden rack, "all you know about your friends." She untied the cloth gag and the man coughed, inhaling deep breaths in between. He spat on the floor but not in disgust, just from the build up of saliva in his mouth from having it forced open during the ordeal.

"I don't know what you're talking about!" he exclaimed, hoarsely and not as loudly as he had intended. "I don't know, please, just... I don't know." His voice was cracking and doleful, the voice of a man breaking under the strain of both physical and mental torture.

"Oh, come on, you know the friends I mean. The fanatical ones." The little blonde woman walked back round the other side of the rack towards the small table in the corner and picked up another cloth. "Everyone else knows the fighting has finished, but your friends..." She approached him again, stretching the cloth taut and looking him in the eye. He began shaking more vigorously as she approached, and started mumbling please for mercy as she knelt down by his left hand.

212

The clamp device had made hideous work of his fingers and the blood was still dripping. "*Shhh*, calm down. This is just to stop you bleeding out on me. I'd get in trouble if you did that. Apparently, the King has quite a temper, so I've heard. Have you met him? He's very tall, and strong."

The man winced and gasped in pain as the woman tenderly wrapped the cloth around his bloody stumps. "I don't know the people you're talking about," he murmured.

The woman squeezed the ends of his mutilated fingers together tightly, holding them for a moment as she replied. "Oh, but you do, my lord. Because they know you, so you must know them."

She let go of his fingers and stood in front of him. She raised her left hand and lifted his chin before punching him hard in the nose again. Blood exploded from the crunching impact, his already swollen nose instantly ballooning as again his head rocked back and he groaned in pain.

"The friends of yours I've spoken to all know you... they told me a lot about you. In fact, they told me where you were, which is why my lord was able to find you. Some of them were very tough. I took six fingers from one of them before she told me where you were headed. Women are always the strongest ones."

She punched him again, across his left cheek causing him to groan again. "Matilda was strong. She had the pox when she was younger... she fought it bravely, and came out of it," she explained to the man, looking at his face as his head drooped and swayed. "Are you listening?" Her voice remained impassive and quiet, completely at odds with the physical exertion required to punch him. "Do you know what it's like, watching your little girl die?" She jabbed him in the ribs on his left side, his torn shirt offering no protection to the bony skin underneath. The man was so malnourished that the blonde woman may as well have hit him square on the bone. The woman seemed to be using punches to signify the breaks between the sentences she spoke.

He moaned in agony. "Yes... I do," he gasped, winded from the savage shot to side.

The blonde woman cocked her head to the side, her gaze moving away from the pitiful and bloody shambles tied up to the wooden

213

frame, and she thought on his answer. After a few moments, measured in the wheezes of the man as he tried to catch his breath, she bent down and picked the clamp up, loosening the jaws so the mashed gore of what was the top of the man's ring finger unceremoniously fell to the floor, like its former neighbour just a few moments previously.

"If you have, then you shouldn't let anyone else experience that," she stated, the first hint of aggression in her voice all day, matched by the intensity of her eyes, boring through the man's dark, matted hair and into his own.

At that moment the long-haired man thought the blonde woman even more terrifying than she had thus far demonstrated; he dreaded to think the brutality she would be capable of with the addition of aggression to her demeanour. He saw her idly playing with the long, thin handle of the vice, slowly turning it one way and then the other, all the while staring at him disconcertingly. Her long fingers twisted and twined themselves around the handle and then slid down the length of the iron rod, before they slowly rotated the handle so that the vice jaws gradually closed. The woman lowered her gaze from the man's face down his body, stopping at his waist, whilst she continued to close the clamp. The man followed her gaze and realised where she was looking.

"Please, no... no," he spoke softly, pathetically, the broken voice of a broken man.

She looked back at his face and stepped up close to him, her head angled up to meet his eyes, so near that his dangling hair nearly brushed her nose. "Some of your friends ratted you out," she sneered, "but not any of their own, which gives you a problem." With her left hand she roughly took hold of the top of his linen breeches and began pulling them down, crouching slowly down without taking her eyes off his. He shook his head and contorted his face as the tears began welling in his eyes.

"No, no... you can't do this," he begged, trying to flail all of his limbs in defiance but ultimately getting nowhere.

The aggression dissipated from the blonde woman's voice as quickly as it had emerged. "It's not a question of whether I can or can't, my lord. It's a question of whether I have to, which I do." She

214

took hold of his member and squeezed hard, eliciting a wince from the bound man. "I imagine it's been a long time, hasn't it?" Her eyes and face remained completely unreadable but the slow movement of her left hand indicated her calculating mindset.

Despite being subjected to starvation, light deprivation and finally mutilation, the long-haired man's body betrayed him.

"Oh, you're not here to enjoy yourself, though it does give me better purchase," she paused, "or moves it out the way for a couple more targets behind," said the woman, without slowing down her hand. The man closed his eyes and wept. She gently slipped the clamp around his member, holding the device in her left whilst she gently twisted the handle with her right.

"So, simply, and if you have any common sense you'll answer, where are your friends hiding?" She left unnaturally lengthy pauses between the clauses in her speech, feigning concentration on operating the clamp but actually just dragging out the act. All the man offered in return was a pitiful arrangement of stifled snivels and pleas for her to stop.

"I'm not sure this will need as much effort as your fingers did, so you don't have much time to answer," she explained casually, again as if the acts she was carrying out were not out of the ordinary, perhaps even familiar.

The pain was becoming unbearable and the terror even more so. The removal of his fingers was traumatic but the next target of this woman's toy was beyond nightmarish; the man felt that his very essence was being crushed between those unforgiving iron jaws. He prided himself on his resolve and fortitude and it had been on these strengths even more than his family name that he rode so far and high. But what man could stand firm in the face of such complete emasculation? The rising agony he could stomach, not without a physical response – no one alive could endure dismemberment with no complaint – but he would survive the suffering. No, it was the total loss of identity that this woman's particular brand of torture entailed. The long-haired man knew he was as likely to die that day, or the next, as he was in twenty, thirty years' time. But he resolved that he would die a man, not a husk of what he had been. The game was up; the King's forces were too strong. His friends would be long gone by the time the King's soldiers arrived anyway. He could play no further part in this war.

"I'll tell you! I'll tell you... I'll tell you!" he cried, tears streaming down his darkened cheeks and mouth twisted in pain and emotional turmoil.

The blonde woman stopped turning the handle and as she had done with the two fingers, left the clamp hanging by its own grip. The man groaned as the pain suddenly increased, adding to the excruciating agony.

Her cold, hazel-green eyes found his once more. "If you lie to me, the King's man will do things to you even I couldn't imagine."

The blonde woman wearily climbed the stone steps, her dark smock stifling in the heat of the subterranean dungeon that seemed to double as a furnace in the summer. She was not one to wilt in the heat; her bronzed skin was testimony to a life spent outside, and this summer's unusually oppressive heat had still not deterred her. Instead, it was the effort of maintaining the bravado, the pretence of brutality for a prolonged period; she felt the sweat run down her body almost as profusely as it had done for her victim. Most regrettable was her use of Matilda; she prayed God that she would be forgiven for using her daughter as a tool in her work. Once the wooden cell door had been closed she allowed her emotions to see the light of day, her heart rate jumping and tears welling in her clear, blue eyes. She did not enjoy the experience nor could she block the memory of the screaming. The screaming always stayed with her; with the recent increase in hostilities, she found herself almost inundated with 'clients', as the earl termed them.

She reached the top step and resolved to reduce her anxiety before walking back through to the sergeant's quarters. In front of her was a bolted oak door with iron railings either side to prevent escape from the cell downstairs. The railings did not leave much space for one to knock on the wood to alert the guards outside, so she had always just rattled the railings.

With her free right hand she rubbed down the tears in her eyes and any perspiration that may have been built up on her brow and cheeks. The little woman had constructed a fearsome reputation as an interrogator, manipulative and cold and the earl always turned to her when extraction of information was required. In this case, she had orchestrated the weeks of solitary confinement, intermittent meal provision and random sleep deprivation prior to her more direct treatment of the prisoner.

In return, she had the earl's favour and was paid handsomely for her work. She was not sure how her father acquired the role, but following their arrival from Cornwall he became gaoler at the castle and upon his death his daughter assumed the responsibilities alongside her work as the milkmaid. The blonde woman considered it unfortunate she possessed such a useful yet stressful and morally repugnant talent so valuable to the security of the realm; in an attempt at atonement, she spent much of her time outside of the cells and away from the cattle in conversation with the Elric, the old priest.

Satisfied her flustered appearance seemed merely heat inflicted and not derived from her possessing a conscience, she lifted her torch in her left hand and rattled the railings with her right. The bolt instantly clanked, as if the guards on the others side had heard the screams cease and were expecting her back imminently. The door swung open and the woman was first hit by the relative glare of the well-lit atrium and then by a cool draught that almost extinguished her torch. Quickly recovering her sense, she looked to the kindly, bearded face of Ralph.

Ralph always had a smile for her. It was a smile of innocence, of a man who had not seen the things she had seen, of a man whose entire world extended as far as the gates of the castle. He was very amiable and carried an honest look that suggested he would not hurt a fly. The Cornishwoman always wondered how it was that Ralph became a man whose job required holding a spear and shield. His toothy grin flashed through his black stubble, his face lighting up as he greeted her.

"All done?" the man asked enthusiastically, his inquiry misguided but well-meaning.

"Aye, all done, Ralph. Is the sergeant in?" she responded, tired. She did not feel like talking to Ralph today.

"He is. He's in his quarters," came the reply from his still smiling mouth. A couple of teeth were missing, and for the woman this usually simply added to his charm but now she was mentally drained and just wanted to get out of the castle.

"Thank you, Ralph." She walked forward into the small hall. "Alfred," she nodded at the other guard to her left on the other side of the doorframe to Ralph. He nodded back. Not only was it unfathomable how Ralph became a soldier but also how the sergeant thought to pair him with the most sullen man in the entire town on guard duty. Alfred barely said a word, which the woman assumed to be appropriate for a castle guard on duty, yet she imagined him to have the patience of a saint when keeping watch with the talkative Ralph. Ralph could strike a conversation with a tree. He probably had done so on occasion, she reflected.

Striding forward with false purpose she crossed the small hall and headed to the corridor to the right, along which the sergeant had his quarters. He was a difficult man at times, but the blonde woman thought this a symptom of trying to run a castle during times of war. Consequently she did not feel entirely comfortable around him and tried to keep their interactions as brief as possible, which he reciprocated.

His door was open. "Sergeant Everard," she announced, returning to her other persona with its deadpan delivery and cold, uncaring eyes.

"Adelaide, please, come in." He did not look up from his papers, but spoke in an affable manner. His speech was authoritative as always, matching his appearance – balding with greying dark hair like a crown on his head, light stubble gracing his cheeks and angled jawline. Everything about him was angular; his jaw, his nose, his shoulders, his arms; in physique and temperament he was a man forged of iron and steel.

She stepped forwards a few paces and stopped in front of his desk, waiting for him to stop writing, which he did within moments. "I have the necessary information," she stated without fanfare.

He looked up, his grey eyes scrutinising her bright hazel-greens. "Very good. Is he in one piece? I have received word that he is to leave for London no sooner had you completed your work."

Adelaide retained her blank expression. "He is. He cracked more quickly than I expected. But that's what happens with these jumped up princes; they surround themselves with a tough shell of retainers to hide their own softness inside." Her monotonous delivery had the effect of amplifying the scorn in her voice.

"Quite. We shall see what the King thinks of the last 'Prince of Wales', Madog ap Llywelyn, in due course, shan't we?" Everard said with a mocking emphasis upon the title that Madog gave himself. "Regardless of his current state, he travels now. Doubtless he'll be paraded alongside this stone that everyone seems to be talking about."

Adelaide was puzzled; she had not heard anything about a stone being paraded in London.

Before she could enquire, however, Everard spoke again. "So where are these 'Dragons' of his hiding? The Earl of Hereford is keeping watch here whilst Lord Richard is in London, and has asked me to keep him abreast of things – it seems the earl wants to make a move on these Dragons before the autumn is out."

"He will need to hurry," Adelaide replied, "they are spread across a number of camps and villages in the southern part of Arllechwedd, in the area around Dolwyddelan, particularly between the Moel Siabod and Y Ro Wen mountains." She could not speak Welsh but Adelaide had regular contact with Welsh speakers both friendly and hostile to the Marcher lords and so her pronunciation of the proper nouns was immaculate.

Everard pondered the information, staring at the blank stone wall to Adelaide's left. The only defining feature that suggested this room was the sergeant's quarters was the sergeant himself. If there were ever a man born to soldier, it was Everard. Not the frivolities of life or the adornments here and there that make a house a home for the sergeant of Clun Castle. The guards' quarters were not particularly homely by any stretch but there were personalised features that distinguished each bunk, each space; Alfred had his two silver spoons, stored under his bedding – he never used them as cutlery, just kept them as tokens – and Ralph had a remarkable canvas cloth that the sergeant graciously allowed him to hang above his bunk.

Nobody, not least Ralph himself, knew where the kindly soldier had obtained such a wonderful weaving; on it was depicted a boar hunt, with three young men all uniquely armed, one with the spear, one archer and one, bafflingly, with an axe, chasing down the fleeing animal. It was a mighty beast, fearsome tusks protruding from its great head, all supported by powerful neck and shoulders. The figures were embroidered in yellow thread on a red background. Neither Alfred nor Ralph had ever encountered attempts of theft of their prized possessions despite just how vulnerable to pinching they were. Adelaide had always thought this was because of their favour with Everard and Lord Richard, both of whom were men one would not want to cross. Furthermore, she reasoned, Ralph's work of art was so splendid and famous that a thief would have to travel a very long way before its appearance in a new location raised suspicions.

The sergeant finally spoke. "Yes, very good." He regarded Adelaide with a close eye. "And another thing, you're going with Hereford."

The blonde woman was taken aback, her acting mask slipping under pressure for the first time today. "I'm going with Hereford?" she asked, disbelievingly.

"That is what I said," replied Everard, finally putting down his quill and leaning back in his uncomfortable-looking chair. "Hereford's arriving in the next week with a small force. He'll be collecting men en route and from here, along with footmen and archers from Lord de Grey at Chester."

Adelaide could feel her heart rate rising once more – she had no business anywhere near a battle! Even Ralph was more suited to war than was she.

The steely Everard continued, "Hereford wants your familiarity with the Dragons. Rest assured, dear girl, what fighting there will be, will be brief, and you'll be nowhere near it."

But the blonde woman could not shake the apprehension, looking at the rickety stonework in the walls and down to the smooth limestone floor and back again, stumbling her words as she tried to broach the topic of the safety of her honour, dignity and person in such circumstances.

Everard was as perceptive as he was disciplined, which is why he was the obvious choice for sergeant of Lord Richard, Earl of Arundel's castle. The steely Everard guessed such an issue was playing on the young woman's mind. "You'll be travelling in the company of Hereford, my girl. Lord Richard has agreed to this, and the earls have also sworn that any man who so much as looks at you will be executed." The iron sergeant picked his quill back up and moved some papers to the top of his pile, no doubt some mundane administrative tasks necessary to the castle's upkeep. There was a professional air about him; every task he undertook, he did so with unswerving attention and integrity.

"Is there anything else?" he not impolitely added without looking up, though suggesting Adelaide be on her way.

"No, no," the woman replied timidly. She silently cursed herself for having let her guard slip to such an authority as Everard. Lord Richard FitzAlan, Earl of Arundel, was a practical man and Adelaide knew his favour for her would extend only so far as she was providing information through her methods; were he to discover she too possessed an inner softness, she would undoubtedly be cast from the castle and back to the hovels in the town. She turned on her heels and exited the sergeant's quarters, back into the atrium. Alfred and Ralph were at their post by the railed door, looking anything but soldierly. Alfred sat fiddling with the leather strap to his rounded blue shield, the precise nature of which Adelaide could not see from the other side of the atrium. Ralph was cleaning down the blade of his longsword with his discarded linen supertunic. It was far too hot for the full complement of armour and clothing required of the castle guards. Adelaide could not even see where their helmets were.

A Welsh attack now would surely be catastrophic… How bad will it be when the two hundred best fighters have left with Hereford?

To rid herself of thoughts about such plausible disasters Adelaide slipped out of the atrium and into the castle courtyard, unnoticed, enjoying the first natural light she had experienced for hours. She looked up to the sky and closed her eyes, revisiting that first wonderful summer with baby Matilda.

Chapter 16

Henry sat alone but for the candles on the table and the torches on the walls, held fast in a stone grip evenly spaced around the top end of the chancel. He had watched the small flame of one candle in particular for a while, unsure of how much time had passed since Brother Edward had retired for the night.

Henry had always found peace in solitude, actively enjoying roaming far and wide away from the bustle, noise and smell of the city. In his experience, London was the worst offender in all Christendom in all three categories. Constantinople was a magnificent Roman masterpiece, not without its flaws but conspicuously planned; Jerusalem stiflingly hot though consequently slower paced; Rome a mosquito-plagued village by comparison. Paris housed more people and had greater sprawl, thus diluting the adverse effects of urbanisation.

London was simply cramped and hectic and loud. It overwhelmed the senses from the moment one first lay eyes on the Tower, even before reaching the Aldgate. The Strand, formally separating old London and Westminster, had become a major internal arterial route within the greater sprawl, which brought the negatives of mass human residence closer and closer to the Temple. Henry still found the Temple to be the only place in the city where one could truly gather one's thoughts without risk of having one's senses battered by a cacophony of experiences, but for how long? He had noticed the changes along Fleet Street since his first visit over twenty years ago. Each new tavern seemed to spawn two more, contributing to the artificial river of water, refuse and who knows what else along the street parallel to the Thames.

For now, though, the tranquillity reigned and Henry remained lost in the dancing yellow flame. He had not left the Temple grounds since arriving two weeks' previously and spent every evening sat in the same chair, alone with his thoughts. Brother Edward had spent much time with the knight and their conversation had wandered far and wide, for Brother Edward was as much an intellectual traveller as was Henry a geographical one. Neither man required much sleep thanks to the fortuitous combination of natural vigour and monastic discipline. On occasion they had continued their discussions until the ringing of the bells for Matins, only a couple of hours before sunrise.

The tanned Englishman lived a generally itinerant life, though this did not preclude him from making meaningful connections with people. Quite the contrary, he had found, for it placed the whole world before him. What he did miss, though, was building upon those relationships, returning to see friends old and new for more than just a fleeting visit, or perhaps even not at all. Henry liked to think that his own and Brother Edward's sleeplessness was a little gift from God, allowing the knight some respite from his endless odysseys.

The ponderous wooden door at the other end of the aisle closed so softly that the knight was not roused from his silent vigil. His chair faced the back wall of the chancel, away from the central walkway up from the main door, so his eyes were not able to pick up what his ears did not. Henry only became aware of company when he heard the soft shuffling of leather soles on the stone steps leading up to the raised area of the chancel housing the ministers' table. Even then he did not turn round, guessing that Brother Edward had returned for further conversation, having had a further thought on the scriptural merits of either Latin or Greek. Or perhaps Master Guy had returned with his entourage. The Master had been at Westminster since three days previous, following the calling of Parliament in response to the catastrophic defeat to the French in Aquitaine and the French king's abolition of King Edward's duchy there. Guy had returned late the previous two nights, and even then he had immediately retired to his study to pursue the work required of him by the Temple. Henry thought it just as well that Guy seemed incapable of experiencing fatigue. He began to wonder if permanent wakefulness was actually an Order requirement.

The footsteps reached the chair to Henry's right and the body to whom they belonged pulled back the small, plain wooden seat once more with minimal noise. The thin wooden frame creaked loudly, finally shattering the faltering illusion of silence that Henry had crafted but had been slowly and accidentally eradicated by his new companion. Henry continued gazing at the candle, loose grip on the end of both chair arms. Master Guy did not require an invitation to talk, so the knight assumed the reticence belonged to the meeker Brother Edward.

"It's unreasonable to assume vernacular versions can be trusted across the entirety of Christendom, but I tell you, Rome cannot maintain its monopoly forever," Henry said unblinkingly, continuing where their conversation left off earlier.

"*Certaines personnes ne seraient pas d'accord avec toi*," replied a soft, feminine voice, shaking Henry out of his trance.

He looked to his right and saw El studying him in the serene way with which he was so familiar, her mouth not explicitly smiling but emanating happiness nonetheless.

"You're here!" he exclaimed in French, smiling wide so El could see almost every tooth in his mouth. Henry then jumped out of his chair and flung himself at the small woman, throwing his arms around her in an awkward hug that nearly rocked both chair and people backwards. El grunted and laughed at the same time, grasping the back of Henry's tunic and gripping tightly as if she were holding on for dear life. The knight released his hug and stood back up in front of her, taking her hands in his and gently encouraging her to stand. "Where have you been?" he asked, smile still on his face before grabbing her close again.

El laughed again into Henry's left shoulder, the happiest sound he could remember having heard. She pulled her head away and looked up at him, her brown eyes wide and smiling.

"We were close… so close," he said reluctantly.

Her eyes and smile faded, as did Henry's. They simultaneously released their grip on the other but remained standing close, Henry looking down and El looking up.

Henry pursed his lips, audibly breathing out, inadvertently and lightly blowing on El's dark brown hair. "They hurt you, didn't they?" he asked rhetorically, bringing his right hand up to her face and feeling her cheek, outlining the slight bruising remaining from the beating she took all those weeks ago outside the quarry at Rhuddlan. Not an hour had gone by when he had not thought about her; he had prayed for her return and the Lord had granted it. Henry said a silent prayer of thanks in his head.

"It is nothing," El insisted, taking Henry's hand in her own and squeezing lightly. "I had worse from my brother when we were children. But our task, we did not make it."

"We were so close," he sighed. The knight suddenly felt self-conscious of how closely he was standing to El and so turned around and returned to his seat, falling back into his chair more heavily than the thin chair was designed for. He looked back up at her and smiled again, genuinely. El flashed a smile in return. "But it's coming to London. So... all is not lost. And it is as the Master said it would be."

El cocked an eyebrow and spun on her heels. She glanced around at the heavy shadows cast amongst the arches of the chancel roof, creating beautifully perfect curved boundaries between the pitch black and the dark reddish-brown of the illuminated stone. "Jacques de Saint-Georges, wasn't it?" she asked Henry, all the while looking around at the ceiling arches whilst settling herself down gently in the chair next to the knight's.

Henry brought his fine eyebrows together at the question. "The King's architect?"

El regarded the knight once more, taking in the familiar sharp jawline and easy eyes. She thought of Sir Edward de Beauchamp, Lord Reginald's man. Sir Edward and Henry both appeared how she would expect such a man to look, and she knew as well as anyone that aesthetics mattered in high society; the little Frenchwoman remembered back to her treatment at the hands of Sir Edward and his men before they discovered her family name. El imagined that Chrétien de Troyes would have men of Sir Edward and Sir Henry's appearance in mind when writing of Sir Lancelot or Sir Gawain, the Green Knight.

But only Henry was a true champion. El knew many knights were morally ambiguous, verging on generally immoral, and Sir Edward was one of the worst she had encountered. Henry was more complex, good-natured and kind-hearted but passionate when riled. There was the crux; Henry was a man of the Church and a godly man. He carried his cross like every man and woman but fought

226

hard, largely successfully, not to indulge it, unlike Sir Edward and his sense of superiority.

She replied to the knight in her small, soft voice. "Yes, he built the King's castles in Wales. You look at a building such as this – the finest masons in Christendom build for the Temple. Is it necessary? But the castles of Wales," she said, her eyes widening again with a sense of wonder at the memory, "Henry, you haven't seen anything like it. Jacques de Saint-Georges is a true master."

Henry raised his eyebrows in slight disbelief. "They keep you in a dungeon, they injure you, yet all you can talk about is how well-constructed the castle was?"

El's façade of self-assurance began to crumble much as had Henry's soundless idyll just a few moments prior. "People... died, Henry. They died." Her calm face began contorting into one of pain and grief, not physical but the torturous, mental kind. "The English followed me, and killed the Welsh, and the Dragons came-"

"It is all part of the Lord's plan," Henry interrupted, looking kindly to his friend but not entirely believing his own reassurances. "When it is time, it is time. Those people, it was their time."

"If I hadn't been there, they would still be walking."

"You don't know that," the knight assured her, trying to instil a little cloistral rigidity into his voice to help persuade the little Frenchwoman of his determinist reasoning.

The candlelight reflected off the tears that were forming in the corners of El's eyes. She lifted her head up to Henry, her voice retaining its level timbre despite her rapidly spiralling distress. "This one man, he died, I didn't even know his name. They killed him with a spear... he was protecting his friend, who protected me, and he might be dead too," she managed to blurt out. Her voice then cracked and the sobbing took over, echoing through the empty, lofty space of the Round Church and recently constructed chancel.

Henry got up out of his chair and stepped over to El, crouching on his haunches in front of her, his long grey tunic folding up every which way around his now-compacted body. He cupped El's face with both hands and used his thumbs to wipe away the tears rolling down her tanned cheeks. He noticed a few light freckles that were emerging as the bruising slowly faded; she had spent much of the

227

previous few weeks on the road and the sunshine had given her a distinct glow.

"El. Look at me," he said, sensitively yet commanding, "the Welsh know that to court trouble with soldiers is to court death itself..." he caught himself, sighing at such an unfortunate turn of phrase and looking down at his feet before continuing once more, "that's obviously not a justification. But it happens. Everyone on all sides is under incredible stress, and I can guarantee if that spark wasn't ignited then, it would have gone off another day – the slightest provocation could escalate. It is only the Church's work, *our* work, that can clean up what the wars wreak. Which is what we'll do. We'll atone for others, as the Lord Jesus did for us. Now, which Dragons did you see?"

El looked down at the kindly knight, simply wanting to fall into his gentle, earthy-coloured eyes and hide away from the guilt that wracked her conscience at every turn. She had not seen repeated visions of the huge man being speared by the man-at-arms but instead experienced a draining sensation of remorse for what she had done, for her role in the man's death.

It ate away at her, wearing down her energy and taking her focus from anything else she had tried her hand at. She had spent much time out of the saddle with her hands to her flustered face, pressing on her temples and rubbing her hair in an attempt to alleviate the anxiety over the sin she had committed, the sin she had committed against the Lord. She had apologised over and over but each apology failed to meet the invisible and inexplicable standard she set for apologies – her mind refused to confirm that her apologies to God, Christ and the Holy Spirit were sufficiently honest, humble and correct for it to move on to the next thought train.

Trying to ignore the apprehension only exacerbated the difficulty, for once her resolve to resist the demands of her conscience collapsed the contrition became even more intense and consequently stressful for both body and mind. As time went on and days became weeks, the fear over the actual incident itself faded to the background and was replaced by guilt over not having apologised sufficiently nor correctly; so that as she had approached London, El had at times

228

almost forgotten what it was that caused her guilt in the first place. She was exhausted and could not find peace.

The extended period of isolation also took its toll. The little Frenchwoman was alone with her thoughts for days with no one to converse with beyond a few words exchanged at inns. Her mind had no rest nor distraction.

She got round to answering the knight. "There were two, a man and a woman. Both with blond hair, strikingly so…" El hesitated as she noticed a glimmer of recognition on Henry's face, "you found them also?"

"Unfortunately, yes. They took Brac," he explained with sinking shoulders and downward stare, still on his haunches. He heard El take a sharp intake of breath and, having realised she feared the worst, continued talking. "He went by his own accord, and I think he will be fine. He is Welsh, after all."

"What did they do to you?" the little Frenchwoman asked, her concern transferred from Brac to Henry.

The Englishman chortled a little, characteristically wheezing loudly before the main body of the laugh emanated from his broad mouth, as if he could not do so without first expelling half of his lung capacity. "I've had worse," he said, and then looked down between his legs, exaggerating the arch of his neck. "I don't use them anyway," he added with a wry grin.

El laughed and rolled her eyes. There were few circumstances about which Henry could not make light, and chastity was one of them. She did not truly know how Henry felt about it, not so much his commitment to or his acceptance of it but rather how challenging he found adherence. A considerable percentage of conversation between men was about women, and between women was about men. But she had known Henry since she was a girl and he was a young teen and never had he mentioned so much as one girl who had stolen his heart, or shared his first kiss, or....

Stop it, El. You're better than this. Time and a place! Her conscience kicked back in, reminding her of the guilt she had carried for the past few weeks. Further, to entertain such thoughts in the Temple Church, of all places! Her conscience was right; she was better than this. Her smile faded as quickly as it had appeared. "What did they want with him?"

Henry lost his joviality as rapidly. "I'm not quite sure; they were speaking in Welsh, and there was some concussion involved on my part, so exact details elude me," he said deadpan.

El's eyes immediately transmitted her sorrowful feelings at the thought of Henry suffering injury and Brac being taken by such a dangerous pair.

"They murdered the three English soldiers, not even in fighting. It was horrific, and they did not seem to even blink," El explained, "and what was almost as bad was that the villagers didn't seem to think anything of it."

"I didn't think things were becoming that bad," Henry said pensively, putting his hands on his knees and pushing himself upwards to return to his chair. He grunted a little at the effort and was reminded of his slowly accumulating physical limitations – a weak left knee, sharp soreness in his outer right elbow. The teachings of the Lord and the Church were so familiar, so ingrained in one's being that the concept of death and the soul's ascendance from this earthly plane was omnipresent, yet almost inconspicuous simply because it was such a huge presence. Henry could see it there and yet he still found himself surprised at the associated decline in physical capabilities as one aged, as if the two were not at all linked. He remained a superior athlete and followed his monastic habits as practically as he could when on the road, a lifestyle that most certainly had extended his effectiveness amongst the caste of warrior monks by a fair few years.

'They also knew who I was," added the Frenchwoman. "I think they've been onto us for a while. I don't know how, because I'm adamant we weren't followed to Rhuddlan."

"Same here, to all those points," sighed Henry. "*And* they know about the stone... too much about the stone."

"What do you mean, 'about' the stone?" asked El with stoked curiosity.

"Ah, you would've missed it all. You would not believe it unless you saw it," Henry said in an illusive manner.

El held her hands out with open palms and nodded at the tanned Englishman, wordlessly encouraging him to continue.

"From what we saw at the abbey of Chester, with Father Thomas and Prior Simon, it seems the stone has some unusual reaction with fire, or sources of heat. Oh, and it's not silver."

"What is it, then?" El asked impatiently.

"We don't know yet. I haven't had a chance to ask Guy about it properly because he's been needed at Westminster, and we were going to invite Brother John Duns at Oxford to investigate with us but Lord de Grey put paid to that venture."

"What's this reaction to fire?" The little Frenchwoman had momentarily forgotten her troubles and was hooked.

"It... makes things disappear," Henry said with reluctance, aware of the incredible claim he was making and unwilling to come across as deluded.

"'Disappear', what do you mean, 'disappear'?"

"I mean, literally disappear. Gone. At one point we poured some candle wax on it and in a burst of smoke the flooring beneath the stone had vanished, and it was sat at the bottom of a hole in the floor of Father Thomas' office. He didn't seem to mind, though," he quipped.

El looked at Henry with scrutiny. She had not risked her life and caused the death of others for the knight to play jokes on her now.

"No, really, Henry, this isn't time for games. What did you find?" she demanded wearily.

"I promise you, my dear girl, I speak the truth. I hear Father Thomas is en route here, he will vouch for me, and Prior Simon if he is with him." The English knight held his hands up in a gesture of innocence. "I tell you the truth. The stone is truly something of heavenly origin, but what it is, I cannot tell you. And now it is coming to London, so everyone will know about it."

"It made the floor *vanish*?" El checked again, incredulous.

Henry nodded deliberately slowly with lips tight together. "There's nothing further I can say that will convince you. I wouldn't believe it either, but you have to see it."

"Are you sure you hadn't been drinking?"

231

Henry scoffed. "Of course I'd been drinking, but that's never clouded my judgement before. I promise you, El. When we see Guy, we'll ask him. He must know what this is, and he must be able to tell me now that I've seen what it can do."

The two sat in silence for a moment and contemplated the state of affairs. The secret task to retrieve the stone had been blown and somehow revealed to not only the English but the Welsh as well. El simply needed some time to compute the tale Henry had just told her.

Henry sat back in his chair, noting the length of candle wick that had burned away in the time he had been ignoring it. He turned his mind back to the Dragons and thought aloud. "They know who we are, and they know about the stone. Somehow, they also know that it is coming to London; for a bunch of outlaws, their organisation and spying isn't half good," he said ruefully.

"They're better than we are," replied El, to which Henry raised his eyebrows and widened his eyes in a silent, reluctant agreement. "But only because we do not know much about them," El added, defiantly.

The knight nodded and leaned forward in his chair. "So, we need to do what we do best. Master Guy may have other contacts with information on them... and if not, we'll discover the information ourselves."

"To what end?" El asked, a hint of futility in her tone. "We're spies, nothing beyond that."

Henry could see the toll her recent experiences had taken on her. He had not seen her so disheartened! The little Frenchwoman was usually steely and determined, and often took the lead on assignments and dictating terms to him but now she was a husk of that woman he knew.

"Because we must work to protect our fellow Christians above all. It is our *raison d'être*. Just because we are roaming the hills of Wales far away from the Temple in Jerusalem does not mean we are not brothers and sisters of the Order," he asserted.

Henry saw that El was fixed on him, eyes darting between his and his bearded mouth. "We are the knights of God and as our lay brothers do, we must cover our Lord's servants with our shield. We are not the brothers and sisters of the saints, Benedict or Francis; our

232

duties take us beyond the safety of the monastery walls. We are the walls of the monastery and we protect the Christians within."

Henry sat back in the creaking chair and gripped the ends of the chair arms in his broad hands. "That is why we must go and find these Dragons. There cannot be a separation between the Welsh and the English, it is too far past the old divisions. It is one island; we must stop those who would have this island divided, Welsh or English."

Henry was silent for a moment and put his hand to his mouth, chewing a little on the middle knuckle of his right index finger, whilst staring into the small candle flame once more, deep in contemplation.

"You do remember it was a military conquest?" El stated, quite disbelieving of Henry's apparent short-sightedness. Again there was scrutiny in her eyes and she almost glared at the knight in the manner she always assumed when questioning particularly slippery characters in the field.

The knight had never received one of these glares and it was more than a little uncomfortable, but on the positive side at least the Frenchwoman was more like her usual, combative self.

"It was. And it was regrettable. As long as I have been alive, there has been fighting in the Marches, there has been fighting amongst the Welsh. What is done is done. We can only work with what we have now. Longshanks is a strong king' he is the man to unite the island. Look at the number of Welsh who fought against the uprising! It is our prerogative to assist the kingdom in helping the Church to create a united Christendom. These Dragons are zealots only out for their own ends. And there are Marcher lords who would see the countryside burn... we will stop them too."

Henry's blood was up. He was a man of action, an all-or nothing personality with indefatigable drive and El knew that it was at a time like this when the knight was almost irresistible in his rhetoric.

El glanced away from him; there was an energy about him like a ship riding the crest of a wave, unstoppable in its forward momentum regardless of her sailors' commands and efforts. What he was suggesting was far beyond their tasks, far beyond the teachings of the Lord Jesus. He was proposing proactive aggression! A knight of many battles in the Holy Land, but never before had he actively sought combat. His Holiness had requested he travel to the Holy Land... no heavenly or earthly authority had sanctioned this proposal!

El scrunched her long cloak in her right hand and chewed a fingernail on her left. She wanted to say all of this to dissuade Henry from his delusions, but did not have the heart to upset her closest friend by dismissing outright something about which he cared so passionately. Henry was a true man of the Church, righteous, pious and just. His words were not idle for they always came from the heart, but these... these were dangerous, not just physically but spiritually too. El wondered just what had happened in Henry's encounter with the Dragons that unsettled him so.

Finally she spoke, slowly so as to not sound accusatory. She wanted to dissuade Henry as gently and subtly as possible yet hoping that her own misgivings would not be lost amidst the cushioning words.

"The Master will not allow this. We cannot judge foe from friend – the hatred is intense, yes, but for this reason we cannot judge who is our friend, because they may one day become a foe. In the instance of incorrectly identifying one group or another, it will inevitably lead to persecution and there are heavy spiritual consequences for that... it is not who we are. We are the Church; the Master needs to rally for the authority of Rome in Parliament. That should be our direction, Henry. We are brothers and sisters of actions but before that we are brothers and sisters of words."

Henry leaned forward once more and reached out with his right hand, clasping over the top of El's left. He locked his eyes to hers and she saw the earlier passion had drained from them leaving a bare, mournful visage. Despite all of his energy, charisma, humour and joviality, in that moment it seemed Henry's essential constituent was sorrow. El wondered how she had not noticed this before, how she could not have seen through the clear waters of drive and exuberance to the distress and grief at the bottom of his being. This realisation was more painful than any punishment she had endured at the hands of gruff Sir Edward de Beauchamp and his men or the trauma she witnessed at Llaneurgain.

The Englishman spoke softly. "I have seen what divisions can cause; it is a nightmare from which I have not woken. I have seen Saracens slaughtering Christians and Christians slaughtering Saracens. I have seen green fields drowned in red and towns and villages burnt to the ground because there is no brotherhood between peoples. We will find the Dragons and we will find the Marcher lords and we will stop them. They will all be stopped."

Henry gripped El's hand tighter, the softness of her skin seemingly impossible to comprehend in a world of brutality and pain. He brushed his thumb over the back of her hand and she responded by slowly turning her hand over so that she could clutch his, holding tight. The two shared a silent moment. Henry longed for something but he did not know what that thing was; all he did know was that he wanted to sit here, at the ministers' table in the chancel of the Temple Church, holding El's hand. They had never had prolonged physical contact as intimate as this and Henry found it deeply comforting for reasons he could not explain. He had missed her and worried for her during the preceding weeks. Was this not an expected response to such potentially and likely perilous circumstances?

The knight had not allowed himself to become close with many people before. His brothers and sister were long dead and with them, so he thought, were his last meaningful emotional ties. He had compassion for those around him and was appalled by the cruelty he had witnessed on his travels, fuelling his desire to serve the Lord. However his concern had always been of a general rather than specific kind and he did not know why, but he did not think anything of it.

This too had been the case with El in all of the years they had worked together. *Or had it?* Henry began to question how he had viewed their friendship. Surely it had been platonic – she was his closest friend of course and he was not so emotionally stunted as to be indifferent to emotional investment, so his care for her was beyond the general concern he held for the peoples of the world. But he believed he still maintained a barrier that prevented El or anyone into the deepest corners of his being; those corners known only to the Lord.

235

On a baser level, too, the knight had not found himself enticed by the temptations of the flesh nor by the vices that came hand in hand with civilisation. He possessed mental fortitude beyond most monks, let alone the common man. So why did he draw such comfort from holding El's hand and gazing upon her gentle face? Was he sullying the Temple Church and his own soul with thoughts of lust? No, it was not that. It was something else.

Before the Englishman could decide what it was the silence of the lofty church was obliterated once more by the introduction of another guest via the huge creaking door at the front of the Round Church.

The tall figure swept along the aisle with dark grey cloak trailing after him and arms behind his back. The Master was the most senior Templar in England and he had a suitably authoritative air about him, striding imperiously through the church as he went. He had a hard face topped with a sheer bald head, solid in keeping with his giant frame. There were not many in the kingdom taller than King Edward, but Master Guy was amongst them. Henry had heard even the uppity lords at Parliament were cowed in his presence, taking care not to conspicuously disagree with a man who was at once one of the foremost churchmen in the land and had also seen more combat than most men alive. He had fought for years in the Levant, carving out a fearsome reputation; known as "The Anvil" by the brothers of Cyprus, Antioch and Jerusalem because iron and steel bent and broke on his unyielding resilience and spirit.

On top of this, he was possessed of near-mythical levels of energy and intelligence – El and Henry knew him well and could find no fault in the way he operated. The highly politicised leadership of the Order represented a microcosm of the secularisation faced by the greater Church body; in Henry's experience it was a place where godliness provided no advantage to those seeking office for altruistic purposes. And yet, travelling throughout Christendom, the English knight could not think of a man or woman more devoted to the faith than Guy. Henry saw the Master as some amalgamation of heroic figures from scripture and legend come to life; to El he was the guiding influence and paternal figure to whom she had been given as a ward by Uncle Jacques.

Hearing their new guest, El rose to her feet, letting go of Henry's hand suddenly and experienced a guilt-ridden rush of blood at thought that she had been caught doing something she should not have been doing. It was the very same feeling she would have as a child upon returning home with her brother after long summer days in the Provencal forests, and Mother would be waiting, furious.

But Guy was no furious parent. El could not recall the Master ever having lost his temper, though her time with him had been largely confined to ecclesiastical locations such as the Round Church and occasional Order houses around southern England. She imagined the Guy of the battlefield was a sight to behold and fear, the dread knight towering above all others in service to Christendom, but here he was an altogether gentler beast. The great man smiled as he approached and brought both long-sleeved arms out wide to beckon El for a hug. The little Frenchwoman's thin lips exploded into a beaming grin and she bound off the raised platform, almost breaking into a sprint towards the giant cloaked man; there was no risk of a dangerous collision such was the gulf in size between the two, though.

"*Ma chère* Eleanor!" Guy boomed, teeth showing through his wide-mouthed smile. He barely noticed the impact with the woman, so little was she. He folded his arms around her and momentarily all Henry could see of El was her legs emerging beneath the sea of cloak sleeves.

"And what has kept you from home for so long? Truly, the work of God is a lengthy task," the Master said to El, joy radiating from his broad face.

El looked up from her vantage point buried in the man's barrel chest. "Then let me go, so I can get back to work," she replied mischievously.

Guy then noticed the fading bruises on El's cheek and around her eye and his blue eyes lost their verve. "My dear girl, what has happened?" He felt a father's concern as if El were his own flesh and blood. He brought his hands up either side of her head and with a deftness that belied his great size caressed her cheeks with his thumbs.

"I had a little run in after we found the stone... nothing more," she responded, trying hard to seem unfussed by the recollection of what had happened.

Guy continued studying El's tanned face, the darker skin rendering the fading bruises only slightly less visible. "My dear child, your work has been magnificent and I pray God and the Lord Jesus forgive me for putting you in harm's way." There was contrition in his voice and El could sense this news had caused him almost as much pain as she herself endured.

She feigned her best smile. "Honestly, I'm fine. Others have been through worse. What about the sacrifices you and Henry have made? The Lord has brought me home."

Deep down, El felt she had been guided home, preserved for another day. She always had been guided home, preserved for future service in the name of Christ. She saw a narrative flowing through her life like a river, inexorable in its passage; she could move laterally across its channel and sometimes she might dig her heels into the riverbed and slow or even stop her momentum but given enough time the pull of the water would drag her ever forwards. After discussing the topic with Guy, he had warned her against complacency in her duties, though – not only was complacency akin to sloth, but assuming to know of God's plans was pride incarnate.

El disputed the Master's judgement of her thinking although chose not to take him up on the matter, figuring it would cause unnecessary friction. She was adamant her line of thinking was not prognostic – she was not claiming invulnerability to the agency of others courtesy of a preordained path of which she had knowledge – instead it was simply a way of retrospectively summarising how historic events had transpired. The little Frenchwoman had not knowingly shirked obeying the Commandments and whilst she had not yet mastered Aquinas' doctrine of predestination, with her travels with Henry revealing there were differing views on its interpretation, she felt the potential for lateral movement across that river channel

238

still represented the opportunity to follow the Commandments within the context of an irresistible journey forwards.

"You know that I will be upset if you are not truly revealing the nature of your injuries," he said again in a fatherly tone.

"There's nothing to worry about, father," the Frenchwoman lied. "I just need to sit down a little, that's all."

"*Hmm.*" Guy could see through El's untruth but for the time being decided against investigating further. There would be opportunity for that later.

"Have you just returned? You still appear bedraggled, and you smell of horse. Come, let's have some wine. I've been speaking all day and my throat needs relief." The tall man clasped El's shoulders and spun her around so that she was once more facing the raised platform crowned by the great ministerial table, peaked with Henry in his chair. El began towards the table and the Master followed once he had reset his grey tunic following their embrace. It was a dark grey tunic, fitted at the arms and emblazoned with a simple white cross stitched onto the chest and abdomen. It was near-identical to Henry's garment with the exception of the size. El thought it interesting the two knights insisted on well-fitted tunics and cloaks; old habits died hard for those who needed maximum agility in the arms. Loose and baggy sleeves as sported by the nobles at court furthered the risk of becoming engulfed in one's own clothing when brandishing sword and shield.

"Any word on arrangements for the King to see the stone?" asked Henry, passing a jug of wine to Guy as the Master walked round him to an empty chair across the table from El.

"Thank you, and they've been made. I spoke with Longshanks today. I hope this relic's abilities are as spectacular as you described, my dear boy, or there will be a great many disappointed noble types," came the reply. Guy spoke to Henry in an endearing manner without patronising him; he enjoyed the knight's company and English sense of humour which translated surprisingly well into Norman French. He poured a cup of wine for El, who had sat in her chair, and then one for himself. Henry's cup remained full, untouched since the rapidly diminishing candle that once again ensnared his attention had been first lit.

239

Guy continued. "Baron de Grey's caravan will be reaching the city the day after the morrow," he said, pausing after noticing El's reaction to the mention of the name. "My dear girl, I'll be having a chat with Lord de Grey to remind him of his duties toward those in his care," correctly deducing that El's bruises had something to do with de Grey having recalled Henry's account of her courageous diversionary tactic in the forest by the quarry.

El gave a smile that both knew to be insincere. She trusted Guy would deal with the situation appropriately – yes, technically she had been stealing – and as for the lord receiving a coolly-delivered dressing down from the Master she had no doubt

"Just as well we aren't needed over the next few days then; I'd rather not grace the lord with my presence," she spoke as she tried to drag her thoughts away from the experience at the hands of Sir Edward de Beauchamp and his soldiers.

The Master slowly sipped his wine, keeping his eyes on her as he did so, leaning forward with both elbows propped on the table and broad shoulders hunched. "Well, that's where you're wrong," he said before taking another sip. Both El and Henry glanced at him. "I wouldn't send you out to find it and then give it up at the first sign of trouble. All the suffering you have endured... no. The Order will have the stone; it cannot remain in the King's hands. Undoubtedly, it is the relic we have been searching for." He drank again, slowly and steadily, measured as was everything else he undertook.

El shot a questioning look to Henry, who continued staring at the candle flame. The English knight knew, however, he was being silently asked his opinion and so responded with a raised eyebrow. No words were necessary for both knew the Master to be sufficiently thorough as to never leave details unconsidered.

"Sleight of hand and distraction will be in order," the great man continued, "and we must pray the good Lord smiles upon us that day. The council members are suspicious of the Order's interest in the stone and these reservations have reached the King. It doesn't help that Baron de Grey is one of them." Master Guy sighed, regretting Lord Reginald's presence in the capital. "There will be a demonstration, public for the most part, but largely excluding the commons, as you'd expect. The King's forbidden our presence in the immediate circle at its demonstration. Unfortunately, it seems the King's council is also aware of our interest in Brother John Duns, which rules out that approach. He'll be watched like a hawk the moment he walks through the Newgate tomorrow."

Henry finally snapped out of his flame-induced trance and rubbed his eyes with the back of his thumbs, momentarily casing his face to go red from the pressure on his skin. "So we're on our own," he sighed.

"We're always on our own," El retorted. Lord Reginald knows who I am, but I'm guessing he's never seen you," she said looking at the English knight, to which he shook his head, "and so it should be Henry with the sleight of hand..." She paused, gathering her thoughts.

"Go on," Guy encouraged.

El squinted at the English knight, but directed her question at Guy. "Where will the King be watching a 'demonstration', if you can call it that?

"On the clearing to the north of the fortress. Wide open so no tricks, yet completely secure from other kinds of tricks," Guy answered, trying to second guess El's thought process.

El pursed her lips, thinking. The candles' illumination of her small face made her seem even younger than she was, vulnerable and abused with the fading bruises. Of course, both her friends there knew the opposite to be true; she was physically and mentally resilient. Henry knew this particularly well; El's account of the previous few weeks would be harrowing regardless of who one was.

The little Frenchwoman spoke once more. "The fortress... the closest houses to the fortress are Aldgate and Eastminster, yes?"

Henry enjoyed her pronunciation of certain English proper nouns. El had never quite mastered a consistent pronunciation of 'Aldgate', stressing the second syllable here, shortening the 'A' there. Listening to her accent was melodic and soothing like sitting by a stream on a hot summer's day, effortless and serene. The occasional English place name represented the slight, mischievous cascade down a jutting rock as the stream makes its way downhill, unexpected and yet at the same time a completely natural aspect of the course as a whole.

The knight answered her. "And the brothers at Crutched Friars." Guy nodded in agreement.

"Of course, thank you," El replied. "Perhaps we should see if any of the brothers would be willing to accept Henry as one of their own for the day? I'm assuming the King will be expecting local dignitaries from the houses." She looked to Guy.

"Undoubtedly," came the great man's response. "I'll find out tomorrow which house will have the honours. I would suspect the Crutched Friars. Those pious brothers are particularly favoured by King Edward."

El nodded in affirmation. "And if you can find out where the stone is going afterwards, if the dignitaries are going with it, then our anonymous brother here can go with it," she planned, nodding her head at Henry.

"I do believe the relic will be taken to St John's Chapel in the White Tower, from what I've heard," Guy offered. He paused briefly with his mouth open a little as if the words he wanted to say were not quite ready to emerge. "I should be able to arrange some sort of decoy. Once Edward realises what he has on his hands, he won't keep it in the chapel for long."

Henry smiled at Guy and then El. "So when am I getting my hair shaved, then?"

"Depends on which order house the King chooses," cautioned Guy, though aware the English knight was as resistant to complacency as was he. "Rumour has it, for what rumours are worth, that some of our brothers and sisters have caught the people's excitement at the approach of the 'Godstone'." He raised his heavy eyebrows at the name, averse as he was to using informal English vernacular.

"'Godstone', not bad," Henry opined. "For once, popular exaggeration may not be unfulfilled."

"It certainly shan't, but we must ensure that popular anticipation does not become popular demand, and I'm including the lords and Longshanks himself in that group." Guy's face seemed to darken a little, replacing his former mellow disposition.

Both El and Henry noticed the change and glanced at one another briefly for a clue as to what the Master could be hinting at. Henry assumed that such capabilities as the stone ostensibly possessed could be used for ill, which so greatly troubled him with respect to the Dragons, but Guy had not yet even seen the object or what it could do.

"Is there... something else about the stone?" Henry spoke slowly at first, hesitant to hear what could only be bad news.

Guy looked Henry in the eyes. "If this object is as you say it is, and is as we have been expecting, then I fear not even Longshanks could rein himself in."

"What *is* it?" El interrupted, shooting Guy an impatient glower that was a little stronger than she had intended.

Guy paid her frustration no mind. "It is something that will create an Ozymandias or Nebuchadnezzar of those who use it. Longshanks is a warrior, and warriors need weapons. This is a relic from God, but with impure intentions, any gift from the Lord could be used for ill. This is why the Order seeks it and must retain it. Even His Holiness is, or at least was, unaware of this hunt. Rome's involvement will further complicate matters."

El was not satisfied with the Master's answer. "Henry says it makes things *disappear*," said the little Frenchwoman with uncertainty, self-conscious at how silly such a claim may sound.

Guy rubbed his hands together and contorted his mouth a little, a sure sign of discomfort. "Henry is right. It can cause all sorts to disappear."

Henry sensed Guy did not want to talk too expansively about the item they had sacrificed so much to locate, but because of that effort the English knight decided an explanation was appropriate at this stage. Guy had always been grey with details or even evasive when the two spies had pressed him on the provenance of his command. All they knew was that Master Guy and Grandmaster Jacques wanted it found.

"How did you know about this?" Henry asked.

Guy stopped for a moment before answering. "I've seen it before."

Both El and Henry raised their eyebrows.

"There's another one. The Temple hid it away, far away, out of the reach of grasping men," the great bald man continued. "Man is

243

not yet ready for these treasures, and it's the Temple's task to keep man safe."

The Frenchwoman and the English knight were unsure how to respond to such a revelation, sat poised with questions that refused to formulate coherently in their minds.

"But we should rest, now. You especially," Guy ordered whilst looking at the exhausted El. "We have much *unofficial* business ahead of us."

Chapter 17

The horses stood with static bodies but their heads and tails waved and bobbed frantically, trying to ward off the late summer gnats that had emerged and converged for their daily task of plagueing man and beast alike. Their riders, the pinnacle of French nobility, encased in plate and mail and decorated with fine cloths, were altogether more disciplined and thanks to their hammered iron casing likely did not register the insects' presence.

Instead it was the eerie *thrum* of bowstrings released in their hundreds that held their attention. The French archers had formed three irregular banks split between two flanks on either shoulder of a seething mass of heavily armoured knights. Raoul de Clermont's horsemen were in the mould of their commander – intimidating and dangerous, lacking only the constable's ice-cool composure. These sons of France, the most renowned knights in the realm, were impetuous and fearless. However, they had not been trained since childhood to loiter at the rear of battle awaiting the arrow storm to subside. They had been trained since childhood to join battle and win. More perfect physical specimens one would not find anywhere, no stronger nor fitter men on this battlefield than they. Seizing the opportunity to demonstrate this physical prowess was as crucial to their identity as was the prowess itself. Frustrated anticipation of joining battle led to their position appearing a veritable wasps' nest of dread iron and steel.

In front of the archers stood an even more disorganised line of spear levies, hundreds of men rounded up from the villagers in the last brief lull before the harvest, barely any of whom possessing a shield of any kind let alone experience of a battlefield. Even through the great helm about his head that deprived his senses their full range, and from two hundred yards away upon their small hill, the Comte de la Marche could sense the trepidation emanating from those spearmen.

He did not blame them for their unease. Across the potholed field a few miles west of Ghent, so chosen by the Comte Dampierre because of its unsuitability for heavy cavalry, lay the Flemish host. Mathieu knew exactly what awaited Philippe's army. Solid blocks of highly disciplined dismounted Flemish knights stood in ranks like the alternating squares of a chessboard, entirely clad in iron grey and steel silver and carrying shields almost as long as they were tall. As the irregular volleys began to fall on the squares, Mathieu could see each long oblong shield rise up and provide cover for both the carrier and a crouched figure beside – a few tiny figures fell to the ground but the French archers did not make much of an impression with their half-hearted skirmishing. The Constable of France had never been one for preliminary archer fire, and with de Clermont's record, Comte Mathieu would not argue with him.

No sooner had the French volley dissipated did those crouching figures scurry out from underneath their shield canopies and begin firing their own arrows, somehow managing to do so in an even more disorderly pattern than did the French archers, much to the Comte's amazement. However, the French infantry were generally far less protected, and Mathieu winced as the first screams went up from the hapless spear levies whose nervous energy was threatening to spill over into hysteria. They appeared alarmed as the hens in their enclosure at the approach of the plunging long-winged goose hawk; frenetically turning this way and that for cover or escape that is not forthcoming. The hawk soars above and picks its prey at will whilst all below is pandemonium. Thus were the poor farmers in the front ranks of the French host.

Mathieu remembered the catastrophic defeat suffered by Philippe's father to King Pero of Aragon at the Col de Panissars ten years prior, almost to the day he noted. Thousands of terrified French infantry were massacred as the army was completely annihilated by Pero's forces. The speed at which mass panic washed over the French army was almost as frightening as the slaughter that followed – with the royal family having already escaped, the Comte and other lesser nobles toiled fruitlessly to keep the infantrymen in a semblance of discipline as they desperately sought flight across the Pyrenees from the murderous and vengeful advance of Aragonese behind them. The Comte was not sure there had been many defeats as comprehensively catastrophic as that he witnessed that terrible day.

Mathieu knew, however that the spearmen were not the targets – the majority of the arrows were falling toward the concentrated box of mounted knights at the centre of the line, though he pitied the spearmen who would find no solace in such knowledge. To his right he saw the fearsome Raoul de Clermont raise a long lance tied with a blue streamer at least ten paces long. The lance itself was fifteen feet of treated ash tipped with a steel fist, requiring huge strength to lift at such an angle with two arms let alone the one hand the mighty Constable used.

It was said that de Clermont had a cast taken of his own clenched right hand so that the war lance became so much more an extension of his fighting arm, though Mathieu also recalled that many soldiers believed de Clermont to have cleaved a horse clean in half with a lance strike, amongst other even more improbable rumours; soldiers had built up an entire mythology around the Constable, unsurprising given his ferocity and monstrous appearance. Ever the cynic, however, Mathieu knew that even the most implausible stories could have the simplest of explanations.

What all accepted, though, was that the blue streamer signalled the advance to the knights up ahead and they broke apart and fanned out towards the flanks, screening the terrified levies and archers. The latter continued firing away sporadically in between helplessly and hopelessly scampering to avoid the incoming Flemish missile attacks. Their own desperate efforts to avoid the invisible death falling from the skies only had the effect of further scaring the levies who were far more densely packed in position and therefore themselves incapable of running no matter how futile such an act would be.

At the sight of the knights breaking out Raoul lowered the lance and his squire rushed forward, a youth of about twenty with long black hair slicked back over his burnished shoulder plates; Mathieu had seen him before and sensed the boy's appearance was a manifestation of hero worship for his fearsome lord. He looked a strong lad and was surely close to knighthood himself, there was a restraint in his expression that the Comte had seen in so many disappointed youths who had to watch their knights ride off to battle as they watched on.

The squire expertly untied the streamer and hastily retreated behind the giant destriers carrying the kingdom's finest knights; at Raoul's side was Gauiter de Narbonne with his symmetric blue red shield design matching the livery draped over his light grey mare; Henri d'Albi, the young lion knight who had the proud beast emblazoned across his chest plate and steel lion jaws clamped shut around his closed visor like a latter-day Hercules; and to his right was Simon de Châlons atop his horse, the animal resplendent in a blue caparison from nose to tail, adorned with tens of golden-stitched *fleurs-de-lis*.

Beyond them came the tourney champion, Renaud d'Angers, brandishing the gold-gilded lance that had won so many victories at the recent tourney on the bank across the Seine from the fortress. Mathieu believed such ostentatious gilding superfluous, but could appreciate the marvellous craftsmanship of Renaud's favourite armourer, the famous Pierre of Angers. Renaud was followed by Guy de Clermont, the Constable's younger brother and a frightening man in his own right; Mathieu often wondered how their gentle father Simon de Clermont, who had tutored King Philippe's father when he was a child, had produced such monstrous issue.

Finally, after the younger de Clermont came the hot-headed brother of the King in his shimmering silver-treated plate, the armour unmarked but only due to its freshness and not through vanity – Charles de Valois was a skilled horseman and Raoul had requested Charles and his bodyguard Gervais accompany him into battle.

Mathieu turned his head to better view the terrible wall of man, beast and steel, flying the finest livery and brandishing the fiercest weaponry in the land. It was both an awesome and dreadful sight, assembled from the beelike work of squires running hither and thither to arm their masters before the advance commenced; the Comte felt a shiver as he took in for a moment the power of such a group. No exhilaration could match the sight of the cavalry charge, that dance of the knights that tore through and flattened enemy ranks as if they were crops in the field.

Raoul once more raised his lance, no longer flying the royal blue streamer, and began cantering forwards followed by the knights either side of him. Another fifty yards or so away was Philippe's bodyguard, the King himself indistinguishable from his guards so he may do battle and avoid undue enemy attention. His bodyguard unit, also advancing on Raoul's signal – as in civil administration, in times of war Philippe allowed his ministers and officers much responsibility – somehow managed to outdo the Constable's own contingent in the garishness of their decorations. Truly, it was as if the tournament had come to the fields of Flanders but there were no adoring crowds nor streamer displays here, no money counters offering odds to possessed gamblers nor women shouting lewd declarations of desire.

Mathieu scowled a scowl that no one could see behind the jaw plate across the lower part of his helm. It was all pointless. The colours, the elaboration, the lion maw around Henri d'Albi's visor. The inevitable and imminent slaughter of hundreds, probably thousands of men. There were so many other ways in which Philippe could achieve his expansionist goals and sate his ego. So many other ways that did not involve rich men in heavy armour atop huge horses running down poor men in no armour and ankle deep in potholes and mud.

Mathieu had little love for rich and poor men alike, but the poor men did not deserve this end. He subconsciously played with the long, coarse hair of Pinto's mane. There was a reassuring fullness about the hair even if the Comte could not experience the fibrous strands through his gloved hands. It was good to grip onto in times of stress and Mathieu knew the mare enjoyed it too, as many animals found such attention addictive.

He narrowed his eyes at the spectacle unfolding before him much like a deadly chess match. Ahead, the centre of the line opened up and the cavalry spurred their mounts into a slow trot, a rolling start for when the King and the Constable's heavy cavalry joined, to gradually accelerate to a devastating gallop that would smash through the Flemish lines.

Fighting wars was an unsavoury business; the Comte found the experience at Col de Panissars mentally if not physically scarring.

But all the same, he had always expected - nay, demanded - people to perform to the highest standards in whichever role they were allocated. Once they were stuck in, the French knights were exceptional at conducting their unsavoury business. They were a different breed of man, living for the garishness, pomposity and superfluous. He pondered the chain of events that brought him to the position of Philippe's spymaster; as an exceptional spymaster no one really knew about his work, a circumstance he highly appreciated. He dreaded to think of the attention he would garner were his specialist talents concentrated in the conduct of war from the saddle.

Mathieu watched de Clermont's small group thunder away across the dry grass toward the rapidly widening corridor through the centre of the French line, the knights at the front branching out left or right and creating the appearance of a giant gate swinging open for de Clermont's paladins. Mathieu wondered how it was that anyone could survive a charge from such monstrous amalgamations of man and animal; like great armoured centaurs with the swift speed of four legs and the terrible warcraft of two arms were the chosen companions of the Constable of France, all at once magnificent and nightmarish with screaming horse and brutal lance. It would surely appear to the Flemings that Charlemagne and his glorious Franks were riding once more, irresistible and unstoppable.

The sounds of screaming came flooding back to the Comte's ears as his attention refocused to the poor levy spearmen at the front, soaking up the Flemish arrow fire with as much discipline and steadfastness as could be expected from frightened farmers. Raoul de Clermont was a hard man and pragmatic but not without compassion; knowing the likely outcome of the opening exchanges he had requisitioned every shield, purposefully crafted or adapted, and piece of armour he could, going so far as demanding of the lords and knights they distribute their personal wardrobes to the levied peasants. Yet still the arrows rained and the farmers fell. But not for much longer, Mathieu hoped – the bodyguard units of both Raoul and the King were fast approaching their designated corridors, accelerating from a canter to a gallop which in turn was the signal for the remaining French knights to turn about and spur their mounts towards the waiting Flemish infantry.

250

The Comte cast his eyes skywards at the pregnant iron-grey clouds heavily looming overhead, darker and more menacing than even the silvery-steel wave of cavalry flooding across the uneven grassy field. He imagined the French knights feared what they could see in the sky more than they did on the earth before them. The Flemings had chosen the field of battle well – if the rain were to start falling the field would become a quagmire.

Mathieu grimaced. When the clouds had rolled in that morning, Raoul had insisted on giving battle as early as possible lest the rains lasted a few days, a week or even longer. The harvest was just weeks away and the treasury empty – Norris and his collectors had moved more quickly than Mathieu had anticipated. Once the fighting had concluded the Comte intended to ride straight for Paris to deal with Le Verre and his failure to provide correct information. Of course, Mathieu did not know his or her identity, but he still held some leverage. As much as the Comte relied on Le Verre for information did Le Verre owe their security to Mathieu's patronage – Mathieu had runners other than Le Gris, who either had split loyalties or none at all, who could shut down Le Verre's circle at his command. The Comte was not happy at being outmanoeuvred by Norris and taking the fall for it from the King. Mathieu and Le Verre knew their work and relationship was based on mutual respect and so the former considered the latter's failure to perform a grave offence to their unspoken agreement.

Presently, retribution would have to wait. All such issues were of no consequence for the time being, the timing of their resolution entirely dependent on fearsome Raoul de Clermont's martial nous and, more significantly, the weather. Perhaps the only feeling Mathieu resented more than suffering the consequences of another's incompetence was that of powerlessness – from his current position atop Pinto, hundreds of yards away from the lines of battle, amongst the elders and non-combatants, he could do nothing. He did not regret sitting out of the combat because he had no inclination towards the savagery that was required of the participants and had not done so since that day at Col de Panissars ten years ago.

No, it was his mental, verbal and aural impotence. He could not pull strings nor manipulate nor treaty; all he could do was sit and watch. Worse, he could not shake the sense of alarm over the timing of the message from his English contact, that message relaying news of King Edward Longshanks' divine discovery.

It affected Mathieu at some deep level but he did not know why. Was Philippe mistaken in his belligerence? Even without the news from England, Mathieu thought he was. Had the English king truly received a gift from the Lord? And if he had, what agency could now resist him? Philippe had not only stripped Edward of his ancient right to the Duchy of Aquitaine, but had demanded personal fealty in Paris! The English king was not a man to take insult lightly.

Even more pertinent, Philippe having publicly claimed the senior Parisian churchmen had taught him the way of peace, prior to marching for war in the name of financial gain, was morally questionable and somewhat out of character. The Comte was by no means naive, probably the least naive man in the kingdom; he understood the rhetoric demanded of a king more than anyone. Keeping a kingdom afloat and a society cohesive required shifts in principles and adaptations to what was popularly considered 'right' and 'wrong'. Mathieu himself would have advised against Philippe's choice of lie - he suspected the Queen and Enguerrand de Marigny had some say in it – but Philippe was not the first king and would not be the last to play the game, though these circumstances were troubling and the Comte could not shake the feeling that the throne's current course was contradicting destiny's flow. He looked up again at the clouds, by now fit to burst. A shiver ran down his spine.

With little in the way of introduction the rain began hammering down. The raindrops pattered against the Comte's armour and found its way through the joints in the plate and the mail rings to further soak his already sweat-drenched under tunic and breeches. He closed his eyes and savoured the refreshing, cooling relief afforded by the rainfall – in one moment the stifling humidity had been obliterated and the temperature fell rapidly. Mathieu opened his eyes again and squinted through shower. The Flemish plan had worked – although the advancing French heavy cavalry were now too far away to accurately judge speeds, Mathieu knew only too well the chaos the mud was playing with the horses' footing.

Raoul's colourful bodyguard with Gautier de Narbonne's red and blue, Simon de Châlons' *fleurs-de-lis* and the golden lance of Renaud d'Angers had merged with the silvers and greys of the knights and the blacks, browns and whites of the horses. The King and his bodyguard were long gone, originally almost indistinguishable and now completely invisible through the opaque rainfall. Mathieu thought he saw a horse fall in the centre of the line. The visibility was further obscured by the mud and grass thrown up by the galloping mounts as the cries of war, impacts of hoof and drumming of rain all merged into one dire cacophony. He saw another few horses upend. Pinto stomped at the ground and the Comte absentmindedly *shhh*ed, far too quietly for the agitated animal to hear, whilst he strained to keep an eye on the swarming French knights.

By now the Flemish line had completely disappeared behind the French charge and judging from the topography, which was more or less flat from the French position leading to a very gentle slope up towards the Flemish lines, the knights, with the King and Raoul, Charles de Valois and Guy de Clermont, were almost on top of the heavy Flemish infantry. The Comte winced as the sickening impact of the frightful cavalry charge crashing into the Flemish human wall announced itself with countless riders and infantry vaulting, spears flying and horses falling. Mathieu had seen firsthand the devastating carnage of a French cavalry charge from behind the lance. The bloodcurdling screams, the horrifying crunch of high velocity steel and horse on soft, stationary bodies and the trail of gore left behind as the unstoppable paladins rolled forwards were indelibly marked in his memory. He was silently relieved when the King requested he stay out of this battle. A preening courtier drunk on the idealisation of stories and poems would take such a request as an affront to his honour but the Comte de la Marche was too realistic and long in the tooth to take offence.

More horses and riders fell. The Comte's grim expression, squashed in by the restricting cheek plates of his helmet and further encouraged by the foul weather, twisted more as he thought he saw an entire section of the left flank go down in a matter of moments. Not trusting his eyesight, which he reckoned had deteriorated considerably in recent years, Mathieu glanced to his right to Roger for affirmation of the turn of events. Roger was dutifully holding Mathieu's lance and shield and had never looked so miserable in his life, completely sodden with rivers of rainwater running down his sloped open helmet onto his shoulder plates and through the joints. Roger wore no armour on his arms or legs, though, offering far less protection from the wet than did Mathieu's full body plate and mail and so whilst the Comte was sodden, his guard was absolutely drenched through. The precipitation was of no concern to Roger now, however, for he was staring at the same part of the line as had Mathieu, mouth opening a little in an inaudible gasp.

"The left..." Roger began before his words faltered into nothingness.

His fears confirmed, Mathieu looked back to the front. He could see it now; there was a significant gap in the left flank where moments before countless knights had been. In that gap could be seen the Flemish infantry, still standing firm and not scattering as had been intended. Concern seeped into Mathieu's mind like the rainwater through his mail shirt.

"Are the Flemings coming?" he asked Roger without taking his eyes off the front.

"They are, my lord," came the sorrowful reply. Both men knew the downed French knights would be no more than meat for butchering for the heavy Flemish footmen wielding their great pole cleavers. The cleavers were horrifying weapons up to ten feet in length topped by brutal steel blades with edges as long as a man's arm. The length of the pole meant that each soldier could generate sufficient downward force to cut clean through plate armour – much as enemy infantry would usually crumble in the face of a cavalry charge, the fallen French knights would stand no chance in the mud against such weaponry. More horses were falling on the left when a horn sounded that signalled the levies advance to their support, driven forward by the Constable's chosen sergeants. Remarkably, Mathieu could hear the individual bellowing of each man, some of them known to him and others not. They were the hardest men on the field and the Comte urged them on in their urging. *"Come on, come on, come on!"* he growled, causing Roger to look over at him.

"You might be needed, my lord," Roger offered matter-of-factly.

The Comte turned his head to Roger and then looked beyond the loyal guardsman to the agitated body of knights twenty yards away, the army's rear guard headed by the wise Duke Robert de Bourgogne, useless and furious and sinking in the mud and rain whilst the great men of the kingdom were being hacked down and slaughtered a few hundred paces to the north. They were the reserve force tasked with watching the caravan and had been instructed to provide support only if the tide of battle appeared to be turning – even with the threat of rain, Philippe and his councillors, Mathieu included, expected a rapid and decisive victory so long as the cavalry charge went without issue.

Issue had been found however and so Mathieu was thankful to the Lord that the King's army had very little in the way of a caravan to look after; such were the benefits of marching through a neighbouring province. Who knew where the King was at this instant; Raoul had taken the left corridor and Philippe the right but heavy cavalry movements were not always precisely executed, and the weather had turned at the worst possible moment.

"We're going to lose this, Roger," Mathieu said wearily as he turned back round to the fighting. He had hoped his direct involvement would not be necessary today. The right flank's momentum appeared unimpeded by whatever tactics had caused the left to collapse and the Comte could see it wheeling round to mop up the rear of the increasingly unnerved Flemish infantry, but then noticed some more horses emerging from a copse off to the east. They were not French knights.

"Do you see that?" he urgently asked his guardsman.

"I do... they'll hit our cavalry side on, my lord." Roger's tone was urgent and not at all like his typically dreary delivery. "My lord," the guard prompted Mathieu for a response again without really giving him time to reply to his first comment.

"Stay here," the Comte commanded as he pulled the reins sharply up and left, urging Pinto right and kicked her into a gallop over to the Duke de Bourgogne. The necessity of testing his martial prowess once more was becoming apparent. Ten years since that ride at Col de Panissars. That must have been the last time he had donned full armour, which still fit perfectly, somehow – a fairly big man already, Mathieu knew from observing the other old hands at court and particularly in high ecclesiastical office the effect of a lifetime's worth of drinking wine on an ageing and inactive body. Yet miraculously he had retained the same appearance for twenty years. Perhaps it was the excellent Bordeaux.

Martial or otherwise, all he had worked for over the past ten years was presently at risk through the twin perils of Philippe's recklessness and inconvenient weather. Who else would keep the kingdom together should Philippe fall alongside his greatest generals? The roar of battle and the incessant, deafening ringing of raindrops on helm and armour vied with Mathieu's rational judgement for his attention, and in this critical moment, with the outcome in the balance, the roar and the ringing won through. The Comte was moving, or rather guiding Pinto, without conscious control – he knew the likelihood of horrendous injury for both him and his mount but something stronger than his own rational mind had taken control of his faculties. Was it duty? Action was required and the Comte de la Marche was responding.

The going was becoming treacherous as the rain fell in sheets, heavier than any fall this season, turning not just the sky but everything beneath it a shade of grey, dulling colours and blurring objects. Indeed from just a few paces away even the vibrant red cross on pure white of Duke Robert's Burgundian coat of arms splashed across his shield and horse's caparison were clouded to drabness through the precipitation and grime. Pinto's hooves slapped through the waterlogged grass as the Comte approached de Bourgogne, atop his huge grey destrier, a truly magnificent beast clad in almost as much plate as was its rider. Pinto seemed an underfed juvenile in comparison and certainly less heavily armoured. Mathieu doubted she could carry that additional weight.

The Comte pulled up alongside de Bourgogne. The two men had great mutual respect for each other, but were by no means close. In wartime as in peace such distinctions were of as little consequence to the Duke as they were to Mathieu and so the acknowledgements were informal and to the point.

256

"My dear Duke," Mathieu shouted through the downpour, the hammering rain creating an almighty din against the metalwork garnishing the heavily armoured riders and horses of the army's rear guard, "what say you join me in ignoring the King's orders for the afternoon?" He spun his head to the left and caught sight of more knights disappearing from view, though he could not be sure whether this was due to the Flemings or the weather's effect on the visibility.

The Duke eyed Mathieu from head to saddle and back again before looking down at his own saddle, as far as the restrictive combination of helmet and shoulder and breast plates allowed. A smile crept onto his broad face. "Once more, my dear Comte," said de Bourgogne rousingly, with the enthusiasm and fearlessness of a youth out on the hunt. "We rally these farmers to fight for their king and yet they are butchered by men they have no quarrel with. Let's put a stop to this."

He twisted in his saddle, again as far as his bulky dark grey suit permitted, and bellowed for his arms. There followed a ripple of shouting and activity backwards and outwards from the Duke to the rest of the rearguard, all calling their squires if they had one, clanking shields onto arms and shutting visors and steadying bristling lances. A number were navigating the churned long grass to positions wide of Mathieu and Duke Robert and squires scurried between horses with all varieties of metalwork, the ruinous instruments of war now appearing even more haunting amidst the miserable deluge.

The Comte heard angered shouts go up as a young squire slipped in the mire and sullied his jacket and fair hair with mud, coating his knight's shield and lance with sludge before they had even been used in battle. The flailing lance struck another horse on the rump causing it to dance and momentarily lose its footing; its rider, who on a clear day would have been resplendent with a burgundy plume from atop his crested helm but instead appeared like a drenched cockerel with feathers plastered to his helmet, skilfully calmed his distressed mount before turning to berate the poor young squire. Tensions were high and Mathieu knew they needed to get going as soon as possible, not just for the King's sake but also for the health and stability of the men here, knights and squires both.

He turned away from the miniature drama unfolding before him and saw Roger already on foot with his arms, lolloping through the muddied grass with lance over one shoulder and shield the other. Pinto shook her head and snorted. Gruff voices cried out and metalwork *clank*ed on more metalwork, periodically drowning out the chaos of the battle across the field.

"It's plenty sharp enough, my lord," Roger stated drolly, handing the dread lance to the Comte de la Marche.

Mathieu gripped and squeezed and was immediately transported back years to his halcyon days of jousting and warcraft. The lance was perfectly balanced - heavy enough to deliver the desired impact but wonderfully weighted so as to be held with just a strong right arm. He looked it up and down as it towered aloft and the rain fell directly through the visor of his great helm into his eyes.

Blinking hard for there was no other way of clearing his vision, Mathieu lowered the lance and beckoned Roger fasten his shield. The shield was angular, wider at the top than bottom and pointed at either end. The lower end was extended to offer a slither of additional protection for Pinto without compromising the maneuverability of man or horse. Upon the shield was the coat of arms for La Marche; the royal *fleurs-de-lis* on a field of azure, supporting a diagonal deep red sash that blazed across from top left to bottom right. Three consecutive lions lined the sash and roared their defiance of the enemies of the county of La Marche, raw spirits in their hearts as they defended the county at the heart of France.

Duke Robert raised the grill to his great helm. "For God and our country!" he roared, prompting a booming chorus of cheers from the remaining horsemen as they spurred their mounts into a canter. Mathieu joined in and felt that old rush. Even though he considered himself far more refined than his youthful self, he remembered why knights could not tolerate delay when the opportunity for the spectacular charge and slaughter was there. It was a shameful concession to his baser instincts, and he prayed that it was only a momentary lapse of character.

Thus rumbled forward the small contingent of heavy cavalry who would turn the tide of battle. Two overwhelmed and hurried squires up near the front of the group had not yet vacated the vicinity and were forced to dive to the side to avoid being trampled. The Comte de la Marche fought to maintain the balance of lance, shield and horse whilst encased in his sensory-depriving armour, and was thankful for the high pommel at the front of his saddle that effectively buffeted him in. He gripped the rein with his free left hand tighter than he would normally have done and Pinto recognised this, instinctively slowing which caused horse and rider to fall behind the others. Mathieu kicked a little harder on the swift beast's flanks to accelerate again, simultaneously attempting to relax his grip, as unnatural as it was.

Consciously trying to relax is nearly always an oxymoronic undertaking and so as they cantered along, slowly accelerating, Mathieu allowed himself to think of the moral concessions one makes in times of duress or under the ideal of duty. His personal dislike of participating in the cavalry charge was deeply rooted in its barbaric consequences - not through any disagreement with its effectiveness as a military tactic, because of that there was no doubt - and yet when required, he stepped up to participate. Was he betraying his own moral code? Or worse? Was betraying one's own moral code a betrayal of God, in Whom that moral code must surely originate?

Render unto Caesar what is Caesar's, and to God what is God's. As he advanced ever closer to the lines, Mathieu worried of the implications of prioritising his obligations to Philippe over God. His plate armour rattled with every bounce in the saddle, shaking him like a rag, and his thighs burned from the intense effort to maintain a steady riding position.

Somehow the downpour intensified; surely a rainstorm of the kind that brought about the Great Flood, treacherous conditions for walking let alone galloping across a field. At first light Raoul had insisted the smiths attend as many horses as possible to apply studded shoes when it became apparent that the weather would force battle, but the smiths were outnumbered by hundreds to one and many, the majority even, trotted out to the lines with the fair weather shoes of the long, hot summer that was most definitely on its way out. The twin perils of urgency and caution tore at Mathieu's heart as Pinto hammered forwards as if riding through an unnaturally extensive waterfall with clumps of matted grass thrown up by Duke Robert's giant charger ahead flying about the Comte's line of sight. They were approaching the advancing masses of French footmen trudging onwards, some using the butts of their spears to maintain balance or wade through the churned field, once relatively pristine and occasionally grazed but now obliterated and left vandalised by thousands of hoof impacts.

The Comte could not hear anything from inside his enclosed helmet except the thunder of Pinto's gallop but he saw the sergeants marshalling the levies clear of the approaching rearguard. In contrast to the cooling rain that had burst the looming humidity in the air, the motion of his horse and the perfect fit of his armour generated tremendous heat that caused him to perspire in ever increasing quantities. His right hand felt as if he had plunged it into a pail of water, such was the grip with which he held his lance. He felt shame at having switched his thoughts, from the possible sin he had committed in renouncing his objection to the cavalry charge, to registering exactly how uncomfortable he had become in these conditions. How did the monks keep their thoughts from straying? Did they manage to maintain focus, or were they as susceptible to distraction as was everyone else, but simply did not tell anyone about it?

Fifty yards away were the Flemish horseman hacking their way through the rear of the French right wing. Duke Robert's relief force took their commander's cue and lowered the lances as one, finally accelerating their fearless steeds to full speed and in amongst the deafening din did they roar a primal bellow; incomprehensible, inhuman and as much in fear as it was in rage.

The reserve force plunged into the largely unsuspecting Flemish cavalry like foxes leaping into a chicken house, felling and scattering men and horses left and right. Mathieu felt the exhilaration of impact, seizing up moments before and gripping the lance so tightly his hand started cramping immediately with the effort. His lance smashed a distracted mounted Flemish knight cleanly in the ribs as he was engaged with a foe the Comte could not see. The head of the lance bounced away almost immediately and the Comte somehow retained his grip of the weapon. The shock of the strike violently and agonisingly jolted through his wrist and up his arm and his weight fell heavily into the pommel at the front of his saddle but Mathieu managed to steer Pinto left and away from the falling knight; given the speed and his severely limited visibility through both grill visor and the rain he could not be sure, but he guessed the Fleming was at the least incapacitated from such a terrible blow if not dead. No man could withstand such an impact from side on, unawares or otherwise.

But there was no time for confirmation because maintaining momentum was so very crucial at this stage. To be caught stationary in amongst the Flemish pole cleavers would be to court death, for they could easily hook a knight off his horse and to the ground. Urging the flying Pinto ever onwards, he frantically scanned the field for his next direction, ignoring the pain in his right arm and the remarkable circumstance that his lance remained in one piece.

A conspicuous path opened up through the chaos of bodies, pieces of metalwork and horses muddled in a churned sea of mud to an island of dismounted French knights under severe pressure from the Flemish footmen wielding their devastating pole cleavers. Right shoulder still reverberating from the collision with the unfortunate Flemish knight, Mathieu kicked Pinto into a direct charge into a body of five or six Flemings, none of whom aware of his approach. Lacking a shield the Flemings had two free arms with which to swing their lethal butchering tools, wildly hacking and slashing at the cumbersome French knights who were practically sinking into the morass under their own weight. The Frenchmen were incapable of balancing or bracing themselves owing to the necessity of holding and hiding behind their heavy shields.

As he thundered in the Comte noticed one filth-spattered French knight desperately throwing a shield up to block a vicious overhead strike from his Flemish foe, the brutal blade lodging in the knight's shield and somehow missing his strapped left arm on the underside of the boss, whilst the Frenchman slashed wildly and hopelessly with his much shorter sword for retribution. Effectively being held at over six feet's length the latter had no chance of returning the strike against his enemy which led to a momentary deadlock before another Fleming leapt in with a thrusting motion from his own pole cleaver, skewering the knight's right shoulder on the steel spiked-tip of the pole.

The knight's legs gave way underneath him but before the Flemish could retract their deadly weapons from shield and shoulder the Comte was upon them, his lance lined up remarkably well so as to batter the first man in the side of the head and catapult him grotesquely, his skull surely shattered inside his helmet and his neck snapped instantly. Still the Comte's grip on the great lance stayed strong and Pinto drove onwards side on into a tight formation of Flemish footmen, pole cleavers bristling but crucially lacking the protection of shields.

The speed at which his brave ride was hurtling through the deluge and the restricting grilled visor blurred Mathieu's vision and so he could not determine where on the next unfortunate footman did the steel head of his lance punch but he crumpled a fraction before Pinto bulldozed through the rest of the men with sickening force, her plated shoulders and chest at the very least knocking unconscious the two or three or four men she practically ran over. Pinto's speed was slowed and Mathieu's heart jumped as he the thought that she had suffered injury in the collision but she leapt clear of the bodies without noticeable difficulty. The Comte himself had very little idea as to his own condition, shaken in the saddle as he was through the multiple hits and jolts, and it dawned on him he was no longer carrying the lance. He looked down as far as he could to his right arm as if his sense of touch were lying to him but an unexpected blow on from the left on his shield sent him flying from the saddle and before he could process what had happened the slits of visibility in the metal box on his head were filled with the rapidly approaching dark brown mud.

Stunned by the unseen attack and incapable of lifting his fatigued and constricted arms even if he had time to break his fall, Mathieu plummeted head first into the mud and horribly jarred his neck as the entire weight of his suited body fell on his neck. The sludge seeped through the grill and into his mouth and he scrabbled his limbs around as if swimming, trying to gain some purchase to lift his head up. The extended end of the shield strapped to his left arm stuck in the ground at an angle that seemed to threaten to rip arm from shoulder – Mathieu had no give to prop himself up using the shield and so his left arm was effectively rendered useless. Furthermore, the agony of his sprained neck lost precedence to the sensation of slowly drowning on land and he could not control the escalating panic that saw him breathe in more and more grass and mud as he began hyperventilating.

All sounds around him fused into a singular hellish din as the high pitch of metal striking metal and man and beast screaming became one with the monotonous thundering of rain and horse. Mathieu did not know for how long his gloved right had been scraping for a surface more tangible than the little remaining wet grass and plentiful slop but clenching his fist he pushed himself up sufficiently to bring one knee up and secure a foundation for balancing and relieving his beleaguered left arm which by now had largely gone numb. With little success he clawed with clumsy ironclad fingers at his mud-saturated visor grill, panting and coughing, desperately trying spit out the disgusting mixture of saliva and mud in and around his mouth.

Having had his eyes closed whilst face down his eyes were mercifully clear though the more the Comte attempted to scrape away from his grill the more he smeared across his helmet and eyeline in particular and he cursed under his breath between hacking coughs and strained breathing. It was then a clear scream to his left caused him to throw his head up and bring his mind back from his own mud-encrusted world to the reality of kneeling amidst a raging battle, the cacophony around him distilling itself into the separate chaotic noises of war, suffering and agony, and in a very ungainly manner he swung his left arm up to hoist the shield up over his head and side to buy himself some time whilst he continued attempting to rescue his visibility. Bodies of unknown allegiances pressed in around him but taking no notice of the crouched figure; on the battlefield a grounded figure posed no immediate threat to standing, warring combatants. A filthy coloured cloth, perhaps from a banner or a caparison, lay half submerged by his right knee which he grabbed and used to wipe down his visor, providing almost immediate relief to at least one of his senses.

Finally able to see, as much as one could in the circumstances, the Comte spun around searching for Pinto but knowing with a sinking feeling there was no chance of finding her. Mathieu sufficiently gathered his composure to draw his sword before heaving himself unsteadily to his feet and took no time in identifying the lion breastplate of Henri d'Albi to his right, scything with his great sword at indistinguishable enemy footmen and throwing up his broad shield with the strength of a man in the prime of youth. He was preening and self-important but unlike certain of the King's circle the young knight was as brave as his lion emblem and as strong as a bull. The war and death cries of men dominated the battlefield as two formerly orderly armies furiously contested a wallowing swamp in utter chaos, all semblance of discipline and formation completely vanished. The Comte had no clue as to the success of the relief charge, nor in all honesty that of the first either; his entire world was concentrated on the few paces around him that were currently filled with lumbering French knights and Flemish spearmen brandishing their diabolic pole cleavers. Mathieu swung his sword in a wide, flat arc at the nearest Fleming who had not noticed his presence, the sword bit deep into the man's right arm as he stabbed at the young d'Albi. He screamed and dropped his weapon, instantly clutching at the horribly maimed limb but did not have time nor space to turn and face his enemy before Mathieu ran him through with his sword, killing him instantly.

Pushing the dead man away with his shield, Mathieu roared with adrenaline as he raised his sword arm high, the heaviness of his lungs dissipating and fatigue of his limbs forgotten as he barrelled forwards. He lunged at another man who met him with poised spear, jabbing at the Comte's chest and stopping him in his tracks, the Comte only just bringing his shield across in time to deflect the blow. The Fleming seemingly danced across the filthy morass such was the ease of his movement relative to Mathieu's graceless locomotion, and he held a further advantage in having a faceless helmet lacking even a grill. The Frenchman did not even see the other end of the pole cleaver as it hurtled towards his helmet, clattering into the temple area with an appalling force and pushing him down to a crouch as he unconsciously sought to protect his head.

Disoriented, Mathieu had no clue as to where the Fleming was and so using up much of his draining energy levels - their depletion only noticeable when he had stopped moving, further underlying the importance of momentum - he blindly spun and lashed out his sword with the hope of hitting someone – and he felt the blade lodge into a man's side. Small lights floating in the periphery of his vision, Mathieu looked up and right to the contorted face of his combatant who still had the deadly cleaver aloft, but it was never to be brought down upon Mathieu's head for the sword blow had been fatal. The man's bright blue eyes were the only distinguishing feature on a grimy and blooded face and body, perhaps on this entire field. Mathieu looked the man in the eyes as black blood began dribbling and then spilling from the man's mouth, the pole cleaver dropping to the ground just before the man did so himself as Mathieu pulled his sword out of the gruesome wound he had unseeingly carved into the man's ribcage.

Dehydrated, coughing through a cracked, parched throat and trying to catch his breath, thinking about how thirsty he was and wanting nothing more than to jump into a cold pond or even the filthy Seine, Mathieu strived to find the next immediate threat with all the composure of a hunted rabbit but without any of its agility. He stumbled on an unseen body and fell to his right, awkwardly landing on his right arm and immediately he felt an excruciating jolt of pain in his shoulder; the Comte tried to push himself up but his right arm did not respond to his commands. Face down in the mud again and exhausted from the exertion of simply trying to stay standing in the mud let alone fighting, the Comte desperately waved his left arm so as to lever himself up using the shield but its shape and weight prohibited such action. Only his legs could move and even they were restricted by the body over which he had tripped. Still the sorrowful dirge of war poured over him from all around in a deafening and incessant volley of noise and suffering.

Perhaps for the first time in his life the Comte experienced pure terror. It dawned that he was prone, face down with no working arms and no way to protect himself against a sword, spear or hooves; perhaps he would drown in the quagmire under the weight of his armour, that which was supposed to protect him; trapped in the suffocating helmet and with a mouthful of the semi-liquid ground he silently screamed with the last of his energy. Knowing that only unseen death was around him, ready to strike unannounced, frightened the hard Comte de la Marche as he pathetically pushed his heavy legs against the body behind him in the vain hope it would keep him from sinking further into the ground. It would be a demise far more horrifying than anything man could do. Mathieu had no conscious control over his movements and emotions, just pure instinctive dread that only increased when a huge weight landed across his back, knocking the remaining breath from his lungs.

He was beginning to suffocate before he was allowed to drown. The Comte felt tears welling in his eyes as the end drew near; a horrific end, one he would not have wished upon his worst enemy. He could only feel the clashes of weaponry and the hoof falls around him as all audible ambience once more blurred into a monstrosity befitting such martial carnage. A particularly heavy *thud-thud-thud* combination resounded near his feet and screams punctuated the droning of battle, followed by an increase in the pressure on his back and then a crunching blow to the right side of his head.

Mathieu felt his brain rattling around his skull and he desperately wanted to cradle his helmed head to alleviate the agony but neither of his arms were of use and whatever it was on his back, man or horse, had pinned his shoulders anyhow. Mercifully, however, it seemed the impact had shunted his face to a small crater pooling with rainwater in the mud where his visor grill was not so submerged – his great helm shielded the crater from the continuing and unfathomably severe rainfall, though this was not immediately apparent to the Comte as he was heavily concussed. Now able once more to breathe relatively freely, and utterly drained, Mathieu's body stopped struggling and he closed his eyes, moaning and whimpering softly as all of the adrenaline that had carried him through the combat following his dismount flooded out of him.

Having closed his eyes, however, Mathieu could not see the blood dripping from his right cheek on to the inner grate of his visor and out into the dirty puddle. All he knew was the pounding agony in his head, so pervasive that his shattered and crushed body no longer registered as part of his entity. The crippling pain about his skull became his world. The last thing he remembered was the image of Jaqueline smiling at him; she was young, probably only a couple of years after their marriage. He did not know where she was but the sunlight streamed in from a window to the right that illuminated her emerald eyes, and her soft pink lips as they opened wide, as always so wide and broad that he could see the lower part of her upper gums. He had never seen anything so wonderful in his life.

Chapter 18

Henry paced back and forth as would a dog sensing danger outside but unable to do anything about it. He rubbed the fresh stubble of his shaved head and enjoyed the satisfying hint of friction produced by the closely trimmed hairs. It had been a very long time since he had received the severe monk cut; a diplomat and a spy needed to look as unremarkable as possible and not draw attention to themselves. A monk, in any circumstance, was always immediately conspicuous. This time round, though, the English knight needed to appear as conspicuously clerical as possible. He already was a monk of course but had not adhered to the common sartorial and aesthetic themes of the brothers of the cloth for a long time.

"Your men are in position? Henry asked, pausing his pacing to look at the great bald man wearing what he thought to be the only habit large enough in the kingdom to fit him.

Guy raised his head and smiled a smile so broad it almost outshone the handful of candles that were illuminating the gloomy corner of the quarters in which they were holed up. "You Englishmen worry. Authority is merely the correct pulling of strings; that's all I do. All of the strings have been pulled. You'll be in this position one day," sighed Guy, reflecting on his advancing years.

Henry rearmed his pacing, and on his return leg towards the gloomy back wall he picked up the tall staff surmounted with the crucifix. The knight considered the woodwork; the shaft was heavy, solid ash, weightier than a lithe spear. He tapped the heavy end on the stone flooring a few times and each was received with a satisfying *thud*. Taking in the momentary gratification before the coming tribulations, he stepped forward once more and quickly picked up his original pacing rhythm.

"Would it be that I shan't have your position," Henry wistfully responded. "How difficult was it to win round our Crutched brothers? I fear for our souls sometimes when I think about the duplicity we have committed in the name of the Order."

"In the name of Our Lord, brother," the Master stated in a manner to remind rather than correct. "We all fear Longshanks possessing such an item. Even the Tatars will be nothing on him were he to wield its power."

Henry had reached the sole window in the room at the other end from the Master's shadowed corner. The small patch of sky visible was pure white; the clouds had seemingly formed one great amalgamation with no beginning and no end. He thought of sunlight and how many days it had been since he last felt its warmth. The knight pulled back his left sleeve to reveal the bronzed skin of his forearm, the dark hairs bleached from a long summer on the road. He lamented the coming of winter, feeling the cold too easily for an Englishman, he thought; but this was his homeland and years in the Levant had not changed that feeling. England's green fields, peaceful forests, grey skies... something about it all was inescapably nostalgic.

Shouting in the street outside brought him back to the present. Green and peaceful London was not, and he wished he had been born without a nose to escape the overwhelming stench, which admittedly had softened since the harvest; the season had turned almost in a day, categorically closing the door on the merciless summer. Regardless of how many days, weeks or years one had lived in the city, every morning the smell would wake one up and linger at the forefront of one's attention until such time as another stimulus took precedence.

Henry silently scolded himself for allowing his concentration on pressing matters to slip back to the odorous ambience of England's capital. And the Tower ward was not even the worst offender! The Crutched Friars' house was close to the river and the wide spaces of Tower Hill and East Smithfield and nearby also was the extravagantly paved Tower Street; the fumes and smoke from the ironmongers' shops behind the Crutched Friars' house on Lombard Street, and the brickmakers on Cornhill Street up near the Aldgate, had plenty of space to dissipate. As for the poor denizens and merchants on Poultry Stocks with the crammed mercers and grocers, or the fishmongers and cordwainers just off Watling Street – Henry wondered how anyone could concentrate on anything but the noxious

269

cocktail of airs combining with the churned refuse and mud that passed as a road in that cramped part of the city.

The Englishman moved away from the window, eager to distance himself from the vulgar shouts of hawkers being ushered out of the way by the King's men-at-arms. The going was better along Hart Street and the Crutched Friars, as the street on which the friars' house stood had become known. But the going was better not through the surface of the road itself – which was as swamp-like as any other unpaved route in the city – but through the smaller population of vermin. Rats were everywhere, but along Thames Street Henry had seen what in the countryside would be considered herds of wild pigs, particularly around the fruiterers and the vintners. The rats at Crutched Friars largely kept to themselves, allowing human traffic relatively uninterrupted passage along their way from the Tower wharfs to the Aldgate and vice versa.

Even so, the hawkers knew there was a large order house here, and there were many other streets in which to curse and argue. But those hawkers and peddlers were just trying to get by; in their world, shouting and swearing was just as important and crucial as stealing a stone from royal possession for the second time in a matter of weeks was in Henry's. Henry never disregarded perspective, remembering that everyone from the King to the prostitutes over on Cock Lane were simply trying to get through life.

"Henry," said the great bald man, a knowing grin on his face and holding up a cup in his right hand, "you've faced worse odds before. Our brother Friars do not want it in the possession of the laity any more than I do. No problem."

Henry walked over and emptied the wooden cup in one draught. It was his first beer of the day, and it was good, the hoppy beer Guy sourced from Peter Brewer on the junction of Tower Street and Bishopsgate Street upon their arrival the day before last; Peter's stock came highly recommended by the Crutched brothers. *This is England*, the knight mused. Green fields, peaceful forests, grey skies and beer. He had gone too long without it in the Levant, where the wine was always too sweet and practically undrinkable in tandem with meat.

Henry wiped some spilled beer from his freshly shaved face with the back of his hand and placed the cup down forcefully on the table. "Where will you take it?" he asked in English, switching from the previous French, a question that immediately removed the genial expression from Guy's face. "Assuming you have a place to safeguard it?"

The Master's brow furrowed and he looked down to his sandalled feet, grey and brown with dirt from the walk over to the Friars' house from the nearby church of St Olave-towards-the-Tower that morning. "It shall be taken to Iceland, with the other stone," he responded likewise in English, a distinctive and pleasant French lilt to his accent. "Immediately." The great bald man raised his head and stared at Henry, his eyes so intent the knight thought they were holding him still with unseen hands.

Henry reflected for a moment on Guy's hasty and unsettling answer. "Iceland? Surely it is too risky a journey for such cargo. Will you study it beforehand?"

"No," snapped Guy.

Henry did not understand the Master's sudden change in demeanour. So rarely had Guy become irate that Henry could not even register shock – his mind simply could not comprehend what had just happened. Struck dumb by an inability to grasp Guy's unusual tone, Henry opened his mouth but had not yet formulated a response.

Guy interrupted Henry before the knight could say anything. "Forgive me, brother," the Master said whilst exhaling loudly and rubbing his eyes with his fingers. In that moment the great bald man looked one hundred years old. "I would not wish you the sights I have seen. The first stone..." he paused, sticking his tongue in his cheek, "there were terrible accidents. I'm sure you can imagine their nature." He lifted his huge frame from the bench and stood to his full height, nearly as tall as the ceiling timbers, and slowly lumbered over to the window Henry had just been stood by. The Master moved in a very tired way, as if he had suddenly become an old man, or the cumulative fatigue and deterioration of years of combat had caught up with him. Henry reckoned Guy was at least twenty years his senior, and even with his relative youth the Englishman sympathised and empathised with the wear and tear, the realisation that one's powers are no longer what they were. It was remarkable enough, Henry considered, that a man of Guy's age and size could keep himself in the condition of someone half his age.

"When did you find it?" Henry asked the question softly, treading carefully around the Master whilst he was quite clearly vulnerable to the memory of the first stone's discovery. But Henry was not going to lay off investigating altogether; to his mind these were the most powerful and important discoveries ever made in this land and the Englishman needed to know as much as he could before the Order shut them away, or Guy refused to talk about them, whichever came first.

Guy looked out at the comings and goings on Crutched Friars Street. The sturdy clothiers' workshop across the road with its new cloths hanging out front, gaudy reds and dazzling golds and blue patterning, drew in passersby like flowers attracting insects in the spring. The street hawkers had moved on and their guttural slang and shouting had once again given way to the general hum of excitement and anticipation so customary of the city over the past few days.

The entire populace knew the Godstone was here, its demonstration before the King in the open Tower Liberties evidence enough of its significance and potential for spectacle. The stone was deemed too valuable to be investigated beyond the grounds surrounding the Royal Palace where it was currently being held under heavy guard. The households of countless lords had followed their masters and ladies to the city and trade was heaving in all areas of the city. London's aldermen were more conspicuous than usual, vying to make an impression on far-flung earls and barons as well as their usual drinking partners, the wealthy Venetian, Lombard and Hanseatic merchants.

Indeed, such was the interest generated that Baron Grey de Wilton, on whose watch the Godstone had been secured, had the forethought to write to His Holiness and Boniface had sent his close friend Bartolomeo Fiadóni as papal legate to observe proceedings. Guy had much to discuss with Bartolomeo beyond the Godstone and had thoroughly enjoyed the Italian's conversation; his scholarly aptitude was second to none and any man who enjoyed close friendship with the great doctor Thomas Aquinas was also a close friend of the Church.

A festival atmosphere had enveloped the citizenry as they awaited word from the fortress of what exactly it was the Godstone could do. Even the brothers and sisters of the city's order houses had contributed to the city's rumour mill, much to the disapproval of order heads including Guy and Abbot Geoffrey, who led the Crutched brothers. Henry had told Guy of his chance meeting a few days previously with poor Abbot Thomas and Prior Simon from the abbey at Chester. They had reluctantly attained celebrity status owing to their eyewitness of the stone's powers. Lord Reginald, Baron Grey de Wilton, they had said, was able to keep himself away from the masses but owing to their line of work they themselves had no opportunity to do so. Consequently, they were practically mobbed whenever they left the enclosure of Westminster Abbey where they were staying with their Benedictine brothers.

The great bald man rubbed his expansive dome pensively as he recollected the discovery of the first stone. "It was during the early years of your King's reign," he began, reverting to his native French, "and, so I was told, a fisherman had stumbled across a shimmering rock half submerged in the low tide, off the rocks by his village. Somewhere in the west of England, I don't know, they didn't tell me. I wasn't told the village either, but perhaps it doesn't matter. He gave it to the local church, fearing such an object of beauty would only bring him trouble, and there it stayed for years as a centrepiece, the local treasure, the marvellous keystone to the altar, in honour of the Lord; a symbol of our Lord's perfection through creation. No one knew what it was, nor where it had come from, they told me, but all agreed that such magnificence was not the work of man."

The Master awaited any hint of reaction from Henry upon the popular conjecture regarding its origins, but the English knight betrayed no response. "Yet, one night, a great inferno broke out in the village and the church was engulfed in flames, and, so the story goes, amidst the conflagration a towering light was seen before the fire vanished and with it the church and the earth upon which it had been built. At the bottom of the pit left behind sat the shimmering stone, untouched as if it were the day it had been freshly carved by the angel who surely worked it. All about the village saw this as a sign of the Lord's displeasure at His creation becoming a source of pride amongst His flock."

"And that's where the Order stepped in," presumed Henry.

"Indeed. News travels fast through official lines."

"You saw the result of the fire?" Henry asked.

Guy nodded before answering. "The villagers feared going near it, as did the priest. And the local lord. I arrived and took it into protection, not before we held services to atone for the village's pride."

"So this demonstration, you think it will end in disaster as well?" Henry had a habit of making even the negatives seem almost tolerable.

"If the experiments are conducted with appropriate caution," explained Guy. "I'm not entirely comfortable that there will be so many people present to witness it."

Henry leaned against the wall. "I thought you were against investigating it."

"I am. But it seems I have no control over that decision for the time being, at least until the time that we acquire the stone."

"I still don't understand why you don't want to study it," Henry declared, his tough hands tending to the solid ash of the staff he held.

"There were brothers and sisters who did not treat the first stone with the respect it deserved," the great bald man replied coolly. "I refuse to run that risk again. It is clear that man is not yet ready for this gift from the Lord. This is why the Order must conceal them until such time that man is."

Henry gently nodded his head as he mused Guy's answer. "Lucky we've found it under your watch, then."

"If you seek, you shall find, Sir Henry. There is no such thing in existence as luck."

Henry crossed his arms against his chest, the staff angled across his body within his arms' embrace. "You have to make your own luck sometimes," stated the knight with a hint of defiance. "If you seek, you make your own luck."

274

"What form would it take? It's not quantifiable, nor does it take physical form," replied the Master. "Agency, however... that is what people mistake for luck. The agency of man as directed by the will of God. And the will of God is quantifiable in the actions we see enacted by man and beast and the earth. Do you not see how we have been moved, seemingly *fortuitously*, to this position? I have encountered two such relics through vigilance and industry, granted me by the will of our Holy Father, so that the Order may take these relics and hold them for man's protection."

Henry unfolded his arms and twirled the staff between his flat palms, as if he were spinning a stick to start a fire. A troubled expression befell his tanned face, emphasising the crow's feet that were faintly visible at the corners of his dark eyes. Something did not quite add up in his mind. "How can you know this is the Lord's plan for us?" he asked, remembering Prior Simon's words in the Taverner's Inn at Chester all those weeks ago. "What if, say, this is a series of events, ostensibly connected, but merely fortuitous in their similarities? Is it not wrong to be so presumptive?"

Guy thought for a moment. "Fortuitous, fortune, luck, chance," he listed ploddingly. "All variations of the same. All superfluous, Henry. The application of fortune to which you refer is in a worldly sense; it is a construct of man to shoulder the responsibility that he himself refuses to take when he commits transgressions, or where he is too proud to acknowledge his own moral failure. Our task is beyond worldly. We are physically protecting man from himself, but more than that, we are undertaking to protect the flock's souls." Scratching his chin, the great bald man tailed off, distracted by some unseen vision or memory. "The pride, arrogance and lust these objects can elicit are far more dangerous than any physical damage."

Guy turned and reached for another cup of beer. Henry had wondered why there were five flagons on the table, when only the two Templars had been present. The Master was nervous, Henry suspected. *Perhaps more nervous than am I.*

"With respect, father, you are contradicting a great many established tenets; unless I am mistaken, many thinkers have taught about the wheel of fortune?"

Henry began to think that Guy was more persuading himself than the knight; there was no doubt the proposed action today was as risky a venture as any he had undertaken. Attributing the outcome to divine determination rather than random chance was more comforting. Further, Henry imagined the fall out should their plan fail. Surely conflict would ensue between the Order and the kingdom. Longshanks had already a chequered history with the Temple, and what ramifications throughout Christendom? So deeply entrenched was the Temple in economic and political matters, so far reaching were its roots, could a kingdom oppose it without facing ruin?

"You are sharper than this, my beloved Henry," Guy responded abruptly, not condescendingly but in an instructive tone. "The wheel simply represents; there's no 'is' about it – it is a symbol for the worldly failures of man. The worldly failures of man are not dictated by fortune, because fortune is the result of that which occurs. Fortune is not the agent, it is simply an artifice of consequence, a retrospective label applied to an outcome, and the wheel is a vehicle for its depiction. The true agent is the free will exercised by man in accordance with God's will."

Guy returned to his chair, which creaked under his great weight. The man seemed as broad as he was tall and the slope of his powerful shoulders could be seen under even the shapeless material of his habit. The men at court fitted their clothes purposefully to emphasise their manly physiques, their virility and their natural dominance over the less well-fed serfs and villeins who constituted the majority of the population. Henry fancied one could put Guy in a wheat sack and his tree-like arms would still retain their definition.

The tanned Englishman looked over to the great bald man and resumed mindlessly spinning the staff between his hands. "It troubles me," he stated, looking back to the twirling crucifix at the top of the staff, mesmerised by its motion, staring at it without really watching it. "Because if we are free and can will things of our own accord, but we are still under the auspices of God's will, then those for whom our artificial wheel of fortune shows to have fallen into disfavour and sin, how have they had any choice but to take the choices that ultimately caused their fortune to fall? How do I know

276

that my deceit today is my own choice for good or not? Do I have another choice? Or, what if I decide to not go through with this? Will I ever have been able to make one decision instead of the other?" The Englishman stopped himself, realising he was tying himself in logic knots with his own questions.

Guy drank another draught of beer. "You have many fine qualities, brother, and your incessant questioning is chief among them," he declared with gusto. "We all exist within the world created by the Lord, and because He created it, He knows what will happen and the choices we will make. This differs from effecting an agency-removing direction on the 'choice'. The choices we have made are our own and the events that have occurred have occurred precisely because our choices determined they would, all under the auspices of the will of God through His creation. Things would never have happened in any other way... Our finding the stones, that wasn't ever going to happen any other way, Henry. It is our *raison d'être*."

Henry stood up off the side of the table and walked back over to the solitary window, planting the staff every second step. He could hear the music somewhere off in the direction of Tower Street, floating above the low murmurs of the crowds and livestock at the meat stalls over on neighbouring Eastcheap and the barely discernible voices at the clothiers' place across the road.

"I think we ought to restrain our thoughts a little, father, lest our choices prove incorrect," the Englishman urged. He turned to find Guy's gaze awaiting an explanation for such a cautionary statement. Henry did not feel threatened by the Master's scrutiny, because he felt justified in nipping the potential for recklessness in the bud. Guy was a great man, the most astute Henry knew, but even the most gifted of men could be blinded by a lifetime of success. So turned the wheel of fortune, Henry mused.

"These choices are our choices, and regardless of how successful we judge our past choices in retrospect, we are fallible... we must remember this, my friend. We could be wrong. We could both be working against God's will." A sorrowful look came over Henry's dark eyes.

Outside, a gravelly cry went up – more soldiers clearing the route to the fortress, no doubt some nobleman and his train coming down from the Aldgate. Guy silently looked to the window and then back at Henry.

"We pray our choices have been made for the right reasons, then," the great bald man said with an air of resignation.

Henry breathed out loudly through his mouth. "I pray this also."

Guy approached him and held out his arm. "You are doing a great service to God and the Church, Henry."

The Englishman looked up to the Frenchman, dutiful servants of the Church both, yet both under no illusions as to the risks they were taking. Henry reached out with his right arm and the two clasped each other's forearm in the old Roman manner.

"I pray you are right, father," Henry said, before he inclined his head and turned away for the door.

Straightening the thick habit hanging over his shoulders, the Templar knight pulled open the heavy door and lowered the towering staff through the doorway, following it out into the dim corridor. The walkway was sparsely populated with thin candles that signified where the walls where and little else. Composing himself for a moment, he turned right down the stone-floored corridor to the tall rectangular entrance door to the Friars' house, thick wooden panels bolted together with iron plates and rivets and acted as an exceedingly effective sound reducer. In fact, the stone walls and monolithic door were so effective that the Englishman was quite taken aback by the humdrum and bustle of the city outside upon opening the door and exposing the deathly quiet of the Friars' house to the chaos of a city positively charged with excitement.

Henry stood his staff and awaited his fellow Friars, who were at a service at the nearby church of St Olave's, visible at the end of the road with its angular presence in the Norse style. All sorts were wandering past; soldiers, peddlars, street urchins running between and around legs, a knight atop his bay chestnut stallion. A clothier across the road, a ruddy-faced man with wild red hair and scrawny limbs, momentarily interrupted a client to wave a greeting to Henry.

Henry assumed the clothier and the Friars were familiar with one another – after all, it had been a few years since the Friars had established their house here. The English knight acknowledged the clothiers' greeting with a slight incline of his head and the briefest of smiles, for he considered it unwise to induce too much unnecessary conversation in his current guise. Continuing to scan the crowds, he spotted bobbing crucifixes to his right, high above the heads of those milling around them like insects around a horse; the horse pays the insects no mind despite their fervoured attention. So approached the Crutched Friars along their eponymous street from the direction of St Olave's, attended by countless hangers on, all desperate for a hint of what the Godstone was about and to be near those whom would be handling it.

A lone man-at-arms walked ahead of the Friars, yelling at all and sundry to make way as they noiselessly marched on like an army, their cross-topped staffs tall spears and their grim silence the contemplation before battle. All about the excited laymen and women beset them, asking questions and pulling on robes, begging for snippets of information. It was a curious sight for Henry, having never seen its like before. The champions of the joust, yes, but friars being mobbed without giving food away? A pang of self-consciousness threatened to overwhelm the English knight; why had no one mobbed him? He, too, was a brother of the crossed staff, albeit temporarily and unofficially, and he too was to handle the stone. Could people see through his disguise?

Get a grip, man, he told himself. No one in London knew what he looked like. Few knew of his existence. Those who did would have taken the Master's word that no member of the Temple was to attend the demonstration. The Crutched brothers, he had been told, were unswervingly loyal to Abbot Geoffrey, and would welcome him as one of their own. Thus far this had been proven true.

He ran through the plan in his head once again, worrying that the guards in the White Tower would recognise him. Again he quickly dismissed this as a baseless concern. Those guards would escort the Crutched Brothers and the Godstone to St John's Chapel in the southeast corner of the Tower, wherein the Friars would oversee the stone's consecration. Only the stone would not be consecrated, because Guy had already arranged for a decoy stone to be placed in the chapel. The Godstone would be hidden in a wall of the chapel.

At such time that the decoy stone was moved out of the chapel at the King's orders, it would be straightforward to remove the original without stirring any suspicions.

Henry thought the plan solid but just feared the loyalty of the Friars to this deception. As he stood and awaited their approach the knight knew it was far too late to back out now.

The human wave washed over and around Henry until its centre reached where he stood, and he subsequently fell in line with his fellow Friars without so much as an acknowledgement between the men. Trudging on, Henry kept his eyes fixed on the city wall beyond the end of the street, soaring up to thirty feet high, ignoring the shouts, comments and hassle of the ever-increasing press around the resolute Friars.

Henry imagined the small army filing up the street to be preceded by an advancing wall of noise, a physical entity in its own right and one that had evidently failed to dislodge the thronging crowds ahead filtering down from the Aldgate – soldiers ahead were shoving and pushing men, women and children to clear a path for the brothers. Fear blazed in the eyes of many, accompanied by haunting cries for help as the crowd behind pushed ever closer forward. He winced as he saw one man-at-arms knock down a dark-haired man in a blue tunic; he did not see what became of the victim but the swelling of the crowd like currents of the sea did not offer much hope for the dark-haired man's wellbeing. It was likely he would not re-emerge from that body of people. *Such suffering already*, Henry silently lamented.

Sweat began pouring down his back as he watched the thin line of soldiers gradually falter and begin to buckle under the sheer weight of numbers. The closer he got to the line, which blocked off the crowds from the approach road to the open grass of Tower Hill, the more chaotic was his sensory experience. Cloth banners of all colours lazily flapped in the breeze above the pandemonium of people and the occasional horse; here some people were using a hay cart as a makeshift viewing platform, much to the consternation of its driver, there a finely-dressed man in a vibrant green jacket was barking orders and pointing at the soldiers from the saddle of his black horse, soon to be accompanied by quickly moving spear tips as more soldiers hurried from the direction of the fortress to the right.

A few enterprising souls had clambered upon the roofs of the clothmakers' sheds, though a large hole in the tiling of one building suggested one adventurer had fallen through. High above on the city walls were the regular mounted torches, blazing bright on a dull day, and the menacing city archers, eyes all trained inside the city for once. Henry had no doubt they were under instruction to spare no one in the event of a riot, the likelihood of which seemed to increase with every passing minute.

Turning the corner onto the Tower approach the Friars were greeted by a paved path mercifully free of detritus and rats but populated with men-at-arms in full armour suits. The soldiers stood abreast of one another across the road, acting as a human sieve to filter out the laypersons from the Friars as the group walked down towards the open grass.

Chapter 19

Adelaide shielded her blue eyes from the driving rain with a sleeve that was soaked through and clung to her forearm, the woollen cloth smock weighing down heavily as she had been exposed to the elements for a few hours now. Her kirtle was drenched and the dampness from both layers had seeped through to her skin underneath, giving her shivers and a longing for a roof, fireplace and hot stew. She had never known a harvest to be so wet and miserable. The rain was practically horizontal, hammering in from the west and feeling strong enough to leave lacerations across any exposed skin.

Nonetheless, her physical discomfort was exceeded by the unease of being so close to the army's vanguard, a situation Everard had promised her would not arise. Granted, the hill ahead was barren with little cover to conceal an enemy, but Adelaide could count maybe ten, twelve footmen between her and the open country ahead. She was not a soldier and even more emphatically she was not supposed to be here with soldiers.

"They'll be back, soon, my girl. Not much longer," yelled the Earl of Hereford, only two lengths to her left but needing to shout to be heard over the rain, referring to the scouts he had sent out that morning. Adelaide did not know how long they had been waiting for the scouts to return, but she did know it had been raining the entire time they had waited. She did not think to question the Earl on matters of warfare but even her robust nature was beginning to wilt from the relentless wet and cold. The flipside of standing in a rocky field with no cover to conceal an enemy was that one in turn had no cover from the elements. She possessed a linen gown that she carried in her sack but putting it on would have been futile by this point; she was already completely drenched and it was likely the gown in the cloth sack was wet as well.

She raised her arm away from her head a little and regarded the earl from the corner of her eyes. He stood resolute against the onslaught from the heavens, a man in his prime with a great dark beard flecked with grey and topped with a whitening moustache.

Hereford chose not to wear a helmet and yet he did not cover his face from the battering meted out to it by the lashing rainfall. Though not necessarily a physically imposing man he had charisma and a presence that demanded one's attention, and Adelaide had seen the esteem in which his men held him. Some of them had been in his service for years beyond their ability to count, she had heard. Some remembered fighting in the Welsh Marches many years prior and the disputes Hereford had become unwillingly embroiled in with the Earl of Glamorgan and the King. He had always stuck to his position, they said, and had always championed the common man.

Adelaide had not noticed such devotion towards the Earl of Arundel at Clun – in the relationship between lord and subject, there was a strict demarcation between obedience and reverence and Lord Richard's men fell toward the former. Arundel was not disliked, at least not conspicuously, and Adelaide considered him a fair and just man, but he did not have the energy about him as did Hereford. He looked majestic, king-like. They said King Edward was the epitome of kingship, but Adelaide had never seen him; surely the Earl of Hereford, a younger man, was even more so?

She looked around. The soldiers here in the vanguard were the toughest, she guessed; Hereford would not go so far into enemy territory, or what Adelaide assumed to be enemy territory because she had never ventured so far west, without adequate protection. Indeed, she had often wondered if a Cornishwoman of her standing had ever ventured so far as she had in general. All around were unpleasant looking men made to appear exponentially more unpleasant by the grim, hard expressions they bore amidst the howling rain. Some wore full plate armour with helms and the rain bounced off them with an incessant ringing. The armoured men were mostly on horseback, a few of the horses draped in the ceremonial colours of the earldoms to which they owed allegiance; a few sported the azure field stalked by golden lions, the arms of the de Bohun family, the Earl of Hereford's line; here and there were Lord Richard's blue-tongued and blue-clawed lion sparring on a red coat, inherited by the FitzAlans upon receiving the earldom of Arundel. During the march, Adelaide had occasionally glimpsed a few knights carrying deep azure banners adorned with three sheaves of wheat;

Hereford had said they were of Prince Edward's household from Chester. Hereford had told her their names as well but she found it difficult to apply names to faceless suits of armour.

Regardless of their armour, the bodyguard to the earl appeared as miserable as did the ordinary foot soldiers holding lonely guards around an imaginary perimeter encircling their position. Adelaide knew the kinds of men these men were; like Alfred and Ralph, destined for a life of following commands, commands that made no sense whatsoever such as standing in freezing horizontal rains for hours with no cover. She coughed and felt a roughness in her throat and immediately the Cornishwoman knew illness was imminent. She suspected the same would apply to any number of the men stood leaning against spears or resting elbows atop the rims of their shields around her, the earl and his officers. A few appeared to splutter, backs spasming violently, but such was the impact of the rainfall on the pitiful soil and bare rock underfoot as well as the metalwork worn and wielded, produced a permanent washing sound that drowned out all other ambience.

Adelaide watched the lip of the gently sloping hill up to the left. Nothing. Nothing either ahead along the flat or further down the slope to the right. Shivering, she turned to her left and caught the eye of Sir Walter Percival, as usual at Hereford's right shoulder and looming high on his colossal white destrier. The horse was surely the largest animal on God's Earth, Adelaide thought. Everyone had heard tales of fantastical creatures from beyond the realms of Christendom, giant grey horses with an arm protruding from their face but she knew these to be nonsense. Sir Walter's destrier was the closest beast to the travellers' tales as anyone would see; it was truly a majestic creature.

Not so much Sir Walter Percival however, one of the ugliest men Adelaide had ever seen. His eyes, which the Cornishwoman believed were unnaturally far apart leaving a vast gap filled with a pig-like nose sporting permanently flared nostrils, glared back at the woman and caused her to sharply look away, back at the nothingness of the rocky slope before them. The Cornishwoman did not know if she averted her gaze through fright of his visage, all the more menacing in the foul weather, or his abrasive nature. On more than one occasion Sir Walter had spoken witheringly of Adelaide within earshot, bemoaning the presence of a woman on a march and in particular a woman who needed guarding, on the earl's orders.

Sir Walter was not alone in this behaviour and Adelaide found herself dreading being left even for a moment without the Earl of Hereford, or one of his salt-of-the-earth sergeants. The earl seemed as straight and principled a man as she had met and had not conspicuously bemoaned her presence. For such a hard looking man the earl was incredibly charismatic and people seemed to gravitate towards him, which was probably why he could get away with marching soldiers from a number of liege lords hard across very challenging land with little, if any dissent. Even during his absence, Sir Walter and the other officers would begrudge Adelaide's presence but never the conditions of the march. Even their disagreement with the Cornishwoman seemed rooted in what they felt to be Hereford's obligation to bring her along; her knowledge of the enemy was a necessary evil for the earl, they said.

Two grey dots moved on the gentle slope to the right. Adelaide peered through the heavy precipitation, adamant in her mind that the grey dots had been part of the scenery for the past few hours. Perhaps they were animals? She had heard the sliding of steel and iron on sheaths around her – some of the men had too noticed the movement. She craned her neck over her right shoulder at the sound of urgent footfalls across the stony hillside and saw a handful, then maybe tens of spear-wielding footmen jogging out of the squall from the rear of the column, as if they were emerging from a cascade of a waterfall.

Adelaide gazed forward again, unable to find the moving grey dots. She turned to her left this time, at the earl. He remained helmetless and retained the resolute gritted teeth, shining through the darkness of his beard, of a man who considered a mere necessity standing on a bleak hillside in a deluge worthy of the Great Flood. By contrast Sir Walter and the other officers had already shut their visors and some were shifting in their saddles, anticipation building at the presumed return of the earl's scouts. Hands wandered to sword hilts and squires emerged from seemingly nowhere carrying great oblong shields of varying designs, largely corresponding to the

285

banners that meekly drooped in the tempest, and the muffled clanking of metalwork joined the clanging of rain on armour plate in creating an eerie, determined ambience.

Not receiving a hint of recognition nor acknowledgement from Hereford, Adelaide turned back to the search for the grey dots. She wondered why the knights had closed their visors already; visibility was poor to begin without having to look through a pockmarked or grated grill. Perhaps they were scared? She herself certainly was, but she was supposed to be. The officers were full of bravado and bluster, and were entirely encased in fitted plate. And on horseback. Yet they were wilfully blinding themselves and carrying an aura of trepidation at what may transpire.

From the knowledge she had gleaned Adelaide suspected the Dragons were outnumbered and, relative to Hereford's army at least, under equipped. The officers were aware of this and also aware that this venture was merely a clean-up operation; an elimination of a pest, an annoyance. Those were the words the earl used.

Regardless of how straightforward the campaign was in military terms, the Cornishwoman knew how crucial it was to end the Dragons' terror. She shuddered at the memory of fire and screaming and the bodies piled up. The tiny bodies, mauled and mutilated. The officers needed to do their jobs and put an end to it; and Adelaide silently willed Hereford to keep his men in line and tell them to man up. The Cornishwoman had encountered Dragons in the dungeon at Clun facing up to the vice clamp who were less frightened than the armoured rabbits surrounding her presently.

The two grey dots gained form and definition as they approached the flatter part of the slope before Hereford's position. Once more raising an arm to protect against the lashing rainfall, Adelaide squinted and could make out two horsemen of indistinguishable attire and conspicuously lacking weaponry. She had earlier seen a number of scouts head out so knew that some remained in the surrounding hills. The entire day's waiting, the entire march was here culminating in one conversation; would the earl have the opportunity to end the uprising today? For Matilda's sake, the Cornishwoman prayed the Lord would grant it. She had waited for this moment and just regretted the earl would not allow her participation in the combat despite her undoubted ability with weaponry.

"My horse!" bellowed the earl, making Adelaide jump a little. She hacked a cough again feeling heaviness in her chest. Just as the officers' squires had materialised from nowhere with their shields, Hereford's squire, a nondescript dark-haired boy with a pale, unhappy face, led forward the earl's destrier, Sunrise. Sunrise was a graceful animal possessed of agility and a temperament that belied its breeding and role in life. With the practiced athleticism of a lifetime in the saddle the earl vaulted onto the horse as if he were not wearing a full suit nor did he have the stiffness that hours of standing in a downpour would give a man over fifty years of age.

"Form up! Adelaide, my girl. Fall in." He flashed her the barest of half-smiles, more so with his eyes than his mouth, before kicking on and rocking back in his saddle as the mighty black warhorse slowly lolloped forwards.

All around the knights and foot soldiers moved as one and Adelaide had to jump out of the way as the fearsome Sir Walter barged her aside atop his own mount. The knight did not deign to look down at the Cornishwoman as his warhorse walked through, though she could sense his bulbous blue eyes following her as he passed. Adelaide was not sure at what position she should fall in, though could feel an excitement build within her at the idea of active participation. Finally! Her presence on the march would become a necessity and not merely an investment.

"Come with us, love," spoke a gravelly voice enriched with sincere friendliness that Adelaide heard above the howling rain and the deep tramping of footsteps. She spun to her left sharply and saw the gap-toothed smile of Hereford's sergeant-at-arms, Will. His unshaven face peppered with blemishes and pox scars and a broad grin had been a constant source of comfort to Adelaide on the march. Day or night, rain or shine, hours from supper or during a meal, that permanent, toothy beam on his face had brightened the circumstances whenever he had been near. As with the earl it was clear that Will was much loved by the soldiers and consequently did not need to enforce his will upon them, even the men picked up from

Arundel and Baron de Grey's armies. He somehow merged the authority of Everard with the joviality of Ralph.

"Thank you, sergeant," the Cornishwoman responded, her blue eyes blazing out of the greyness. To Will, they appeared as if the clouds had finally parted to allow the heavens to once more appear to man.

"The earl wants us to have a chat with the scouts, see what they have to say," he continued. His gravelly midlands drawl undulated pleasantly and seemed perfectly suited to a man of his friendly disposition. They stepped aside for another unidentified knight to pass, this one carrying the shield of the earldom of Chester with its golden wheatsheafs but utterly sodden and lacking the gold design's intended verve. "Hang in with the lads, there'll be nothing to worry about. Between you and me, these highborn ponces on their horses are scared of the rain, which is why they've got their helmets closed." He winked, knowing none of the knights would have been able to hear through their helms and the hammering rain. Will himself wore a leather cap that covered down over his ears, the only protection he had for his head. He had not removed it for the duration of the march as far as Adelaide was aware, so she wondered if he actually had leather hair.

The Cornishwoman giggled at such brazen and good-humoured insubordination from a man in Will's position, not to mention how similarly his views were to her own. "Funny you should say that," she replied with a mischievous grin of her own, "I've left my helmet over there actually. Have I got time to put it on before my squire brings my horse?"

Will laughed a hearty laugh and for a moment it seemed as if they were sharing drinks in a tavern rather than standing on a cold and wet rock field goodness knows how far into Wales. He shouted at a footman wearing a similar leather cap and clad in thick hide across his chest and shoulders trudging past, "Oi, Rob! Where's Sir Adelaide's horse? What kind of fucking useless squire are you?"

"Fuck off, sarge," yelled Rob through an equally big smile. "I thought all the horses were needed for that carriage you're supposed to drive for us?" Rob and a few men around him guffawed deep belly laughs.

"Only proper soldiers get horse-drawn transport, mate," piped up another man, whom Adelaide remembered as Big Steve. "You'll be walking with the sarge." More deep laughs went up and Adelaide smiled at the humour that managed to cut through the miserable weather.

Rob piped up again. "And you'll be on the wagon, 'cause you're too fucking fat to march." The men laughed again and Adelaide saw Big Steve clap Rob on the shoulder as they marched past. "You coming, sarge? I'm sure there'll be loads of women to chat up just on the other side of this empty fucking hill," Rob asked as he grinned through thick red stubble at Will and Adelaide.

"I'll save them for you. You need the practice," Will chuckled before turning round and bawling at an indeterminate number of soldiers. "Get a move on, you lot. We've got gentlemen to look after."

Will awkwardly hefted his shield from his back, not easily loosening the straps that clung to his shoulders tightly and he struggled with lifting his arms high enough owing to the layers of leather hide covering his upper torso. It seemed the leather padding he wore was even more restricting than the plate in which Hereford and his officers were swathed, whilst offering less protection.

The roles in life we are assigned, thought Adelaide. Could any of us really make a choice? She would like to know more about how these men came to be here - her professional curiosity never ceased. Bowing her head down she hacked another dry cough and felt the acute, grating pain in her chest, eyes streaming before she raised her head and was immediately hit once more by the turbulent rain. Yet the Cornishwoman found the sensation soothing; having her face completely dowsed with rainwater negated and distracted from her eyes watering and for a moment brought relief from the horrid feeling in her chest, as if the thrashing rain itself had cleansed her body of its ills.

She hoped the storm would also cleanse her mind of its restlessness and poisonous desire for vengeance. She knew she should turn the other cheek, and she prayed forgiveness for her inability to do so. *Poor Elric*, she thought, the old priest had many in his flock but the Cornish daughter of the gaoler demanded more time than most for advice and comfort and above all else, reassurance. Reassurance that her abilities would not see her condemned to hellfire; reassurance that her willingness to cloak normal sensibilities during her work, during the punishment she meted out to prisoners in exchange for information would not lead to damnation. Reassurance that the weeds of retribution that thrived inside her and suffocated her mind and judgement were not sown by the devil himself, and that she could cut them away so that when her time came she would be reunited with Matilda.

She stepped carefully but quickly across the stony ground, slippery in places but otherwise completely devoid of any characteristics; a few sporadic tiny shrubs tried desperately to forge an existence out of the lifeless rocky soil, but otherwise the hillside offered pitifully poor earth and a generous helping of rocks large and small. The soldiers marched unevenly but with purpose and at a more or less uniform speed. Walking next to Will, Adelaide sensed the sergeant was the glue that held the disparate band together. Sir Walter with his bulbous eyes shouted a great deal and postured like the lord of his own kingdom but there was no bond between the officers and the infantry.

It was a relationship, if it could be defined as such, based on a lifetime of conditioning and fear – fear of repercussions and punishment if commands were not carried out, and they would not be consequences relating to the task itself but from the commander for simply disobeying the command. Adelaide could see how the common theme of subjugation could bring the soldiers together in times of hardship, which she knew was practically all the time, but it took a special type of leadership to transform shared experiences into a watertight attachment. After all, she mused, was not life an experience of subjugation for all commonfolk? And yet by no means were relations as happy between the inhabitants of a small town such as Clun, let alone across a whole kingdom. Indeed, if they were, would the commonfolk remain in subjugation?

She did not know what it was in Will that made him so effective a leader but she knew the men could see it, and, crucially for his own position, Hereford could see it too. Adelaide counted herself largely fortunate to have been surrounded by good men during her life – her father, Elric and his endless patience, Ralph and Alfred at the castle, even Everard, who was a professional soldier through and through. Lord Richard and Hereford, two lords who held true to the ideals of nobility. Smiling sergeant Will who had time for anyone and everyone. The Cornishwoman thought about the grim existence she and everyone else of her station had to eke out, but she was in very good company and that kept her warm inside as the rain lashed and she coughed some more.

The smiles and bonhomie melted away as the soldiers steeled themselves against the twin difficulties of marching head on into the driving rainfall and navigating the increasingly treacherous hillside – the battering gales were dislodging the already loose scree and underfoot the thin earth, beyond saturated from the downpour, provided no grip for the soldiers' leather boots. Ahead and on the left, further up the slope, the mounted knights and soldiers made painfully slow progress, slower even than the footmen slogging on two legs.

Adelaide could sense the shift in attitude from one of joking to business, but she did not detect any of the nerves in the footmen as she had a little earlier in the officers. It was remarkable that the knights, those with a lifetime of preparation for climactic moments as these and all of the support in the world, seemed more apprehensive in such circumstances than were the lowborn, for whom such a life was merely employment rather than duty. The joking and laughing died down beneath the howling wind and heavy tramping of countless feet so that the momentary façade of a warm tavern was washed away and the reality of war returned. An eeriness descended and the army took on the appearance of a horde of sleepwalkers, or ghosts, wordlessly edging forwards.

The Cornishwoman noticed the two grey horseman and their mounts had gained form but only one was recognisable – Harold? Was that his name? A rangy youth probably as tall as the spear he carried, and almost as thin. Adelaide thought he was too tall to ride a horse and she had never before seen a more uncomfortable gait in the saddle as the leather-capped stick of a man hunched forwards, facing the approaching cluster of Hereford's infantry and cavalry. To his left was the unidentified horseman wearing – *is that a Dragon?* – a red cloak. Adelaide has seen them before, during the massacre and on the prisoners at Clun. Dyed scarlet and red cloaks were relatively cheap and readily available, but she had learnt to trust not only her instincts but also the most obvious explanations.

The red-cloaked rider wore a hood over their head thus shrouding their gender from view, and nor did their size give any clues - both a man and a woman appear small of stature besides Harold – but regardless, what did it mean, this Dragon's presence? Adelaide's heartrate increased. Finally, she had encountered a Dragon in the field, unchained and unbound. Yet the cloaked figure was completely unlike anything she had expected, because they were apparently not belligerent.

What had she been expecting? Even under torture they were resilient and concise, everything about them apparently calculated and meticulous, rarely displaying any sense of emotion, even pain, in order to minimise the loss of information. Therefore an enigma of undetermined sex in an unpredicted circumstance - side by side with one of Hereford's scouts - was surely precisely what Adelaide should have expected.

About forty paces or so from Harold and the unknown Dragon, Hereford turned to his left and spoke inaudibly to Sir Walter, who promptly brought his horse about and yelled, "Halt!" to the column. The ill-defined mass of men ground to a stop and as one readied spears and swords in a highly aggressive posture. Hereford's horse slowly lumbered forwards alone towards the pair of horse and riders. Once more the earl's army found itself stationary in a rainstorm, though mercifully the intensity seemed to be lessening so that Adelaide no longer needed to shield her blue eyes.

The wind too was dying down but not enough that the individual hoof falls of Sunrise could be heard as he carried Hereford towards the scout and the Dragon. With about ten paces between them the unidentified rider pulled their hood down, either as a sign of trust or because the rain was easing off, and Adelaide saw a woman's head with what seemed to be long, scraggly hair tied back, oak-brown like the horse she was riding. The oak-haired woman raised her arms aloft either side of her body, displaying empty hands, before shaking them violently up and down in what Adelaide interpreted to be a demonstration that she was not concealing any weapons. Adelaide noticed that in the meantime, Hereford had not so much as moved for the sword hanging in its scabbard at his side. Her suspicions increased; did the earl not intend harm to the Dragon? Something was definitely not right here.

All around the Cornishwoman were the soldiers of Hereford's army; motionless as the hills they had traversed. Their horses too were statuesque and could do as little to get out of the rain as could their masters. The hillside was truly barren with the nearest trees hidden from view by the mist. Adelaide sensed many a held breath as she saw the oak-haired woman open the top of her cloak a little, but the extent to which she did was partially obscured from Adelaide's view by Hereford and his mighty warhorse. After a few moments the Cornishwoman saw to her left and right a few heads turning to each other, and where beards were not concealing them she saw mouths moving and tongues wagging.

Without facing his army, Hereford raised his right arm and made a waving motion with his gloved hand. Sir Walter instantly swivelled in his saddle and lifted up his visor, his bulbous eyes now practically spilling out of the front of his helmet, and bellowed in his thick west country accent.

"Sergeant! And gaoler. With me." He returned to a comfortable sitting position and gently urged his horse forwards, stepping clear of the lines. Adelaide shot a confused expression at Will, remembering Everard's promise that she would be nowhere near the fighting, but Will did not return the look. Shorn of his usual brightness, the sergeant-at-arms cleared his throat in what seemed both a natural occurrence and an unhappy response to taking an order from Sir Walter.

"Let's not keep the lord waiting," Will grunted as he kicked through the loose stones, looking down as he went so that his leather hat took the majority of the rain that so desired to strike his face. His footsteps were heavy yet not reluctant; a career soldier's footsteps. He may not have taken any pleasure in receiving orders from Sir Walter, but the sergeant knew his place. By contrast Adelaide stepped lightly but almost unwillingly, her body not eager to advance towards a potentially dangerous situation and only moving as if Will were the dutiful current of a river and she had been caught up in it.

They edged closer along the slippery hillside with unsure footing. Will chanced a look up from the placement of his next footstep and saw the crimson cloak about which so many of the soldiers had heard stories; he also knew that the crimson cloak was the reason for Adelaide's presence. "Is she one of them, do you think?" he asked, knowing the answer already.

"If she is, why has the earl not killed her?" Adelaide wondered out loud.

Will glanced at her. "I've never seen you look like you don't know what's going on," he commented. "And if you don't know what's going on, then what chance do we have?" His question was not quite as rhetorical as he intended for he himself was rather taken aback by the Dragon's peaceful appearance.

Adelaide thought the oak-haired woman looked to be carrying something in the front of her cloak; perhaps she was overweight? Highly unlikely, she thought. And if she were, she would not look like that. What was it? Finally she and Will reached the parlay ground where Hereford and the woman on the horse were still talking, and it became clear that the woman was not overweight, yet something was definitely peculiar.

"… need *strong* assurances on your part. You claim to speak for your people, yet you are not a sovereign nor lady?" asked the earl of the woman, Adelaide not catching the first part of his question owing to the death throes of the howling rainstorm.

"If it is evidence of the authority I hold over my people you would like, I can provide it, right now, my lord Hereford," stated the oak-haired woman in a tone that riled Will to the point that he flipped up his sword from his side and adopted a wary, prepared posture.

"Please, good sir," spoke the woman, unalarmed by the sergeant's escalation of tension, "I am unarmed and mean the lord no harm. As I have explained to your lord, I have brought this with me as a sign of my trust." She unfolded the top of her cloak with her right arm, bringing it back over her shoulder and revealed an infant wrapped in linen at her chest with just the top of its thinly-haired head visible.

The woman looked down at the babe and smiled, retaining the smile as she lifted her head back up to Will and Adelaide.

The Cornishwoman glanced to her left at Will who looked stupefied as he lowered his sword. His eyes shot to Adelaide's and then to Hereford, though the earl was not watching his sergeant's reaction.

Instead, he had already resumed the exchange, an exchange that Adelaide already found unusual before the revelation that the woman had brought a child with her.

"Evidence of your authority, now? You will regret taking me for a fool, if you so intend," snarled Hereford.

"This agreement is as beneficial for us as it is for you, my lord," replied the woman calmly, "and it is not in my interests to create enemies when we can create friends." With no warning she swung her right leg over the back of her oak-brown mount and jumped down so numbly that barely a sound could be heard upon her boots hitting the rocky soil. Adelaide thought of nothing but the baby – which, she reflected, was unlikely to have registered any change in altitude or positioning such was the grace of the woman's dismount – this was not a war, it was a negotiation!

Before the Cornishwoman could mull the situation further there was a flurry of movement on all sides of her peripheral vision. Will spun and instinctively raised both sword and shield, and Sir Walter drew his sheathed blade with a swift *shhhhing* that emphatically cut through the damp atmosphere.

Adelaide shuffled a little closer to Will and the sergeant responded by bringing himself round so that the Cornishwoman could stand, as much as possible, behind the great bossed shield. The sounds of metal scraping on metal and the rustling of plate and jingling of mail from the main column of the army tore through the air, replacing the newly-absent cacophony of driving winds and lashing rain. She peered out above the rim of the oblong shield and saw a large number of people silhouetted in the lingering mist, stretching in a huge crescent around their position from up to downslope, where previously, and all morning, there had been no one.

"What is this?" barked the earl. His body was the picture of cool in contrast to the chicken impersonation being displayed by the uneasy Sir Walter, all rapid head jerks and wide eyes darting back and forth which Adelaide presumed to continue after he had once more shut his visor. But the urgency of his question betrayed his own fraying nerves.

"These are the sons and daughters of Wales, under my authority, and they have accompanied me as a sign of our honesty and, so important to you, a demonstration of our unified cause," the woman explained, her high tones, almost girlish in their softness but with the wisdom and experience of someone much older, seemingly cowling the assembled English leaders before her.

The earl stammered his response. "But, how..."

"It is not so difficult to imagine, when you see the clothes on their backs," the woman interrupted, fiddling with the arrangement of the crimson cloak around her shoulder and round the child bound safely to her chest. "When we have achieved our task then perhaps we will have to source clothing that allows us to hide so well."

"They are to drop their weapons, immediately," Hereford growled to the oak-haired woman. "Sergeant, have your men form up!" he commanded Will. Adelaide found herself back at the village, butchery everywhere, the flames and the bodies, the tiny bodies. And here she was again, trapped in the middle of it all. The escalating fear of conflict only compounded the confusion over the dialogue she was hearing.

"You have brought armed men to our country, lord," the oak-haired woman said serenely but with an edge of threat in her confidence. "Your men are to drop their weapons in turn. I'm as little inclined for this relationship to get off to a bloody start as are you." She walked up to Hereford's horse, scratching around its jaw underneath the plate head protection.

Hereford stared with mouth agape at the oak-haired woman's brazen attitude to the safety of herself and that of her child. The soldiers around him were edgy, spears and swords pointed at the woman whilst others faced out at the ghostly army surrounding them in the mist and none of those weapons held level or steady owing to the rising adrenaline pumping through each man. Hereford paused for a moment at the sight of the placid woman, representing the enemies of his king, idly caressing his destrier and surrounded by men brought up with tales of her kind's savagery and barbarism. And she had her child with her! Swaddled to her chest as if she were out working in the field. "Bring your people in and then we can talk," he snapped, eyes burning into the woman before surveying the horizon around him, a horizon that sat uncomfortably close due to the mist.

The woman's face hardened. "We have more to fear from you than you do from us, lord. No harm will befall you nor your men; those who would come to help us have our friendship, the Lord will see to that." Her voice dropped in tone and her eyes narrowed. "Though you will learn, lord, that you've no authority here without my say so." At that she spun away, arms cradling around the sleeping baby at her chest still wrapped in the cloak and the linen underneath. "Drop them!" she cried in Welsh, understood by none other than her followers.

Adelaide jumped a little at the shout and within seconds the deathly quiet hillside rang with the tremendous clash of metalwork on stone and rock as the still unseen Welshmen and women released their swords, shields, bows and spears in a gesture that was more audible than visual. Soon the *clang*ing and *clank*ing was joined by the solitary cry of a young babe awoken by its mother. The oak-haired woman hushed her child and apologetically kissed it lightly on the head, bobbing it up and down to soothe its fright at such a startling awakening.

Adelaide lowered her head so her mouth was hidden behind the rim of the shield that Will was still holding in front of her. It was the first time she had noticed that the sergeant had been holding the leather and wood shield almost straight-armed out to his side to cover her, a remarkable feat of strength from a man not conspicuously large; indeed Will was barely taller than she, and she had always considered herself on the small side.

Behind the cover of the shield, the Cornishwoman whispered to the sergeant. "Are they surrendering? This doesn't feel right."

"It's no surrender," came Will's reply. He switched his eyes between the woman before them and the grey silhouettes over her shoulders now about thirty paces away. "It's not done this way, they've got no need to surrender – they haven't been defeated."

Adelaide warily watched the advancing ghostly ranks to the left and right. "She's a Dragon, isn't she? It's not their way."

Will nodded, though Adelaide did not see. "I know. I reckon something's up here."

By chance the mist began lifting as an intense of beam of sunshine burnt a hole through the clouds further down the hillside, fleetingly producing a dazzling vista where the light reflected off the hundreds of thousands of wet stones and rocks that populated the desolate landscape. The sunlight advanced up the hill and then illuminated a line of metalwork straddling the slope where the Welsh had dropped their weapons; the iron and steel glinting as if God Himself was endorsing the disarmament.

Looking to her right, Adelaide had to raise a sodden arm to cover her eyes once more but this time to protect not from wind and deluge but the glare; she had always thought that sunshine was brighter, finer and more intense after rainfall. She saw a straggly line of people shuffling manfully up the slope, some with arms outstretched through effort or want of balance on the scree. There was little in the way of helmets or plate armour flashing in the sunlight, and most wore dark cloaks or tunics – it was not difficult to see how they could have stayed hidden in the conditions, but the endurance to remain motionless and, as far as Adelaide was aware, silent in that downpour! The Cornishwoman could see temporary streams of rainwater still snaking their way down the hill. So many Welsh must have been lying in those cold streams for hours.

Sunshine continued to burn the clouds away, and soon Hereford's army was too revealed to the hillside. It was equally gloomy in appearance but with a predominance of black and brown leather and far greater instances of sunlight reflecting off plate; altogether a far better equipped force. The Cornishwoman knew as well as any of them, however, that all of the armour in the world did not matter if the English could not actually see where their enemies were.

"There are so many of them!" she whispered urgently to Will.

A little before them the earl exchanged silent nods with Sir Walter Percival, still visored, and Hereford jumped down from his mount. Sir Walter lifted his visor and roared to the army behind him. "Stand down! Stand down."

Will lowered the shield with a grunt and carefully slid his sword back into its scabbard. Adelaide looked incredulously at him.

"What is going on?" she hissed, though a little louder than she had hoped for it drew the attention of the earl.

Hereford overheard Adelaide's question. "Alterations have been made to our original plans, my girl," he said matter-of-factly but with an underlying hint of stress to his voice. He appeared to have aged ten years in the minutes he had been speaking with the woman and Adelaide could not tell if she saw regret or uncertainty in his lined face.

"Alterations?" enquired the Cornishwoman.

The crimson-cloaked woman walked slowly but purposefully towards Adelaide with long and careful strides suggestive of someone carrying a fragile load across uncertain ground.

"Yes, friend, alterations," the oak-haired woman clarified, staring at Adelaide with hard, dark eyes. "The lord has graciously chosen to abandon his king's penchant for slaughter and we encourage his vassals to follow suit."

Adelaide initially thought she had misheard the woman. "Abandon... his king?" She looked to Will to her right and she could almost see the sergeant working over the woman's answer in his head.

"There is no obligation on any man here to stay, as will become clear," the woman began explaining as she walked, "but if you would listen to us, you will see there is no choice to make." She stood a yard or two away from Adelaide, her long brown hair lank and damp with more of it untied than controlled. She looked to be perhaps thirty years of age with dark eyes that gave away no clues as to her thoughts and motives. Just at the top of her chest the baby's head could be seen, a few wisps of hair floating on its bobbing head and occasionally a high pitched infantile sound or gurgle could be heard.

Adelaide found the experience of talking to this baby-carrying woman profoundly disturbing and felt embarrassed at how easily she had been disarmed by the situation; at Clun she was the queen of her world and always knew how to think on her feet and adapt to situations as they arose, but on this hill the Dragon had the upper hand and, even worse, the Dragon knew it. And who was the Dragon to parade a child in front of her? She felt her rage building. Was it a set up? Had she been dragged all the way to this bleak hillside with the pretence of retribution only to endure the same grief all over again? The stab of humiliation was almost as painful as the memories of Matilda stirred by seeing that crimson cloak.

Adelaide could not hold her emotions in check any longer. "Slaughter! And what do you think about slaughter?" she cried, the volume of her voice increasing as she continued, "You murder children!" Tears began forming in her eyes and Will put his arm across her shoulders as a symbolic act of restraint, for she was not moving anywhere, and also to show to Hereford that the situation was not getting out of hand.

The oak-haired woman was taken aback by the outburst and though Adelaide herself could not deduce it at the current time, Will saw that the vitriol thrown at the woman had cut through her serene exterior and struck a nerve.

"Child murderers!" Adelaide screamed in the woman's face, drawing the attention of scores of the soldiers in the main column back along the hill. Hereford and Sir Walter watched on in stunned silence whilst the bemusement on Will's face evolved into full open-mouthed and consequently gap-toothed confusion. For Adelaide the scream was like a wave of a relief that washed away layers of tension that had gradually accumulated during the march before accelerating at the appearance of the oak-haired woman, but the self-consciousness that followed at being the subject of hundreds of eyes was acutely embarrassing for the Cornishwoman and she tried to shrink under Will's arm and into his body for protection.

The oak-haired woman, eyes fraught with emotion and beginning to water just a little, stepped forward again until she was separated by just an arm's length from Adelaide.

"Let he who is without sin, cast the first stone," the oak-haired woman seethed with her deep brown eyes locked on Adelaide's.

The woman's attitude sparked one last burst of emotional tumult to surge through the Cornishwoman. This Dragon was dictating terms and claiming circumstances were agreeable and peaceful, which Adelaide knew to be untrue. How dare this woman say these things? How dare she preach on sin? But this was not the worst of it. No, this Dragon dared to brandish her child before Adelaide. This woman, this Dragon, was responsible for Matilda dying! *How dare she flaunt her child before me? This woman had killed my own!*

Irrepressible rage descended over the little Cornishwoman's fair eyes and seized control of her faculties; with no warning she sprung forward from Will's leather-padded refuge and punched the woman in the face with a lightning hook across her nose. Adelaide immediately winced at the pain of impact, her small fist instantly cracking the cartilage in the oak-haired woman's nose which caused the latter to stumble back a few paces but without crying out in pain.

The crunching hit immediately snapped the Cornishwoman out of her anger; she stood stupefied at the realisation at what she had just done – punching a woman holding an *infant*! She watched for the woman's reaction, hoping, praying that the child was unhurt.

The Dragon woman held her nose and checked her hands for blood before remembering the infant at her chest; she looked down as the child began crying from the abrupt jolt its mother had suffered.

After a moment of shock the whole countryside erupted in uproar as the encircling Welsh responded to the assault with shouts of outrage. Intermingled with the cries were the occasional clanking of worked metal as a few picked up their discarded weapons.

"Enough!" Hereford boomed, restoring silence to the desolate hillside once more. His face was like thunder and his massive mouth opened wide so that he bared his teeth as he roared, their light yellow colouring sharply contrasting with the thick, black beard that covered the lower half of his face. Rapidly drained of expressive energy, both Adelaide and even Will took no little fright at the earl's terrible anger.

"I will have the head of the next miscreant who acts out of line!" he raged, somehow growing taller and more menacing as the ever increasing sunlight caused dark shadows to form under his heavy eye ridges, only adding to the monstrous transformation he was undergoing. The regret, uncertainty or both of a few moments previously evaporated in the cauldron that had just been lit.

He stalked towards Adelaide, completely ignoring the oak-haired woman who was being steadied by Sir Walter, though she regained her balance and composure quicker than the knight could dismount and tend to her. She coddled her baby, kissing it on the head and soothing its cries.

Hereford raised his gauntleted right hand and backhanded the Cornishwoman across her right cheek with the force of a blacksmith striking his hammer, instantly reddening the woman's face and bringing tears to her eyes. The pain seared through her head as it snapped back from the intensity of the strike. Openmouthed, Adelaide dared look back at the earl who stood hulking and menacing, anger writ large across his darkened face.

"You are lucky I am a merciful man," he sneered at Adelaide as she sobbed quietly. "Sergeant, she stays with us," the earl barked at Will before turning around and surveying the surrounding Welsh, whose agitation and volume were rising conspicuously. He returned to Adelaide, fire in his eyes and teeth still bared. Hereford's presence was overwhelming and his fury even more so. He leant forward, looking down at the small blonde Cornishwoman, nostrils flaring.

"This is bigger than you and your fucking vengeance, *girl*," he hissed, placing particular derision on the noun. "You have no idea what we are doing here and how crucial it is to ensure that no slaughter and killing has to happen again. Do you see these people here?" he asked, raising his right arm with an open palm in a vague indication of the Welsh fighters. Adelaide flinched, expecting a strike that never came. "Do you realise you could have got all of us here killed? Aren't you supposed to know everything there is to know about this fucking country?"

Leaving the Cornishwoman rattled the earl spun and paced toward the oak-haired woman, his armour clanking with every step. "How is the child?" he asked, with little enthusiasm but plenty of annoyance.

"Fine," replied the woman, her voice more nasal thanks to the damage dealt and subsequent blood flow that her right hand was failing to staunch.

"Good. Tell your people to disarm. The girl here will be dealt with." Hereford looked at the stones by his feet and linked his hands behind his back before surveying the Welsh host once more as he beckoned his captain over. "Sir Walter," he said, plainly and with the composure for which he was usually renowned.

The knight marched over to the earl's side. "My lord."

"Have it known that we are under a truce, and any harm dealt to the Welsh will be punishable by death. Let it be known to the Welsh as well. They will do you no harm." He spoke calmly but loud enough for Adelaide, Will and Gwenhwyfar to hear.

"Right away, lord," Sir Walter affirmed.

"Sergeant, take the girl away before I change my mind about taking her head," he ordered Will as he returned to surveying the hillside.

"My lord," responded Will, who turned to Adelaide with eyes a little wider than usual and his face entirely devoid of his characteristic cheer. "Come on, let's get you somewhere less horrible."

The Cornishwoman nodded, still frightened at the earl's wrath but more so at her own loss of composure and control. In her line of work aggression was always practiced and limited, even when she had before worked on Welsh who had been there at the village. She had always thought of herself as in control regardless of how emotionally drained it left her afterwards. Her face throbbed but the true pain was deeper and the blonde Cornishwoman did not notice Will tenderly taking her arm as they started back towards the army.

Chapter 20

All around El a milling aggregation of humanity and all of the sights, sounds and smells that accompanied it slowly swirled. Filtered into every nook and cranny by the sturdy workshops flanking Hart Street, the solid mass of men, women and children – most of whom were on the shoulders of their parents lest they become lost in the mayhem. This was as far as the hopeful crowd would get, though, in their quest to witness the demonstration. Men-at-arms had penned in the commons along the streets and so the vast majority of the city would come nowhere near the Godstone.

Even so, everyone else could talk of nothing but the Godstone and what strange properties it might possess, but the little Frenchwoman was entirely preoccupied with another hypothetical – how would she watch the spectacle? El could not hope to see anything over the swelling crowd of hats and fillets that would amass around her on the edge of the Tower Liberties, the wide cleared ground to the north of the fortress outer curtain wall and moat.

Consequently, she had asked along Maxwell, the stable lad at the Temple, to accompany her and to provide a platform for observation, be that through a piggyback or sitting on his shoulders. The little Frenchwoman held no qualms about adopting certain practices not necessarily becoming of a young woman – physical contact such as this was entirely practical and represented no ulterior intentions. Her practicality was further demonstrated by her choice of companion. In spite of having given her adult life at the Church and the Order, El was not so naïve to not recognise infatuation and so convincing the stable lad to abandon his post for a few hours was not difficult. He was a tall youth, round of face and shoulders with straight black hair that grew in all directions, giving him the permanent appearance of having just woken up. He was solidly built but the wisps of hair about his mouth did not quite connect with the budding whiskers on his cheeks, betraying his age. The boy did not even have concern for the inevitable punishment he would face when old Amaury, the head husbandman, noticed his disappearance. El had told him she would do her best to appease the cantankerous horseman, a grizzled long-haired man with a thick, barrel-like body and twig-thin arms and legs. Privately though, she did not think even Guy could charm Amaury; forgiveness did not come easy to the old man.

Nonetheless, that was a problem for another day. Here and now, she thought vigilance was essential, not against Amaury but the altogether more subtle and considerably more dangerous Dragons. Guy had not officially sanctioned El's presence, which made her task that much more difficult. The Master had spoken with Longshanks about a threat from such an organised outlaw group but the King had waived away such concerns. El had not asked Guy for the King's reasoning, but suspected the King saw no risk in the shadow of the Tower. Or, more likely, Edward simply did not trust the Temple – it had already tried to steal the stone, after all. El suspected the Temple's favour with the King was entirely dependent upon Guy's personal relationship with Edward; from what she could deduce there was great mutual respect between Guy and Longshanks and the King's well-known disagreements with the Temple had largely died down in the years since Guy had been ordained as Master.

Instead, the Master had given her free rein to undertake surveillance on her own terms, on the proviso that her own cover remain anonymous, a clause the small Frenchwoman would have insisted upon herself. Lord Reginald had not yet made an appearance as far as she could tell, spying through the ever shifting gaps between people's heads, a man's cap, another's shoulder, a woman's bunched hair.

Further, El had insisted that her presence at the demonstration be kept a secret from Henry, and Guy had agreed. Neither had any intention on unnecessarily worrying Henry after the English knight had made it clear that he was not happy with what he termed as the 'risks' El had taken recently. Her work in and around Granada had been an exhausting and almost deadly learning curve but the very personal nature of her recent tribulations had caused part of her to think that perhaps Henry was right; she had been placing herself and others in unnecessary danger, taking too direct a role in situations for which she was not prepared. In Spain she had rarely seen the faces of those who would technically be considered her 'enemies', let alone directly interacted with them. But in England and Wales, it had all been very direct. El had no idea if Dywel was alive, if his son still had a father, if Morwen still held a grudge against her. The guilt over the deaths at the village paralysed her on occasion, forcing her to retreat alone to shadowy corners to hide away from company and seek the forgiveness of the Lord.

The little Frenchwoman felt her face and lamented that it was no longer tender from the beating she had received from Sir Edward's men, guilty that her physical penance had all but disappeared. The intensity of the treatment that night in the forest at Rhuddlan and the fighting in Llaneurgain was disturbing but in retrospect El considered it entirely deserved.

But Guy had told her to go outside the walls of the Round Church and into the crowds and to range through the city as she had always done. "Get back on the horse," he had said, his huge hand softly cradling the side of her head. "The Lord has allocated us all duties in life, and we do not shirk them nor judge ourselves before the duties are fulfilled, for it is not our place to judge," he had said.

As usual the Master's prescription had proved effective. A renewed focus had offered the little Frenchwoman respite from the maelstrom in her mind that had been lacking during the traumatic journey across country back to London. She was not entirely free of her mind's compulsive reluctance to rest but, perversely, El found a kind of mental solace in her assignment here.

Not that it was a straightforward assignment. Searching for hints of suspicious behaviour or things out of place in these conditions, along the crammed streets that led to the Tower, was near-impossible. And yet the risks attached to an innocent public demonstration of what both Guy and Henry had said was a potentially devastating weapon were too great. The King's hubris in assuming security through proximity to his mighty fortress was unacceptable but officially inadmissible. El would have to do things the way she had always done them - right in the thick of it herself.

Thus here she was, sat atop Maxwell's wide shoulders like a little sparrowhawk perched in the gently swaying upper reaches of a full grown oak, her sharp eyes scrutinising every movement as she scoured the street and the walls up ahead for prey. She may not achieve anything today and hopefully she would not need to, but El felt comforted that she was doing *something* at least.

Confident in the boy's stability, the little Frenchwoman was craning her neck this way and that, not entirely sure what she was looking for but trusting her judgements, for she had found her instincts had generally served her well in the past. It was a liberating experience, level as she was with the prominent joinery between floors in the flanking stone workshops that lined Tower Hill Street. For once, she rose taller than any man in the kingdom, probably in all Christendom.

With the round-shouldered stable lad securely planted on the road, standing firm amidst the ebb and flow of so many excited and agitated hopefuls, El had a commanding view up the road and back down it, whilst keeping the city walls in sight on her left over the clothiers' shops. Ahead, she could see the bright patchwork of tunics, coats and cloaks give way to the more monotone collection of blacks, browns and greys worn by the brothers and sisters of the city's religious houses, or at least those who had been permitted to attend the demonstration, gathered at the top of the slope out in front of the Tower; although it seemed the entire city had gathered, El knew a number of houses were absent.

Notable amongst these, of course, were the Temple brothers. El was thankful that on the whole the men and women of the many houses throughout the city understood that any perceived sin committed by the Temple in their attempt to acquire the stone was the attributable to those who ordered and carried it out only. On her rounds of the city over the past week or so she had not picked up any ill-feeling toward the Order members, much to her relief. It was understandable yet regrettable that the King was punishing the Order for what had happened at Rhuddlan, but she was relieved that the other communities did not hold it against the Temple brothers based in London, who had no association with El and Henry's mission.

Further along she could see the assorted nobles, aesthetically at odds with their religious neighbours and the grim sky above them, a dull pallor that gave everyone a greyish hue about their faces as if the clouds themselves had robbed the world of both the shining sun in the heavens and the colour on the Earth. The barons and earls were fighting back, though, against the monochromatic conditions. Even at a distance, El could make out the magnificent hats of the bishops amongst their humbler brothers and sisters, the tall conical headdresses of the duchesses towering high like the spires of so many churches, the ostentatious fur linings of a wealthy earl's studded green jacket that doubled the width of his shoulders.

The chaotic mix of colours was only a symptom of the disorder that reigned all around. Faces turning left and right, excited voices drowning the occasional aggressive shout, here a laugh going up and there a ribald riposte. El looked down at the dark brown hair of the stable lad who was gripping her shins assuredly befitting a boy with a lifetime of handling mighty horses behind him.

"Are you well?" she asked Maxwell.

Maxwell awkwardly tried to look up at his passenger but the angle was too steep so he abandoned the idea. "Yeah, I'm doing well. I've carried sacks of wine that are heavier than you. You should pay closer mind to meals," he replied jovially.

"That is easier for some than others," she responded.

The joke was lost on the stable lad. "I know how to get extra portions, you know," Maxwell offered, swaying a little as the ripple effect of soldiers wading through the crowd reached their position.

"Is that so?" El replied with humour in her voice, her eyes still scanning the crowds and walls.

Maxwell gave a half-offended laugh. "Ha! What's that supposed to mean, hey?" he exclaimed, clocking on to what El had been hinting at.

The little Frenchwoman did not answer the lad's rhetorical question, her attention momentarily captured by a group of people on the roofs of some workshops back down towards Hart Street. She studied them for a while, watching as a couple of figures looked to secure the tiling around a collapsed section of roofing whilst another peered into the gap. Many people had clambered atop the closely packed buildings with the hope of watching over onto the hill. El knew that like the hundreds, thousands maybe, who crammed the streets leading to the east of the city, those on the rooftops along Hart Street would be very unlikely to see anything at all, but equally she knew hope was an inextinguishable concept and all the more potent when enhanced with excitement and anticipation.

The buzz of the occasion was both welcome and unwelcome as a distraction. It was wonderful to see the city united in enthrallment at the gift bestowed by the Lord unto His people, from the loftiest earl to the most humble hawker, and on an individual level El enjoyed the charming straightforwardness of her young companion. By the same measure, however, she did sense the potential for something ominous afoot and the same festival atmosphere rendered surveillance an almost impossible task. She knew it was a token role; the unavoidable presence of the city's men-at-arms was as ubiquitous as the peddlers flogging their food and wares to the swarming multitude, so she hoped the King's soldiers could handle any trouble should it arise. The image of Morwen cradling her prone husband flashed into El's mind once more. Guilt washed over her again. If trouble did flare during the demonstration, at least she was at hand to assist in dealing with it. Conscious abstinence from assisting those in difficulties was categorically not an option for the little Frenchwoman.

The faces in the crowd blurred into one and El imagined once more she was back in southern France, this time sat on her brother's shoulders. There was that time he had tripped whilst carrying her so, and they both fell to the dirt. She had scuffed her knees badly, she remembered, but she did not cry and neither did her brother. El recalled looking up following the fall and see that man stood there - where had he come from? He was the tallest man she had ever seen. Who was he? El thought perhaps she was simply confusing memories. The man was reminiscent of Guy because of his height, but this man had a full head of hair. Obviously it was not Guy because she had only met him years later. A most peculiar transposition of memories, she thought.

A familiar voice much closer to the present interrupted her accidental daydream.

"El...?" she heard the stable lad tentatively ask, "El, there's someone who wants to talk to you."

She looked down. The round-shouldered youth had given up attempting to make eye contact whilst talking to her, so she saw he was aimlessly speaking to the air, loudly so as to be heard above the raucous din all around. The little Frenchwoman also noticed a pale white face of a young woman looking back up, framed by the white wimple of a nun covered with the black veil of a sister who has made her vows. El took a moment as she studied the face, with its dark brown eyes and an intriguing expression; an expression that seemed to suggest the woman was awaiting information, news, the bestowing of knowledge – she looked poised to carefully listen. The little Frenchwoman could not work out who was this nun. She found it a little disconcerting that someone knew her identity and not vice versa. This was not supposed to be the way things worked. Especially on a day such as today, when she was explicitly forbidden from the Tower Liberties on the King's orders. She was also a little annoyed that Maxwell had used her name in public when she had explicitly asked him not to do so. Such issues would be addressed at another time.

"El? There's someone he-"

"*Oui, merci*," El interrupted with forced kindness in her voice, knowing the boy could not tell if she had heard him.

"Oh, shall I let you down?" Maxwell asked.

"Yes, please," she replied with a smile on her face that was reflected in the inclination of her voice.

The burly lad stooped down in the little space available amongst the crowd and El awkwardly jumped off his shoulders practically into a man standing in front of them. He either did not notice or paid her no mind, and having bounced back into Maxwell she realised that the stable lad's head was still caught under the long wool of the bottom of her circle coat. It was hardly the most practical of garments for climbing, least not when climbing over other people. This caused him to flail around somewhat before he was able to stand tall once more, red of face and grunting as his body was relieved of the additional burden it had carried. He puffed his cheeks and blew out of his mouth, recovering his composure from having been tangled up in El's long coat and from the strain on his legs when lowering the little Frenchwoman to the ground.

"Blimey," he said whilst smiling to her, "think we need to practice that."

Turning to face him, El shot him a straight look with raised eyebrows and pursed lips. "I don't think that will be necessary, but thank you."

"Excuse me," said the veiled woman in English, her tones clipped in comparison with El's strong French and Maxwell's London inflection. "You are Eleanor, is that right?"

El looked at her, blanking any emotion from her face. "Good afternoon," she said neutrally, "it depends who's asking."

The woman flashed a quick grin, her head slightly leaning forward as her small mouth curled into a mischievous smile, before returning to the intriguing look it had before. "It does, I suppose," she responded with wide eyes not quite as dark as the gently arching eyebrows above them. "I am Sister Diane of St Helen's Priory, but who I know is of greater interest to you. Please, could we talk somewhere a little more secluded than this?"

El looked around, suspicious of this stranger's interest, and particularly of how the stranger found her in a crowd numbering pretty much the entire population of the city. She did not like it and with her right hand, hidden away behind her shapeless sleeve and behind her back, she grabbed hold of Maxwell's tunic, tugging slowly but firmly to signal her concern. Partially redeeming his earlier slip from the rules of El's game, the stable lad leaned in conspicuously on the two women's conversation and placed a left arm around El's back in a show of genuine protection.

El knew Diane could sense the discomfort. "If I told you that old Brother Edward has concern for Sir Henry, would that make you trust me?"

El was taken aback by the namedropping, figuratively and physically as she inadvertently backed her head into Maxwell's shoulder.

"I don't like to hear of concern for Henry. Has Edward sent you?" The Frenchwoman referred to old Brother Edward at the Temple, Henry's late-night conversation partner. The kindly old monk had always just let the world go by outside the Round Church's doors, for as long as El had known him; she could not quite grasp that he had conversed with this enigmatic nun. When did Brother Edward last leave the Round Church? Even if he had

311

ventured outside of those walls, St Helen's Priory was up by the Bishopsgate, which was on the complete opposite side of the city to the Temple.

"Not quite, but Abbot Geoffrey has," came the answer from the nun.

Abbot Geoffrey? Why was the order head of the Crutched Friars sending messengers to her? He was a close friend with Master Guy. Any business with the Temple would presumably go through him. El looked up at Maxwell, who in turn replied with a puzzled appearance, either end of his mouth sinking down and his eyebrows raised in the visual expression of 'I don't know.' Moving her gaze beyond the stable lad's confusion, the little Frenchwoman saw a longhaired man practically hanging out of the window on the first floor above one of the clothworking shops. She wondered again at how his sharp-eyed stranger had found her amidst the throng. There must have been countless brown-haired women in the crowd, many of them in a long blue coat. Everyone in the crowd was a suspect, everyone in the crowd a potential enemy. Everyone could be out to get her. The sparrowhawk was both hunter and hunted.

"Come, let us talk away from here," commanded El to Maxwell and Diane. "Over there." She flicked her head up, indicating the direction straight ahead of her gaze, a shallow enclave in the wall of a workshop between two mighty vertical wooden beams.

Maxwell saw it immediately and grabbed El's hand before bundling forwards through the solid wall of commonfolk with very little difficulty. El followed in his footsteps, and behind her trailing circle coat went Diane, herself nimbly slipping between the jostling crowd.

The two women leaned into the wall between the supporting beams either side of this section of the wall. The beams acted as two barriers to the rest of the crowd and Maxwell himself stood resolute as the third barrier.

"Why has Abbot Geoffrey sent you? And how did you find me?" El asked, straight to the point and not willing to spend any more time than absolutely necessary in conversation. The little Frenchwoman's guilt was unceasingly pushing her determination for vigilance and she could not bear to abandon her surveillance for too long.

312

"The Abbot warns of an infiltration of the Crutched Friars by an external order, and he believes there are malevolent intentions around the demonstration," Diane explained hurriedly with a hushed voice. "He caught me running errands by the Priory – he was hiding between some shops. I think he is worried about who knows he is aware, and wanted to send someone he could trust who is also less conspicuous than him."

It was a lot for El to digest.

"Infiltration? How does he know this?" the Frenchwoman demanded in a decidedly less understated tone. She was also concerned about the elderly Geoffrey wandering the streets of London looking for couriers.

"All I know is that the Abbot accidentally overheard a conversation between some of his brothers and an unknown voice, good lady," the nun replied.

Diane had barely finished answering when El recommenced her inquisition. "And infiltrated by whom? Does he know any more?"

"Again, I'm not sure exactly," Diane offered helplessly. Her face was pulled in contrition for being no more than a simple messenger. "He said something about 'Dragons' but I don't really know what he was talking about; he was urgent and insisted I come find you straight away."

El's mind raced. Henry was definitely in danger. Or had Abbot Geoffrey simply confused Henry's plant and explained it with a fictional subversion? She had not seen him in a long time but had heard the elderly abbot's sharpness was deteriorating.

Then again, the Dragons are everywhere...

Maxwell's round shoulders barged into the women as his body rode the swell of the crowd, and the stable lad responded by bracing his arms against the beams on either side and swiftly apologising to his wards.

El paid him no heed, however. "How did you find me?" she asked again.

"Geoffrey knew you would be here."

Perhaps his mind isn't going, after all, El thought of the ageing abbot.

Sister Diane continued. "He told me to look for a woman of your appearance in a blue coat, sat on a dark-haired youth's shoulders. He said you wouldn't be relaxed and would be looking the wrong way half of the time."

El conceded that Abbot Geoffrey had powerful powers of intuition and this nun impeccable perception. She looked around at the crowd, or at least the parts of the crowd she could see past Maxwell's bodily blockade, and wondered just how many other eyes noticed her presence so easily.

"Who else knows this?" demanded El, lowering her voice to an audible hiss.

Diane's worried face became increasingly panicked, unsettled as she was by the ire she detected in El. "I don't know, I'm sorry, I can't tell you any more than this," she reiterated, brow furrowed and sorrow in her eyes.

The little Frenchwoman exhaled heavily through her small nose, huffing in frustration at the tantalising yet wholly unsatisfying morsels she was being offered here. She looked around again on the off chance that a Dragon would come into view and make her job that much easier. There was one lurking in and amongst the crowd, there had to be.

Chapter 21

There already was a tall, grey-haired man, stern of face with a seasoning of iron-coloured whiskers on either side. Baron Reginald de Grey, the only layperson in the immediate group around the stone, conversed with the finely dressed churchmen around him. Henry recognised the sombre Archbishop of Canterbury and his mighty mitre to Baron de Grey's left. The knight had met neither man but knew from Guy they were both intense and principled, not given to idle chatter and apparently renowned for not suffering fools. He could imagine the conversation between the two was either stilted or meticulously boring. There were three other figures with them, their backs to the higher slope from whence the Crutched Friars walked, whom Henry could not identify.

The brothers marched in silence across the short grass and Henry felt thousands of eyes follow him from the crowd to their left. Out in the middle of the grass, though, no one would recognise him. None of the senior delegates had ever met him, such was the Temple's highly successful policy of concealing its members' identity from *any* conspicuous exposure to the population.

The Dragons have got round that, though, he mused.

The Crutched brothers, staffs aloft and proud in the white-grey sky, filed alongside the stone and opposite Baron de Grey, the Archbishop of Canterbury and the three other men. Henry guessed that at least two of the men with their back to him were senior churchmen judging from their ornate attire, and the third man was possibly of foreign origin, perhaps Mediterranean? The disguised knight could not tell.

Baron de Grey welcomed the Friars with open arms, belying his firm reputation. "God bless you, brothers. I assume you are familiar with our distinguished guests, his excellence the Archbishop of Canterbury, his excellence the Archbishop of York, his excellence the Bishop of Durham and the honourable Brother Bartolomeo Fiadóni, here on behalf of His Holiness."

The brothers bowed solemnly before their seniors and Henry felt apprehension as Lord Reginald's gaze crossed his own, but the tall baron's eyes did not linger long on his. The English knight tried to convince himself that there was no reason the baron would recognise him simply because he had never seen him before. So long as the Crutched Friars held their nerve, which Master Guy had assured him they would, Henry was safe.

"So to continue, Bishop Anthony, you would say your initial opinion is that some exaggerations must have been made?" Reginald enquired of the Bishop of Durham, Anthony Bek. Bek was a tough man with bright, alert eyes. He practically ran the north of England as his own kingdom, holding responsibility for both ecclesiastical and military matters in the area. If anyone would dare question Reginald's storytelling, it would be the Bishop of Durham.

"I'm just not sure how it can be as you say, Reginald. It defies logic. Something must go into something else; something cannot go into nothing. Even with the Lord – if someone ascends to Heaven, they are going *to* something. But swords and armour? Surely they cannot ascend?" The blue-eyed bishop debated calmly as befitted one of the King's most trusted ambassadors.

Reginald did not take Bek's hesitancy as an affront. "I did not believe it either, father. Perhaps if you observe it here, your mind might be better served with suggestions," he said encouragingly.

Among the silent and unmoving brothers, Henry observed the tall baron. Based on El's testimony he had expected someone akin to a monster, but this man seemed reasonable. *Early days, though*, the knight thought. There had not yet been anything for Reginald to get angry about.

The Archbishop of York, the jowly John le Romeyne, opened his flabby mouth to contribute to the discussion but was instantly cut off by the blaring of trumpets from down the slope. All spun round and saw the King's troop escorting the man himself as they marched up from the outer gatehouse, the only land-based entrance to the fortress that dominated the river and the city.

The crowds further down by Tower Street cheered their king, a hero warrior who had pacified the island of Britain. Henry observed that those same people cheering seemed to have forgotten that the

316

King had taxed everyone harder than at any time in living memory in order to do so, and even then the officially declared 'peace' was a rather generous term. But London was a long way from the recent fighting; the city's population would not know any different.

Nonetheless, onwards the soldiers marched and knights rode to the chanting and shouting of the commonfolk, the guards in a box formation around the King mounted upon his destrier in the middle. The soldiers came to a halt about twenty paces from where Lord Reginald and the churchmen stood and the King dismounted before striding towards the stone. The assembled dignitaries knelt as one as their monarch approached.

King Edward paced like a colossus amongst the throng, with the proud bearing of a champion warrior and resolute leader, and with the physique of a man in his prime. Twenty years on the throne and twice that time that warring had not deteriorated the man's vitality. His long brown hair, curling down around each ear from beneath the golden crown, had barely silvered even in his mid-fifties. Even through a chestnut beard that grew thicker towards the chin his iron jaw jutted proudly, Henry thought; he could not imagine anyone, not even Master Guy, able to resist the King's rage.

With the exception of Lord Reginald, the men milling around him appeared barely half his height – Edward cleared well over six feet tall, and was so broad of shoulder the white fur-trimmed cloak cast upon him, infinitely deep black with gold embroidery, seemed barely able to contain his arms. He wore black leather gloves from within the well-fitted sleeves of his tunic, a brilliant red again with gold embroidery that seemed to flash with fine rays of light as he moved despite the heavily overcast conditions concealing the sunlight. The King approached Lord Reginald and the two tall men clasped forearms with the firm familiarity of years of friendship, exchanging hushed words imperceptible beneath the tumult of both church and lay crowds.

The King turned to the gathered senior churchmen and the brothers of the Crutched Friars. "God bless you, fathers, brothers," he announced with vigour, approaching the Archbishop of York and the Bishop of Durham and bowing before them, apparently without

317

reluctance. The bishops bowed in return, or as much as their ponderous headwear permitted.

Henry found it fascinating to watch the mighty King Edward supplicate himself before the men of God. There had always been debate over the primacy of secular or ecclesiastical rulers; that both parties were showing respect was welcome.

The King reached the Archbishop of Canterbury, Robert Winchelsey and suddenly lost his smile. The man transformed from benign to malevolent in one moment, and the crowd hushed noticeably as many saw the inevitable meeting between two powerful men who detested one another - everyone knew Edward's attempts a few years prior to tax the clergy had drawn resistance from Winchelsey and even more significantly that resistance largely succeeded. Bad blood had continued since; the first clash had started a rot that would sour all following discussions.

Curtly bowing, King Edward greeted the Archbishop coolly. "Archbishop Robert, welcome to London once more. I trust we may put aside our differences in the light of the Lord's blessing here today."

Winchelsey lowered his head whilst expertly balanced his towering mitre. "God bless you, my lord. It is time for all of us to bask in God's love and that of our Lord Jesus Christ with this wonderful gift," he responded sincerely, not taking his small eyes from the King's face.

The King signalled his satisfied with Winchelsey's reticence with a cursory *hmm*, before walking on to Bartolomeo Fiadóni, the Pope's representative. He was a tremendously tanned man, remarkably so for someone so scholarly and tied to a desk within the abbeys and cathedrals of northern Italy. Appearing to be at least sixty, Fiadóni's skin was leathery and tough, quite in contrast to the pale and soft appearance of some of the English brothers present. Even at his age his shaved head appeared to be covered in thick hair, such was his dark complexion.

"It is an honour to host such an esteemed friend to so many of the finest Christians to have lived, Signor Fiadóni," spoke the King grandly. He did not know Italian and so retained the French that had sufficed for his previous exchanges.

318

"My lord," Fiadóni replied with a dramatic bow and a broad, practiced smile, "His Holiness welcomes your most gracious invite to this most portentous event. As Papa Boniface's and the Lord's most humble servant, I thank you for your hospitality." The man's Italian accent was thick and coursed through his excellent French.

Henry observed Fiadóni. The Italian was a fascinating character and Guy had told Henry much about him. Any man who formed such a close friendship with Thomas Aquinas so as to be his confessor was worth meeting, Henry thought.

King Edward smiled warmly to the papal envoy. "We must converse afterwards, Signor," he added with warmth before turning and striding towards the stone, finally giving in to temptation. Lord Reginald walked over to join him.

"The moment of reckoning, Reg," said the King, warmth in his voice for his old friend who had staked his arguably heroic reputation, his position as a true English champion, on a successful demonstration. As far as the King was concerned, the entire kingdom was present. This was not a time for failure.

"I've risked more for you before," Reginald replied bluntly, the gravity of the situation weighing heavily on his proud shoulders.

The King nodded and looked around at the expectant crowd, the noblemen and ladies in their multi-coloured finery like a great stained glass window, and the church orders on their right by the approach road, all sombre in appearance but for the ostentatious prelates and bishops with their great hats and staffs, and their splendidly ornamented cinctures heavily decorated with stones, silver and gold. "No pressure, then. Let's see what you have found," said Edward gruffly.

"What we have been *gifted*, my lord," Reginald reminded Edward with a nod of the head and raise of the eyebrows.

"Of course, may the Lord forgive my slip," responded the King, crossing himself. Turning to his right, he addressed the Archbishop of Canterbury, viewing him icily. "My dear Winchelsey, would you like to initiate proceedings," he commanded; there was little love lost between Edward and Archbishop Winchelsey.

"My lord king," responded the Archbishop with the respectful grace expected of the leading churchman in the realm, irrespective of

319

the enmity between him and Edward. His demeanour was matched by the trim and restrained appearance that represented the ideal of leading churchmen – his well-fitted alb, the basic white tunic, gave no hint of fat around the stomach, nor did he carry loose jowls on his taut face, quite in contrast to the other primates beside him. The senior churchmen were essentially noblemen anyway and had a reputation for living as such. The bishops and archbishops generally matched their lay counterparts' lifestyle in all but the martial requirements; consequently, the churchmen tended to be much softer in body, and so apparently greedier.

But not the trim Archbishop Winchelsey, that stern and frugal man, a true son of the Church. Though considerably paler than Signor Fiadóni – who was not? – Winchelsey was akin to the Italian in how *strong* he appeared; his very aesthetic spoke of a sharp man, physically and mentally. Winchelsey was a man of action. Spinning on the spot and raising his hands, palms to the crowd, he somehow drew the murmuring and chattering of the assorted spectators to an almost immediate cessation, leaving in the air only the buzz from the common folk penned behind the churchmen on Crutched Friars and Hart Street who could not see his request for silence. They were too excitable to have paid attention even if they could see him.

"My fellow brothers and sisters of Christ our Lord, my lords and ladies, my lord king. We have been blessed with a gift from the Lord, surely worked by His angels if not the Lord Himself, possessed of miraculous properties in accordance with reputable and honourable eyewitness accounts."

His voice was not particularly deep but it was commanding and Henry imagined the Archbishop could lecture on any topic and keep his audience enthralled. "It is surely an indication of the esteem in which our great kingdom is held by our Heavenly Father, that our efforts to bring the peace of the Church to all corners of this island are succeeding. But the work is not complete; we know we must remain vigilant and ceaseless in our labours. If the Lord blesses us in such a way now, how great the reward in Heaven for our evangelical work?"

Winchelsey walked back to the stone and ran his hand over the surface, smoothing his palm around the soft curve at the near edge.

320

Henry watched as the stone passively and invisibly worked its mesmeric charm on even the infallible Archbishop, a man of principle renowned throughout Christendom for his piety and propriety. He thought Winchelsey had lost his train of thought, as had El, Abbot Thomas, Prior Simon and Lord Reginald when they regarded its finery.

But Winchelsey was not so easily distracted. Standing up to his full height, around five and a half feet not including the gargantuan mitre upon his head, the Archbishop walked back past Bartolomeo, Bek and Le Romeyn to once more face the fascinated observers. The commonfolk could still be heard, penned in by soldiers behind the churchmen. Who knew what state that crowd was in? Of course, it was no concern of the nobles ahead, thought Henry.

Winchelsey raised his hands once more. "We have in our midst some of the finest minds of the age, esteemed doctors of the Church tasked by God Himself with divining the mysteries of this relic. And once we have determined the meaning and workings of this gift, let knowledge of its teachings be spread forth to all corners of Christendom and beyond, that the message of Christ be further strengthened through what we shall witness here today." He paused, composing himself and allowing his message to sink in. Henry admired the Archbishop's strong oratory and guessed the blustering King rued having been cursed with so often having to face such a compelling opponent.

Winchelsey continued, incapable of keeping his arms by his side, making grand arching sweeps to either end of the assembled onlookers. "We have today been blessed with the presence of so many friends from lands near and far, not least His Holiness' personal representative, and of course his majesty the King."

Cheers went up from the nobles, interrupting the Archbishop's flow. "Such gatherings of great men and women beloved of the Lord are uncommon and so we thank our Father for safely bringing together so many of His children, themselves tasked with shepherding the people through the responsibility they have received from the Lord God. This gift is a reminder of those responsibilities we have in marshalling those under our care; as we learn from the

321

teachings and knowledge provided by this gift, so those under our supervision shall learn from us."

The Archbishop patted down his attire and checked the security of his mitre as a slight breeze picked up on what was otherwise meteorologically a very dull day. The motionless, endless clouds matched the whitewashed fortress walls and the White Tower itself, surrounded by the dark murk of the moat. Even the green of the grass seemed to lose its verve in the leaden conditions, and in spite of the imperious fortress providing a backdrop the setting seemed underwhelming for what could prove a momentous event in history. But the colourful garb of the nobles and churchmen provided some relief from the gloomy environment, and above each bright outfit was an eager face impatiently anticipating the demonstration to come.

As the Archbishop began to lead the assembly in prayer, a small movement caught Henry's eye to his left. He glanced at the friar beside him, a small man with a high hairline that meant his shaved hair seemed to merge seamlessly with his forehead. The man was very slightly moving his right arm inside the long sleeve of his habit. Ever wary, the English knight suspected a concealed weapon; he had been around quite enough people carrying knives up their sleeves that he suspected anyone with long-sleeved clothing, ordained or otherwise.

Returning his eyes forwards, Henry considered what he had just seen. The Friar was slowly and very gently moving his arm back and forth, as if trying to inconspicuously loosen something underneath the dark cloth of the habit. Henry himself gently and with considerably greater subtlety loosened the blade around his outer right forearm in preparation to foil some attack, should the brother be contemplating such a move. He worked it to a point where it remained secure in its strap, but free enough to slip immediately into his hand if moved rapidly – under the cover of his long habit sleeves the knight repeatedly clenched and unclenched his fist and wiggled his fingers in a wave motion, working the tendons and muscles of his forearm to gradually shift the blade forwards.

Archbishop Winchelsey continued with his sermon, entrancing the crowd and King alike. Henry thought he noticed another friar gently rocking his arm within the habit, much in the same manner as the brother to his left. Henry assumed the same explanation. Had he stumbled upon an assassination plot against the King, or one of the high bishops? Guy had assured him of the Crutched brothers' loyalty to the Order's cause, and Abbot Geoffrey was one of Guy's oldest friends. Henry did not expect disloyalty, let alone such a base crime as assassination! It could be that the Dragons had already reached London and were possessed of influence beyond even that of Guy, persuading the Crutched Friars to forego their loyalty to the true Church in favour of a zealous and violent sect.

But surely there was some other explanation. Perhaps they were nervous, which would be understandable. The friars had heard the same rumours as had everyone else – a stone that could make armour disappear, earth disappear, buildings disappear; some said it was a test sent by the Lord, others a contraption sent by the devil to ensnare the weak-willed. And here they stood, awaiting the lighting of the torches to clarify these rumours.

Henry had always trusted his gut instincts, however, which in this case were of suspicion and trepidation. A public attack on the King in the shadow of the Tower would be a logical culmination of the recently escalating attacks undertaken by the Dragons. More sweat ran down the centre of his spine, further indication of nerves and anticipation, and further agitating the English knight. He had already seen an overwrought commoner beaten down by a jumpy man-at-arms, nerves fraying whilst attempting the daunting and thankless task of keeping back a mass of excited bodies. The narrow streets funnelled the swell, concentrating the pressure on the creaking human fence of the King's soldiers. Who knew what had happened to that man; Henry shuddered a little at the thought of being trampled to death by so many unaware feet, feet that could belong to your own family and friends.

Guy was right about the stone. The Order needed to seize it, to protect people from themselves. Still the two friars shifted their arms, almost imperceptibly but in stark contrast to the statue-like bishops, other friars, Edward and Reginald. Henry darted a glance down to the end of the friar's sleeve and a tiny cascade of liquid made itself visible below the friar's habit, running down the outside

323

of his leg and over his sandal. Henry suppressed a groan of disgust; assassin or no assassin, relieving oneself in such a situation, during a sermon and before God's earthly representatives was deplorable behaviour!

But how was it on the outside of his leg? A slight glistening in the grass at the friar's feet extended a little way back in the direction of the Tower Hill approach, and Henry's eyes darted to the other friar in front – he too had liquid streaming down the outside of his leg, pooling around his right sandal, again glistening in a trail off from whence they had came.

Henry turned his gaze to the as yet unlit fire torches in the hands of the other friars. A horrifying realisation hit him like an arrow to the chest. In one lightning motion, practiced countless times and executed to perfection he reached into his right sleeve and drew the blade in his left hand, turning and slashing open the friar's habit across the front. The sliced material practically fell off to reveal wine bags strapped to his body, one of which was by now rapidly leaking clear liquid all down the friar's front. The balding friar was dumbfounded, a startled fox at the hen house caught in the act by a wary dog, spotted before he even knew there were eyes on him.

"Don't light the torches!" Henry boomed, face contorted with anger and determination. A gasp went up from the front rows of nobles and churchmen, and the dignitaries around the stone all to a man spun at the shouting.

"What is this?" roared the King, his ire erupting spectacularly quickly. Reginald, who was surely deafened in one ear by the outburst, put a hand to his sword hilt and eyed Henry maliciously.

Breathing heavily due to the sudden attention focused on him, Henry shouted again. "Don't light the torches!" he cried, pointing his dagger at the bag-laden friar. "My lord king, you must move away at once! These men will burn the city down with this much oil," he hurriedly explained walking towards Edward as he spoke which prompted Reginald to draw his sword.

"No further, brother," Reginald growled, holding his longsword out to his right, not ostensibly threatening but giving the grey-haired baron the option of an immediate swing should the situation escalate. "Drop your weapon!"

Henry obligingly let go of the knife, not caring where it landed and indeed almost costing him a foot as it plummeted blade-down into the soft grass beside his open sandal. "My lord, we don't know the effects this much fire would have, this is all oil!" Henry said almost breathlessly, gesturing back at the friars. They all carried pitifully clueless expressions on their faces, one or two occasionally studying the slashed brother's modified and un-monastic attire. Henry looked over Edward's shoulder and saw a few men-at-arms running towards them, armour clanking and rattling, dark blue shields the only colour of an otherwise dreary appearance.

"Guards!" thundered Edward Longshanks, unaware his soldiers had already taken the initiative. "Have these men arrested!" His face was a picture of fury, reddening cheeks flanking his great cavernous mouth, jaws wide open as if he were taking the form of the lions on his arms. Henry had heard tales of the King's legendary volcanic temper; one churchman who incurred his wrath had supposedly fallen down and died in terror at his feet earlier in the year, and though he did not usually give credence to apocryphal stories with little opportunity for genuine investigation, the terrifying force of nature exploding before him gave him no doubt as to the man's bark.

A number of the Crutched Friars started to plead their innocence with supplicating gestures and clasped hands, with the exception of the two assuredly guilty men. One of them, a tall, sad-faced man with mournful eyes, spoke louder than the rest. "My lords, there is some mistake; we are men of faith and loyalty! I know not of what this brother speaks. He is not one of us!"

Henry's game was rumbled but he did not begrudge the sad-faced man. It did seem likely that only a few of the Crutched brothers had been compromised and the sad-faced friar was probably not one of them. On the other hand, being rooted out as an imposter would now be received even worse given the developments.

The open-mouthed shock of the senior churchmen was accompanied by an outburst of disbelief from Winchelsey. "Brothers, is this true? This is an abomination!" he stammered, all the fluidity of his earlier delivery gone in the sudden onset of confusion, as was his composure and grace.

The men-at-arms were approaching and the tumult of the crowds continued to rise, an air of discontent enveloping the open grassy area. Henry resigned himself to also being arrested; fear truly took hold of him for the first time since he had donned the dark habit and crossed staff of the Friars.

"My lord king, my lords, we must move away from this stone," the English knight urged again, his eyes frantically darting between the lofty nobles standing before him and the mesmeric silvery block. The Godstone had a serene and peaceful essence yet possessed a capacity for chaos and disorder, dangerously mischievous for those unaccustomed with its nature.

Lord Reginald, resplendent in his fine scarlet jacket, stepped closer to Henry and looked him closely in the eyes. "How do you know...?"

Henry cut him off. "My lord, I believe the man here with the oil may have sympathy for the Dragons," said the knight hurriedly, but at that moment two men-at-arms appeared and flanked Henry, taking hold of his arms and forcibly bending them behind his back.

"My lord!" Henry exclaimed, grimacing but not actively resisting as the men-at-arms tried to bundle him away from the King's presence, "you need to move away, now!"

Reginald looked to the stone, thinking for a moment before a light of comprehension was lit in his mind. "Sir Henry of the Temple," he stated hesitantly, loud enough for Henry to hear but not so for the King who continued blustering and barking orders to anyone who would listen.

The soldiers bundling away Henry too heard the cryptic comment and paused in their manhandling, turning around to face Reginald again. Henry nodded in response to the baron's half-question, half-statement.

"Reg, what is the meaning of this? Get these men out of here!" commanded King Edward, looking as if he would actually blow his top if someone did not remove the crown to relieve the pressure of rage building in his head. "You have offended the Lord God and your king!" he spat at the Crutched Friars being carted off by the grim-looking soldiers, all but the wine bag-laden two begging forgiveness for a crime they pleaded no involvement with. Their

326

pleas and supplications were barely audible over the increasing hostility of the crowd, the majority originating with the boisterous earls and barons closer to the front of their unofficial enclosure. The church representatives were not entirely silent either, though; Henry could see a number of brothers, sisters and even an unrecognisable prelate pointing and mouthing their displeasure.

"We must go, Edward," said Reginald, calmly yet firmly, slowly moving his gaze along the trail of oil glinting on the grass. The more he looked, the more oil he noticed; every which way he looked, unless his eyes deceived him, they seemed to pick up a new trail or patch.

"Now! And get the stone out of here," he ordered another two soldiers freshly arrived from the perimeter, who immediately dropped their arms and went to the stone. They initially stared at its impossibly flawless surface with its magnetic attraction before putting hands to the object and lifting. Reginald looked to the senior churchmen, heads turning like frightened chickens unsure how to proceed in the midst of confusion, Winchelsey aside, who retained his face of fury. "Out of here, now, fathers. This is an assassination attempt on the King's person, we must go!"

Henry managed to look around briefly at the scene before a hand roughly grabbed the back of his head, forcing it forward so he could be manhandled more quickly towards the assorted nobles and whatever fate the King's officers had in store for the immediate time being. Edward himself was already twenty or so paces away from the stone in the opposite direction, heading southwest for the Lion Gate across the moat and surrounded by a number of men-at-arms and a few mounted guards.

The shouts and curses of the crowd became increasingly distinguishable from one another, and all manner of insult fell down on Henry's head. *"Shame!,"* *"Traitor!"* and others interspersed with boos and jeers. A burning sense of injustice rose within Henry, the heat of anger filling his head and his painfully locked arms as he scanned the innumerable disgusted expressions focused on him. But they did not focus for long; he saw their faces look up to the sky in the west almost as one, the jeers and vitriol dying down as one. The sudden silence brought the soldiers and consequently their captives

327

to a halt, all craning their necks upwards following the gaze of the churchmen and the nobles.

Once Henry had wrestled loose of the slackening grip on his arms and shoulders he too turned and raised his eyes to the white cloud-covered sky. Two large, dark bundles trailing flames streaked over from an unknown source behind the churchmen and commons penned in along Crutched Friars, Hart Street and the routes down from the Aldgate. Henry found the sight incomprehensible; in that moment he could not fathom what they were nor whence exactly they came. They arced through the still air, burning intensely and appearing to fly too slowly to remain airborne. It was a sight that did not make sense because they were so very much out of place in this setting.

They bore similarity to some indistinct figment of his memory, as if he had seen similar somewhere before. He could not remember the when nor where of the memory and so neither the why of the familiarity. The flaming objects began dropping, the first followed closely by the second, diving like a hawk swooping on a poor creature of the field, terrifying yet graceful in equal measure. The first thundered into the moat sending up great plumes of water and vapour as its fires were instantly extinguished, but the second had a different trajectory and crashed onto the open grass, not far from where the party had gathered around the stone. It exploded on impact, sending fragments of wood flying, adding to the flaming embers and what looked like hay straws floating along the path it had flown.

A moment's silence followed the crash before a crackling inferno erupted around the grassy slope, the fire shooting along the myriad trails of oil left by anonymous conspirators. The fire burst forth from the grass at an impossible height and intensity, burning far more furiously than Henry believed possible from such short poor grass. The outbreak of fire instantly provoked screams of panic and terror from the packed crowds, both ordained and lay alike, and Henry ducked instinctively and covered his face as the fire shot along invisible paths criss-crossing the grass between him and the moat. Soldiers and others started running this way and that and the crowd began to flee, backs turning away from the flames.

Henry peered through the ever-increasing walls of fire before him, the smell and heat of the blaze almost overwhelming after only a few moments, trying to spy where the King and the stone were; he could not imagine the consequences should the beautiful silver object become engulfed in the conflagration.

A searing *whoosh* swept behind him, shaking him out of his momentary focus and forcing him to spin away from a freshly forged scorching wall that shot past his position and into the previously packed enclosure – flammable materials had been dropped into the crowd's enclosure as well! The shouts all around were momentarily overcome by the roaring field of fire, a place of peace and dullness mere moments before, once green but now all orange and red.

Henry was staggered as he watched the fires spread around, weaving into the areas vacated by the nobility of England and abroad, the fiery tongues lapping at the legs and cloaks of those unfortunates unable to escape as the first wave of alarm rippled through the spectators. The knight looked on in horror as the area further cleared to reveal a number of bodies lying motionless; a finely dressed lady, face down and tunic muddied, not moving, and further on a man in a blue tunic attempting to crawl, both presumably crushed in the crowd's frightened surge. Snapping himself out of inaction, the Templar knight jumped through the fire in front of him and ran to the woman, dodging past stumbling stragglers who were running in all and no directions all at once, like game birds scattered by the unwelcome approach of the hunting dog.

The air was becoming thick and acrid with smoke and the knight hacked a coarse cough whilst sliding to a halt on one knee by the body of the woman. He gently turned her over and was greeted by unseeing eyes and an open mouth dirtied with mud; she was ghostly white and her hair clumped with grime. The knight did not know if it was blood or dirt, but at this point the distinction was irrelevant, for the poor woman was dead. Henry closed her eyes gently before springing up to the crawling man, running into another man in a painful collision that floored both. The Templar was winded but wasted no time in getting back to his feet and helping the other party find his.

Breathing heavily, Henry stumbled onwards across the balding grass, stamped away by so many fleeing shoes and sandals. By now a dark hue was hanging over the area that blocked out the white of the clouds and adding to the nightmarish quality of the circumstances. The shrieking and yelling did not subside with the escape of much of the crowd; many had escaped the fire on Tower Hill but were now trapped on the narrow roads surrounding the area, along Hart Street and Tower Street. The scene en route from the Crutched Friars earlier had been bad enough, Henry thought, as he glimpsed the horde of people to the west trying to escape back towards that very same road. In doing so he noticed another dark object fall from the heavens, billowing black smoke as it tumbled earthwards.

Unlike the apparent lethargy of the first two this projectile hurtled towards the ground and only at the last moment did the English knight see the people running around no more than twenty paces away before the bale of flaming wood and cinders smashed into them, instantly igniting widespread debris and the clothes of people nearby. He found himself once more staring as the pitiable figures flailed helplessly and their hideous screams tore through his heart like the sharpest of blades, little to no chance of salvation from burning to death as everyone else looked to secure their own escape from the bedlam. How many more had fallen from the sky? He had no idea. He could only see and hear that upon which he specifically focused – everything else was anarchic ambience.

A woman with her bonnet half pulled down her head and her long red-sleeved tunic dishevelled ran past, crying for someone by the name of Richard. The crawling man groaned besides Henry; perhaps this was Richard? Grunting under the strain and from the oppressive heat that caused every movement to be that much more laboured, the English knight hefted the crawling man to his feet by supporting under the man's right shoulder, staggering to the left as the clearly concussed man did not immediately realise he was standing.

Righting himself and his new ward, Henry raised his head again to scout a route through the inferno. Another unexpected view greeted his gaze. *Surely not.* It could not be. Was that – no. Was that smoke pumping from one of the barbicans of the fortress wall to the south, beyond the moat? Or was the increasingly clogged atmosphere casting illusions upon his eyes? The answer would have to wait – navigating the fiery maze was the first priority. To the north and west the buildings had apparently caught alight, all of those wooden workshops, the clothiers' workshops full to the brim with highly flammable cloth. To the south lay the burning grassy slope down to the moat above which floated an intimidating curtain of black smoke. Henry turned possibly-Richard around so they headed east.

As he did, the earsplitting detonation erupted across the hill.

He felt the shockwave, an almighty blast the like of which he had never before experienced. The shockwave knocked possibly-Richard over, who nearly dragged Henry with him, and momentarily blew away the heavy ash cloud over the burning slope. Stunned, the English knight gasped as he saw the mighty middle gate that crossed the moat wobbling - buildings were not supposed to wobble - before it sank into the water as if the very earth beneath it had swallowed it whole.

"Screams fused with relentless roaring fire. Henry had seen this before, somewhere far away and long buried in his memory. That experience, seared indelibly into his very being by the fires that had spread so viciously, had seemed to him to be what the end of the world would look like. As it was then, so it was now, here in London; the end of the world.

Chapter 22

Reginald marched with long strides down and along the slope towards the outer gatehouse, the newest and outermost addition to the fortress' primary entrance, standing tall on the cityside of Edward's grand new moat. Checking the King's party was still advancing ahead towards the outer gateway through the scrum of commonfolk down by the opening of Tower Street, just to the north of the outer gatehouse, he saw the tall spears of the King's guards waggling as they ran, shields raised in their other hands whilst mounted spearman and a few knights bulldozed a path through the poor spectators not quick witted enough to move out of the way for their superiors. The baron's rage bubbled away just beneath the surface at the heavy-handed approach taken by the knights but he knew it was too late to help those in the way now. The delegation of churchmen were not far behind the King's group though they lacked an armed guard and at this Reginald was relieved; tempers in the capital will already have been frayed by the disruption to the demonstration, let alone the inevitable casualties caused by Edward's boneheaded knights in escorting their king to the fortress. *And it will all fall on my head*, the scarlet-coated baron rued, gritting his jaw.

The delegation of senior churchmen had overtaken the soldiers carrying the stone, lumbering as they were with its awkward shape; it was beautiful to behold but very unwieldy to move quickly because of its very beauty – so flawless an object, worked curves beyond the capability of the finest human smiths and masons, had no obvious handling features, and so the soldier at one end had to walk backwards with it. It would have been easier to carry it unceremoniously in a sack, as Reginald had seen Sir Edward de Beauchamp do when bringing the stone out for the demonstration in the courtyard at Chester Abbey, though it did not seem proper to treat such a relic in this manner, even in a time of emergency. In any case, no sack was at hand.

The two soldiers were now joined by a number of other men-at-arms commanded by Sir Edward de Beauchamp, imperious in his black armour atop his pitch steed, himself now galloping up the hill to meet the ambulatory Lord Reginald. The men-at-arms marching alongside the stone included a number of archers trotting around the outside of the perimeter group, bows in hand and arrows poised but with slack strings. They were fast approaching the surging sea of curious cityfolk who had gathered in the hope of spying a miracle. How poetic, thought Reginald, that they would see the famed Godstone closer than the nobles had. He looked back up the slope to the two banks of privileged spectators, the hum of jeers thrown at the arrested Crutched brothers filling the emptiness of Tower Hill like the drone of a thousand disturbed beehives.

"The stone is safe, my lord," shouted Sir Edward breathlessly as he approached, his voice hoarse from a day of yelling at subordinates. Black armour like a moonless night sky and visor raised so his dark beard was nearly spilling out of his helmet below his straight nose, he looked every inch a knight of the calibre of the heroic Roland or Tristan, upright in the saddle, huge and menacing. He brought his horse to a halt before Reginald, the great animal shaking its head in excitement; so many people and horses moving amid so much noise was enough to agitate man and beast alike.

Reginald looked up at the knight with disapproving eyes. "Your archers, they shan't be firing on the crowd, Sir Edward?" he asked dryly like a man nearing the end of his tether.

"My lord, I... the stone, it must return to the Tower... we cannot lose it," Sir Edward replied, uncertainly.

"No one dies today, Sir Edward, not on my watch," Reginald stated slowly and firmly.

"Yes, my lord," Sir Edward nodded, his voice deeper and more forceful. The knight motioned his mount to return back towards the outer gate when Reginald saw his eyes catch something further up the slope, causing the dark-armoured knight to pull on his reins to hold the horse steady.

An instant passed as Reginald realised Sir Edward seemed to be studying something to the north that had caught his eye. The baron slowly shifted his right leg back to pivot round to see what Sir Edward was looking at. He then saw them; two great hulks scorching through the sky, flames streaking behind them and trails of smoke further back still, flying over from left to right as he looked, west to east. Reginald looked on, not noticing the silence that fell upon the hill as suddenly as these missiles had appeared.

The first object smashed into still surface of the moat only thirty or so paces away from Reginald and Sir Edward, startling the latter's horse, but the second hit the grass on the slope and was obliterated and instantly erupted in a gargantuan flash of fire. Within moments the flames had reared up and shot across the slope in all directions, the height and reach of the fire inexplicable to the iron-stubbled baron looking on with mouth agape. The roaring inferno cut off both visibility and audibility of the crowd on the other side, so Reginald had no clue as to the extent of the fire's reach beyond its initial burst. A sense of horror welled inside him as he understood his own impotency in this situation – he had no buckets for water and no idea how far the fire would spread; it was behaving in a seemingly impossible manner! The grass was too short for it to burn at all, let alone rage.

His head spun round to look back down the slope towards the moat, Tower and the crowd by the entrance to Tower Street. Between these people and the baron was Sir Edward as dumbfounded by the blaze as was Lord Reginald himself. The baron set off towards the knight, wishing he had not left Arthur back in the Tower stables.

"Get the king and the stone through the gatehouse!" Reginald boomed at Sir Edward with a face of thunder, the red of his cheeks matching his fine long coat. "And none of those people die today!"

Sir Edward kicked on his horse and thundered away down towards Tower Street and the outer gatehouse without acknowledging his lord's command. Reginald did not notice this slip in deference and instead began running across the hill towards a few soldiers idly staring at the erupting fire, spears in hand but with no action to match the disciplined aesthetic their appearance suggested.

"You!" the baron bellowed, the sound shocking the men-at-arms more than the onset of fire, "gather the other companies, have the hooks ready to bring these buildings down. This fire doesn't touch the city. Where's the constable?"

His tone was urgent and volume excessive so as to be heard over the roar behind him, embers of which had begun to float farther afield. Reginald saw a few sparks harmlessly land on the tiled roof of one of the clothier workshops that lined the western edge of Tower Hill. It had long been decreed that no thatched buildings were permitted in the city, but this law alone did not fireproof the capital – bringing the buildings down would be the only guaranteed way of containing the blaze.

A bearded soldier with a leather cap over his curly brown hair spoke up first. "Yes, my lord, but I don't know where the constable's gone, I haven't seen him since this morning, sorry my lord," he explained, bowing his head repeatedly in a clear indicator that he did not know how to deal with the presence of nobility.

The soldier's companions milled about, one or two shuffling from one foot to the other awaiting a response from the baron but were rudely sent on their way as Reginald bawled, "Go!" The baron turned to regard the crackling flames once more, jutting his jaw and rapidly blinking as his mind raced through the causes, explanations and solutions to this disaster. The fire had not yet reached the sturdy stone-built clothiers' workshops but he did not want to risk greater conflagration through complacency.

Another flaming missile crashed onto the slope from an unknown source further within the city. The baron traced its path back and suspected there were at least two catapults somewhere in the ironmongers and bricklayers' district, perhaps the clothiers' district; his eyes widened as he remembered that the Crutched Friars' house was in the midst of that district! They would have to be investigated later though, of course. So many thoughts streaming through his mind as his ears were buffeted from all sides by the terror of man and nature, the tall baron watched more soldiers and a number of other men running up from Tower Street with poles and ropes in preparation to bring down the workshops.

The King! He looked further to his left and saw an indistinguishable multitude swarming around the front of Tower Street and the outer gatehouse on the landside of the moat. Had the King made it through the three gatehouses to the grounds of the White Tower? He must have done – his escorts were uncompromising and to Reginald's sorrow the baron saw some people crawling, presumably having been trampled or battered aside.

The stone too, was nowhere to be seen; those guards would have been equally unbending even without a mounted escort and so it must surely have made it through the gatehouse and away from the oil-laden and fire-ravaged Liberties grass. Nonetheless, Lord Reginald resolved to ensure both king and stone were within the Tower and began running towards the outer gatehouse.

He had only covered a few yards when he saw a wisp of dark cloud, conspicuous against the rest of the endless white that covered London like the awning of a great tent. It drifted quickly, and seemed to move in a nonsensical manner - clouds were not supposed to move upwards, surely?

Despite all the chaos around him, Reginald was halted from his run and momentarily transfixed by the horrible dark and snaky trail before realising the trail was emerging from the top window of the middle gatehouse tower - *Oh God, no* - the gatehouse was burning! Where was the King? Edward might not have made it through the gatehouses yet, and if he had not then the stone was still somewhere along the path across the moat as well!

Lord Reginald took off again at speed, hurtling down the hill towards the moat and the crowd around the walled gate approaching the fortress' first gatehouse, bellowing hoarse commands that took the few soldiers attempting to move people in any direction but the slope by surprise.

"Get away! Move away from the gate! Get away!" he yelled breathlessly, waving his red-sleeved arms manically. He saw a few people had noticed the smoke issuing forth from the upper window, a subtle trail that one may not have noticed in the pandemonium unless one were looking for it. The crowd around the outer gatehouse and Tower Street, panicked already by the fire further up the hill and the ensuing pandemonium as they watched the spectators attempt to flee, broke out into complete anarchy when the first few to notice the smoke down by the Tower began screaming.

Reginald saw the flock scattering like so many insects from a swatting hand, dispersing in all directions but mainly toward the heaving mass on Tower Street - the street was already almost completely blocked, the widest street in the east of the city but woefully inadequate for the volume of traffic on market days, let alone when catering for what seemed to be half of the city's population.

Still Reginald ran on, his athleticism equal to the demands of his duty to his friend and king. Approaching the tall, whitewashed walls of the gated entrance with shouts and yells ringing about his ears as men, women and children sought to fight through the scrum of bodies before them, Reginald eyed three spear-wielding men-at-arms nervously attempting to herd people away from the section of wall across from the approach to Thames Street, just south of Tower Street.

"Where is the stone?" he yelled, just audible above the disorder. The frantic waving of the finely dressed baron in red, amongst a sea of drab blues, burgundies, browns and greys, had caught the eye of two of the soldiers. The man closest to Reginald, about twenty paces away, looked up and let go of a small woman and presumably her child he was trying to shield from the worst of the swaying tide in that hellish bundle. He instinctively looked back around for his temporary wards, realising they were no longer safe in his grasp, but could not locate them. His pained, fair-bearded face turned back to the lord shouting to him.

"*Where is the stone?*" Reginald bellowed again, his exhausted patience now fully in depleted.

"It's just gone in the gatehouse, my lord," the fair-bearded soldier shouted back, his voice not so sure if he had given the correct or expected answer.

Between heavy breaths did Lord Reginald continue his hurried questioning as he slowed to a jog and then walk. "And the King?"

"The King entered the gatehouse a while ago, my lord," the soldier responded dutifully, nerves from the stress of the situation clearly eating at his fidgeting limbs.

"Good," Lord Reginald asserted. "Get these people out of here; move more of them onto Thames Street. Now!"

"Yes, my lord," the fair-bearded soldier mumbled, having almost broken into a run in the opposite direction before having finished acknowledging the baron's command.

Eyes wide and breath quickened with apprehension and physical exertion, the Baron de Grey had his head on a swivel as he bellowed at anyone who crossed his path or happened upon his eyeline. He had commanded over many battles and was in his element amidst the noise, confusion, terror and screaming, regrettable as the circumstances were. A light haze of smoke was sluggishly drifting down the gentle slope that began enveloping those down by the outer gatehouse. Briefly taking the time to check on the chaos back up the slope, the tall baron saw what he thought to be a congregation of silhouetted individuals in the middle of the field, amidst the hedges of fire and the blanket of smoke, entirely conspicuous by their immobility whilst all around them were losing their heads. *Poor wretches.* Perhaps they had attempted to escape downhill and were trapped by the flames; all Reginald or anyone could do was pray that their end was quick.

A thin, weathered man with messy, greying hair lurched past and nearly collided with the baron, causing Reginald to spin to avoid him, more so to protect the visibly frail old man than himself – they were probably of similar age though differing fortunes throughout their respective lives had rendered Reginald a colossally strong and resilient warrior. The spin now caused him to once again face up the nightmarish vision of the smoking gatehouse tower.

It was then the nightmarish vision became tangible.

The first sensation was a blinding blue flash that extinguished the flames licking at the windows of the middle gatehouse. Like the others who noticed this strange phenomenon, Reginald was bewitched by the effervescence, surely heavenly in origin because no fire of earthly derivation could attain such an icy brilliance. Nor could the baron recall any element that could quench a raging fire so swiftly and so completely.

A gigantic boom then exploded that reverberated about Reginald's head like no sound he had ever experienced, numbing his mind and his body with an immediate sense of foreboding that very quickly concentrated in the pit of his stomach; in the moments following a huge wall of wind crashed through him and threatened to knock him over; all around him people were bowled over and scattered like toys cast to the ground by playing children. Reginald tried to rationalise what had happened but could not do so as he stumbled to gather his balance, whilst the echoes of the monstrous sound rattled his skull and very quickly doubled him over in queasiness. He wretched twice though his body had nothing to offer, for it had been hours since the steely baron had broken his night's fast with bread and ham that morning.

The muscles and blood vessels in his neck strained and Reginald felt fierce pressure around his eyes as he hacked and coughed to reset his body to a more agreeable state. The iron-stubbled man wearily rose back to his full height, suddenly feeling every one of his sixty years. He had no awareness of those around him, blind to their presence, deaf to their groans and cries, for a sickening creaking sounded out from the middle tower that soared above the moat up ahead. The twin peaks of the whitewashed tower, three stories of Kentish ragstone dressed with sandstone and topped with crenellations offering unparalleled commanding views of the Tower Liberties and in both directions along the river, wobbled as if it were a hazy mirage, or the tower had been robbed suddenly of its mortar.

Even as Reginald urged his mind to comprehend the increasingly bizarre stream of events he was experiencing, handicapped as he was by the stupefied paralysis afflicting his body, the tower collapsed in on itself and entirely disappeared from view behind the outer curtain wall rising up from the moat. In its wake it left nothing but the white of the clouded sky and a few wisps of dark grey smoke that had escaped the miraculous erasure of the fire effected by the fleeting blue illumination. As his eyes searched for the gatehouse keep in the place he knew it should be standing Reginald sensed an eerie calm, which gave him a perverse sense of satisfaction that he was *not* hallucinating, that he did *not* imagine such destruction. It was as if the booming detonation that followed the flash of light had blown away all of the background noise, sound proofing the immediate vicinity against the cries and shouts from the fleeing crowds and leaving Reginald and those near him in an enhanced state of awareness regarding what was truly unfolding here on this day. Shorn of the instinct to panic or abscond, the audience could now not only watch and appreciate the magnificence of destruction; the tearing down of that which was designed to be indestructible.

The red-sleeved baron was coaxed out of his inaction upon noticing the stocky guardsman by the outer gate stagger a couple of steps backwards in disbelief at the tower's collapse.

"What the *fuck*...?" Reginald heard the man say, unconsciously elongating the vowels in his incredulity.

Focusing on the man for a second, with eyes widening as he took a sharp breath in, Reginald bawled at the guard and another equally stunned man-at-arms to open the outer gate even as the baron strode forward, heart hammering in his chest and cheeks reddening as he regained full command of his faculties and limbs after the shock.

"Open up! Open up!" he boomed over and over, feeling his head might burst from the twin pressure of shouting and the ringing pain resonating throughout his skull, all the while craning his head up and left in a vain attempt to spot the missing gatehouse over the outer wall. On his right came running a number of men-at-arms, some burdened with spears, others having either lost theirs or discarded them in prudent anticipation of their uselessness in any rescue activity. Some men on horseback approached too, weaving through the throngs and dressed befitting a range of statuses, one of them instantly recognisable in his black armour as Sir Edward. The gate guards screamed at the gatekeeper atop the outer gate to raise the iron portcullis and he did so agonisingly slowly, limited by the weight of the grille and the size of the spool around which he furiously pumped the winch handle.

"*Come on, come on!*" Reginald yelled, pounding a gloved fist on the rising grille, producing no extra speed in its upward movement nor any lateral shuddering – Edward Longshanks had invested the greatest expense in expanding the Norman fortifications and it would take an entire army to hammer through the fortresses gates. Fifteen or so yards ahead the second, inner gate began rising with the cranking and clanking of metal chains on metal pivots, grinding steel-lined grilles sliding up grooves carved into the limestone interiors of the gateways themselves.

The baron and soldiers bundled through the two gateways no sooner was there space enough for them to squeeze underneath the grilles. Reginald remained at the fore, scarlet cloak flying behind him as his long strides took him through the archway at the back of the outer gatehouse and onto the wide, semi-circular staging area behind it. Running into this area he immediately cast his eyes left and saw the Byward Tower, the 'inner' and final gatehouse on the moat; however, he should not have been able to see this from the staging area because the middle gatehouse ought to have blocked that view. The middle gatehouse was now a crumbled pile of ruins, an artificial island in the middle of the western entrance to the moat, spread wide and piled as high as the elevated walkway that connected the three gatehouses.

Reginald slowed to an immediate stop and the tightly-packed men behind him responded in kind, not without some shoving as they blundered to a halt in a short space. The baron scanned the rubble, as if he would be able to see anything of the King or anyone in fact, but all he saw was fractured stone and brick. The demolition of the gatehouse was total and unlike anything he had seen before. The men behind him too were silent as they jostled to best view the carnage, their mail *clink*ing and other metalwork softly *clang*ing in their midst. From the north and northwest the screams and cries of the fleeing and frightened drifted down to the river and filled the deathly quiet of the scene on the moat. Reginald feared immediately feared the worst. Anyone who had been in that gatehouse would be dead.

"*Reg!*" came a ferocious bellow from the entrance to the Byward Tower about sixty yards away at the other end of the walkway.

Startled, Lord Reginald looked up and saw a distant figure in red and black with a white lining, flanked by two others in grey-blue get-up – King Edward stood alive and tall, shouting away at his old friend on the other side of a newly wreaked chasm in London's defences.

"Reg!" the King cried again, as bewildered as anyone at the Tower, "*what in St George's name was that?*"

Chapter 23

The little Frenchwoman's eyes were everywhere, sifting through the crowd for malevolent faces and indications of trouble. What she did see in that moment, however, was considerably more troubling than spotting a Dragon. Through the narrow gap to the heavens, between the overhanging upper stories of the flanking houses and workshops, El saw a great flaming bundle of unidentifiable form and origin scorch through the sky, followed momentarily by another.

She could not comprehend what her eyes had just witnessed; it was nonsensical, a moment her mind could not comprehend because those objects seemed so thoroughly out of place.

Many others saw them, too, and the rabble was reduced to a hushed whisper, only occasionally punctured by the excited chattering of those who did not notice the objects. El's brown eyes darted to Sister Diane, herself as alarmed as was the Frenchwoman. Concerned questions broke out amongst the tightly packed mass, frowning faces sharply turning back and forth like so many frightened hens in a coop.

"What... was that?" the round-shouldered Maxwell asked no one in particular. The broad lad, head and shoulders above the two women, urgently looked up and down the street for any hints but was greeted only by a resurgence in the volume of the crowd.

"There're your Dragons," El affirmed to Diane.

Before the sister could gather her wits to reply a man's voice could be heard up ahead with that most terrible of cries – "*Fire!*" The acceleration of fear in the closely confined number was palpable and already Maxwell could see a ripple of people attempting to move back down the street away from the source of the original shout. Further cries went up, now accompanied by screams of terror and the subsequent wave of motion pressing to escape by exacerbating the already uncomfortable crush.

Fire?

Another flaming missile flew overhead from the same direction as the first two. The sudden and frightful appearance of these

342

monstrous projectiles had touched nerves in those crammed into the streets around the Tower Liberties area, nerves that would only snap with that dreadful word, *fire*.

Overhead, another missile.

"I think it is coming from behind these shops," clamoured El, trying to escalate her gentle voice above the din.

Maxwell looked up. "You want to find where they're coming from?" he asked in surprise.

"Of course! I must stop this," El stated, leaving no room for doubt in the stable lad's mind.

"I think I should go," interjected Sister Diane, fear written large on her face. "The priory will be called upon to help the injured." The nun's eyes were wide and darted back and forth, trying to catch a view of every person who flooded past in terror to check for any wounded.

El knew the nun was right; if there was a fire and these missiles were landing anywhere near the crowds gathered at the Liberties, then the sisters of St Helen's would be among the first on the scene. The priory was one of largest houses within the city and almost as large as the Temple grounds, not to mention the closest to the Tower ward.

The little Frenchwoman took Diane's hand. "Thank you for your work, sister. God bless."

Sister Diane's troubled eyes relaxed a little hearing that melodic French accent in the middle of the surrounding shouting and crying.

"God bless you two," she said with a temporary yet genuine smile from her small mouth, before slipping past Maxwell's left arm and into the flow of the human river that endlessly rolled westwards down the street.

El watched the dark-haired nun disappear and then darted her eyes eastward to the source of the commotion. She could see faint smoke rising above the roofline of the workshops across the street.

"Mark Lane. We'll look there first," the Frenchwoman instructed Maxwell. "Why are you waiting, let's go!" she added, pushing the burly youth into the jostling multitude.

Maxwell was a highly effective battering ram, not aggressive by nature but round of shoulder and bulkier than much of the crowd

343

through which he barrelled. He did not want for food at the Temple and though the brothers in the kitchen were generous with their meal allocations, the young stable lad had often been caught in the refectory or kitchen on Tuesdays and Thursdays, snooping around for extra portions of meat and the magnificent Gascon reds sourced from the renowned vintner Antoine of Coggeshall, down where Cordwainer Street met Thames Street. El weaved behind him, her left hand tightly enclosed in his right, her nimble frame altogether more crowd-friendly in its movement than the stable lad's burly frame.

Bundling their way round the corner and up Mark Lane, the two quickly clocked the great wounds to the roofing of the workshop to the right in a small cut-through off the main street. The flow of people was lighter and so the stable lad found navigating less stressful than on Hart Street, though the street's surface was as swamp-like as anywhere else in the city and made worse by the thousands of extra footfalls it had endured over the morning – tripping would be a death sentence. However, neither El nor Maxwell tripped and onwards they battled.

"There!" shouted El as some great flaming object erupted from the hollow in the workshop roof at a seemingly impossible speed; what could be throwing out such sizeable missiles at that velocity?

"We go now!" she yelled at the lad in front of her. Maxwell redoubled his efforts and flew through the mass, apologising as he did so. El could not see who the youth was knocking aside; all she saw of them were the briefest of glimpses of their tunic or coat colour and perhaps a flash of hair. The *'hey'*s, *'ouch'*es and *'watch out'*s amongst the audible reactions, intermingled with cursing and shouting, were the only clues to the genders of the victims of Maxwell's haste.

They reached the front of the workshop from which El had seen the missiles launched and through themselves flat against the wall for the greatest protection against being dragged along with the flow of people. The windows were blocked up with wooden panels though none adorned the street side of the door at least.

"Go back to the Temple," El ordered Maxwell, catching her breath a little from the tiring trek from the neighbouring street.

"How are you going to get through that?" the lad asked incredulously, nodding his head in the direction of the doorway. "It's probably blocked in." The stable lad was breathing a little heavier than usual but would quickly regain his physical composure.

El regarded the door and agreed with Maxwell's prognosis. "After you," she said with little courtesy, sliding over to the other side of the doorway to allow Maxwell to shuffle sideways along in the same direction.

He hammered his fist on the door and did not feel reverberations nor a sound indicating the use of single-beam thickness in its manufacture. Rather, the door was unnaturally firm, suggesting that multiple reinforcements had been made to the inside. Maxwell slammed his shoulder on the unyielding wood a few more times as best he could in the crush to no avail, grunting with exertion.

"No more," shouted El over the din, Maxwell turned and stood flat against the door upstream of El, shielding her against the current of terrified people flooding away from the Tower. "I'll find a way in," she half-yelled in his ear, unaware of how ill-prepared the stable lad was for such volume.

Pulling her head away from his, El wondered exactly how she was going to find a way in, and found herself distracted and disturbed at the mass panic from the Liberties what with Henry in the middle of it. As she pondered she caught the eye of a sour-faced man with matted brown hair approaching with the flow. He was no more than five yards away, staring at her. The Frenchwoman did not recognise him but there was something about his approach and focus that cleared her mind of its previous worries. El sensed it was not right. She immediately determined his expression was not of fear, like all those around him – fear of fire and of uncontrollable crowds – but of concentration and intent, and it chilled the Frenchwoman.

But in response, a cold calm came over her mind that blocked out the pervading din of the rammed street. El could see and hear nothing but the man's approach, her vision a tunnel concentrated on the man's sour face. Unconsciously she reached for the knife strapped to her belt beneath her loose coat and unsheathed it, gripping the smooth hilt in her right hand. Nimble fingers slipped effortlessly into the faint grooves whittled into the polished oak

345

handle and her right arm smoothly rose from within her tunic to Maxwell's side, bent at the elbow and poised to strike.

The man, still watching her, was now two yards away and pushing across the crowd perpendicular to the flow of people but seemingly moving slower than he should have. The little Frenchwoman heard Maxwell say something without understanding what it was; her entire world had rapidly and unexpectedly boiled down to just herself, her knife and the unknown threat approaching. Even the broad stable lad in between her and the sour-faced man was just a murky and formless mirage, like a fog partially obscuring El's target.

The man was now directly behind Maxwell. "How are you going to-" Maxwell began, inclining his head to look at the brown-haired Frenchwoman and responding to her proposed plan, before he was cut off by El lunging at him and ramming her shoulder into his midriff, throwing her arms around him – "*Ooff*! What are you doing?"

El looked up from his chest but not to the stable lad's face. She peered round his right shoulder, prompting the stable lad to follow her gaze. There they saw the sour-faced man with matted hair standing unsteadily, all focus absent from his eyes, and El's arm extended towards the man's stomach. Her hand seemed buried within his heavy jacket. The man spluttered and his own gaze dropped slowly to see El's blue-sleeved arm affixed to his front.

Maxwell did not have much space to move, sandwiched as he was between El and the unfocused man behind him.

"What's...?" he began again, when El pulled her arm away from the man's body – it was as if her arm had been all that was keeping the man upright, for he slumped against the door beside the young lad and drew his hands towards his stomach with a grimace. In one, a large knife blade could be seen just as he dropped it and shortly afterwards his body followed suit, sliding down the door to the filthy street's edge.

Finally able to turn round fully, the stable lad nearly tripped over the prone man. "What the...?" he shouted, brown eyes wide with fright for the first time despite the chaotic nature of events already that afternoon.

346

El blinked and at once regained full awareness, shaking her head a little and glancing at her hands, one of which was darkly stained with hot, black blood.

"It's not safe for either of us," she stammered in a flustered voice, struggling to focus on the appropriate words to use in what was not her native tongue and trying to stop her body from shaking. She could not, however, and nor could she remove her gaze from the bloodied knife blade in her right hand.

The stable lad turned to look at her and saw the blade in her hand. "El... what have you done?" Maxwell stared into her eyes as if he were actually awaiting a response to the question with his mouth topped with the wispy moustache hair of youth ajar. The pair shared shock at the sight of the bloodied knife and the crumpled body, physical verifications of another terrible dream suffered by the brown-haired Frenchwoman.

Someone in the crowd stumbled over the sour-faced man's prone legs, unconscious as he was in the mud and effluence of the street's edge, and knocked into Maxwell's back. The broad-shouldered youth himself lurched forward into El but managed to right himself before completely losing his balance. Literally jolted out of her stupor, El quickly wiped the blood away on the long sleeve of her blue coat and resheathed the knife. "Get back to the Temple," she ordered the lad, a stern front without that did little to conceal the turmoil within.

"What... what are you going to do?" Maxwell asked hurriedly, unable to swallow the rising panic within him nor stop himself from glancing at the unmoving man at his feet. By now, El thought, the sour-faced man would be beyond help as his body was gradually trampled into the grim river of sludge that constituted streets in London, only by virtue of their running between opposing rows of buildings. The press of the crowd around them was so great she could no longer make out the man's face; she prayed he had already succumbed to the stab wound before he helplessly drowned in the horrific cesspit under a thousand leather boots.

"I'll be fine!" the brown-haired Frenchwoman snapped at the youth, "You must go now – get away from me. It's not safe, if someone sees you with me!" The concern in her eyes was palpable.

Even if it were not, as a senior ranking Order member El's command would have to be obeyed.

"Who is coming for us?" Maxwell asked, ignoring El's question or simply so scared he did not register her responses.

"*Go away!*" El screamed.

Horrified by what had just unfolded right beside him, the stable lad nodded and clasped El's narrow shoulders before locking eyes with her. His deep brown irises conveyed sorrow, like he feared seeing her for the last time. "Yes, of course," was all he could manage before slipping into the bustling crowd.

El turned her head to follow the lad's dishevelled hair until it vanished over too many other heads and shoulders. Steeling herself against the morbid temptation to inspect the body on the floor one last time, she slipped along the wall to the gap between the workshop and the neighbouring building, an alleyway wide enough for just one person to pass down at a time. She poked her head around the corner and was hit by a terrible smell from the accumulated filth that lined the walkway, a stench even worse than that of the main street. Where heavy rainfall might on occasion partially cleanse detritus from the arterial streets, the roof-covered alleyways and narrow paths between houses and shops were often completely unaffected by such natural irrigation, leading to years of waste build up. El saw a few sizeable rats rummaging around in the litter, silent in their movements but as large as cats and much stockier.

As she loitered by the gap between the two buildings, the never-ending stream of people flooding away from the Liberties jostled the Frenchwoman and her ears were still beset by cries of *fire! You have a job to do*, she told herself. This was the way she would help Henry. Henry was always fine. He had survived worse odds than this, surely.

El craned her neck upwards and saw the narrow stone walls both culminate at the same height. These two buildings could not have been built more conveniently for climbing! She took a deep breath of the relatively fresh air in the street and slipped into the passage, hit immediately by the revolting odour. Continuing the assault on her senses, the stone walls were uncomfortably damp to the touch and the smell was strong enough to make her wretch. The little

Frenchwoman continued into the darkness, however, regardless of her body's automatic revulsion at apparently everything in this alleyway.

Stepping carefully in the semi-darkness with her ears quickly tuning to the sound of scurrying rodents, El soon made it half way down the alley, at which point she checked over her shoulder; all clear. She mused on the likelihood that any killers sent to dispose of her would have a far easier job in here than they would out on the street. *But I am about to climb into a building potentially full of killers, so it doesn't make any difference.* The brown-haired woman backed against the workshop wall and pushed one leg, then the other, against the opposite wall and shuffled herself up. Initially shuddering at the almost slimy texture of the cold, damp stone, El quickly worked herself into a routine the regularity and control of which concealed just how precarious her grip was on the frictionless stones. Maintaining a sure grip on either surface was difficult but her leather boots were crafted by the finest shoemaker in London, John of Cordwainers Street, and in months of trekking across country, through cities and fording rivers they had not so much as scuffed.

El found her coat and skirt, on the other hand, to be less practical. She struggled with her body moving upwards against the workshop wall without the coat doing the same with each shuffling movement, dragging down on her shoulders and tightening around her neck. Every slide upwards she was forced to take on hand away from the wall to her back and unbunch the linen at the bottom of her back. Still the masses streamed past the buildings and El wondered if truly all of London had come to witness the stone's miracle. As far as she was aware, no one had so much as glanced down the alleyway. El thought it unlikely anyone would in any case – those fleeing a fire did not seek shelter in narrow walkways close to the conflagration.

Some distance away rumbled an unusually heavy booming sound that instantly caused the hairs on her arms to rise, more audible than the din of the frightened cityfolk in the streets. It was not something El had before heard, but she instinctively knew that no good could come from a sound of such magnitude. She paused, attempting to deduce its provenance for a few moments before a renewed volley of screams from the street redirected her focus back to the task at hand.

Breathing heavily and profusely sweating as much through concentration as much as exertion, El had shuffled about three-quarters up the buildings by the time her left hand first slipped. She yelped, catching the sound too late to completely suppress it in her throat, but her lithe legs were too secure for her to fall, burning and slightly shaking as they were with pain. The small Frenchwoman chanced to look down at the pitch filth, fifteen or so yards below. In that moment she felt young again, instantly transported back years to her childhood and the days she spent climbing trees and walls just because they were there to be climbed. She would tease her brother when she reached the top of the tree before he did, and then jump down from increasingly dangerous heights to avoid the punches he would throw at her in retaliation once he too reached the top.

Her current vocation did not lend itself much to climbing trees or walls, and she contemplated the consolation that if her curiosity and zeal did lead her to trouble inside the building, then at least the route into the workshop had been more a pleasure than a chore.

Resolving to double her efforts to reach the roof, inspired by the competitor chasing her in the imagined form of her brother, El pushed on and soon found herself able to escape the foul corridor and breathe in less polluted air above the roofline. She hauled herself atop the tile roof, seeing in the uninterrupted daylight the grubby mess her skirt had descended into. A few tiles were dislodged, careening back down into the crevice below, leading to El unthinkingly holding her breath that no one down was down the alleyway and therefore at risk of being struck.

Hearing a *splat-splat-splat* as three tiles landed in the muck, the little Frenchwoman exhaled and then scolded herself for her natural concern – anyone in the alleyway would be likely following her, probably looking to do her no good; them being hit by some roof tiles would be of great benefit for her! ... what was she thinking? The preponderance of death around her was becoming almost overwhelming for the fair-natured young woman, regardless of Guy's reassurances. She regretted that her calling, for so long risky without being essentially dangerous, was now, in the midst of the

Dragons' insurgency, becoming a lethal vocation. This was not what service to the Church should entail, she thought. Or did she think that? The Order *was* a military organisation; yet she was a non-combatant.

But Henry, he certainly believed in the martial responsibilities of their role. Master Guy had officially forbid her direct combat responsibilities though seemed somewhat ambiguous about his own feelings on the matter – explaining what had happened in the Llaneurgain through determinism, Divine Will; did Guy truly believe it? El had never before thought to question the Master's guidance but equally she had never before been directly or indirectly involved with death.

If she was not so sure before at Llaneurgain then El knew now, she knew that she was responsible for the death of another person. Crouching atop the roof of the workshop far above the crowd, and the trampled, mangled body into which she had driven the knife that now hung at her belt. The man's blood she had wiped on her sleeve, staining the linen dark brown and was now irredeemably merged with the mud and dirt from the streets and walls and now roof that she had traversed over the day so far. The little Frenchwoman shuddered as she thought about how easily her knife had sunk in to the man's midriff, both physically and the ease with which her personality switched to that of a retrospectively disturbing killer.

Why had she done it? Was the sour-faced man truly a threat? He was armed with a knife and tracked her down at a time when *everyone* else was fleeing a fire.

"Dear Lord," she said in hushed tones, "I'm... so sorry, I..." She stopped, unable to find the words, trying to explain her actions. But the Lord knew her reasons, she as sure of it. What use was there explaining to the Lord when he knew all already? "I thought he... he had a knife. I'm so sorry. I have sinned, Father, please forgive me, dear Lord, thank you, dear Lord...," she sobbed quietly, shedding two tears before closing her eyes tightly to stop the salty tears falling. "Amen."

Opening her eyes, the little Frenchwoman sighed, trying to exhale away the stress of anxiety that filled her to the brim, trying to reason with herself that her actions *were* justifiable, *were* necessary for the safety of so many who might otherwise suffer were she unable to continue working to prevent the Dragons committing further atrocities. The Lord knew that El would have to make sacrifices to continue her work, though the nature of those sacrifices she did not know. And yet, the gnawing anxiety that had so afflicted her since Llancurgain would not cease. Its intensity had subsided since that first talk with Guy upon her return to the Temple, but it had never truly disappeared. All thoughts of overcoming this corrosive and crippling affliction fell apart like the man she had killed, no, *murdered.*

What could she do now but throw herself back into her work? That, El, concluded, was the one way to redeem her soul. Deeds, not words. She would find the Dragons in this workshop and bring them to the King's justice, and more importantly, the Church's justice.

The gap in the roofing was substantial, half the length of the workshop roof and almost as wide. At first sight the gaping hole could easily be mistaken for the result of a collapsed roof or someone having fallen through – after all, tens of people had clambered atop buildings in varyingly successful attempts at seeing the events over on Tower Hill and there were no legally enforced regulations enforcing building quality in the city beyond the requirement for tiled roofs; El imagined more than a few slate tiles had been dislodged over the course of the afternoon. Further, there was no good reason to suspect anyone would deliberately pull down their own roof. Part of El admired the ingenuity, but mostly she resented the devious nature of the operation; for the terror it caused amongst the people of the city.

Lying flat on her front she peered down beyond the edge of the tiling, past the crudely shorn roofing beams and into the workshop's first floor. The bitter smell of smoke was heavy in the workshop and a number of open flames shone around the edges of the room, as far

352

as El could see, illuminating piles of wood and stones and buckets filled with unidentifiable liquid.

Careful not to lean too far over and expose her presence to whomever it was scrabbling around, she saw two men attending to a jumble of wooden beams in the centre of the floor in a hurried manner, seemingly dissembling a large piece of machinery that looked like it could once have been a large but crude mangonel. El's eyes widened at the size of the bucket at the end of what she presumed to be the arm, surely greater in volume than any of the siege catapults she had seen during her travels in war-torn Granada. And this was a catapult constructed on the first floor of a building! Reconsidering her earlier appreciation of these men's ingenuity, El viewed their idea as very short-sighted – both the size of the missile fired and its size could easily have set fire to the building itself. She did not know the damage caused to the other parts of the city around the tower but a fire amongst all of these workshops would be catastrophic.

Resolving to finish this murky business, El took the knife from her belt and placed the blade between her teeth, before slowly lowering herself over the edge. Fortuitously there was an exposed roofing beam from which she could hang by her fingertips without too much discomfort. Her fingertips were raw from her shimmy up the wall but the roof beam was well cut and did not offer any splinters to her troubled skin. She repeatedly turned her head to check on the two men who remained occupied with wrapping up all sorts of pots, implements and tools, as well as different powders in small vessels and what looked to be a metallic siphon connected to a large flask; presumably the materials that created the combustion for their projectiles.

El looked down past her billowing skirt at the floorboards that lay five feet or so beneath her leather boots. Such a jump was child's play, quite literally, for the woman who spent all of her free time in trees during her childhood. The tricky part was landing without the men noticing, and then somehow apprehending both men or rendering them ineffectual.

She glanced round again. Neither man looked to be armed, but the floor was strewn with timber pieces that presumably originated from the roof and any of these could be opportunistically used as a weapon. A sizeable plank lay to the left of where she clung, certainly within easy reaching distance once she had her feet on the floor. It looked as if it could be wielded with two hands, if not one. El visualised the plan of action. Having that piece in hand before the two men knew she was even there would allow her a moment to cover the five or so yards that separated them. Then she could strike one about the back of the head and the other across the face as he turned round in response, the little Frenchwoman imagined.

El felt the resolution of her current predicament was intrinsically linked to the favour she held with the Lord. Hanging on to safety by her fingertips both literally and figuratively, with a blade between her teeth that had ended a man's life, she was neither supposed to be here nor aware of what she would do upon discovery. But investigating this very suspicious event and set up was the right thing to do. With the grief and guilt she carried, doing the right thing was the only course of action.

It's what Henry would do. El did not know what fate had befallen her friend, out there in the midst of the chaos that spurred hundreds of people to flee back into the city. She felt she owed it to him to do this. If he was risking his life to stop this terror, then so should she.

The dangling woman craned her neck to the left for the umpteenth time, looking down the room at the crouching men next to the partially disassembled catapult. They still had their backs to her. El considered that if they were to turn round now, she would at least have a moment to act whilst they tried to comprehend the bizarre sight of a woman wearing a long circle coat hanging from the roof with a knife in her mouth. *Seize every opportunity*, she reminded herself.

But they remained oblivious, and she prayed they would continue so. Five yards *was* a long distance to cross, though, before either reacted. After all, they were two men who presumably knew how to look after themselves - a fair assumption given their line of work – and armed or otherwise, El did not like the odds. Driven forward by duty, guilt and grief, and hanging by her fingertips, there was no turning back now though.

She heard them murmuring to one another before the man on the left as El looked at them appeared to straighten a little as he began tying a large sack. His companion on the right stopped moving his arms in front of him, concealed from El's view, and he turned his head to watch the first man. They seemed to be finishing whatever task it was to which they were attending.

El needed to act now.

Yet as she braced herself for the drop and roll, the manoeuvre she had executed so many times before from various branches in various trees, a sudden gurgling sound broke out from where the two men were crouched. Upon turning her head round again she saw that the man on the right had his arm extended towards the other man's throat, whilst the latter desperately clawed at the former's arm. He could not stop the arm juddering closer toward him, though, and the thrust was matched by a gargling choke that caused the clawing man's panicked arms to freeze. The man on the right jerked his arm back with a nauseating *squelch* to reveal an entirely red knife and then the majority of the other man's throat as it sprayed and fell out all over the floor. The throatless man's frozen arms dropped to his side and he fell forward from his kneeling position, landing across the great sack that he had just tied.

El watched the man on the right, who was now drenched in his former companion's blood, casually drop the knife and start to shove the lifeless body away from the sack. There were no words that signified the instigation of struggle. All El heard was the frenzied choking of the man having his throat ripped out.

The murder did not elicit any emotional response in the Frenchwoman, however. The lack of emotional response did not even register with her either. Instead, numbed to bloodshed and violence from the event that had just occurred outside the workshop, El decided to exploit the halving of the odds against her. She dropped to the ground, twisting in mid air before landing on bent legs that crumpled beneath and then launched her forward. The momentum of the fall was transferred to the roll over her shoulder and in one movement she was on her haunches, her long coat momentarily covering her face but quickly patted down and out of her eyeline.

El had judged the fall perfectly and upon finding her feet she was just a few yards from the murderer, with her hands pressed down on the very plank of wood she had spied from above. The killer turned round to reveal the face of a young man with short dark hair and a gormless expression; he evidently did not expect to see a furiously snarling woman carrying a knife in her mouth dropping from the ceiling. The killer went for the knife that would have been at his belt had he not just cut out his companion's throat and discarded it on the floor.

Adrenaline was now surging through El's body and she picked the timber up as she shot forward, swinging the makeshift weapon back over and past her right shoulder. Her little eyes bulged and she shrieked through the gritted teeth clamped around the knife blade as she leapt at the man. The man realised too late that he had dropped the knife just out of arm's reach and did not have time to raise both hands as the Frenchwoman brought the timber crashing down across his face with brutal force. The plank splintered with the impact and such was her forward momentum and subsequent loss of balance, El went flying over the man's rapidly collapsing body and landed on his legs, the plank dropped from her grip.

Stunned only briefly, the killer lashed out with his left elbow behind him as he screamed in pain from both a badly broken nose and the many splintered pieces of oak that speared into his face. His bony elbow connected poorly with El's leg, drawing a grunt from the woman as she herself scrabbled around, trying to disentangle her legs from the man's. The rapid disorientation suffered by both parties was exacerbated by the quantity of the dead man's blood spilled across the floor, creating a hazardous surface upon which neither could find grip to stand without great difficulty.

It was El who got to her feet first and she kicked out at the man's legs as she did, as much through aggression and pre-emptive defence as it was to shake out the soreness arising from the man having elbowed her. She desperately looked around for the knife that had dropped from her jaws as she tumbled; the splintered plank was no longer a suitable implement for defence and not for the first time today the little Frenchwoman felt terror in her heart - the man was not incapacitated as she intended and was evidently capable of great violence. The man, however, was severely concussed and could not see too well through the swelling that was already emerging either side of his mangled nose. The treacherous conditions underfoot did not help him either as he groped for the sack to his side and unsteadily got to his feet with the grace of a newborn foal, utterly disorientated and himself panicking as much as was El.

El saw the knife ahead of her, lying in a fresh pool of the dead man's blood as the body continued to bleed out; she saw up close the extent of the killer's attack - it did not seem possible that the head could remain attached to the body. Diving forwards, the Frenchwoman snatched up the knife and span, legs burning from the exertions she had forced them through this afternoon, only to be met by the murderer's shoulder as he blindly and wildly bouldered through her with the sack in his left hand. With a surprised cry she was sent sprawling onto her back and the man flew over her, somehow continuing upright but not at all in control of his forward motion, which was abruptly stopped by the far wall.

He grunted with the impact but regained his balance very quickly, bouncing off the wall and shambling towards the stairway door at the other end of the wall. El had cracked the back of her head on the floorboard that immediately sent a dull ache shooting through her skull. Gingerly she rolled over to push herself up off the ground, for a moment forgetting her reason for being there. Her coat was now smeared with the dead man's blood and she looked down at her ghastly state with revulsion before gathering her senses and wearily getting to her feet, leaning forwards and swinging her arms to gather acceleration for the chase after the man with the sack.

The Frenchwoman reached the top of the stairway and saw a passage of light streaming through the otherwise darkened downstairs workshop - the man must have escaped through the previously barricaded door. The sounds of the street were also allowed in, amongst them the crying and shouting of people separated from family or friends in the chaotic flight from the Tower Liberties. El's own chase had just become exponentially more difficult. Steadying herself and ensuring her footsteps were assured, lest she fall again and not escape serious injury with the knife she held - she would thank the Lord for His protection in her prayers - El purposefully advanced down the steps two at a time.

Upon reaching the bottom step the passage of light in her peripheral vision vanished and darkness reigned once more. Heavy footfalls accompanied the resurgent shadow and she raised her head to find her path blocked by a number of armed soldiers, grim helmets behind dark round shields, their bosses grey and foreboding at the centre. Overhead swayed spear tips, their silhouettes against the white-grey light outside altogether more menacing than if they had been fully illuminated.

"Don't move!" bellowed an impossibly deep and gravelly voice from somewhere amidst the helmets and shields, an atmosphere of malice filling the dusty workshop air.

El knew her presence here did not look good.

Chapter 24

The tired army had billeted around a lofty bluff dominating the gentle south slope of the hill. Mercifully they were shielded from the sporadic wind that raged out of the north by the rising crag atop the hill above the village of Dolwyddelan, an outcrop that obscured the rest of the mountains from view. Lookouts had been posted in double strength atop the hill and in a wide arc spread across the surrounding high ground to ensure the camp's safety. Most of the soldiers were more concerned with ill-health than the likelihood of combat; many had fallen sick during the march and most of those since the morning of the meeting with the Dragons.

Adelaide's throat tickled her, bringing forth another cough and with it another wad of phlegm. She could not decide which of the railing cough in her chest or the throbbing bruise on her face was worse.

"I'd be in better condition in the Clun dungeon," she said to Will and Rob as the three tramped into a position not too far downhill from the bluff, in and amongst a number of congregating soldiers. She felt the material of her kirtle and could still feel the damp; it did not matter how many hours or days clothing was hung over a fire in the Welsh mountains, it would stay wet. The Cornishwoman had grown up with an appreciation for coastal rain but she could scarcely believe the propensity for showers in this part of the world.

Rob looked at her and sniffed. "That's only 'cause you've not got as many bits to lose as if you were a bloke," he responded, his eyes shining with mischief but his puffy face too fatigued to comply.

"Shut up, mate. Heffer says we have a truce, so we should probably get used to not thinking of them as animals waiting to get butchered," Will spoke as he scanned the horizon, searching for any sign of the Welsh. "Though we haven't seen them in a few days so fuck knows if we're still supposed to be mates with them."

"I bloody hope Heffer knows what he's doing," offered Rob as he palmed a handful of red hair from his forehead. Having moved his hand away the hair fell back in the exact same place it always did. "Otherwise we're all dead."

Adelaide looked to the red-stubbled man. "You think you're dead? At least they'll kill you quick. The Witch of Clun has some delightful treatment coming her way."

"Is that what they call you?" asked Will between coughs.

With a grubby hand she brushed a loose strand of long dirty blonde hair behind her left ear. "Well, I *think* that's what they call me..."

Will smiled. "Are you making names up for yourself? How shit company must we be if you've resorted to that."

"I've got some suggestions for the lady," Rob chimed in, his delivery increasingly cheeky even if he himself did not look too well.

Adelaide raised an eyebrow at him. "No thank you, Robert."

"Witch of Clun it is, then," he concluded. "So what's this meeting about, sarge? I've heard rumours from some of the knights, is all."

Will was shifting his weight from foot to foot, treading in the gravelly earth to create two distinct boot prints, claiming this one small patch of Wales for himself. "Hef's going to explain the whole Welsh thing, I guess. Never seen him or any lord gather so many soldiers together. But he's nothing but honest, and if the other lords and knights are still with him, then I don't see why we shouldn't be either."

Adelaide turned to the gap-toothed sergeant with a sceptical look on her face. "So what's good enough for the lords and knights is good enough for us?" She shook her head gently.

"He'll do right by us, you'll see. He even bothers to speak English, which isn't bad in my book."

By now large numbers of soldiers had arrived for the assembly called by the earl, himself striding past his officers to the centre of the rock outcrop in his burnished plate mail and wielding his longsword in his right hand. Even from a distance he looked every inch the leader, his helmetless head mighty and bearded upon those plated shoulders. With his flat left palm raised to the assembly Hereford wordlessly called for silence. The mixture of bass conversation sounds punctuated by higher-pitched coughs, splutters and sneezes all came to an abrupt halt – even illness stopped for Hereford.

He lowered his palm and gazed across the massed army, hundreds of men strong. Dotted here and there were men on horseback and more regularly the deadly spear tips that towered above their wielders.

The earl did not warm up for his oration. It was straight to business.

"The portents have spoken of a new king of the Britons having risen in the west, a most Christian king to depose the Angevin pretenders who have held sway as foreign conquerors for so many years. Arthur is reborn! Not that false Arthur, the warlike Edward, holding together his kingdom with an iron grip and at the point of a blade, taking gold and silver and blood as payment for his rule; no, truly, Arthur himself has returned as promised so many years ago."

Hereford's eyes blazed with passion; it was impossible to determine whether the man was driving forward the words, or the words the man. The inflammatory opening brought forward murmurs of surprise from the assembled army, and all around muddied, tired faces looked to each other briefly before the next blustering flurry of oratory crashed down upon them like the irresistible rainstorm.

"Men, I ask you, why labour in the fields for French kings and Norman lords, in the land of your fathers, when your fathers themselves lived under the auspices of men of their own blood; men who led them to victory over the invaders from across the sea?" The Earl jabbed his sword to the sky. "Now is your chance to follow where your fathers led; expelling the invaders back over those same seas! Take back the lands you work and the lands your fathers worked for yourselves. Why should Norman kings take what you've worked because they hold the power, a power they took by force?"

Intermittent 'ayes' went up. Adelaide could feel an energy building amongst the gathered soldiers, men of the land from all across the Marches, men who had followed without question their entire lives. She guessed that many of them had never even thought of questioning the status quo, why they were required to labour for their feudal lords, why those who ruled over spoke a different tongue. Yet here he was, a son of the de Bohuns, a family as old as old Normandy, rallying the commons in the English tongue against the Crown. And the Cornishwoman could not help but feel the dynamism of the Earl's treasonous, nay revolutionary, bombast. Dynamic they were and yet somewhat discomforting - there was a reason why the status quo was the status quo; did the Earl of Arundel know of this?

Adelaide reflected on her position as gaoler to an Earl's castle, and specifically the individuals she was responsible for keeping. They were usually enemies of England. They fought against King Edward and his marcher lords, earls and barons, against the Plantagenet hegemony. They had known a political system other than the imposed Norman-English model. Adelaide spent much time with dissidents who questioned the system under which they laboured – it struck her that she, a gaoler's daughter from Cornwall, had somehow acquired far greater consciousness of social and political rhythms than perhaps any other lowborn in this entire army. Perhaps all of England! And now she stood as close to the beating heart that dictated these rhythms, whether or not she wanted to be so.

"Is it not against God's Will, that a man holds another man in servitude? When did you invite the Normans to hold sway in the houses, courts and manors of the Britons?" The Earl's voice rose ever higher as he asked each rhetorical question. "These Norman kings, they are not even their own lords! Edward himself is but a vassal to some French king who has never visited these fair shores, never tested himself against the men of Somerset or Gloucester, Worcestershire or Herefordshire. See how the Great Charter is abused and ignored, the Provisions flouted and neglected by the Angevin thirst for war and blood. Even the earls and barons who rally you to march leagues from your homes, to battle those with whom you have no quarrel, even they see the defective nature of this foreign dynasty, and have done for decades since the barons' wars of our fathers, and the greed of kings past before even they. Which of your families have not suffered the ravages of civil war and the merciless vengeance of Edward and his father before him?"

Low-pitched affirmations went up from the army. Against her will, Adelaide felt the hairs on her neck stand as the excitement in

362

the crowd continued to build. The claims made by Hereford, the man who would make peace with the murderers of her child, were truly shocking to her ears and the common men-at-arms around her. She saw Will nodding beside her. "Did you know this was going to happen?" she asked him.

The sergeant stopped nodding and gave her a bemused look. "Did I know what was going to happen?" He looked at Adelaide but his attention seemed to remain on Hereford's speech.

"Treason!" she hissed, lowering her voice so only Will could hear it. It was such a potent word, so distinctive and noticeable when spoken; ripe for identifying in a crowd of ambiguous speech.

"No... I suppose not. But it sounds alright by me," he drawled in reply. He had that morning shaved for possibly the first time since they had met, revealing further pox scars around his cheeks. They slid up and down as his jaw worked whilst talking, the movement of each mark inexplicably fascinating to the blonde woman. She thought the sergeant wore a truly interesting face; there was so much going on all at the same time. Will leant over to Adelaide again. "Heffer's had disagreements with King Edward before. He missed out a lot, which meant we missed out a lot. He's a good man; sticks up for us, you know."

Meanwhile from the elevated natural stage Hereford continued in grand manner. "The Welsh, the Scots, they are Britons. You Saxon men of England, you are Britons. All of our lives, we've been told who is the enemy, the ones we need to fear. It is not the Welsh, defending their ancestral homes. They are the last of us who would protect the British lands from the Norman conquerors. During the age of our fathers, the Welsh and the English were united against Henry, father of Edward. Once more I call on the English to unite with the Welsh and with one great push can clear the land for you and you can live in peace, no more uncertainty, worry that you will be called away fighting in a foreign lord's war."

Distinct cheering became apparent from the general excited humdrum. "No starving in hard winters because your lord has taken food as dues." The cheers became louder still. "And the taxes! Oh, men of the Marches, what burdens we carry, high and low alike, for Edward's campaigns. You need look only to his majesty's concerns for his French possessions, stripping you bare to defend his vanity in a land where he himself is but a vassal to the French king. What says this of England's status, a land kneeling before the effete French? I know of many brave men who have opposed the king in his demands for more money and more servitude. Where they were solitary, we are now an army!"

Adelaide noticed a few of the mounted knights beside Hereford look to each other with solemn faces that betrayed unease over the mounting boisterousness amongst the rank and file, nonetheless they remained by Hereford's side as he continued rallying the troops with his magnetic charm and enthralling delivery. She turned once again to Will. "This is dangerous," she said, quieter than before. The Cornishwoman did not desire any of the partisan crowd hear her negativity.

"There's no coming back from words like these in front of an army," he explained in his droll voice.

"What will you do about it?" Adelaide asked.

"He's speaking for us, love. If Heffer says it, he means it... I'd follow the man anywhere. If he says the Welsh are our friends, they are our friends."

"Men of England! Even now, earls and barons are rallying to our cause. The great men of the kingdom are congregating in London and still I hear word from all corners of the land of a shared sense of grievance. Leicester, Lancaster, Norfolk; these grand earldoms rally to our side.

"The stone of Rhuddlan is the sign that change is afoot, heralding the arrival of the King of the Britons, God's chosen man to lead our countrymen from the darkness of destitution and war, starvation and a hundredfold social ills and grievances visited upon us during the plague of Angevin rule. You have freedom to choose your own destiny, men of England!"

The earl bellowed his message with zeal, whipping his audience into a frenzy of cheering and hollering. "If you want no part in this, we will grant you leave to return to your homes, and guarantee safe passage. Harm will come to you from neither English nor Welsh. But those of you who stay, you shall be crowned liberators of the Britons, this I promise you. What say you, free men?"

The soldiers cried out in support, deafening Adelaide with their fevered and rowdy cheering. Will began chanting '*Hereford! Hereford! Hereford!*' in a slow, rhythmic fashion and was soon joined by others following the lead of their beloved sergeant-at-arms. A little along from the sergeant, Adelaide spotted Big Steve raising a gloved fist above his head, pumping the air in time with the melodious repetition of the earl's name.

Hereford! Hereford! Hereford! Over and over his name was sung until it seemed the voices of thousands had come together and the country itself was bellowing the name of the earl and that no other word existed. Adelaide resisted the popular surge to join the singing, unhappy with and disturbed by the proposed friendship with the Dragons.

Hereford raised a flat right palm to the crowd, requesting their attention once more. His name reverberated through the morning air a few more times before the vigour began to fade once the soldiers noticed their commander's silent order. "There is work to be done if we are to save this land we love. Already we have sent letters far and wide, to all of the hundreds and to the people in them, requesting they join our campaign. Our scouts tell us the countryside is flaring in revolution against the Angevins and even now men are flooding from the towns to join our ranks, patriots all. But this is not a march of conquest; it is a march of deliverance. We shall deliver your wives, sons and daughters from their oppression. We are a free army of free men, and we will not cause injury without suitable provocation. There will be aggression and opposition, with cruel fighting and hardship, but it shall not last and you can return to your homes and farms before too long. The King will move soon, so we need to strike sooner - I shall take you to the new Arthur."

Hereford sheathed his sword and stood with arms wide, palms open and a great smile on his bearded face whilst his bright teeth could be seen the length and breadth of the camp, such was his broad beam across that mighty jaw. The army responded to him as if he were a conquering hero or had won gloriously at the tournament. The cheers and shouts of the soldiers echoed around the empty valley and even the unconvinced Cornishwoman felt the atmosphere crackling with energy and exuberance, completely at odds with the serene surroundings of the silent Welsh hills.

To her side, Will beamed his toothless smile and even Rob's puffy face was lit up with raw emotion. *What a moment*, she thought. The Cornishwoman paused for an instant amongst the frenzy of movement that exploded with the arrival of the drums ordering the assembly disband, considering her presence at a moment of history. What a dream to have! Surely it could not be done, tearing apart the very structure of society to rebuild it in a simpler manner, under the auspices of native rulers. If any man could forge such a future it would be the kinglike Hereford. She watched the Earl disappear from view as he descended down the bluff and into the crowd, apparently oblivious or ambivalent to his own safety following such electrifying yet also treasonous oratory.

A hand caught her left arm forcefully, enough to shock her out of her inner monologue. "We've got marching to do, girl. Come get your things," said the pockmarked Will with a grin. He really did love soldiering, Adelaide mused.

"I'm the earl's special guest, I can't imagine he'd leave without me," she replied with raised eyebrows, rubbing the swelling on her cheek.

Men dashed in all directions, the heavy tramping of countless leather boots on the hard, stony soil adding to the chaotic visuals and pungent odour created by an unwashed army packing up camp. "And if he leaves without you, I'll be hanging by me own insides," Will quipped with a grimace, "so if you could hurry up, that'd be lovely."

The sergeant noted Adelaide's lack of enthusiasm for moving out and immediately knew the source of her discontent. "We all have to do things we don't like," he explained sympathetically.

"They murdered my child," she replied coldly, her sad eyes looking downwards.

Will shared in her grief. "They murdered a lot of people's children," he said gently, "and we've murdered a lot of theirs. Look at these men here, they are all someone's children, and they've got a chance to make sure no one else loses their children. Look what it meant to them," he gestured to the re-energised soldiers rushing around, "and finally we have lords who want the same as us."

He was not eloquent but he was honest. Adelaide remained grief-stricken, though, and she raised her doe eyes to the sergeant, worry engrained into her brow.

"It's up to us who's left to make things better," the sergeant continued. "We have the chance to protect the ones we have left. That's why we're here, that's why you're here." He smiled a small smile, genuine but more in hope of Adelaide seeing his point of view than in expectation.

Adelaide took a deep breath. "I need to find out if Earl Arundel is part of this," she stated suddenly.

"Let's find that out, then."

Will let go of her arm and turned away, narrowly avoiding bumping into a small man wearing a similar leather coat underneath a dented breastplate, grimy and mud-spattered. Where the sergeant led, Adelaide followed, weaving through the ants' nest of meandering soldiers.

She could feel a hundred sets of eyes following her every move and did not enjoy the sensation. As had happened every day since joining up with Hereford's army, a few unsavoury offers of relations could be heard from the men as she walked through the camp, at best unsubtle and at worst almost vomit-inducing. The blonde Cornishwoman knew there was little chance of any trouble so long as she remained by Hereford or Will's side, and the incidence of comments had subsided following the punch she landed on Gwenhwyfar, but to whom would she turn when those two were required to fight? She did not think Rob would make a good bodyguard, and for such a massive man Big Steve was very inconspicuous in a crowd. There was no doubting his physical presence but the more pertinent question was whether that presence would be present when needs be.

"Adelaide!" a heavy voice rang out behind her, a voice she recognised as belonging to Sir Walter Percival. For once his voice did not carry any malice, and mercifully it also silenced the small chorus of innuendo and ribald comments that followed her wherever she walked. Turning around, the Cornishwoman saw the tall knight atop the giant white destrier armoured but for his helm, carrying no weapons. His longsuffering eyelids still appeared barely capable of restraining his bulbous blue eyes, but he appeared considerably less ugly now that he was not sneering. "The Earl would speak with you. Sergeant, you too." With no further ceremony he turned his horse and trotted away without deviating his course for any of the pedestrian traffic before and around him.

Adelaide glanced at Will over her shoulder, who gave the impression of being as much in the dark as was she.

"Rob, get the boys in line. We move out this afternoon," Will barked to the flame-haired man-at-arms."

"Sarge," Rob affirmed.

"And sort my kit out whilst you're at it."

"Sarge," the man-at-arms acknowledged again, all hints of the usual joviality absent from his chirpy voice and puffy features.

Adelaide sensed greater sobriety in Will than minutes earlier, the order to attend to the Earl instantly draining the drunken delight of Hereford's speech from the sergeant. Rob scurried away with the hulking Big Steve in tow, no doubt an effective deterrent against lethargy and ill-discipline amongst the men. Will approached and put an arm on Adelaide's shoulder.

"I suppose you can ask him now about Arundel," Will offered.

"So where did you find him?" Hereford asked out of curiosity as he reclined in the chair by the table. The ham in front of him tasted more succulent than he remembered. Had it really been three weeks since they had worked through the last of the swine?

Across the table the oak-haired Gwenhwyfar had barely touched her meal. Hereford did not assume ill manners on her part; her cloak completely concealed her body but the lie of her face suggested the woman was stick-thin, so probably did not need much feeding. The earl also knew from experience that it was difficult for one accustomed to an infrequent and unsubstantial diet to gorge oneself on too much food once it becomes more plentiful.

"I'm not sure where it was," she replied politely.

"How do you mean?" the earl asked, puzzled.

"He hasn't arrived yet," she said in a softer voice.

The earl put down his ham. "He hasn't arrived yet?"

"He hasn't arrived yet."

The earl stood up and leaned over the table towards Gwenhwyfar. "You mean to tell me that I'm staking *everything* on someone who may not even exist?" Hereford's eyes were wide in disbelief both at this bombshell and his own recklessness in gambling on the Dragon leader telling the truth – actually having amongst her ranks the new King of the Britons.

"He will be there in good time," Gwenhwyfar said reassuringly, keen to avoid too great a scrutiny on the risk she was taking.

"It's an unacceptable gamble! Do you realise what this could do for both our people?"

"I thought you were of the view that we are the same people?" Gwenhwyfar scathingly retorted as she stood in response, not accepting any attempt at bullying from the bearded man.

Hereford was not amused by the oak-haired woman's pedantry and stalked towards her with menace in his eyes. He stopped just before her, looming like a great bear standing tall on its hind legs, such was the stature he seemed to take in that moment. Hereford's expression was dark and he subconsciously bared his teeth before he spoke. "I can make this work for you or I can crush you in my one hand," he growled, more than a little alarming the Dragon as he brought his hand up and clenched those thick fingers into a massive fist.

The Earl glowered for a moment before turning back to the table and the ham he had left to address the Welshwoman. He was hungry and the sight of the slab on the bread platter made him salivate. Because of the march's originally belligerent intentions, which would assume frequent raiding and pillaging of supplies, it had been weeks since the army had been fully provisioned and it was only thanks to Gwenhwyfar's intervention that a number of pigs and sheep were purchased from initially hostile local farmers and shepherds. Committed to fostering improved relations between two groups brought up on tales of the other's demonic behaviour, Hereford had strictly forbade raiding and pillaging by any of the men under his command, threatening execution for any man caught with illicitly-sourced provisions. Discipline had largely held after four early beheadings; consequently, however, what would normally represent a marching army's supplementary rations - the fruits of locals' labour – was not forthcoming. Hunger was rife and Hereford knew this to be more dangerous than any foe in the field.

As he moved to sate his craving, Gwenhwyfar was allowed a moment to recompose herself away from the Earl's scrutiny. "I'll bring him to you," she offered in a voice far more confident than she felt.

"I need more than that if this is to appear legitimate," Hereford snapped back.

"He is legitimate," Gwenhwyfar insisted. "Our finest rangers have been tracking him. Everything is as they say."

Hereford looked round at the oak-haired woman, who was now wearing defiance across her face. Gwenhwyfar marched towards the tall, bushy-bearded Earl, striding so close she had to crane her neck to see his dark eyes.

"You think that this is only a gamble for you, coming out of your grand castle and turning on the king you served, bandying about promises of food and land and emancipation? You have no idea. We have no country, no land, no voice, we're considered animals by all of your type, by most of your army, by you yourself." She spat at him, her eyes as venomous as her tongue. "These partisans I bring with me are following me, trusting in me that I have found their Arthur. It is all on me – if he is not, then I have failed. If your army cut our throats in our sleep, have failed and will be held accountable for the extinguishing of the Welsh people. There will always be an England, no matter what you do here today, tomorrow or in one year. If you fail, you can find yourself a home with some allies in an English castle or even a remote Welsh lord's homestead as a friend of the Welsh. If we fail, we *die*. We are fighting for an existence that has never been guaranteed and still isn't guaranteed. So if you want to worry about legitimacy, or how you'll appear to the other earls and barons and all of those Normans, then you can, but remember that we are *all* in. We have nothing left."

Gwenhwyfar pushed closer to the Earl, snarling like a trapped wolf. "If you want to threaten me then let me tell you that wild animals are very dangerous when backed into a corner."

Only when the oak-haired woman broke her gaze away from Hereford's eyes did the Earl feel a pressure lift from his chest, as if the woman's presence itself had an asphyxiating effect on him. He watched her retreat out the back of the tent towards her quarters. Hereford had heard tales of the Dragons' fanaticism and intensity and had always attributed it to their tribal barbarism. The bearded man admonished himself for being so wrong.

Slumping heavily into the plain chair besides the table, the Earl pondered the balance of his relationship with the Dragons; he remained confident in its potential and in his own superior bargaining position, but Gwenhwyfar's defiance chilled him somehow, encouraging caution within him. Peering into the darkest depths of the Welsh fears for the first time did not leave Hereford unaffected. He had not previously acknowledged the magnitude of the risk the Dragons were taking with this unexpected alliance. The hungry man picked up the ham again and began eating once more, oblivious to the action as he mulled over how to deal with his new friends.

Trailing the bulbous-eyed knight by a few paces, Adelaide and Will reached the Earl's enclosure. It was a plain tent only a little larger than those of the men-at-arms, but Hereford had the luxury of turning in for the night alone. Adelaide saw two sleepy looking guards lolling either side of the tent door, dressed in matching dark blue leather coats with ringmail vests over the top, topped with dark brown leather caps similar to Will's signature garment. The Cornishwoman had taken to spotting the soldiers in the camp who did not have any visible indicators of battle experience, such as scars, missing digits or eyes and damaged armour. These two had no such indicators. Adelaide still could not decide whether she considered battle scars to be a positive in the circumstances - dreadful fighting surely lay ahead and those with battered chest plates and holes cut loose in the iron rings of their mail vests were not green; Hereford would need to counter his small numbers with all of the experience he could garner.

Equally, however, she pitied the man shuffling past with a painful limp, leaning heavily on his spear, and the chef putting out the fire burning underneath a great pot, the squint in his left eye presumably derived from the jagged purple scar angrily slanting across his cheek, bisecting the greying stubble that otherwise grew uninterrupted.

Without announcement the earl emerged from the tent, sweeping back the canvas with disdain. He was a man for the elements, Adelaide thought. Being cooped up inside came as naturally to Hereford as it would to an eagle. Still, he appeared dry and warm, or at least not cold, in contrast to the sodden clothes she was still wearing from the night's rainfall. She coughed again and her throat felt as if it were full of sawdust. Sir Walter nodded to the earl and turned about, eyeing Adelaide as he trotted back past them to go order some other unfortunate minion to do his bidding.

"My lord," Will greeted the earl with forced cheerfulness.

"My lord," parroted Adelaide with a bow of her head, causing her blonde ponytail to fall over her shoulders. Dirty blonde it may have been, but her hair had been the most vibrant aesthetic of the army's march since reaching the barren earthy slopes of the central Welsh hills. As she bowed her head forwards, the pressure around her bruise increased. It was an unsightly blemish but the Cornishwoman considered it a physical reminder of her guilt.

"May I ask, my lord, what exactly is happening?" Adelaide asked snappily, much to Hereford and Will's surprise – a commoner was not supposed to speak first to a lord, especially not having been summoned.

Will's eyes widened in shock and the earl looked down at the little Cornishwoman with interest, noting the result of his gauntlet's handiwork on her face but not paying it much heed. "I was hoping that you would have learnt your lesson regarding that tongue of yours, girl," Hereford spoke with a tinge of exasperation in his voice.

"I am sorry, my lord," she replied contritely. "But-"

"You will learn your lesson, woman," the earl interrupted.

Will looked to the ground and shook his head slightly as he recognised a slow build up in Hereford's ire once again.

"I'm sorry, sire, I just want to know why we are no longer fighting the Welsh when they've-"

Hereford interrupted her again. "Gwenhwyfar is offering us an opportunity for peace; it's an opportunity I'm not going to dismiss."

Such rhetoric held too little substance for Adelaide. "You're committing treason against the King on account of them?" she asked with a hint of incredulity.

Will grabbed her by the shoulder and pulled her back to face him. "Stop this, now!" he warned her through gritted teeth, or at least through the teeth he had left to grit. "You're lucky you're useful to him, at the rate you're going."

"I would listen to the sergeant's counsel; I trust few men more than he, and he speaks for me. I like your spirit, girl, but not your insolence," Hereford emphasized. "Sergeant Will is right; you are useful, otherwise you wouldn't be here. And it's because you're useful that I'm telling you this. The Dragons are key to the peace in these lands but not how you imagine. Do you know Lord FitzAlan was in London, girl?"

She shook her head, resisting the temptation to speak under any circumstances.

"The Lord FitzAlan had been summoned by the King, along with every noble of note in the kingdom, to London to view the relic found somewhere near Rhuddlan. The Dragons know all about this relic, and having a read a report from Lord de Grey, who has seen what it can do, I share the view with many others that the King is now in possession of a very powerful weapon indeed. I believe that many in the camp have heard rumours of their own about the nature and power of this 'Godstone', as it seems to have been named."

"Is that why we're here?" Adelaide asked innocently, her innate inquisitiveness getting the better of her caution. The earl had mentioned the stone to Adelaide on a number of occasions but had never divulged the report from Lord Reginald.

"With the aid of the Dragons, we shall retrieve the stone. It is essential to the prophecy of the King of the Britons. You are witness to a new age, girl."

"It was never your intention to fight the Welsh?" she asked.

Hereford paused, shifting his weight onto him left foot, his suit clanking with the slightest of movements.

"I didn't know what I'd find. Gwenhwyfar has given me assurance on the life of her child that the Dragons share our concerns. My officers have vowed to follow me in this venture. And once we have the Godstone, you will see yourself that it is a venture blessed by the Holy Father and His Son. There is no side to choose, girl," the earl said in an almost fatherly tone, "for the King of the Britons is returning."

The earl's presence seemed to have a persuasiveness of its own, as if he could talk over anyone with this understated enthusiasm and idealism cunningly disguised with a glean of pragmatism. As was the case in the crowd earlier, Adelaide felt the energy of the man's delivery.

"I need your help with the Dragons, Adelaide," continued the earl, striking whilst the iron was still hot. He looked her square in the eyes, no hint of shame on his thickly bearded face at conceding weakness to a gaoler's daughter.

The Cornishwoman could never have expected such an admission from such a magnate as Hereford. The Lord Richard had asked things of her, of course, but they had always been *commands*. In a sense, Hereford's request was a command, as well; she did not expect the earl to take too kindly to a rejection nor did she have much hope for her own chances of freedom in the same situation, for all of the promises of freedom he had just made to his army.

But she felt there was a subtle difference between the Earl of Arundel requesting Adelaide assist in the rounding up of prisoners at Clun, and the Earl of Hereford approaching her to help plug a gap in his own competencies. The former was impersonal and generic, a request made because Arundel did not have the *time* to sort to the prisoners and nor was it a task appropriate to his station. In the case of the latter request, however, Hereford actively sought Adelaide because she had knowledge of something at Hereford's own station, despite her own relatively lowly position. Irrespective of the circumstances, being in demand with such a man felt good.

"I, how can I help, exactly, my lord?" she stumbled a reply.

Hereford turned his dark eyes away to the floor and conspicuously exhaled. "Plainly speaking, you know them better than I do."

"But you're friends with them already, my lord," Adelaide grumbled, consciously swallowing the resentment that rose from her stomach at such a situation.

"*We* are allies, girl. Not friends. Which is why I need you."

"I wouldn't say I've been a great friend of theirs recently..." she trailed off and looked to the patchy cloud overhead.

"Just as you know how to be their enemy, you know how to be their friend; just behave the opposite to how you have been. Which should be easy, because there aren't any torture dungeons around here." He gestured with his right hand to the hillside around, populated here and there by intermittent camp fires around which sat his men in groups of three and four. Smoke rose from a number of pots suspended over the fires and the low hum of chatter drifted as lazily as did the smoke up towards the sporadically clear sky.

Adelaide did not know whether or not the straight-faced Hereford was joking and so attempted to avoid the awkwardness by taking a deep, open-mouthed breath and looking back down to the gravelly ground. Did anything grow on these hills?

After a short pause Hereford began speaking again. "You haven't answered me, girl. Because of the nature of the task at hand, I cannot force you to acquiesce to my request." His tone became a little more serious, not impatient but tending towards expectant.

Emboldened by what she perceived to be a position of bargaining strength, the Cornishwoman gazed back up to the majestically-bearded earl, her long blonde ponytail swishing dramatically as she moved her head. "May I ask, my lord, why you didn't tell me you wanted me for this? I've come a long way from home on false pretences." No sooner had she spoken did she regret it, fearing the fearsome man's temper again at a time of such emotion and stress. Would she ever learn?

Hereford though did not react in the manner Adelaide feared. His face seemed to soften and his hard features relaxed, his eyes seemingly no longer straining in concentration. "I admire your spirit, girl, but I should preach a little caution when speaking to superiors. Even my sergeant knows that."

Adelaide thought to Will's words regarding the 'highborn ponces' and wondered if that type of comment was to what Hereford referred.

"And I also expect greater savvy from a potential advisor." He looked away from the blonde woman almost in contempt. "Why would I place all of my cards on the table before we'd left? I could not trust you with such knowledge so early on, so close to England. I still can't trust you now, actually, but at least here I have failsafes in the event that your loyalty to the King means more to you than does the freedom of the English."

Adelaide frowned. "And what failsafes are those?"

"Your return to England will be permitted," said the earl, "but I cannot afford to provide you an escort. And this Dragon territory." His voice became grave once more. "And if any Dragons or partisans got wind of your presence, alone, in their lands..." Hereford raised his eyebrows, asking Adelaide if she understood the implications of this with just a facial expression.

Understand it she did, and a small panic rose in her at the injurious prospects ahead of her, flushing her cheeks red and causing her throat to go dry. Slowly, though, she gathered her thoughts and composure to answer the earl, eventually acknowledging the symmetry of the gaoler being imprisoned to ensure the freedom of those whom she had kept in gaol. This bitter realisation served improbably to soothe her tension and even forced a smile on her reddened face. "So all the English are to be free, except me, my lord?" she asked with more than a hint of cynicism, emboldened as she was by the earl's earlier tolerance.

Hereford ignored her tone again and turned, slowly walking away from the Cornishwoman and kicking stones as he went. He raised his head to the crest of the hill, observing how the shadows of the clouds floated effortlessly across the craggy ground, hindered by neither rock nor man.

"'Freedom' is a relative term, my girl. Pure freedom is an illusion, perpetrated by the proud birds in the sky and great fish in the sea, and those men who strive for it are fools." He paused both his slow stroll and his speech, dropping his head to again view the stones at his feet. "We are all tied to the path laid out before us by the Lord, the path that takes us to judgement at the gates of Heaven. How we acquit ourselves on that path is the true freedom we possess, the freedom to remove oppressive burdens from our fellow man." Hereford turned to face Adelaide once more, moving close to her so that she could feel the warmth of his breath on her cold face. "This is how we shall be judged at the end of days, Adelaide. Your commitment to this cause, this crusade against the feudal state, is your true exercise of freedom."

The little Cornishwoman gazed up at the earl, who was holding her gaze for longer than she expected. It seemed to her that Hereford's dark eyes were trying to bore through hers into her mind, to gauge her thoughts, lingering too long for his mind to have remained entirely concerned with the conversation the two had just had. He broke eye contact and turned away, signalling for Will to return the woman to the camp.

The Cornishwoman wondered if she had seen longing in his eyes? The Earl had a wife! Adelaide speculated for the first time as to the whereabouts of the Lady Maud, Hereford's wife of twenty years and mother to Hereford's heir, also named Humphrey. Nascent it may have been but Adelaide considered the earl's venture already to be highly dangerous, particularly for less combative family members of the participants; a stab of guilt struck the small Cornishwoman as she grasped that the earl had taken her but not his wife on this campaign. Or was she getting too far ahead of herself? It was in her nature and central to her work to assemble information from scraps of evidence. Usually it served her well.

Will marched over, his leather cap covering his ears as usual. One hand shielded his eyes from the morning sun that had finally conquered the patchwork cloud, casting his pox-marked face in shade. "Come on, love. We're moving out soon," he said to her, his more cheery intonation returning.

"Lord Hereford," Adelaide called out, looking past Will to the broad-shouldered Earl who had just reached the door to his tent. "What of the Lord Richard?"

The question stopped Hereford in his tracks, his head dropping a little. "Arundel had not responded to my correspondence by the time he left for London," he replied with sorrow in his voice. "We can but hope the letter did not reach him on time."

A pang of fear struck Adelaide. "Why didn't you leave word when you left Clun Castle?" she asked impertinently.

"Remember your station, girl," the Earl snapped, spinning around to glare at the blonde Cornishwoman. His tenacity and fearsome appearance shocked her into timidity and she involuntarily lowered her gaze. "How could I leave word of such a venture with anyone at the castle, when I could not guarantee their reliability?" he asked incredulously. "Only a man I could trust could carry the letter, as has been the case in all my correspondences on this matter. I pray as much as you that my man was late and arrived after the Earl had departed." Nothing more to say, Hereford stared a little longer at the woman before looking down in contemplation, finally returning to his tent.

Adelaide and Will shared a glance for a moment until the latter turned his head away and shifted onto his right leg, physically hinting that they should leave. Concern was carved deep into Adelaide's face, worry for what would become of her home and the people she knew. That Will's eyes wandered anywhere but to her own told the Cornishwoman that the sergeant recognised the cause of her anxiety. The leather-capped man sighed and trudged away from the tent. "Come on," he mumbled.

Ignoring the occasional leer and cat-call, and judging them to be safely out of earshot of the earl, Adelaide grabbed the sergeant by the shoulder as he walked, ready to burst if she held in her thoughts any further. "He's going fight against the Lord Richard, isn't he?" she exclaimed, more a statement than a question, unable to slow down the sergeant's pace. "That's my home! He's taken me from my home and now he's going to fight against them!"

Will stopped abruptly and faced his ward, greeted immediately by watering blue eyes brimming with confused distress. Acutely aware of the attention her outburst was drawing from the milling soldiers around them he took her by both shoulders in an iron grip. The small blonde woman felt the strong fingers through the leather gloves and her own woollen smock digging into her angular shoulders, as if his hands were made of iron.

"Adelaide! Wake up," he barked, lightly spraying her face with spittle. "You heard the earl. You need to make a choice. Whose side are you on?" He looked to either side and scowled at the one or two men-at-arms who had stopped to observe the exchange; very quickly did their sergeant's silent glower send them scurrying. "Your friends in Clun will make a choice, and if they're anything like you say they are, they'll make the right choice." His face matched the hardness of his words, for once that warm, toothy grin absent; Adelaide had never received anything but from Will.

"What choice have they got?" she responded quietly, acquiescing to Will's unspoken insistence that she not create a scene in the middle of the camp. "They've got the same as you and same as me; following their lord where he tells them," she sneered.

Will blinked slowly in exasperation, riling Adelaide up in doing so. "When they hear what we are marching for, they will not follow their lords," he countered with an equally hushed voice.

"We march for treason, that's what they'll be told!" Adelaide hissed.

"And which poor man or woman is going to hear the freedoms we're offering them, and think it's treason?"

"Don't be so blind, man," the Cornishwoman snapped. "You know what happens to people like us when we don't behave how the lords want us to!"

"This'll be the last time people like us don't behave how the lords want us to, because after this there won't be no lords wanting us to behave how they want," Will emphasised, eyebrows dancing and forehead wrinkling as he stressed the aspect of change.

Adelaide shrugged off Will's slackening grip about her shoulders and let her own arms slump to her side. "So what happens to the earl then if there'll be no lords wanting us to behave how they want?" she asked expectantly.

Another male voice interceded before Will's already-opened mouth could respond. "There's a difference between there being no lords, and there being no lords wanting us to behave how they want," came the weasel-like speech of the now-dismounted Sir Walter Percival, black armour all but still lacking a helmet for his frightful face.

"The earl is no fool," Sir Walter continued. "He'll keep the realm together. It will just be less rotten." He glanced at both Adelaide and Will with a curious expression, not his usual sneer but more benign, before stalking away in his dread plate mail suit.

Chapter 25

For a man who had just had a tower collapse on him, King Edward was remarkably chipper, energetic as always and never short of bluster. That was as positive a spin as Reginald could put on the situation, because the energy meant the King's fury had a means by which to project itself unto the world. This fury represented an outlet for the inferno raging inside his body that surely kept the almost-sexagenarian so vigorously active. Now stripped down to his white leggings and vest and yet still maintaining a hue of grey dirt from the collapsed stonework of the middle gatehouse - looking as if he had rolled around a chalk quarry - the King appeared as plain as any farmer would returning to his homestead at the end of a warm autumn's day. The farmer would remove his rough tunic and lie down for a while, cooling in the shade of the daubed wall besides the implements he had dragged back with him, wearing just the undergarments that he had not removed since they were freshly stitched for him by his wife two months' previously. So was King Edward sat on the sturdy oak chair, shorn of crown and finery, in that rounded room in the southwest corner of the White Tower, above St John's Chapel. Yet, observed Lord Reginald, Edward *always* appeared kingly; there was something about his bearing, his voice, his tenacity. The legendary King Alfred's penchant for convincing disguise that King Edward would never achieve. Edward was too obviously kingly.

Watching on from the side of the room with granite face and fixed eyes, Reginald observed that today's regal characteristic was that old favourite, anger. Usually the Baron de Grey would think nothing of the King's outbursts, so regular an occurrence were they, but the residue of the headache he had suffered earlier following the blue flash rendered him more sensitive to volume than usual.

It was fortunate that the fire had not spread beyond the open grass to the north of the fortress complex – for which Reginald thanked the Lord, both for sparing the city the terror of a mighty conflagration and also those in this room what would inevitably be incomprehensively furious rage from the King.

"I assure you, majesty, the maximum number of available men were on station, and all-"

"*Available* men?" Edward growled, interrupting poor Sir Ralph Sandwich, the constable of the Tower. "What about competent men? What do I pay you for, Sir Walter?" He glared at his household steward, Sir Walter de Beauchamp, face was as red as the Gascon wine he had not touched since pouring it nearly an hour previously.

"How is it the man who ran this city for so many years has been outwitted by a group of monks who know nothing of military organisation? Despite having *all* available men?" The King's voice rose to a crescendo and wads of spittle flecked his lightly dusted chestnut beard as he retrained his ire at Sir Ralph.

Lord Reginald believed Edward to be a little harsh on this point. If anyone would know the city inside out then it would be the brothers of the Crutched Friars, those itinerant holy men visible as likely to be spotted with the cowkeepers on Milk Street as they would be along the Strand. That was, indeed, a reason the King chose the brothers to attend to the demonstration; a brotherhood with whom the entire populace would be familiar. Lord Reginald had agreed on this decision. The city's denizens knew of most of the orders, but many of them only indirectly to the strict geographical restrictions the predominantly socially withdrawn monks worked under. The baron had always thought it odd that the holiest of us would shut themselves away from the world when the Lord Jesus had lived in precisely the opposite manner.

Sir Ralph was four years the King's senior and not blessed with similar vitality nor physical stature, yet he stood resolute to avoid shame before his fellow eminent peers in the King's household. Face flushed with acute embarrassment, the constable swallowed before speaking again. "I, we, believe the Welsh have infiltrated a number of cells in the city, sire," Sandwich explained, keeping his voice as level as he could under the scrutiny of possibly England's most terrifying man.

"The Welsh!" the King roared, startling the others like grouse in the field jumping at the hound's first bark. "A group of outlaws helped the monks outwit you."

Reginald saw that Sir Ralph was desperate to respond, and imagined it was to do with King Edward's own decision to invite a cell from without the Tower to officiate over the demonstration. Fortunately for his own safety, Sandwich was sufficiently long in the tooth to know when to bite his tongue.

"Reg," Edward addressed the baron, "you've not brought the bloody outlaws across country, have you?"

"I fear they may have a greater influence than we might think," the baron conceded. "We are pressed by foes on all sides, my lord."

"Yes, I bloody know that - did you notice I had my own fortress brought down on me today?" barked the King.

Reginald did not take any personal offence at the savage riposte, knowing he himself would harbour equal distress at suffering such an experience. The iron-stubbled Baron de Grey looked round the room, at the beleaguered Sir Ralph Sandwich; the dislikeable Sir Walter de Beauchamp, for once sheepish in the light of the day's events - even as proud a man as Sir Walter recognised his own culpability from time to time; the grand old Earl of Surrey, John de Warenne; and the colourless John Droxford, the newly appointed keeper of the wardrobe. Droxford, a man of average height and build and lacking any distinguishing facial features, was almost perfectly camouflaged into the dingy stone wall behind him - even were he to dress in the garish finery of de Beauchamp or Surrey's spectacular fur-trim jacket, his drab personality would still conceal him from anyone's attention.

Droxford aside, Lord Reginald had always found the King's inner circle to be a fascinating mixture of belligerence and eccentricity and the current roster was no different. This was all without the master gambler, the treasurer Walter Langton. Even if he were not the senior figure in charge of coin, Langton's inclination towards speculation and property acquisition would be cause for concern.

And yet with all of the belligerence and eccentricity of England crammed into one room, it was an awkward stillness that pervaded the small Tower room as the personalities of the royal household were cowed by King Edward's ferocious bent.

The Baron de Grey broke the silence, always the most likely to do so in such situations. His lifetime of friendship with Edward, and a superior grasp of delicate political and social matters to Surrey, gave him a privileged position from which to advise the monarch. This was sometimes a poisoned chalice, but more often than not the steely-eyed baron found the appropriate line of approach to Longshanks.

"If I may, would we call the Templars to questioning?" he asked the room, glancing at the King only cursorily.

"That bloody Order, of course," grumbled Edward. "That monk was one of them, wasn't he?" he asked Reginald, referring to Henry's presence at the demonstration.

"I believe so," the baron replied. He clasped his hands behind his back and began pacing before the other men. "Unfortunately, we have lost him, in the ensuing crush..."

Reginald paused for a moment, aware of the grievous losses suffered by many during the stampede. He looked around and was met by no eyes, for all heads were in that instant bowed at the terrible memory, except for the King whose fury seemed to fix his bearded jaw aloft and his teeth gritted.

The baron continued. "However, we know where Master Guy is, and he shall not be so elusive in giving us answers - how else would a man achieve such high office in the religious orders if he were not honest?"

"*Hmph!* guffawed the Earl of Surrey, recognising Reginald's cynicism.

Lord Reginald raised his eyebrows, looking at the King. "The Master would also help explain why another of his charges, the niece of the Templar Grand Master, no less, was found in a workshop from which the projectiles were launched at the field."

The King's eyes shot to Reginald's at the mention of the Grand Master's niece, causing the steely baron to stop abruptly, his last sentence hanging in the air and leaving his audience expecting further explanation. Audible breaths went in and the tension of the room changed from iciness to intrigue in an instant.

"The de Molay girl again! What are you suggesting?" enquired the King with narrow eyes.

"Now I don't think the Temple has anything to do with this attack - that much is obvious, and aside from anything else, the girl has been apprehended having apparently killed one of the perpetrators - but I should like to know why they are still sniffing around whenever the stone turns up," Reginald explained, "especially when they have had *royal* orders to stay out of the way."

Sir Walter de Beauchamp was leaning on the great triangular shield that he had picked up upon entering the room. Finding such fine armour simply lying around the castle had caused him to look daggers at poor Sir Ralph, but the constable had not noticed, so concerned was he with the King's condition. Having failed to gain the constable's attention, Sir Walter had rather shamefacedly realised his focus was misdirected at that time.

"I wager she was simply gathering information. We know the Order have fingers in all of Christendom's pies - any enemy of the Crown, any Christian crown, is an enemy of the Temple. The Dragons are as bad news for the Order as they are for us," suggested Sir Walter.

Reginald bristled at Sir Walter's haughty assumption of the de Molay girl's motives, but could only agree with the steward's succinct conclusion.

"Be careful of Master de Foresta," advised Surrey, his great red beard almost entirely concealing his mouth. "He's a powerful man. And a useful ally, if we could find some common ground, against Philippe."

The others murmured their agreement, even the wallflower Droxford.

Lord Reginald liked the old Earl, the archetypal grizzled warrior with decades of fighting experience and diplomatic know-how. "My dear Earl," he said warmly, "you are precisely right. We stamp out their misbehaviour and we gain leverage against Philippe with both the Order and the larger Church."

The King tutted. "Should have kicked them out of the country when I had the chance! They've caused me untold trouble." He sat back in his chair and drummed his fingers on either arm. "But the

French and Welsh are dangerous… bring him in for talks. Droxford, sort this for tomorrow. Or today. Whenever is least convenient for him."

Droxford nodded almost imperceptibly. "Yes, majesty," he replied in his hoarse voice.

"And if we can locate Signor Fiadóni, we may bring greater leverage to bear on Master Guy," offered Reginald, finger on his lips has he thought, hoping the Pope's envoy was as worthy as his reputation suggested.

"Bring them all in," replied the King brusquely.

Fiadóni had not been accounted for, as far as the baron was aware. For the briefest of moments he allowed himself to think of the dreadful toll of today. Consequently, for the first time in weeks he was glad Matilda had not joined him in travelling to London, perversely grateful she had come down with illness before he hurriedly left Chester. What chance would she have stood in that crush?

"I already have men tracking down the whereabouts of the noble families and the Church's representatives, my lord," Sir Walter de Beauchamp announced. It was an honest declaration but both the knight's delivery and reputation for arrogance meant that even his most genuine intentions were often misconstrued.

The King's eyes, windows to his tumultuous soul, were calmer following the counsel of his old friends and a suggestion to one of the many problems that beset his kingdom. Reginald was relieved – he knew Edward was an achiever and had been since first leading an army for his father as a teenager; the completion or even serious contemplation of one task or issue would put him more at ease. If there was one thing - alongside the French and Welsh and Scots - that the King could not tolerate, it was inaction. The King never flustered, he just raged; but by removing an obstacle his council had reduced to a mere simmering the unbridled fury of a man who often struggled to compartmentalise difficulties.

As Edward warmed to Surrey's suggestion, Lord Reginald reflected on those difficulties that required compartmentalising. Yes, a burning building did crash down on Edward today, but he was alive, thanks be to the Lord, and physical suffering was water off a duck's back to the warrior king, this Arthur reborn. No, it was the impunity with which England's enemies could strike at the heart of her power, at the Tower fortress - the most impregnable in the land - killing and maiming and burning England's most noble men and women, striking terror into the commonfolk with such ruthless brutality, infiltrating the Crown's favoured religious order.

Edward turned his great bearded head to the upright Walter de Beauchamp, his household steward, a relative of the de Beauchamps who held the earldom of Warwick. "I want everyone vetted – no one enters the fortress without your say so," he commanded.

"My lord," de Beauchamp dutifully replied, courteous as he was only to the King.

The Baron de Grey watched the exchange with interest. Being related to the Earl of Warwick's family, Walter de Beauchamp was also a cousin of Reginald's own man, Sir Edward de Beauchamp. Reginald could see a strong familial connection; both were knightly in bearing if not character, tall, imposing, dark of hair and fixed of scowl. Much like Sir Edward de Beauchamp, Reginald thought, Sir Walter had ideas above his station. He had it from Surrey that Walter essentially believed himself to be monarch in the King's absence, a distasteful taint on an otherwise excellent administrator and fine soldier in the field. Surrey had joked that it was fortunate that Sir Walter was attached to the Edward's household – Longshanks' absence from his own household was a rare occurrence by definition, thus limiting the opportunities for Sir Walter to foist his delusions on those around him.

"And Sir Walter, please tell me you've recovered that bloody stone," Edward asked but sounding very much like he did not want to.

"I think Sir Ralph is seeing to that, Sir," Walter replied acerbically, attempting to pile further pressure on the poor constable.

"Well, there's no chance of finding it then," Edward deadpanned.

Lord Reginald and the others looked to the red-faced Sir Ralph, his cheeks nearly matching his fine dark burgundy jacket and stockings. Baron de Grey thought it an unfortunate choice of colour to be wearing when he knew there would be shame and humiliation before his peers during this council meet.

The constable pursed his lips and blinked slowly, retaining his composure under the unrelenting slighting from King Edward. Reginald considered the King's snide comments, unhelpful as they were, to be infinitely preferable to his terrible haranguing; *at least he can't give himself a heart attack with bitter sarcasm*, the baron thought.

"The men are individually checking every piece of rubble and stone that they pull away, sire, and others are being sent into the moat to recover what is now submerged."

"Good man," said Edward approvingly, finally giving the constable some respite. "I want to be informed as soon as it is found."

"It might be best leaving it in the moat!" exclaimed Surrey in his customarily theatrical style. Even the most mundane observations could be rendered interesting thanks to the old warrior's charismatic delivery.

"All of this fuss and then to leave it under water? Half-tempted to do that," reasoned the King, giving the impression he was considering following Surrey's suggestion, though in reality he was merely humouring his good friend.

King Edward rose from the chair and wandered over to the slim window, hoping but ultimately failing to find an angle sufficient for viewing the recovery operation further around the wall down below. The King breathed deeply of the fresher air, a meagre admittance through the narrow slit though it was, but even so it was still easier on his dust-filled lungs than the stuffy and odorous ambiance of the impromptu council room. No sooner had he filled his lungs then he coughed horribly, wracking his sturdy frame in a manner that countless battles had not.

The old earl turned his palms upwards, trying to physically emphasise his point. "I mean it, Ed. That thing goes up when set on fire - why not keep it under there?"

Reginald nodded unconsciously whilst also wondering how he had not thought of that idea himself. He knew, however, Edward would not treat a gift from the Lord so dismissively.

Longshanks gave a contemplative *hmm* as he moved away from the window and shook some more dust out of his dirty grey hair.

"My dear John, it would be to squander a wonderful gift, were we to drown it away from man's eyes," he said with poker face and the embers reigniting in those eyes bored deep under strong brows. "Droxford!" he called, amplifying his voice as if the keeper of the wardrobe were in another room, "also see to it that the great Duns Scotus is invited with whomever he sees fit to assist him in investigating the stone's mysteries. We shall fathom the purpose of it, but this time without all of London watching." The King nodded at Lord Reginald, causing de Beauchamp and Surrey to eye the baron suspiciously.

"So we are to harbour this relic within our walls? You saw how many people were lost today! It is a wonder the city has not burnt down – praise be to God for the quick wits he bestowed upon Reg - it is not an object to display in pride, that much is clear. You see the displeasure of God that has been brought down upon our heads, Ed?" Surrey's heart was heavy with grief – his family were found safe following the crush but the same could not be said of many others.

"There shan't be any demonstrations," the King replied forcefully, customarily resorting to defiance in place of mourning. He felt for his friend, and for those who had lost someone today, but most of all King Edward felt for his kingdom. He paced back towards the window with slow feet, scuffing his boots as he went. "But," he began grandly, "if there has been a greater portent for this realm than the appearance, no, the *bestowal* of this fine relic unto us, than I know not of it." He quickly and triumphantly spun round to face the five men in the room.

"Remind me how today could be consider-"

Edward quickly cut off the Earl. "How many times does a man fall off his horse before he is proficient enough to master even the most ferocious of stallions? It is not anyone who can take on the mighty warhorse. Our realm, my lords and knights, it has stumbled before – the untimely death of the Richard the Lionhearted, or indeed my own father's capture – but it emerged stronger for it! Let our foes know that the English lion is most dangerous when he is wounded."

Reginald listened closely and could visualise the King clad in his battle armour before a baying host, stirring the hearts of each and every vassal under his command. The man was a force of nature.

"Perhaps more so, these foes dare to use God's gift against us? Woe be to those who stoke the wrath of St George *and* the Lord." King Edward glanced from man to man, unnecessarily checking each had paid attention, as if their minds could have wandered from the subject at hand. "Well, what are you waiting for? Go on, get on with it." He nodded his head in the direction of the closed door, expression darkening as that infamous temper seemed to stir once again.

All bowed their heads in deference with one or two "*my lord*"s mumbled before sloping towards the door to take their leave.

"Reg, John, not you," the King clipped.

Droxford, Sir Walter and Sir Ralph stuttered at hearing further instructions from the King before realising their presence was still no longer required. Lord Reginald and the Earl of Surrey both redirected their path towards the wooden chairs around the edge of the room. Meanwhile the constable, steward and the keeper of the wardrobe silently exited the room and de Beauchamp, carrying the shield he had found lying about, closed the door surprisingly softly behind him, leaving the three most influential men in the kingdom alone.

"I'm going to have to sit down, it's been too long a day," commented Surrey through his great red beard that somehow defied the years that was greying the hair on top of his head.

"Get yourself comfortable, then," suggested Edward.

The earl sighed as he parked himself on the unforgiving wooden chair. "Was this room intended as a gaol?"

The King ignored the comment. "Firstly, where in the name of St George did that fire come from? I've never seen anything burn like it."

Reginald and Surrey looked to each other in expectation that the other would provide an answer.

The Baron de Grey spoke first. "We're not entirely sure, either," he answered slowly, thinking through the possible explanations as to why the fire raged so strong.

"Maybe it's the stone," the King suggested. "In which case, we are best off keeping it under the moat," he said, looking at Surrey.

"It needs to be kept away from the city, Ed," Surrey advised. "The fire it brought with it was burning through the middle gatehouse like it was made of cloth."

"I've never seen a tower collapse so quickly. And the way it burnt on the grass. Remarkable," added Reginald.

"Have the teachers look at it," commanded the King, "and find out whether the fire was added to it, or whether the stone brought the fire with it."

The baron and the earl nodded in turn in acknowledgement.

"And the other thing is, what is the news from Flanders?" Edward put a bruised hand peppered with scratches and cuts to his temple. "Bloody hell, my head hurts." He coughed and felt the dust scratching his throat once more.

Reginald imagined the King to be akin to a bag of sand in this moment, entirely full of sediment. "I'm not going to suggest you lie down, Ed," said Reginald bluntly, knowing that no man but King Edward could tell King Edward what to do, even if he had endured a building collapse that day. "Twice I've been around that stone and it's given me a pounding headache both times. Regarding Flanders, I've heard reports that the French have defeated Dampierre and taken him prisoner-"

The King interrupted Reginald. "Someone needs to teach Philippe a lesson," he growled. "Where were the Germans? What did we pay them for?"

Lord Reginald resumed. "I've not been informed as to where Adolphus was, or what he's planning. In that respect, all we can hope is that Philippe continues to alienate the Pope. Adolphus is the Pope's pet, after all."

"See to it that the Pope's man, Fiadóni, check his version of events from today," ordered the King, keen to keep Pope Boniface on the English side of the Angevin-Capétien divide.

"Of course," Reginald affirmed. "The same reports also suggest the French lost the majority of their knights, though, and a number of Philippe's council members," he reported, lingering on these considerable revelations. He knew their significance.

391

They were revelations that indeed sparked the King's interest. "The majority? Those Flemings don't half know how to fight. I'd bet old Dampierre was at the front. Who fell?"

"The Duke of Burgundy was slain," answered Reginald, "though no confirmation of who else. Philippe himself is fine. Burgundy's loss will be keenly felt, though."

"That boy is looking this way," Surrey asserted, contemptuously referring to King Philippe.

The King nodded. "And when he comes, I'll be waiting for him. Nothing like an invasion to unite the realm. The damn French coming over might be the best thing to happen to this kingdom in years."

"That won't be for a while, they have to get through Calais first," corrected the Baron de Grey. "It might be prudent to lend some support to the Calais burghers because if the city falls, and Ghent's fall is imminent as well as Antwerp, then our wool lines are in trouble."

Reginald carried a troubled expression that matched his mood. Today's disaster was a grave, yet singular impact; the fall of Flanders to Philippe would be an ongoing catastrophe for the realm.

The King recognised Reginald's concern. "If it's not one thing then it's another. Let's clear this mess first, before we go jaunting off to stop that boy."

Baron de Grey recognised that the King was finally compartmentalising the issues facing his kingdom, but the longer he thought about it the more he believed that attending to the issues in turn was not entirely advantageous.

"I'll go to Calais, Ed," offered Surrey, all drama lost from his tone. The grand old earl had been thinking along similar lines to Reginald.

King Edward studied the earl, more beard than man. "We haven't got the money for another expedition right now," he lamented.

"All the kingdom is in London right now, Ed," Surrey replied, "and you said it yourself. Nothing quite like a foreign invasion. We'll raise the money to stop the foreign invasion before it starts." The earl thumped his fist on the arm of his chair, rattling the old thing. In his mind he was already at war. "Or, at least hold it up."

"Reg?" Edward asked.

"You're more likely to get something from the southern nobles now that Dragons are on the loose and Philippe is at the door," the baron opined.

"Very well. I'll call a special parliament. *Everyone* will be in attendance, but there shan't be any mention of Aquitaine. This is defensive. John, you'll raise the militia immediately. I want you in Calais before the weather turns."

The Earl of Surrey inclined his head in acquiescence.

Reginald was relieved to hear the King was at least publicly willing to distance himself from talk of Aquitaine, that hereditary territory of the English kings. Most requests for finance faltered when the noblemen refused to pay for Edward's campaigns to clear his own duchy of the French - Aquitaine was not 'English'; strictly speaking it was Angevin, a relic of the House of Anjou from which descended the current English king.

Edward coughed again. "Where's that wine? I feel like death. Are you having any?"

"No, thank you."

"Go on, then."

Reginald and Surrey looked at each other as they answered simultaneously. The baron was not interested in having a drink at this moment – he was still inexplicably nauseous and suffering from the same mild headache that had plagued him since the middle gatehouse's collapse - but the ruddy-faced earl could not think of anything more welcome.

Edward scoffed a small laugh. "After this, go and check on the tower, will you. You'll have to take a boat out; the Byward Tower gate is somewhat ruined."

As their small rowboat approached the jetty, Reginald could see the flurry of activity even before he had rounded the waterside curtain wall that spread out from the Watergate on the riverside of the fortress wall. The Tower had two entrances and because the collapsed tower had rendered one of those impassable, Reginald and Surrey, together with two guardsmen, took their rowboat from the grand Watergate, reversing the journey they had earlier taken into the Tower. Both noblemen considered it fortuitous Edward had added the Watergate entrance a few years prior. A fortress with one impassable entrance was not a fortress at all.

There were people everywhere by the jetty; soldiers, labourers, anyone the officers could round up to assist with the clearing and repair work. Small boats bobbed around in the river and entrance to the moat like birds in the fields observing the hardworking farmers, milling, never still, always just staying a safe distance. To the men's right was the jumble of whitewashed stone and greyed brickwork piled up, creating an island between the outer gatehouse and the Byward Tower. The debris was strewn across the moat on both sides; on the riverside it was sufficiently extensive that one could walk from the jetty on to the rubble island. Previously, the moat between the jetty and the middle gatehouse had been at least twenty yards wide.

The two lords and a couple of men-at-arms climbed out of the small boat and clambered on to the jetty. The jetty protruded out a little way out into the Thames, the inside edge roughly marking where the original riverbank would have laid. They saw people scurrying everywhere, scrambling all over the mound like ants across a nest.

The guards nearby stood to attention as the baron and the earl walked along. A young man-at-arms missing his helmet and coated in dust stood closest to the lords. Reginald strained his mind to discover how exactly the tower could collapse; during the demonstrations at Chester, the stone had not displayed any explosive properties nor any attributes that suggested it could provide a great displacing force.

"How many have we lost?" Lord Reginald asked gruffly without looking at the dusty man.

"Not sure yet, my lord," the soldier replied, solemnly. He carried the look of devastation, so that when the baron turned to him, Reginald realised there was no need to press the man further. The tall baron looked back at the gaping chasm in the otherwise impregnable stone cliff that cut off the fortress from the miniscule houses and workshops that otherwise populated London. Save for the wall and a number of churches, no other structure in this sprawling hive of stone and wood came close to the Tower in terms of height and grandeur.

Yet now in the fortress' midst, there was a huge pile of rubble in the freshly assembled fortifications, burying unknown numbers of men beneath its remains.

Then it hit him; the reason why the middle gate had collapsed. The iron-stubbled man shuddered upon recognising that some of the men would never be found – he had not considered the consequences of the stone's power. *It took away the tower* and *the men.*

"What was that?" Surrey asked through his beard.

Reginald was unaware he had muttered his conclusion aloud. "It brought it down!" he exclaimed. Taking Surrey to the side, out of earshot of the distraught guard, the tall baron leant in and spoke in hushed tones, urgency coursing through his voice. "They won't find anyone, John – they're gone."

"I know they're dead," the earl said drolly, bemused at what he thought was Reginald's surprise.

"No, they will be *gone,*" the baron stressed. "Their bodies won't be there. That's what the stone *does…* The tower itself will have gone. That blue flash, when that appears, the things around it disappear. Stones, earth, armour… bodies. In Chester we saw that it makes things *vanish.*"

He lingered on the last word as he tried to comprehend what it entailed. How does one consider what it is to *not* be? Reginald had not thought about a person being subjected to the stone's power; the earth and armour that had gone at Chester were inanimate, they were *objects.* People were not objects; they could not be disappeared like that.

It was this blurring of boundaries between subjects and objects that frightened Reginald more than the actual disaster itself. No mightier or more terrifying a weapon had man ever before wielded against another man. The instruments of old – swords, spears, lances, arrows – they were all tangible, if you were quick or fortunate enough, you would see them coming. But this stone with its blue flash was quicker than lightning, and no one knew what it did. Would even the doctors of the Church? He doubted it was an agent of ascension; if bodies – people – were ascending to Heaven through the stone's agency, then why too would pieces of armour or the soil of the earth? No one knew the purpose or nature of its effect.

But there were those who knew how to catalyse its effects – those who started the fires. If it were the Dragons, Reginald thought, then they were a far more dangerous enemy than first assumed. With every ambush or village raid did the resounding English victory at Maes Moydog become an increasingly distant memory.

"When you say, 'vanish', you mean to say..." began Surrey, interrupting the baron's musings but trailing off. His old face crinkled as he too attempted to fathom the literal application of the word in everyday life. "Something doesn't just vanish, surely. Burnt to ash, perhaps, yes." His furrowed face contorted so much that it seemed only his nose and beard would remain by the time he found a satisfactory answer.

"They vanish," stated Reginald, wanting to sound stern and authoritarian with the old earl but finding his voice unwilling to comply.

At the water's edge behind them an expression went up from the soldiers, different in tone to the orders and grunts of the excavation labour, a groan of discovery. It was sufficiently dissimilar from the humdrum of work for both lords and soldiers to notice it. Baron de Grey and the earl turned around to find most movement had stopped except for a grey-shirted soldier with dark hair atop one pile of stonework. He was leaning forward, hands resting before him on some angular slabs of the demolished limestone. The soldier wretched and vomited, his bread and pottage breakfast decorating the bleached white stones.

Lord Reginald immediately suspected the cause of the man-at-arms' heaving and brushed past Surrey and through the scattered pockets of momentarily distracted soldiers. One or two noticed the baron's approach and awkwardly stepped aside as best they could on the unstable and often jagged stone. The baron clambered up to where the soldier was regaining his breath and posture, doubling his efforts to do so upon noticing the iron-stubbled man.

"Lord de Grey," croaked the dark-haired soldier, a youth probably no older than twenty, green in experience and complexion. His voice almost reached soprano, through nature or shock, Lord Reginald did not know. The soldier wiped some residue of vomit from his mouth with his bare arm and pointed down with the other at the horrifyingly dismembered corpse lying on the rocks.

Reginald regarded the dead soldier for a few seconds before looking away and swallowing hard. The dead man, having been uncovered by the dark-haired youth, only had the right side of his body – the entire left half was missing, nowhere to be seen; half of his head, torso, the whole left arm and leg, all gone, as if a great blade had perfectly bisected him head to foot. Stranger still, there was no evidence of bleeding from the man's insides as they appeared to have been completely cauterised, so much so that the innards were a smooth black like a polished marble. No blood, muscle, tissue, organs, bones.

Reginald glanced back again at the corpse and at the one lifeless eye staring ever upward at nothing. One side of the man's body had been completely removed in whatever it was that happened in the gatehouse tower. Reginald inspected closer and saw the soldier's clothing and armour had been flawlessly cut down the middle with not even a frayed linen strand or twisted mail ring to be found – the grotesque severing was remarkable for its cleanliness, a precise operation with no ostensible mess.

"Give him a burial," grunted Reginald with a dismissiveness not born from disrespect for the dead, but displeasure with having to observe the ill-effects of the stone's operation and disgust with his own fascination at the cleanliness of the bifurcation.

"Sir, we can't find… the rest of him," came the quivering voice of the young guardsman, his face whiter than the clouds overhead.

Lord Reginald sighed, unsure how to explain the seemingly impossible to an already disbelieving and grieving friend. "It's gone, lad. Bury him."

For now willing to let sleeping dogs lie and aware he could not provide the young soldier with further enlightenment on the matter, he nodded to the youth and stepped back down the mound of rubble, struggling not to slip on the crumbled masonry. The other soldiers watched him silently, forgetting all decorum in the presence of their superior by not bowing. The baron did not care for their accidental insubordination; the artificial social graces of man were trivial in such circumstances. Who cared if one man did not salute another when investigating phenomena unheard of in modern times?

No, acknowledgement *should* still be necessary, he reconsidered whilst walking past the soldiers. These social graces were a construct crucial to the polity of the realm, a realm beset by enemies without and harbouring within an unknown power that could tear asunder kings and farriers, earls and guardsmen alike. Maintenance of the realm's social structure and stability was essential in weathering whatever destructive or debilitating effects this potent relic could produce should the stone continue to be mismanaged as it had been today

With all eyes following him, the iron-stubbled baron halted and turned to the right, glaring eyes set above the gritted jaw so characteristic when he pondered troubling matters. The stare fixed upon a heavyset man-at-arms stripped to the waist, dust smeared across his thick arms and massive hands. The man-at-arms awoke from his daze and snapped his head forward in an automatic gesture of respect, setting off a bizarre wave of head bowing that surged up the mound of rubble as in turn each soldier clocked on to their mistake, and within moments the social status quo had been restored.

Satisfied with the response, the baron spun and his scarlet cloak swirled over the dusty stones that formed a temporary bank to the otherwise sloped moat's edge. Upon reaching the grass he looked up and noticed people walking around the scorched field to the north, across the deserted Tower Liberties, emerging from the smoke that still lingered low in patches as if another reminder of what had come to pass that day was needed.

"I have never seen anything like that," said the grizzled earl, shaken by the sight atop the mound so that his voice was devoid of the verve that so characterised his contributions to any exchange. "The King needs to see this."

"It will only fuel his fire," cautioned Reginald.

"It's too late for that," Surrey stated reluctantly. "You know that he knows what he wants and he'll get what he wants. Let God decide whether he should or should not use it. All we can do is steer him through this with as little damage as possible."

"The Church will doubtless oppose Edward's intentions." The baron deliberated for a moment. "I'll talk to the Temple Master. He'll be key in this question of ownership, or possession – mediating between Edward and the Church, perhaps. Both sides will know the Temple are interested in it and this very fact will prevent the Temple obtaining it anyhow. Which makes him an ideal adjudicator in our little discussion."

"We have to find the stone first, my dear Reginald," Surrey replied as he surveyed the once-again busy moat side, taking an appearance halfway between a waterborne quarry and a construction site. "Which could have disappeared as well," continued the old earl, giving Reginald a sly look as he did so.

The baron immediately picked up on Surrey's intimation that the stone could have been removed by an agency other than the King's and replied with a grim jutting of his jaw. "If only it were so – it'll still be there. And there's no chance for anyone to keep it from the eyes nor ears of court nor Church, as desirable as this would be."

The two experienced statesmen watched on as the soldiers painstakingly cleared the rubble brick by brick and stone by stone, many hesitantly for fear of unearthing and somehow setting off the Godstone once again. Baron de Grey sighed deeply, unaware that he had done so. He knew London would not be the same after the events of today, nor England. He resolved to ensure the future would not follow today's precedent.

Chapter 26

Mathieu could not tell if he were truly awake, or just dreaming, or just drunk. If he was drunk, he thought, he must have had far more wine than at any time in the previous twenty years. Given his propensity for putting away the fruits of Gascony, the Comte considered outdrinking himself to be a truly remarkable achievement.

The atrocious headache that eliminated all awareness of the outside world suggested that it was likely he had been drinking, anyway. Though it would not explain the sounds that slowly made themselves more obvious to him. Shouts of agony, or anger, the Comte could not tell. There was a low murmuring of a conversation somewhere nearby. Mathieu did not want to open his eyes because he feared exacerbation of his headache, so was reliant on his ears. Sobbing? He could hear sobbing. Where was that from?

Someone coughed nearby and the smell of sweat rapidly approached. Mathieu sensed movement beside him and felt an unexpected, excruciating pressure on his chest, which reminded him that other parts of his body existed aside from his head. Though he would have preferred to not be reminded because suddenly the pain that seared through every fibre of his being came alive – across his shoulders, his mangled arm, his neck and chest. Mathieu remembered that he had not been drinking, but fighting.

His discomfort suggested he was not dead at the very least. But as for where he was, the Comte had no clue. The murmurs of conversation around him were too monotonous and indistinct for the language to be identified, and there was no focus to be had at all upon opening his eyes for the first time.

"My lord!" an excited voice cried out. It was the first clear vocalisation Mathieu had heard since, well, he could not recall. And it was in French!

"My lord," came the voice again, "you are well. I'll be right back."

Mathieu closed his eyes again. *You are well* was perhaps an exaggeration, he pondered, but upon reflection displaying the signs of life was definitely of considerable import to presumably concerned onlookers. The Comte wondered if it had been Pascal. Yes, he decided, it had been.

Now conscious if not fully functioning, the Comte de la Marche tried to sit up on the makeshift bed he found himself on. Looking around he saw plain canvas walls close by, a rather enclosed space that would explain the persistence of the overpowering stench of sweat and other waste. His mind warming up in spite of the dull ache threatening to tear his head asunder, Mathieu began thinking more clearly – the presence of Pascal in such a buoyant mood indicated a French victory. Pascal would be nowhere to be seen had the Comte woken up in the Flemish camp.

A number of bodies entered through a canvas doorflap to his left and it took a substantial effort for the wounded spymaster to turn his head in that direction. It was the King! Mathieu felt his heart jump at seeing the fair face and blond hair, caked as it was with dried mud and quite probably blood. France had won and the King was alive. Mathieu was grateful and thanked the Lord in his head.

Mathieu really did not want to talk to anyone, though; he could barely move his head and his jaw throbbed, but in his state there was nothing he could do to prevent the King from imposing his will onto proceedings.

"Sire," Mathieu croaked, vision blurry but gradually focusing on the tall, mud-spattered suit of armour with a human head stood before him. *At least he's come to see me straight away*, he thought.

"My dear Mathieu!" exclaimed the King with a hint of warmth. "I do hope the Flemings spared that mind of yours."

Philippe laid a hand gently on Mathieu's left shoulder, barely any pressure for fear of aggravating the Comte's injuries. The King did not know the exact extent of those injuries but it was immediately obvious to anyone that Mathieu's body was wrecked.

"I haven't seen your face in such bad shape," joked the King, trying to get a reaction from his old friend. It was not forthcoming. Philippe did have a point, though; Mathieu's face was battered and bloodied despite the surgeon's best efforts at cleaning it, and as

Philippe studied the black, red and purple covering the Comte's visage he could not tell where the bruises and cuts ended and the trails of blood started.

Philippe carried on, looking the groggy man in the eyes. "Your actions saved the battle, my dear friend. The story of the old knights is already doing the rounds amongst the men, I am told; the *chevaliers* de Bourgogne and de la Marche leading a gallant Frankish charge to victory. They shall sing your name for years to come."

Philippe spoke quietly and without the vigour that his effusive words might have required. The muddied King, blond hair dark with sweat and rain and face red somehow retained the look of a man nicknamed "*Le Bel*," yet there was something in his voice that suggested all was not fair.

Mathieu's mind laboriously went through the permutations that could explain the King's essential moroseness but the temptation to just close his eyes and sleep remained strong. The Comte looked past Philippe, as the King went to pick up a cup of water on the next bench along, and saw Raoul de Clermont. *Of course he made it through.* If Philippe still looked fair, Raoul looked positively hideous; his dark, terrifying features lined with grime and blood, heavy lines and scars running along stubbled cheeks. Mathieu could not imagine facing a more chilling foe, an entirely apt attribute for a Constable of France.

The King handed Mathieu the cup, clasping the injured man's left hand around the plain wooden vessel.

"I would rather my name were not sung for years to come, for in my profession that would suggest I haven't performed very well," Mathieu deadpanned. He spoke slowly - the thought process in formulating the sentence was painful, let alone speaking it. He had not before experienced a headache like the one that assaulted his brain in that moment.

De Clermont approached the bench, all glower, menace and the smell of horse and sweat. The humidity and lack of ventilation in the tent exacerbated the vile atmosphere generated by so many sweat, blood and filth-drenched soldiers throughout the hospital tents. Another cry rang out somewhere beyond the canvas walls of the tent, mingled with the continuous sobbing and ceaseless coughing. The presence of the loftiest men in the kingdom could not detract from the despair and misery in the surgeons' pavilions.

Mathieu slowly turned his head to face the Constable. "You look worse than I feel," the Comte commented, again without emotion.

De Clermont did not react to the jibe, his face remaining still like a fearsome stone gargoyle. "We have suffered grave losses," Raoul said in his bass voice.

The King's head dropped to his chest, the long golden hair falling down from behind his ears, and he pursed his lips. Mathieu knew this heralded ill-tidings.

"How many?" the injured man enquired.

"Hundreds," came Philippe's solemn reply, still looking down at the muddied floor, a slick morass of filth and blood only marginally more traversable than the field on which battle was given.

The response chilled Mathieu to his core – the manhood of the heart of France itself, the Ile-de-France, scattered in the fields of Flanders. He prayed that the Lord would forgive Philippe his mercantile ambitions.

"Duke Robert is dead, Mathieu," King Philippe continued in a very matter-of-fact way.

The Comte de la Marche was already numb with the magnitude of casualties but the Duke de Bourgogne's death was a shock he did not expect. Mathieu closed his eyes in regret at the passing of his old acquaintance, unwilling to countenance any further ill tidings. Robert was a fine man who should not have died in a field of mud but in twenty years' time in a warm bed back in Dijon, Mathieu thought.

Philippe stood straight and looked at his wounded spymaster. "Robert was a hero of France. There is no more glorious a way for him to have been called to the Lord than in the cavalry charge, saving his kingdom."

Mathieu forced his eyes back open, in spite of the intense discomfort of even the dim torchlight that barely illuminated the tent. That Philippe lacked appreciation of the Pyrrhic nature of his victory was more than a little perturbing.

"Did he die well?" he managed through wheezing breaths.

"Lance in hand," said Raoul, with approval.

Mathieu reflected on the news, trying to absorb the information in the manner he absorbed all other information: analytically and impassively. It was just the implications of the Duke's death that shook him – he considered how it could just as easily been him lying dead in the field. The two of them led the attack together. *Why have I survived instead of Robert?* He had not been so close to death since the battle at Col de Panissars; had the Comte de la Marche forgotten what it was to be a noble cavalryman?

The King ambled round the bench to face Mathieu and interrupted the latter's introspection. "I want you recovered before too long, Mathieu," the King strongly suggested, "because you are now Grand Chamberman of France. I expect you will perform as admirably as did Duke Robert."

The Comte managed to raise his eyebrows at the revelation. "An honour, my lord," he spoke, nodding his head slowly and painfully.

"Very well. There's much to discuss, Mathieu. We have Dampierre and I'm going to speak with him now. I think the old man is invincible." With that the King strode out of the tent, trailed by Raoul, who nodded to Mathieu as he exited.

Alone with his musings, the Comte tried to put thoughts of the Duke de Bourgogne's death aside so as to concentrate on the matters of state; actively attempting such detachment made him feel guilty, particularly because Robert was as close to a friend as Mathieu had, but Duke Robert was with the Lord now and had no need for Mathieu's thoughts.

In any case, Duke Robert would not have cared that Mathieu was not paying him any mind because he knew the Comte was working. Work was what required attention at this time, irrespective of the previous Grand Chamberman's death or the current Grand Chamberman's debilitating injuries.

"Pascal," the Comte croaked, "where is Pinto?" He braced himself for the worst. Investing emotions in animate subjects was a highly risky venture.

The mouse-like man smiled, perhaps the first time Mathieu had ever seen him smile. "Pinto is well, my lord. She is being looked after. We found her, without you, on the outskirts of the fighting, no injuries to speak of."

Mathieu sighed in relief, though the action was uncomfortable. "And who found me, for that matter?"

"I'm not sure. One of the sergeants. You were buried beneath all sorts, though your shield was a dead giveaway." The Comte's angular shield was quite unique amongst the French army not for its design and colouration – azure and gold were common themes amongst the French nobility – but its shape was instantly recognisable, contrasting as it did with the more modern and more compact round-bottomed shields favoured by the other nobles.

"I should like to find that sergeant and thank him. In the meantime, send for Le Gris. No, send instructions to him."

Mathieu tried sitting up a little higher on the makeshift bed but had neither the energy nor the requisite functioning arms to execute such movement. Pascal watched on dispassionately, not offering any assistance to his bedridden liege. So preoccupied was he with his own efforts that it did not occur to Mathieu that Pascal could help him. Even if it had, the Comte would not have expected his secretary to move; that was the essence of Pascal's being – small, quiet, out of the way. There, but not there.

Mathieu gave up with a grunt, slumping back against the brown sack that acted as his pillow, supplemented by a blanket for comfort. "Tell that little upstart that I have a proposal for Le Verre that will make Le Verre very wealthy, and give him an opportunity to atone for his failure regarding Norris and the Temple loans. This time, he shall act immediately."

"Very well, my lord. I assume we shall be preparing some sanctions to levy in case he refuses our offer?" asked Pascal in a small and low voice but certainly not timid. His was not a presence that dominated, unlike many of the King's councillors yet he did not need to. His shadow stretched far further than the few people who ever noticed him would assume.

"Unnecessary for the time being," responded the Comte. He closed his eyes in an attempt to ease his relentless headache. "The King's advance on Flanders, for all of its faults, will have sent a message. Le Verre will see no choice but to continue doing business with us, because we are now his only partners." Mathieu continued

405

in his laboured tone. "And this monopoly will have the added benefit of strengthening our position *vis-à-vis* Le Verre."

"Because he will become easier to locate," offered Pascal, interrupting the slow-speaking Comte.

The Comte breathed deeply, at once drawing great satisfaction from the sensation of overly full lungs but aching in doing so. "I shouldn't think a man, or woman, in Le Verre's position will be straightforward to locate. In fact, it would be a surprise should I ever encounter him or her. Perhaps in your lifetime, you will. But deprive a wild dog of any food bar that which you provide and it will become trained, and with training it loses its fearfulness." Mathieu coughed and recoiled at the pain. "Le Verre is our enemy, Pascal. Not the Flemish or the English or the Templars."

"He is useful, my lord," said Pascal.

"He is our *raison d'être*," replied Mathieu. He cleared his throat, trying to suppress a cough he knew would bring further discomfort. "I expect the Emperor to send an envoy in the next few days, as well as the Danes and the Norwegians, if they are not too busy killing each other to notice what happened here."

His head hurt but the Comte increasingly found the demands of his responsibilities a soothing tonic that eased his mind, a reversion to a more natural setting in which his bodily ills were trumped by the puzzles of diplomacy and espionage. More importantly, he thought, combatting concussion with work was simply *enjoyable*. It was counter-intuitive, because his body was telling him to sleep, but Mathieu increasingly found his mind winning round to the idea of staying awake and attending to the issues that had arisen during his unconsciousness. He rode a wave of inexplicable excitement, knowing not whence it came nor for how long it would last.

This was not to say that the trauma he had received to his head had not entirely unaffected Mathieu, however. Thoughts came and went as insects buzzing on a late summer evening, and each one he concentrated on with his mind's eye for the briefest of moments before having his attention seized by the next.

"And have Lemaître informed of the Hansa and Flemish cloth traders' responses to this victory, however they react. Their moves will dictate how Lemaître treats the Flemish traders," Mathieu explained with a sigh, knowing complicated economic wrangling lay ahead. "These are interesting times," he concluded.

"Of course, my lord." Pascal waited a moment before speaking again. "There's one more thing, the Emperor's ambassador is already here."

"Already?" questioned Mathieu, expressing surprise that the Holy Roman Emperor's envoy had reached Ghent quite so soon.

"Chancellor von Aspelt arrived in camp this evening, my lord," said Pascal. "The King is to meet him tomorrow, and would like you to be present."

Mathieu grimaced, the necessity of being somewhere that was not his bed hurting him almost as much as being that bed was to begin with. "What was the Chancellor's disposition? I'd be very surprised if he hasn't crawled from Aachen on his knees."

"Flustered," explained Pascal, hands behind his back and occasionally bouncing on the balls of his feet. He was man of great energy, always doing something, attending to this or scurrying around after that. "He did not seem to expect such a comprehensive capitulation from his Flemish friends. In fact, I don't even think he expected to be visiting us at all; I suspect he was expecting to treat with Dampierre. This victory has taken him by surprise."

"Well, he is ripe for the picking, then," the Comte insisted. Send him in and we'll prep him for his meeting with Philippe tomorrow. Bring the Comte de Clermont, also. He'll add a nice aesthetic to the occasion."

Upon waking from another unplanned bout of unconsciousness Mathieu had found a finely-carved high-backed chair placed across from his bench that Roger had somehow sourced from somewhere in the camp. Mathieu was impressed by the guardsman's resourcefulness. The Comte half assumed the rangy guardsman had won it in a game of dice with one of the King's house servants - Philippe would surely notice before too long. Mathieu did wonder how long it would be before someone else caught the guardsman playing the types of games he knew he should not be playing.

Presently, the chair was occupied by one of the few people in the camp who had not fought at the battle.

"So the rumours were true, my dear Peter?" Mathieu croaked in French.

Peter von Aspelt, Chancellor of Bohemia and ambassador of Adolphus of the Holy Roman Empire, looked perturbed, pursing his lips in anticipation of attempted humiliation from the prone Comte. In such intimidating circumstances the ambassador felt as if he were the envoy of a nation defeated by the French, supplicating for peace, not the representative of the undefeated Romans and treating between equals. Peter stretched out the fingers on both hands before clenching his fists in silent resentment against the thick arms of the high-backed chair.

"The whispers suggested the Emperor was not entirely loyal to the friendship proposed by the English king and Comte Dampierre," Mathieu said softly through narrow mouth. The pounding in his cranium reverberated throughout his skull, restricting the movement of his formerly strong jaw.

Peter's face did not stir but he continued pressing down his clenched fists into the arms of the chair, an action not unbeknownst to the still concussed Comte.

"And so it has come to pass, the mercenary has fled in the face of a more lucrative offer. How much *did* he receive from Edward Longshanks?" Mathieu was as equally stony-faced as his opponent.

The ambassador's eyes were like fire. "I should remind you of your station, my lord Comte," he sneered, his accent thickening on the hard sound at the end of the word 'Comte'.

"And may I remind you of your Emperor's declaration of hostilities last year, my dear Chancellor," Mathieu snapped back with vigour that pained him in its physical delivery. It was a sore point in relations between France and the Empire – Emperor Adolphus had declared war on Philippe only to almost immediately rescind the decision following a threat of excommunication from Pope Boniface. Indeed, King Edward of England and Comte Dampierre of Flanders had paid Adolphus tens of thousands of pounds for an alliance against the French. The Empire's lack of military contributions to the English and Flemish cause had been noted across Christendom.

Von Aspelt blinked slowly in exaggeration. "No hostilities broke out between the kingdoms, no hostilities were ever to break out. You know this. Don't play the fool with me. I prefer our discussions when you are not acting as someone less capable."

"Quite so. But how does Adolphus' rhetoric appear to everyone else? How does it appear to those who lack my network of information peddlers? Is not the wise man he who has but does not tell, rather than he who tells but does not have?"

Peter snorted a laugh derisively. "Your discussion of rhetoric is more than a little ironic given the deceptions and misrepresentations you yourself peddle, though whether intentional, I cannot tell. Pascal, has your master rested sufficiently from his exertions?"

Mathieu managed a wry smile as far as his jaw would allow him and as his cheeks crumpled he could feel the dried blood cracking on his skin. Peter looked back from Pascal to Mathieu, catching Raoul's granite visage en route. The brooding constable had motionlessly observed the exchange with nary a flicker of interest in contributing. De Clermont's frightening appearance was more than enough to just knock the Chancellor off his stride for a moment, causing him to stumble a word as he went to reconvene his parrying and counters against Mathieu's verbal barrage.

Mathieu picked up on this. *Raoul is doing his job*, thought the Comte.

"This is an embarrassing about-turn... I wonder how it shall be received in Austria and Bohemia?" asked Mathieu, ostensibly to Peter but realistically to no one in particular.

The Comte continued. "I hear those rivals, Albrecht von Habsburg and King Wenceslaus, are nearing an accord, but you were probably already aware of that, I'm sure. And how would Adolphus cope with news that the good King Wenceslaus is abandoning him in favour of his old Habsburg rival?"

Well-connected as he was, the Comte de la Marche was not above completely fabricating information when it suited the purpose: King Wenceslaus of Bohemia had favoured Adolphus' election as emperor ahead of the Austrian Albrecht, owing to decades-long territorial feuds between Bohemia and Austria. In truth, Mathieu's sources suggested Wenceslaus and Albrecht were barely in contact let alone in cahoots. However, von Aspelt was rattled and Mathieu wanted to further unsettle the beleaguered ambassador with some elaborate falsehoods.

"Domestic concerns of the Empire are of no significance in this instance, my lord Comte. I should like to know how you intend to proceed with this exchange; I pity your short-sightedness, your focus on the particulars. Your King will be delighted to hear of the welcome provided by his top court official to the Emperor's personal envoy," Peter warned, "as will the courts of Christendom. Perhaps Pascal can help ground you a little more."

Mathieu lost all semblance of joviality. "Pascal is a fine man, but I can better myself only through the love of the Lord God and Lord Jesus Christ, by the power of the Holy Spirit, all of whom I believe are above the courts which you hold in such great regard."

"And you would remember that His Holiness, Pope Boniface is the representative of the Trinity at these courts," Peter shot back with narrow eyes and gritted teeth.

"It seems you are claiming the Empire's ascendancy over other states because of Pope Boniface's patronage for your Emperor. In which case, I would ask as to why the Empire is currently supplicating to France, my dear Chancellor?" Mathieu sneered, not entirely convinced of the reasoning behind his argument but required to go along with it in any case.

Chancellor von Aspelt could see this troubled reasoning as well. "Are you suggesting that strength on the battlefield is indicative of spiritual superiority, my lord Comte?"

"The vitality of France is a sure indicator of God's favour," Mathieu answered plainly, trying to believe his own words.

The Chancellor himself was not convinced. "The bravado you carry is admirable and only to be expected in such a warrior as yourself, Mathieu. Yet it behooves me to warn you away from too great a demonstration of hubris and intimidation so soon in your new position. You are only as strong as your master allows you to be. Philippe could fall tomorrow or in fifty years. Then where shall you be? I'm sure the Empire will have user for such a repentant and talented individual."

Von Aspelt maintained his rigid posture, head inclined forwards so that he seemed to be talking to his chest, eyes all the time fixed on Mathieu's and no longer close to being distracted by the brooding de Clermont.

In his mind, Mathieu conceded that the chancellor had a point. The constitutional election of officials within the hotchpotch Empire, including to the office of emperor itself, offered greater temporal security in office than did the purely patronage-based system exercised by the absolute monarchy in France. Patronage was important everywhere across Christendom, but that Mathieu owed his status in the council entirely to Philippe's favour, regardless of how many contacts he had created and roots he had planted since, was inescapable and a fact of life he preferred not to entertain. Philippe's eldest son was barely six years of age so there was no telling who would emerge as his favourites, and the death of Duke Robert had opened up the court further to dangerous cretins such as de Troyes and d'Hainault. The patronage system was built entirely on the whims of those already in power; an elective system at least had some permanence to it.

Having nearly just lost his life in the name of his patron, however, meant the Comte was not prepared to take lectures on the fragility of high political office in the country of his birth, not least from a supplicant.

"That you are correct is not in doubt, my dear chancellor," he began, as grandly as his aching jaw would allow. "We should all envy the bureaucratic wonder assembled by the Diets and benches of the Saxons, Bohemians, Austrians and Swabians. But it was only an hour ago my master was stood before me in this very tent, in all his radiance and fresh from the dreadful battle; surely Philippe is favoured by the Lord Himself. He looked very much alive and eager to recommence the business of ruling and kingship from which this recent here battle had distracted him."

Mathieu felt he had built a head full of steam, the fog of concussion dissipating with every sentence. "And here we sit in the victors' camp, the last opponent to my master from La Manche to the

Mediterranean vanquished, the politics and economics of Western Christendom united under a fine and strong ruler invested with the guardianship of its peoples by the Lord God."

Mathieu recognised he was straying far into the realms of rhetoric and even demagoguery but he knew that deploying a wide range of attacks against a beleaguered and flustered opponent would prevent that opponent from settling. The element of surprise and invention was the Comte's most effective weapon in the espionage game. Overwhelm an opponent with all of the verbal moves and tricks, and that opponent will be more likely to collapse.

The Chancellor scoffed. "Throwing around coins that you do not own is all well and good, my lord Comte, until such time that you are required to invest what you yourself truly do own. I wonder, my dear Mathieu, did the King source his silver himself?"

Mathieu bristled at the comments, aware how accurate the accusations of insolvency were, but his battered appearance was an effective mask for his emotions.

"Consider the payment of silver a token of the King's benevolence to *loyal* friends, and treaty well with him tomorrow and you shall find your position immeasurably strengthened, Chancellor," spoke Mathieu with no little effort. "Should your talks progress smoothly and to the King's liking, will not the Emperor and Wenceslaus save face with the Habsburgs and the Emperor's other opponents?" The Comte coughed, his energy faltering following the excitement brought about by the verbal tussle.

The Chancellor watched Mathieu, hands still on the arms of his chair. Behind Mathieu and to the right still sat Raoul in the shadow, like a bodyguard not allowing the Comte out of his sight. Raoul had his arms crossed, his long leather gauntlets appearing to barely contain the barrel chest beneath. The light from the nearby lamp flickered in strange shapes across the scarred man's face.

Peter reminded himself not to look at Raoul again. He sighed, closing his eyes momentarily as if troubled by the necessity of responding to the Comte. "I have learnt not to take promises from men such as yourself without expecting repercussions."

"I'm not fond of terms such as 'repercussions'," the Comte retorted. He grimaced and felt a fresh wave of fatigue wash over his head, forcing his eyes shut against his will. Weakness must be hidden. "We live in an exchange economy, do we not? Service for service, service for payment, it is all the same. You will give Philippe what he demands tomorrow, and I will ensure the Habsburgs remain where they are, far away from your Emperor's throne."

However, Mathieu was holding back his ace card: the cloth trade. Everything seemed to revolve around the cloth trade. Mathieu knew how integral this industry was to economic fortunes of kingdoms across Christendom. The cloth trade was the very reason the two were meeting in a tent outside Ghent. The Comte paused, awaiting a reaction from the ambassador.

Upon failing to receive an answer, Mathieu continued. "You will be particularly well-rewarded should you reduce the levies on cloth exports going east from Flanders... the Hansa merchants in Cologne and Hamburg are becoming too self-important. See this as an opportunity to remind those hawkers that no man is greater than the realm."

Astounded, Peter raised his voice. "The Hansa will never agree to the Flemings' demands. And even if they would, we could not force them to any more than could you. How do you think these guilds work? Please, Mathieu, take some rest. This is not the man I know." His Luxembourgish accent emphasised words spontaneously - he was fluent in French, of course, but the disbelief at the Comte's words seemed to throw him a little; the Chancellor could not believe the demands he faced.

"What you ask for cannot be done," Peter insisted.

"Have you tried?" Mathieu interrupted.

Peter remained defiant. "The Hansa merchants are as widespread as Christendom itself. See how your King Philippe struggles with the Church in France? The Church is beyond the polity of government, just like the Hansa merchants, and the Flemish merchants. The Empire will not bow to external demands for constitutional reorganisation."

Mathieu arduously raised his right hand to rub his temples with fingers and thumb either side of his forehead. "The Empire needs to clamp down on these merchants, Chancellor. You know it as well as

I. I guarantee it, you allow the guilds to bloom and they will grow exponentially, strangling and subsuming royal authority. It will be subtle at first – why, to whom do the Hansa's private armies swear fealty?"

Now it was von Aspelt's turn to interrupt. "I think you misunderstand the circumsta-"

"Ask your master to have these problems fixed otherwise France may take steps to fix them on your behalf. *Our* Flemish cloth traders must protect their industry." The deliberate lack of malice in Mathieu's speech only seemed to increase the threat of his order.

The Chancellor raised his eyebrows at the Comte's words, initially taken aback by the sharp increase in rhetoric. "*Hmm*," the Chancellor pondered as he took a moment to reflect. In doing so he encountered a profound realisation; a realisation that he did not give voice to at this time.

Instead, he directed the conversation back towards the belligerence of his French counterpart. "One victory does not make a conqueror, my Comte; this you will learn very quickly in your new role."

The contorted frown seemingly impressed onto the Comte's face by his injuries could equally have represented his feelings on being patronised by the tall Chancellor in matters pertaining to the games of state. Who did von Aspelt think he was? Preaching to him like a child in his own tent, in the victor's camp. Mathieu was the gamesmaster. He decided who spoke to whom, which faction held which town council. According to Mathieu's Flemish source, the burghers of Ghent were already embroiled in deep divisions thanks to the Comte's meddling from afar.

In truth, the conquest of Flanders would likely follow much smoother than he originally could have hoped, if the outcome of the battle was as comprehensive as Raoul was letting on.

Oh for goodness' sake, Mathieu. Sort yourself out. The Comte was dismayed with his own rising ire. This man was nothing but small talk with no substance. Mathieu wondered if his senses had truly been knocked out of him by some Flemish lance, spear or club, or whatever it was that had de-horsed him.

The Chancellor continued. "It's easy giving orders to faceless underlings with no responsibilities of their own, only conveying information like so many pages in a book that you are writing." He firmly grasped the middle of the chair's arms in great, pale hands, ready to propel himself up.

"I must bid you goodnight, my lord Comte. It grieves me dearly to see you so terribly wounded, but by the grace of the Lord He has carried you to safety. Tonight, I shall pray for your recovery, my lord Mathieu." In contrast to the entire exchange just prior, genuine warmth enriched the Chancellor's voice.

Here was a man who had dedicated his life in service to the Church, and for the first time in the exchange it became apparent that perhaps von Aspelt was a churchman first and politician second. Of course, anyone could have express sympathy and compassion, but Mathieu had not really received so much of either in his present state from the visitors who had come before.

On the other hand, Mathieu thought, von Aspelt could simply be acting. Either way, his personality was irrelevant to their sparring, aside from the ease with which Comte Mathieu riled the Chancellor. Mathieu resolved to learn more about this man.

The ambassador swiftly bowed out of the tent door, that most rudimentary flap of canvas that could be tied with thick leather straps through and around holes in the adjoining canvas wall for a sealed entrance in times of disagreeable weather, such as the area had just experienced during the battle.

Mathieu had instructed Roger and Jean to leave the door loose and untied lest their presence or assistance was urgently required; he did not think it likely - Mathieu had known of von Aspelt for a while but had not found it necessary to move anyone close to him. Though it was clear from the few occasions they had met that they did not see eye to eye on almost any topic, Mathieu had garnered the impression the Luxembourger was an honourable man. However, the greater the power of the state became, the greater likelihood figures such as Mathieu would become prized scalps for foreign assassins. He had no doubt that in the unlikely instance Raoul was not ready for combat, Roger and Jean would step in without delay. The Comte had requested the guardsmen hand over any dice in their possession to ensure full focus whilst their lord was in such a vulnerable state.

Mathieu heard a few words of German as the ambassador mumbled an order, presumably to his own guards, followed by the squelching footsteps away from the tent in an unknown direction. A few shouts were heard in the distance, and a horse whinnied. For a moment, though, there was tranquility in the dank surgeon's pavilion, in stark contrast to the heated exchange that had gone before it. The unfamiliar stillness threatened to overwhelm the three men sat gathering their thoughts Mathieu resting his eyes to relieve the headache, de Clermont resting his weary limbs from the trials of combat, and Pascal running through the myriad tasks that awaited him. It was a crushingly quiet end to a tumultuous day.

Finally the Comte broke the silence. "Pascal, have you heard from our contact at Saint-Germain-des-Prés?" It was the first time Mathieu had thought about Jaqueline since waking.

"I have, my lord. I shall fetch you the letter," the mouse-like man replied dutifully.

"Very good," the Comte affirmed. "These are indeed interesting times."

Chapter 27

"Fuck me, this is grim," the dark-bearded man complained with the sharp inflection of his Kentish origins. He pulled his fur-lined hood closer over his face, attempting to completely cover the parts of his face that his beard did not reach. The wind made his eyes water, chilling his skin like nothing he had ever experienced.

His companion turned to face him, having to rotate his whole body as his own head was buried deep within a pure white fox pelt hood and very limited in its movements. "It's better than the ship, no? The land is better than the sea, I think. Look, I haven't been sick since we come to land." His mellow Norse accent added a gentle rounded lilt to his pronunciation that made him seem cheerful in almost any situation, particularly when mixed with the sporadic grammatical and semantic inconsistencies to which he was prone. The wet in the air, partially drizzle, partially seawater whipped up by the incessant winds, darkened the man's usually blond beard to a more ochre colour, contrasting strongly with the white skin it protected underneath.

The dark-bearded man continued looking ahead at the mounds of grass under which lay the fishing village that spread up the gentle slope from the boulder-ridden coast around the bay. Even as a veteran of tens of naval odysseys across featureless stretches of grey seas, a drearier visage he could not imagine.

"Aye, it's better than the ships, I'll give you that. We'll make a sailor out of you one day." He sniffed in a vain effort to stop his nose running. "The great thing with the sea, right, is that you can go *anywhere*. That's why I prefer the sea. Because it's not this. This is shit."

The blond man shifted his body back round to face the village once more. "I will tell my mother how you speak of her town. She makes your King Edward Longshanks look like a little girl."

"That'd be a fight. Longshanks against your mother. Bring her back with us?"

"No. She thinks your land is shit."

"It is a bit. Where are we going, then?"

The blond man raised a gloved hand towards the east. "Not far that way. On the other side of the hill, but maybe she moved to be closer to less-shit sea."

The two men simultaneously hauled their fur-lined trouser legs forward along the sharp, black rocks that lined the cove's shoreline. The footing was secure enough so they would not easily trip or fall, but the rocks themselves seemed heavy and each footstep required far greater strength to rise up from than on the wooden boards of their ship.

"I'll give you that, though – that's quite interesting," conceded the dark-bearded man as he pointed at a terrific plume of smoke proudly resisting the gales, climbing high from its subterranean origins, over on the way.

"Oh, yes – the vents keep us warm when everything else is frozen. We are in the Smoky Cove, of course. All year round, warmth," the blond man explained.

Onwards they trudged, encountering further vents that emitted a potent odour not unlike rotting eggs. Walking downwind of a vent was particularly unbearable, so the two weaved along to avoid the smell until they reached the first indicator of a rough pathway as the black rocks gave way to wild and untamable grass.

"There it is," shouted the blond man through a roaring gust of wind that tore between the two companions like a galloping knight plowing through footmen on the battlefield.

The house was like so many of the other buildings in the village, completely concealed under a turf roof with only the wooden door and surrounding frame visible at the end nearest to the approaching men. A small smokestack poked out of the top but otherwise, from a distance, the village largely resembled a particularly choppy dark green sea, each wave crest signalling its presence with a rapidly dissipating trail of smoke from the chimneys.

"You grow up in one of these?" asked the dark-bearded man, waving his arm at the collection of turf houses on their left as they walked up the treacherous path that had been walked into the hill day after day, week after week, year after year. Removing one of his body's balancing counterweights nearly caused him to slip on the muddy path but his friend steadied him with a strong arm.

"Thanks, mate."

"No problem. Yes, I did, and it was the most warm I have ever been. You do not think you are at the coldest place in the world when you are safely inside."

"I'll bet," replied the dark-bearded man, his words drifting off into the wind as he cast an envious gaze over the turf mounds, each one lacking windows but surely housing a family eating bowls of broth around a hot fire.

The Kentishman did not have to wait too much longer to find a turf house to shelter in as they approached their destination. His blond-haired companion hammered a heavily padded fist on the great door, each blow bringing forth a deep thud that suggested assembly from the thickest of birch panels. Certainly, the door on this lowly turf house was more magnificent than any the dark-bearded man had seen in his own country, even on his liege lord's manor house. It was not long before a latch could be heard scraping on the inside and the hefty monolith was dragged back, lumbering like some beast of burden straining in the field.

The warm glow from further inside the building was partially blocked by a dark figure peaking from around the door. The silhouette seemed to wave a hand before disappearing behind the great door and without a word the blond man walked in, ducking under the doorframe as he did so. The dark-bearded Kentishman was a little surprised by the wordless exchange, particularly given the two were not wearing anything pertaining to their identity, but followed all the same. These were not conditions to avoid a fireplace.

Closing the door behind him, the dark-bearded man pulled his hood down as he turned and looked into the room. It smelt strongly of smoke, almost chokingly so, but it was not unpleasant, especially in comparison with the lower deck of the ship during the storms they had encountered over the past weeks. Immediately catching his eye were the massive birch beams holding up the ceiling; imposing, it was if entire trees were holding off the outside world. The room felt very subterranean yet not claustrophobic. The residents had managed to convert a dugout into living quarters, drawing space from where there was none and generating homeliness from hefty earthbound birch timbers.

The former silhouette turned round and stared with ice blue eyes set in a gentle face, neutral in expression. She was unusually tall, considerably taller than both men, but it was not this fact that so shocked the two guests; they had known the woman a long time and did not notice such characteristics. Rather, it was the child on her right arm, a tiny swaddled lump of furs with the smallest hint of a tiny pink face poking out next to the blue-eyed woman's chest.

The babe was asleep, completely oblivious to the world. The child's mother realised the men were staring at it, and she dropped her eyes to the object of their gaze, unconsciously smiling at the sleeping child. The woman seemed the very essence of serene - she had always been graceful in her movement and gentle in her ways, and now a sleeping infant in her arms seemed the most natural, beautiful thing the men had ever seen.

Except things were not supposed to be like this.

"Well, you haven't changed a bit," stated the Kentishman bluntly.

"A fish diet," the woman replied, still smiling. "Keeps you young. And ice baths."

The men laughed. "I told you, you would become one of us!" exclaimed the blond man cheerily, his big smile fighting through the fine moustache hairs that had grown unimpeded since embarking - none of the blond man's crew had shaved since a wager had been placed upon boarding on the longest beard growth over the course of the journey. He himself had frowned upon the suggestion of gambling but ultimately could not force his men to part with a vital source of warmth, particularly not in such frightful conditions, and so simply turned a blind eye.

His companion nudged him whilst nodding his head towards the woman and baby, concerned over the volume of the blond man's voice. He had always been heard before he was seen.

"Oh, sorry."

"It's fine, this one will sleep through anything," the blue-eyed woman explained, lightly and subconsciously rocking on the balls of her feet.

A moment's silence passed between the three. The dark-bearded man felt uncomfortable at that moment for it had been a long time since they had seen the woman - and the journey over had seemed barely shorter than that - and so he was unsure how to break the ice. In a sudden moment, it seemed all of the warmth in the room had melted into ceiling and walls, as if the mighty birch door had flung open and years of familiarity dragged outside by the screeching northerly gales. What would one say to an acquaintance after so many years, when there had been relatively little common ground to start with? Nor did they know each other well enough to hold out during the silences as friends could do.

But most significantly, she had a child! He had not even considered that possibility. She was not supposed to have had a child.

"Why have you come?" the woman asked quietly yet urgently, as uncomfortable with the silence as were her guests. She was suspicious that both men had arrived; such an occurrence was surely indicative of grave tidings. The two would have sailed on separate ships and each carried the same message. If one ship were lost in the unforgiving northern ocean then the other could continue. It was treacherous but there was no other way.

The blond man flashed his eyes at the tall woman and rummaged through the inside of his jacket, tongue poking out as he searched for something by touch. He removed his hand from the furs and with it came a letter stamped with a large red seal. Behind him, his companion already had an identical letter and seal in his hands.

"These are for you," said the blond man, little emotion in his voice. All three recognised the considerable gravity to this exchange but none knew why it were so. The men approached in turn and handed their letters to the tall woman who took them in her free left hand. All those weeks on the ships and both men had resisted the temptation to break the seal and read their copy – how would he know if they were to do that? For sure, he would not know, but the Lord would. They were godly men by vocation, after all.

The dark-bearded man went second and when passing the letter to her paused to look at the baby. "Is there a name, yet?"

The blue-eyed woman shook her head. "There's still some disagreement."

He nodded, pursing his lips in contemplation, before turning and walking back to the door.

"We will go to the church, now, and give our greetings," said the blond man as he pulled up his foxskin hood. The white fur was pure like driven snow and seemed to glow in the warm light of the fire crackling softly at the far end of the room. Saying nothing else the two men left the house, closing the door slowly behind them and leaving the woman to her own thoughts and the sound of the spitting fire behind her.

She sat down wearily on the stool at which she spun and carded wool, absentmindedly swaying her body smoothly back and forth. The infant in her right arm had quickly become like an extension of her own body and so she became accustomed to carrying out tasks and errands around the baby when it slept. The two letters in her hand, each stamped with the same seal, fully occupied her attention. After all of this time, why now? So many years with only passing news, a generous term for rumours carried by sailors, but now this - direct correspondence! The woman could not remember the last time she had received a letter from him. All this time she had been making a home here, half a world away from him. Reflecting on the conversation just gone, she was sure her accent had begun to change too - it had been months since she had spoken anything but the local tongue. At that moment, the woman celebrated a small victory; learning the language was easy but for some reason she had always struggled with accents, despite the advantages she held.

Anyway, what does he want? A shot of anticipation surged through her body. Remembering the baby in her arms, she placed the infant down gently on the deep straw at her feet and took to the letters. She guessed they were identical, one for each ship that sailed, such was the risk of the journey. She ripped carefully along the edge of the fold, preserving the solidified seal where she could with her customary compulsive manner.

It was apparent that before setting the liquid red wax had run only a little from the circle containing the familiar double-knight motif within the abbreviated Latin that encircled it, and the woman felt it important to keep such a symbol intact though did not know why. Keeping the wax seals intact served no purpose beyond satisfying her compulsive mind.

Her fingers began trembling as she unfolded the vellum of both letters.

Bring the wheel with you.

One sentence, no more, yet it shouted louder than the united voices of one hundred people. She dropped the letter to the table as her heart jumped and tears swelled in her eyes, putting her hand to her mouth in disbelief. Her baby did not wake as she sobbed through pure joy, a joy greater even than that she felt at first seeing her newborn child; elation she never thought possible. How had Aurelius done it? At the beginning, neither knew where or how to start. The woman looked down to the sleeping infant - the first of a new generation, a unique treasure. The woman resolved there and then, through the trickling tears that wetted her reddened and rounded cheeks, the child would go with her. Aurelius' opinion would count for nought, because returning home was what mattered.

Even her husband's opinion was of no consequence – she would be gone before he returned. She did not belong here; this was not her home. The child would have to stay with its mother, because a child should never be taken from its mother. And, the woman determined as she read the letter back over again, what future could her husband provide the child here, compared with where she was going? This was no place for an adult, let alone an infant. She had still not figured out why and indeed how people lived here. It was survival, mere existence; little discernible contribution to civilisation. That was an obligation of every man and woman, was it not? She admired for its openness and novelty the local governance of the assembly, especially relative to the rest of Christendom, and yet still the assembly was under the auspices of a Norwegian king who lived many hundreds of miles away. Representative government only got so far if it was constrained by tyranny.

The woman's worldview was skewed in favour of social and political advancement. Accordingly, she did not understand why the Norse had always roamed the known and unknown world, for purposes both genuine and nefarious, yet here they remained, concealing their enlightened democratic system as a puppet of a foreign monarch.

But 'here' had served its purpose precisely because so many other people would also question why and how people lived here. Everyone else, she guessed, did not deem the questions worthy of consideration; the village by the smoking cove would remain anonymous. Anonymity was the cover she needed to keep the wheel hidden.

The woman sat up straight on the stool and dabbed her cheeks, breathing deeply and taking in the familiar smoky ambience of her home. She sighed deeply and sniffed following the tears. It dawned on her that the immediate future would be arduous. Separating from Aurelius had already been hard enough and every day for years she had thought about him – on her wedding day, when she lay with her husband, when she looked at her child. She could not bear the thought of experiencing another separation. Her husband would return in a few days, two at the minimum if previous trips were anything to go by. But this was the last trip of the season and conditions were ever worsening, so it was not beyond the realms of possibility the party could return this evening; it was essential she acted now.

A slither of daylight remained when the men had left. How long ago had that been? No matter. She had waited long enough.

"I want the boats ready to leave before first light," she commanded even before greeting the small congregation huddled

424

around a table. Her Norse was practically flawless, the hint of an exotic accent concealed by the uncompromising tone of her delivery. The tall woman could just about make out the plates of fish and bread not yet touched by those around the table, backlit by a comforting fire that gave the ceiling a reassuringly familiar hazy quality; reassuringly familiar for no more reason than signifying a haven from the storms outside. Accordingly, the woman found no complaint with the mugginess and mildly choking effects produced by each hut's singular fireplace, having grown accustomed to the tickling in her throat and the watering of her eyes. As tall as she was there was no chance of avoiding the canopy of smoke that topped every room in the village, so the she was thankful her body was as accommodating to different environments as it was; the cramped smokiness had been initially unpleasant but she had always hoped – but crucially without expectation - it would be merely a temporary arrangement.

The dark-bearded man was facing her from the far side of the table, shorn of his fur-lined coat and now dressed simply in a heavy grey tunic, no hat atop his thinly-haired head. He very quickly grasped that the woman with the icy eyes was not open to compromise.

"Uh, of course, that can be arranged," he sputtered, his own Norse as competent as was the blue-eyed woman's but with a far stronger foreign tilt, trying to think on his feet whilst sat down half way through a meal. He knew it would be a long ask to locate the full complement of both crews at this time, given the cover of darkness and the very high likelihood of extreme inebriation after so long at sea. In fact, racing through the situation in the short pause between his initial reply to the woman and her response thereto, the Kentishman concluded what she was asking for would not correlate with what would actually happen between now and sunrise.

The priest sat to his right also knew this to be the case. He was an ancient man from Norway with a weather-beaten look so wrinkled that it was not immediately obvious which line in his face was his mouth.

"My fair Thorfridr, child of the seas, these men are industrious to a fault. They'll endeavour to meet your request, but don't you think the crews might need some leave from the boats?"

His thinly veiled suggestion was cheery, a genuine reflection on the ancient man's general demeanour. No one in the village could hold on to positivity like the ancient priest. This indomitable spirit served as a primary weapon in his preaching arsenal; his flock saw his unrelenting resolve and extraordinary age as sure signs of the Lord's favour in recognition of such a pious existence. Some believed him to have been among the first settlers, a bastion constructed with the first turf houses and a sentinel of the Lord watching over the courageous and hardy pioneers of the north.

The ancient priest knew Thorfridr to be strong of will, however, and did not really expect his platitudes to hold water with the icy-eyed woman. Neither was he wrong in his expectation.

"I have been summoned," she growled, bringing her right hand up and pointing her right index finger to emphasise her message, "and I have been waiting for *years*." In that moment the vivid orange fire illuminated her sharp features, the light dancing across her cheeks and brow and the flames reflecting from her ice-cold eyes; so perfect a mirror were those bright blue topaz gemstones set within that fair face did it seem that Thorfridr was herself blazing forth in her smouldering anger, a veritable Valkyrie come to collect men from their struggles.

"Can we wait one day, or so?" pleaded the blond man sat opposite the ancient priest, putting down the bread he had absentmindedly held to his mouth for the duration of the exchange thus far. His request and misjudgement of the mood was met with a raised eyebrow from his Kentish friend and an elbow from his sister sat beside him.

"I'll help round up the men," said the blond man's sister and daughter of the godi, the local representative to the assembly.

"Thank you, Hulda," smiled Thorfridr as her expression softened at once, the previously haunting flames that had cast dread shadows across her flawless face now bathing it in warmth that reflected her maternal side.

426

"I think Haraldur forgets what it is to be home," Hulda suggested before taking a bite of the hard bread before her.

"That's a little unfair," the blond-haired Haraldur protested, his fair eyebrows contorting. "I do my duty by the Church; I go where God tells me." He looked over to his dark-bearded friend, expecting some display of support.

"And I have my duty to carry out, friend," stated Thorfridr, her face hardening again after a brief thaw. "I have not been able to carry out my duty for too many moons now. It is my turn – the Lord commands it. Your duty and mine are entwined now."

"And pray tell, what of your duty by your husband, child?" asked the ancient priest, ever the voice of counsel in social or political discussions amongst the villagers.

All eyes fell upon the tall, blue-eyed woman who still stood just inside the doorway. Her gaze dropped to the floor to the right, noticing the piles of sawdust disturbed by tiny tracks, presumably a mouse living somewhere in the timbers of the priest's turf house. Thorfridr did not see fault with the creature's choice of abode as did some; she did not see the rodent as an occasional thief of food but more a creature merely trying to get by on an island as unforgiving to animals as it was to man.

"I am as married to the Church as I am to my husband," she said. The blue-eyed woman's voice carried with it sorrow and reluctance, averse as she was to confronting this issue. "I love my Church and I love my husband, and my child by him. Tell me, father, what would you do in my position? I am asked to choose between my Lord and my husband – I have not said that I am leaving my husband, have I?"

The ancient priest slowly raised his head to address Thorfridr. "But we know that you shall not be returning, Tova," he stated plainly, using the diminutive of her name. The priest was not aggressive nor condescending for that was not his way. He was not one to strike fear into his flock's hearts.

"I am not breaking my vows, father. I am being called back to the Church. This is grounds for a dissolution, you know that."

Hulda, Haraldur and his dark-bearded friend glanced expectantly at the gentle priest and were greeted with a furrowed brow that took on the form of crumpled old paper.

427

"You are right, fair child. Of course, you are right. But I am not appealing to you from that viewpoint – it's more an appeal to your heart. Einar is a good man, he is very fond of you. And your babe! What of your own sweet child?"

Thorfridr resolved to not allow the priest's emotional plea any foothold in their discussion and yet, as usual, his honey-like words flowed and seeped into her ears and mind, working to dissolve the emotive blockade she had constructed against the memories of her life here in the village.

"The child comes with me," was all she could say. "I will take the child. I have been called back by my first love, my greatest love. Einar knew my position. I didn't make a secret of it."

"But you gave him hope that it was a secret that would never be fulfilled," countered the priest, firmly without being confrontational.

The tall woman exhaled softly and felt her face flush red as the priest hit the nail square on the head. She blinked slowly before facing the dark-bearded man at the end of the table. "Richard, you received the letters directly?"

Not anticipating involvement in the subject of Thorfridr's marriage given he had only just heard about it that afternoon, the dark-bearded Richard was caught off-guard.

"Uh, we did. I saw him write and seal them."

Thorfridr turned back to the priest and his glum visage. She knew they would miss her, and the priest was arguing Einar's case as much for Einar as he was for himself; and whilst it could not be said by any stretch that the village was thriving – the brutal winter was ever a hindrance to any economic advance beyond that of small farmholdings – her own contribution to village life since arriving had been immeasurable in its own way. The blue-eyed woman had brought with her suggestions for insulation, fireproofing and shipbuilding to name but three, implementations resisted by none and lauded by all. The blue-eyed woman felt frustration rising that the enterprising villagers were not as open to the premise of her returning home as they had been to her advice in domestic matters.

The priest's stance was the fulcrum of these frustrations but she did not begrudge him this role. If the village represented one person, he would be the conscience and many said he had been remarkably effective in maintaining order during his decades of service, a more potent tool for social cohesion than any of the godar who represented the village at the national assembly.

Yet, as the priest regarded her with mournful eyes, Thorfridr could not help but think this question was of greater significance than any the priest had considered within the domestic context of the village. This indeed had been the precise reason for coming to the village in the first place, a sleepy outpost on the edge of civilisation itself, yet still sufficiently populous relative to the surrounding settlements to blend in.

"This request has been personally delivered, father," she started, "so I ask again, what course would you follow in my situation?"

The gentle priest pushed back his chair to make room to stand from the table, moving with the grace of a much younger man. Richard went to assist the old man but was waved away with thin, bony fingers covered by taut skin with the appearance of coarse parchment. *They make them tough here*, Thorfridr thought.

He stood to his full height, not as tall as the blue-eyed woman but still imposing like so many of his fellow Norse, towering men carved from the oak trees that birthed their longboats. The priest's shoulders were stooped but carried the considerable weight of the skins piled over them with ostensible ease as he approached Thorfridr.

"It is not my place to answer that question, dearest Tova," he counseled with soft words and a placidity that seemed out of place with his craggy form. He took her hands in his. "Neither do I know your purpose in hiding here with us, nor the nature of your instructions to return from whence you came. However, I do know that whatever purpose you serve as an instrument of the Church, should you truly believe in the necessity of your return, it is likely to have significance over a population greater than that of this place. But beware temptation sent in the guise of opportunity, temptation to stray from the enlightened path you tread now, here with us. A sin remains a sin even with great and commendable actions afterwards. So, my fair girl, I beg you make a decision with the consideration of your serving the Lord God and His Son at the forefront of your mind, for the sake of saving your mortal soul."

The ancient priest's eyes glinted in the firelight, a momentary flash of reflected light shining as they watered. Thorfridr could feel her own eyes welling up and they took on the appearance of melting ice. She hugged him tightly, wrapping her long arms around the old man's back and clenching the thick fur over his shoulder into her fists. After a few moments she released and gazed down to the gentle priest and his craggy face, the wrinkles of his cheeks glistening with tears for the first time in many moons.

"I must go home, father," she whispered to him, rubbing her eyes and breathing in deeply to restore her poise. The priest responded with a slight nod and the most serene of smiles, radiating wonderful warmth from the man's very soul. Truly, this man has been blessed with the spirit of Heaven, the blue-eyed woman thought. The blue-eyed woman let go of the priest's fur coat and looked over his shoulder to the three sat at the table behind, none of the three having moved during the exchange by the door.

"There is something I need to do," she declared, sniffing as she wiped her eyes one more time. "Please gather the crews."

The remaining three sat at the table nodded slowly in affirmation. Thorfridr pursed her lips pensively before looking to the old priest one more time and nodding almost imperceptibly. Nothing further to say, she spun and heaved the door back to expose the hut to the darkness and howling wind of night for the briefest of moments until the door was slammed shut, resolutely sealing Hulda, Haraldur, Richard and the old priest inside their thoroughly insulated shelter.

She paused for a moment to pull up her hood and glance around, as if greater focus would allow the blue-eyed woman to determine any shapes through the blackness. With no moon in the night sky it would be a little more challenging to navigate to the church though she had traversed the route countless times by nightfall; non-existent visibility held no qualms for her. The ice wind bit into her cheeks as she pulled her hood tighter over her head and set off for the church just down the slope from the priest's turf house.

No longer would she have to endure the sting of windchill so potent it would lacerate the skin as if it were boiling water, she thought with relief.

The vault had been cast into the rock deep underneath the church, only accessible by a treacherous stone stairway that spiralled down in the opposite direction to the conventional direction. This was so those at the vault's entrance could retreat downstairs and still use their sword arm to fight, unlike the design used in towers across Christendom that allowed defenders to retreat upwards. Thorfridr knew that specifying the direction of the spiral was, in practice, superfluous because the stairway was barely wide enough for access in the first place, let alone for two people to swing swords at one another. A spiral design was necessary in general, however, simply because of the lack of space; a directly vertical shaft was easier to maintain and construct in than a sloped shaft.

Everyone in the village knew there was a subterranean vault beneath the church; concealing its excavation and construction would have been impossible and so the Order did not even attempt to hide it. Only Thorfridr knew the purpose of the vault, though. Only she had the three keys required to unlock the door at the top and the vault itself - one of which she kept on her person at all times on a necklace, and the other two hidden in the Church itself.

The woman's unusual position in the village offered her secret considerable protection. This foreigner had been settled here by the Order with no uncertain terms of residence; any intervention with the woman's business would be treated with not just immediate and undetermined imprisonment but more significantly, excommunication. The Order had specified the significance of this woman and her cargo to the work of the Lord, but no more.

By and large the threats had been effective; not least because of the woman's exotic appearance itself encouraging all sorts of rumours regarding her providence. Thorfridr had told them she was a Norse, but even by Norwegian standards she was of towering height and impossibly blue of eye. Her lithe movements were fluid and easy and she did not seem to have aged a day since arriving, despite the brutal winters - she had seen thirty winters but barely looked older than twenty. Some of the more inquisitive of the village, well-versed in the old tales, had questioned her heritage – implying she was of divine parentage, a daughter of Heimdallr or even Odin. Of course, openly asking an Order member if she was born of the old gods was inadvisable in a place where everyone hears everything, but she had always not unkindly laughed off such absurd notions.

Her breath quickened she walked to the door at the back of the church, taking in the familiar musty smell of the great timbers used for the skeleton of the village's largest building. She looked up and tallied the number of ribs crossing the ceiling as she had so many times. Countless candles produced the hazy yellow-orange glow that constituted one of the very few colours one ever saw here in the colder months; the black of night and the grey-white of snow being the other two. The woman with the ice-blue eyes tried to remember what other colours existed in the world. Green was one of them, was it not?

As a substitute, the yellow-orange haze was sufficiently reassuring. Beyond the curtain across the back of the altar did the haze immediately give way to damp shadow. Thorfridr knew this to be a foreboding for the dank blackness of the stair well and the vault, so she took her dormant torch and fired it from the last light on the wall before the curtain. This last light was a safe distance from the highly flammable wool of the curtain and so the rear of the small building always seemed to hold a haunting appearance, which she reasoned had deterred at least some would-be inquisitors from inspecting the great doorway at least.

Turning to check no one had followed her, the woman pulled out the key on her necklace and found the covered lock three timber frames in from the left of the altar curtain, an inconspicuous carving in the stonework that actually housed a convoluted locking mechanism. Crouching down and turning the key in the lock, Thorfridr felt the lock spring and she carefully slid the stone out from its resting position at the base of the backwall. She could not see anything – the risk of carrying the open torch this close to the curtain was too great – but had executed the maneouvre countless times before.

The stone scraped along the wooden flooring with little resistance. The woman had always been careful to scour the floorboards when cleaning the church to eliminate any hint of repeated movement from the moveable stone piece, but there was no further need for such care. She picked the stone up in her left hand as she always did. In the same movement the clasp carved into the top of the stone she picked up in her right and locked it into its latch on the door at the back of the altar, twisting to open the stone door to the darkness of the vault beyond.

Taking one more look around the empty church as she returned to pick up the torch and replace the removed stone, Thorfridr drew in a deep breath and prepared to walk down that spiral stairway for the final time.

Untouched by the warmth of naked flame, the stairwell was ice cold and seemed to almost smother even her torchlight. It did have its charms, however; the stillness of the spiralling stairway was unparalleled anywhere in the village and the blue-eyed woman welcomed the calm. She found it soothed her regular headaches whenever she checked the vault, but this evening the silence only amplified the pumping she could hear within her ears.

One last time, she told herself, and then she would be going home to see the one she loved so dearly.

Holding the torch in her left hand and tracing the curve of the central column with her right, Thorfridr glided down the stairway with grace and finesse far beyond that which the conditions should have allowed. She did not recoil from the slimy touch of the damp basalt nor did the lack of traction underfoot slow her down, but ever downwards the blue-eyed woman swept; impatient to retrieve her quarry in order to set sail before the dawn and simply to escape the cramped space of this subterranean catacomb of the Order's secrets - she could barely stand to her full height for fear of cracking her head on the roughly hewn bare rock above.

Nimbly negotiating the final steps with the surefootedness of a rabbit darting amongst the clubmoss and low-growing ferns she reached level ground and raised both torch and eyes to the redoubtable door. It bore no decorative markings nor patterns, no symbols of the faith, adorned only with a great ring handle and three key slots down the right hand side, evenly spaced along its edge. It was a simple design for a simple task and as far as the tall woman was concerned, it had done its job.

She took the key on her necklace once more and inserted it into the topmost key slot, turning it right and pulling the ring handle back once. This action was repeated with the bottom key slot, and then as she had done hundreds, thousands of times before, the woman pushed the handle back into the door again and turned the key in the middle slot. A soft *clunk* emanated from within the monolithic gate and Thorfridr was able to pull it open.

She moved the torch in her left hand into the newly revealed abyss behind the door.

It was empty.